Advance Praise:

"There's a serial killer on the loose, and in the fishbowl setting of Robert Schirmer's *Barrow's Point*, 'shadow selves' of fear overtake the town's residents. No one can be trusted. Schirmer peoples his remarkable book with characters conflicted by their own discordant passions and prejudices. The writing is sensuous, the plot unpredictable, and the upshot brilliantly captures the unease of our times."

—Ann Cummins, author of *Red Ant House* and *Yellowcake*

"Already distinguished for his short fiction, Schirmer now has given us *Barrow's Point*. Schirmer's fans will find, in addition to well-earned suspense, a richly nuanced portrayal of the McGregor family, Iris and her three sons, whose complex, private troubles raise an eerie echo of their small town's responses to the murders of a series of gay men."

—Elizabeth Evans, author of *As Good as Dead* and *Carter Clay*

"*Barrow's Point* is an eye-opening, engaging and emotionally touching novel. Ostensibly, it is a murder mystery: Gay men are being killed one by one in a college town in Wisconsin. A gay cop and the rest of the police force have few, if any, leads in their search for the killer. Within this frame, a complex story of family dynamics and intimate relationships emerges. There are incidents of rage, sorrow and reconciliation. We learn how gayness or straightness brings people together or, more often, pushes them apart. There are no simple answers in this story of several people who live with or close to each other, but for whom intimacy is a state that is needed but not easily achieved."

—Thaddeus Rutkowski, judge and author of *Violent Outbursts*

BARROW'S POINT

BY ROBERT SCHIRMER

WINNER OF THE GIVAL PRESS NOVEL AWARD

Gival Press

ARLINGTON, VIRGINIA

Published by Gival Press, an imprint of Gival Press, LLC.

For information please write:
Gival Press, LLC
P. O. Box 3812
Arlington, VA 22203
www.givalpress.com

First edition
ISBN: 978-1-940724-07-2
eISBN: 978-1-940724-08-9
Library of Congress Control Number: 2016939867
Cover art: © Vincent Giordano | Dreamstime.com
Design by Ken Schellenberg.

To Alice Worden Matthews Schirmer, my
mother,

for giving me, among so many things,

the love of reading.

(1)

On the morning the first body was found, with head crushed and one eye open toward an overcast sky, Reed McGregor woke staring at his face in the glass of an empty picture frame. For a moment he was disoriented, unable to remember his own life. He lay chilled and alone in a bed alien to him, coiled in a stranger's sheets. Just beyond this room he saw, in his mind, a tangled wet forest of rain and dripping trees. A sharp breath caught in his throat, and his mouth tasted dry. "All in all, just another brick in the wall," he muttered before he moved his eyes away from the picture frame and reality shifted gradually into place. He sat up on the side of the bed, *my bed,* remembering with relief that he was still young, and that the ache in his back had nothing to do with age. What the picture frame revealed had not been reflection so much as distortion. He turned the deceptive frame on its side and stared at the police uniform that hung from his bedroom door, badge still affixed to the shirt's front. More and more, he was beginning to question what that uniform really meant to him.

A photograph of Reed and Alex had been inside the picture frame only a few weeks ago. Soon after their breakup, in a spell of anger and regret, Reed had removed the picture from the frame, held it over the kitchen sink, and lit a match. But even then he'd known he was just pretending. He blew out the match before a flame could catch and hid the picture, without irony, in his underwear drawer.

Had he really been in love with Alex in the first place, or Alex with him? They'd wrestled with that question for some time without coming to any convincing conclusion.

The morning was cold, dank, and still as a prairie. Thick mist cloaked the neighborhood, reducing houses and trees to vapor. By the time Reed reached the station it was past seven and barely light. He met Casey Saunders in the hallway, a rugged good-looking officer with a pensive half smile, a dent in his chin too small to count as a cleft, and a bed-head whorl of hair sticking up from his scalp. A blue neck scarf was looped somewhat rakishly around his throat. "Dead man down at the Balsom Warehouses. How's that for a morning wake-up call?" He lifted up his Styrofoam cup of coffee in an imaginary toast.

Reed groaned, still bleary-eyed. "You're serious?"

"Get some coffee first. I made it, so brace yourself."

They drove across town without the emergency siren because traffic was still sparse. Built along a swelling bank of the Mississippi River, Barrow's Point, Wisconsin was a small college city of 30,000, named after the town's founder, Jeremiah Barrow, who died under mysterious circumstances when trampled by a horse on his fiftieth birthday. A narrow offshoot of the river snaked through the city, dividing it into two unequal segments. The smaller section, comprised mainly of industrial buildings and low-income housing, was gray, dusty, and somewhat lifeless, lacking trees or flowers or any vegetation other than unkempt shrubbery and occasional outcroppings of thistles and weeds. During the winter, this side of town suffered the most brutal wind chills; in summer, heat accumulated as if trapped in a bottle, turning the air bone-dry and stagnant.

The larger section of Barrow's Point was a fusion of the picturesque and the practical, of historic riverfront property, several rambling parks, and orderly residential neighborhoods. A liberal arts college mounted the crest of the steepest hill in Barrow's Point, giving the town a steady, ever-shifting influx of youth and culture. This cosmopolitan atmosphere stood in stark contrast to the open fields, sedate farms, and moody woods located just outside the city limits.

An old-fashioned bridge suspended by thick steel beams separated the two divergent sides of town. As Reed and Casey drove across the bridge, Reed glanced down at the river with the same enjoyment and fascination he had when he was a boy, as if he were living in the 1980s again and not 2005.

"Fucking miserable March," Casey said. He dabbed at his stuffed nose with a clutch of Kleenex. "I'm a walking contagion. A biohazard."

Reed loved the scratchy timbre of Casey's voice, a film noir detective's voice. Strange that he and Casey had started out as enemies, back when they were twelve and had bloodied each other's noses in a dispute over Pam Larson, a girl who'd receded from both their minds as their own friendship grew. Yet after fifteen years of constant companionship, they still didn't openly address certain things. The blizzards of their past, for one thing. Sometimes Reed woke with a pounding heart from dreams of the snowstorm that had stranded him and Casey together for 38 hours in northern Minnesota back when they were seventeen. He remembered the steep ravine their car had crashed into, the desolate sweep of land in all directions. He remembered the cold; their increasingly desperate hunger; Casey's broken collarbone; the whiskey bottle they'd passed back and forth to kill the pain; the way he and Casey had huddled together for warmth, Reed's arms folded around Casey from behind.

They had spent the whole bitterly cold night in that position. Once Reed had awoken, shivering from his tattered sleep, and found his head leaned forward over Casey's shoulder in such a way that Casey's mouth was rested against the side of Reed's neck. He adjusted his head slightly so he could inhale Casey's exhalations, intimately linking himself to Casey through this simple exchange of breath. There had been only this moment between them, unceasing. But eventually Casey had stirred and opened his eyes. "Dream, Mercury," Casey whispered and brushed his lips—accidentally?—against Reed's. Then he shifted his weight so they were breathing alone again.

Mercury: Casey's nickname for Reed. The nickname had been invented that night—Reed's body heat was the one thing that could "raise the mercury in this fucking tomb," or so Casey had said, grimacing in pain from his aching collarbone. All the survivalist movies said so and it was the only way.

Reed stared uneasily out the patrol car window, remembering this. Did Casey remember? Eleven years later and Reed was still left to wonder. He turned to Casey, who was examining his face in the rearview mirror, deftly brushing aside a flake of sleep crust from the corner of his eye. "I think I'm turning bronchial." Casey steered onto the sloping road leading down to the warehouses. "Maggie's uncle almost died from bronchitis once. She ever tell you? His lungs became inflamed. He started drowning from the inside."

And then there was Maggie, still an awkward fit in Reed's past. In college he had half-heartedly dated Maggie for eighteen months. Soon after he broke up with her, she began dating Casey, and eventually she and Casey had married. Reed, Maggie, and Casey were a somewhat complicated threesome, actually, when he took the time to think about it, which he tried not to, much.

The Balsom Warehouses were located on the outskirts of town in a featureless area of storage buildings and smokestacks. A lean silent man in a mud-spattered jacket was waiting for them in the parking lot. He stared as if he suspected them of high crimes their police-issued rain slickers meant to disguise. Reed and Casey followed him quietly, sipping their sluggish coffee, both remembering back when they were teenagers—Mercury and Case!—and had haunted the warehouses and loading docks with their friends, drinking and smoking pot and setting off bottle rockets across the river, all in cheerful defiance of the law. Now they were the law, but the docks had remained relentlessly the same, crude and hinting at darkness. The man in the spattered jacket walked them around a grain elevator to an area of shallow brush and a partially cleared footpath that led up to a largely unused frontage road. The light rain turned to an icy sleet, the last fatal gasp of winter.

The body was sprawled face up just off the footpath, the man's long coat tangled in the gnarled overgrowth. Reed guessed the dead man was in his thirties, with darkly Grecian features that looked out of place in Barrow's Point. Yet he seemed familiar in a way that was imprecise and a little haunting. Reed crouched down for a better look and noticed the one open eye, or rather the combination of the open eye and the firmly shut one, as if the man were caught in the purgatory between living and the waking dead. The open eye with its dark pupil drifting upward. *An awakening eye*, Reed thought, as if the man had been asleep and just begun to grope his way to reality, his eye ascending to focus on the blurred shape above him, when he'd been murdered.

And it was evident that he had been murdered. One side of his head was caved inward in a way that suggested a severe blow more than a bullet wound. The blood disoriented Reed, although as a police officer, this wasn't the first time he'd stared headlong at spilled human blood. He breathed, conscious of the wet storage sheds nearby, casting off the vague smell of damp grain and dusty cement mix.

A balding man stepped out of the nearest warehouse and limped toward them. Despite the weather, he wore only a tousled gray T-shirt that read *My Son Died for Oil*. Reed wouldn't have minded hearing this father's hard luck story, but it wasn't the time for politics or the release of personal grief. "I slept back there last night," and the balding man indicated the warehouse. "I didn't hear a goddamn sound but wind and rain and my own moaning. When I come out this morning, I thought for a second he was just a bunch of clothes, you know, that someone had tossed there. I almost walked off till it seemed like maybe them clothes had a *shape*."

While Casey sealed off the crime scene with yellow tape, Reed remained crouched beside the corpse. The man's lips, dimly parted as if to whisper, had turned blue. A rogue wind rippled across the dead man's coat, stirring it slightly, giving Reed the uncanny sense he was watching the man breathe one last time.

Was that a thread of phlegm listing from the dead man's nose, or just melted ice and condensation? On instinct Reed moved to wipe the moisture away, then thought better of it.

A few crows passed overhead, black and soundless.

After an interval, the man in the mud-spattered jacket led another officer over to them. Detective Arnie Granger was one of those heavyset men with just enough muscle to be considered bulky instead of fat. A few warehouse workers—the heavy lifters, the crane operators and cement mixers—had gathered a small distance away, hunched in their jackets and flannel shirts, shuffling their booted feet, watching with keen interest and measured dis-passion as Arnie studied the scene and the corpse, made notations in a small hand-sized notebook, talked into his police radio, and suggested to Casey that if modern pharmaceuticals were failing him, maybe it was time to step back-ward and give home remedies a shot.

"Like what?" Casey asked. "Horse urine?"

Reed paced back and forth, trying to shake the tension from his limbs. He crushed the empty cup in his hand, but there was nowhere to throw it. He glanced up at the hilly incline to the frontage road, partially obscured by mist, then back at the spread-eagled corpse.

When the paramedics arrived to take the body to the coroner, Reed watched, uneasy, as they lifted the body onto the stretcher, their movements brisk and indifferent. Arnie lowered the lid over the man's open eye; Reed felt a peculiar pang, the dead man reduced now to a commonplace corpse. A sheet was tossed over him, completing his divide from the living.

*

The body was identified as Zach Solomon, a 34-year-old man who had moved to Barrow's Point last year to work at a fledgling architectural firm. Solomon had no immediate family in the area, no wife or kids, and few friends other than the contact who had hired him. But neighbors and acquaintances spoke highly of him—his politeness and good manners, his unforced generosity and habit of looking away shyly when he smiled.

For several days Solomon's murder dominated the local news. An autopsy determined the cause of death as blunt force trauma. No one in Barrow's Point had been murdered since Thomas Gardenia had shoved his wife through a sliding plate glass door during a Friday night barbecue two years ago, and that had been "unintentional," or so Gardenia had claimed. He'd meant only to push her away, end her ceaseless physical and verbal assaults, *not* to send her crashing through the hot shimmering glass, and certainly not to kill her. Besides, in the summer's heat, the shimmering glass had resembled his hallucination of water. Didn't anyone see that, in his mind, he'd pushed her toward water and not glass?

After a couple of tense weeks passed without additional leads to fuel the story, the Solomon murder began to fade from the town's consciousness. His death caused some anxiety and a great deal of gossip, but he hadn't been well-connected in Barrow's Point, so few people were shaken by the violence at any personal level. The police could find no motive for murder among the sketchy details of the man's life they'd managed to scrape together. Possibly he'd fallen victim to a robbery attempt or a drug deal gone sour, although no drugs had been found on the victim, and there was little if any sign of struggle. He had lived unassumingly in an apartment building near downtown; he had no traceable enemies; the crime scene had yielded little concrete evidence and was clearly only where the body had been dumped, not where the murder had taken place. Arnie suspected the man had been "homosexual," given the speculation of some of his acquaintances, although no one seemed able to confirm this.

One night Arnie asked Reed to accompany him while he questioned patrons of the two bars in town known as "gay friendly." As the only gay man on the police force, Reed knew he was intended to make any potential witnesses they encountered feel comfortable opening up. The first bar, Oyster, was located near the university campus and packed with college students, some gay and some not, the clientele so youthful that even Reed felt out of place. He and Arnie asked a few questions and passed Solomon's picture around, but no one recognized him. A girl with lavender hair and a bauble stapled into her nose volunteered that he looked a little like her Uncle Oliver, "but my therapist says I see Uncle Oliver everywhere. He's in the trees, for Christ's sake! He's under the trees! *Woodchucks* look like Uncle Oliver."

The bartender at Quench, the town's one openly gay bar, recognized Reed and greeted him warmly, smiling at the police uniform with dry amusement. Arnie passed Solomon's photograph around to the few random barflies, but again no one could place him. Finally Arnie gave up, ordered himself and Reed a couple of beers, and they retreated to a booth in the back, unfortunately lit with a crimson candle that cast a romantic aura and embarrassed them both. "Don't be getting any ideas now," Arnie said as he pushed his stomach into the booth.

Reed let the remark slide. Living in Barrow's Point for as long as he had, he'd become a master at letting such jokes slide.

"We're hitting the wall on this one," Arnie admitted. "I thought maybe this Solomon had picked up a bad trick somewhere, but I can't find a shred of evidence to support that."

Tricks, homosexuals: Arnie's vocabulary sounded stuck in the seventies, but again Reed didn't comment. Arnie had been a good friend of Reed's father, and was still friendly with his mother. Even though Reed was now a 28-year-old man, he felt somewhat tongue-tied around Arnie. Still, the absurdity of sitting in Quench with Arnie, nursing a Guinness, made him want to laugh outright. "Tell me something," Arnie said. "You come to this bar a lot?"

Reed shrugged. "All right, I know I ask personal questions," Arnie added. "Ask the ex."

In bed that night, with insomnia hanging over him like a weighty fog, Reed's thoughts drifted back to Zach Solomon. He couldn't shake the man from his head. That ascending eye, for one thing. And what if he'd seen Zach at Quench one night, after all? The bartender hadn't recognized him—no one had—but people were overlooked all the time. Reed pictured Zach sitting in a stool across the bar, gazing back at him, possibly sharing a moment of interest, of sizing each other up. Reed turned over onto his back, folding his hands behind his head, and stared up at the ceiling he couldn't see in the darkness. All of this left him with a bad feeling. It was about more than a quiet man's inexplicable murder. It was the sense that something was *beginning*, that something larger had been set in motion.

(2)

"The bowels of the earth!" Sandra Locke cried from the corner of Findley and Sackett. "Man's hatred boils forth when we turn our backs against the lamb!"

Every morning when Iris McGregor stopped for coffee on her way to work, Sandra was standing outside the coffee shop, tossing around bits of twisted religious doctrine and holding out to passersby her paper cup punctured with two pencil holes. And she was there again that balmy Thursday morning in early May when Iris first heard about the second murder.

Spare and hungry-looking, Sandra wore a tattered Bible somewhat cumbersomely attached to her hip with a wide silver belt, which seemed at odds with her long and very straight, flower child hairstyle, the hair of a graying anti-war activist. Over the years Iris had started feeling sorry for Sandra. After her husband died, Sandra had a difficult time making ends meet, scraping together what charity she could from handouts, food banks, and odd jobs. She'd turned to evangelism, or so Iris always suspected, to give her luckless new life shape and meaning. Iris had lost her own husband, a minister, many years ago, so she knew firsthand the desolation that followed such a loss. Fortunately she'd had three sons to raise, and they had kept her from losing traction in the world.

As usual, Iris dropped the change she'd received from her latte into Sandra's mutilated cup. Sandra smiled, only instead of her customary and deferential "Bless you," she said, "Do you hear Jesus' wrath, Mrs. McGregor? Like a heartbeat galloping near? Veer from the path of the righteous, and this bloodshed is what we'll see."

Iris was startled Sandra had veered from their canned script. And bloodshed, galloping heartbeats? "Let's hope not," Iris said and hurried away.

Yet Sandra Locke's words were like a seed ominously planted. As Iris drove to work, balancing her latte in one hand, she realized the day was not as ordinary as it seemed. The girls behind the counter at the coffee shop had seemed distracted, whispering among themselves, barely remembering the niceties of greeting customers. Also, Iris was running late, which was unlike her. Nothing in particular had made her late, she just seemed to move with less efficiency today, some caution slowing her limbs. Minutes slipped by, unnoticed.

Normally she listened to music on her drive to work, but today she daydreamed, transfixed by the unnatural silence.

By the time she reached Fairview Hospital she was fifteen minutes late. She hurried through the lobby and passed Emergency Admissions, where a doctor with a tiny Band-Aid over one eyebrow was saying something about "blood-stained hands." A nurse, in vigorous ascent, added, "Just goes to show what we don't know about this town." She gazed at Iris so oddly that Iris ducked into the nearest restroom to make sure her face looked all right, that she didn't have toothpaste smeared on her chin or a speck of something indiscreet peeking from her nose.

She peered at herself in the mirror, trying not to think too unfavorably about the crow's feet around her eyes and the skin beginning to sag around her neck. *Fifty-four,* she thought and, as always, was somewhat jarred that such an age could apply to her. She ran her fingers along her collarbone, and noticed only then that she was wearing her blouse inside out. She gasped, shocked and then amused, as she ducked into a stall to make corrections. Surely this was the answer, then, to the off-balance feeling she'd carried around all morning, the reason people were staring with such troubling insistence.

Only when she slipped into her office in the billing department, now over twenty minutes late, she was still restless. The blouse clung to her skin, a more awkward fit now that she was wearing it correctly.

James Parsons, her boss, a tall and broad-shouldered man who loped more than he walked, stuck his head into Iris's office, armed with his own coffee and a newspaper. "Your son is a cop, right?"

"Reed? Yes." Iris picked up a random file from her desk to cast the illusion she was busy. Or had he noticed already that she was late?

"So what does he have to say about all this?"

"About what?"

He smiled almost savagely beneath his shaggy moustache. "You haven't heard?" he asked. And then, as an afterthought: "*He* didn't tell you? Your own son?"

*

"You should have told me."

"Mom, I didn't have all the details—"

"Everyone knew before me, your own mother. I think, maybe, even Sandra Locke..."

*

The second victim was Anthony Tull, a man in his late twenties and a former bartender at Quench. Reed had known Anthony from several casual conversations over the past few years. Anthony's body was found dumped in some brush near an empty lot on the outskirts of town, in the opposite direction from where Solomon's body had turned up.

Until Anthony's body was discovered, everyone had assumed Solomon's murder had been an anomaly, one of those mysterious and violent incidents that happened from time to time on the edges of everyday life. But the second murder suggested the first had not been just a case of a man who happened to be gay who'd been murdered, but that gay men were the specific targets. Both dead men's skulls had been crushed with baseball bats or "some equivalent," the police speculated, and Iris had no reason to doubt them.

It was after the second murder when people around town began whispering *serial killer*. It was then the stories about the "Barrow's Point murders" started popping up on news channels across the state: *Two men murdered in Barrow's Point within weeks of each other. News at ten.* Or, *Are gay men the target of a serial killer?* As the news spread, overtaking the headlines and clogging the local evening newscasts, the town's shock and confusion didn't skyrocket so much as insidiously deepen. Soon, people were locking their doors even during the day. Parents enforced harsher curfews on their kids, and even the most bold of men, if forced to walk alone at night or out to the street to his car, did so now with a guarded vigilance, as if aware only now, *now,* of how much the darkness might conceal.

"But how can this be happening?" women whispered behind closed doors to their husbands, their relatives and friends. "How can this be happening *here*, to *us*?" And their unanswered whispers grew louder and more emphatic until they became like a low hum echoing over the town.

"Maybe we're safe, though," a few argued. "I mean, if we're straight, right?" But most of the townspeople assumed nothing when murder was involved.

Iris had been living for nearly thirty years in Barrow's Point—known more for its desirable waterfront views than for explosions of homophobic violence—and had never felt more disquieted than she felt now. All her sons were gay except possibly for Eddie, her youngest, who had not declared himself yet, so how could she not worry? Christian was eighteen, set to start college in the fall, and her most visibly vulnerable son. Christian (and the irony of the name was not lost on her) was delicately built and effeminate, with pale skin, gray flat lips, a bony chest, and a voice that gave the impression he was always somewhat out of breath. He was *on the surface*, or so Reed had once noted with an affectionate laugh, the very cliché of a gay man, a Midwestern version of a young John Waters or Quentin Crisp. Even as a baby, Christian was the son who had rejected her breasts, preferring manmade formula to the milk her glands naturally secreted for his benefit. Although Christian's effeminacy had disappointed Iris at first, in time her needling disappointment had given way to concern that he would stand out as prey for the bullies that

stalked most schools, pushing and punching and bloodying whatever misfit
was breathing within arm's reach. Just how much Christian had or had not
been tortured by his classmates Iris never knew, but he remained levelheaded
and calm throughout most of those years, and never once showed an inclination to act like anyone other than who he was—an unashamed gay male,
interested more in history and the fanatical consolidation of power that had
led to the persecution of Jews, Poles, and gay men in Hitler's Third Reich than
in whatever persecution he was inadvertently generating around him. It was
this—Christian's steely stubbornness, his willful self-possession—that Iris
considered his most masculine trait.

Still, with Barrow's Point now gripped by a wave of inexplicable violence,
she feared Christian wandering around after dark. "How about you invite
some of your friends over," she proposed one evening while Christian was in
the living room raiding the laundry basket for a fresh shirt. "I'll play Houdini
Mom and disappear into my bedroom."

"Then there's Eddie," Christian reminded her.

Iris couldn't pinpoint why she wasn't as worried about Eddie roaming the
night streets. For one thing, he didn't go out as often as Christian did. And
although Eddie was only fifteen, he seemed less touchable. He was a wrestler.
He knew body slams and chokeholds.

"He hates us," Christian continued, tossing his arms into a T-shirt and
slipping it over his head. Then he stared at it on him, already having second
thoughts.

"Us, what do you mean, us?"

"Not you and me, Mom. Me and my loser friends."

It was true that Christian and Eddie had drifted apart over the years. As
he'd grown older, Eddie had started hanging around with a tougher crowd,
other members of the wrestling team, and Christian was a frank embarrassment to him. "That's his natural machismo talking," Iris said. "Don't take
it personally. That's just his loser mother's opinion, of course." She giggled,
charmed by her own glibness.

Christian positioned his pale slender feet into a pair of sneakers. "I *have*
to go out tonight," he said. "We have tickets to hear the Intimate Thrashers at
Oyster."

He didn't mention who "we" were, and Iris didn't ask. The world seemed impossibly large to her then, crowded with billions of men and women she didn't and could never know, any number of whom might be harboring secret hatreds and ugly rages, all ready to direct them at her son with the aid of a baseball bat. Odd that she should think *son* and not *sons*. But then her tendency to worry about Christian had started even before he was born. He was the first child she'd had after losing her only daughter years earlier. While pregnant with Christian she had walked about in a light and creeping manner, fearful that she would misstep and fall, that the slightest wrong movement would steal another child from her. "You need to be careful," she cautioned Christian.

"I know," he said carelessly. "A fag killer's on the loose, I know, Mom."

Fag killer. A ragged shadow crept to mind with a hand hewn out of marble. "I'm not hiding like half the town just because some nut job thinks he's taken over," Christian added.

"Stick together then. Hang out in a crowd."

After Christian left for Oyster and the Intimate Thrashers, she phoned Reed on an impulse. "You're the police, couldn't you maybe follow him now and then, just to make sure he's okay?"

Across town, she heard Reed chewing noncommittally on a piece of toast. One of her sons was always noncommittal at just that moment she was most urgent.

"I mean unofficially. No one would have to know. We could just be vigilant."

"You have a very homespun perception of the police, Mom."

"This is Barrow's Point, not—I don't know--Chicago. And I'm not saying follow him nonstop. You're a cop, Reed. Be stealthy. Stay far enough away so Christian won't know you're tailing him."

After she'd hung up the phone, she still wasn't satisfied she'd accomplished anything. Maybe she was asking too much of Reed. Since Carl's death fifteen years ago, Iris had grown accustomed to relying on her oldest son. Carl had been an earnest and decisive man, although somewhat demanding and quick to note fault. He'd possessed the uncanny ability to see past things, beneath their surfaces. During their years of marriage, before his sudden death of a brain aneurysm, she'd turned less observant, yielding to the power and majesty of Carl's vision. When they'd attended college together, she'd fallen in love first with Carl's face, chiseled and finely wrought, with a wide brow and strong bone structure. A mesmerizing face, bright with hope and compassion, with a desire to seize an unjust world between his hands and wrest some humanity out of it. He'd never been more than a perfunctory lover. Often his hands had been tentative, and he'd approached lovemaking like an assignment he had to complete before a due date, and he was willing to settle for a C. Sometimes the physical seemed to baffle and exasperate him. The body—what was it other than petty mortal flesh? He'd seemed more resigned to lovemaking than actively engaged with it. Yet this lack of physical passion had only briefly deterred her from becoming his wife.

After several years of marriage, she'd started noticing a strange dichotomy in Carl. While he remained gracious and receptive to his congregation, he was more chilly and remote at home. Sometimes he seemed to forget her presence in a room. At other times she caught him examining her with a faint chastising air. A critical edge crept into his voice. Behind the pulpit he could spin that edge into brimstone and fiery indignation, a call for his flock to wake up, the world was drifting rightward toward chaos and hate, were all too blinded to notice or too sated with convenience to care? But at home, that edge, stripped of its spiritual context, came across as harsh and impatient. He never punished Reed physically, but relied on the more standard Biblical weapons— guilt, emotional excoriation. Once Carl found a matchbook with several missing matches lying discarded near the radiator. At the dinner table that night, he held up the empty matchbook and asked Reed if he knew anything about it. Reed shook his head but refused to look either parent in the eye. He clutched his fork, spaghetti unraveling from between the tongs. "All right," Carl said, his voice steady, betraying nothing. "But if you're not telling me the truth, that fork in your hand is about to turn very hot."

Almost instantly Reed felt heat shoot through the fork. He stared at it in panic, this deceitful magical fork, and dropped it onto his plate.

For days Carl ignored Reed, who moped around the house like a condemned child. "Why are you punishing him like this?" Iris asked, incensed.

"Think if he'd burned the house down. Or worse, hurt himself."

"But you're carrying it too far. Carl? You're acting…Draconian…"

"Draconian?" He laughed, and she caught a flash of his old, less demanding self. "That's a word you don't hear every day. Dungeons and torture racks, that's me."

Yet at times Carl had been almost painfully vulnerable. Three years after Reed was born, Iris had given birth prematurely to her only daughter, Melissa Rae. The child had lived for sixteen hours in an incubator, every breath a struggle, before she'd relented and died. Carl had cried so powerfully that the sobs racked his chest, battering him with the force of physical blows. He rocked Melissa Rae's body, frail and still, in his open hands, whispering to her, his hot tears splashing over the baby's face, soiling the linen sheet she was wrapped inside. When he passed Melissa to Iris, she held her daughter's body to her chest almost stoically, all her emotions shut down, as if in awe of Carl's grief, so seldom seen. He baptized the dead child with a Dixie cup of tap water that he'd prayed over, although a hospital chaplain had baptized the living Melissa only a couple hours earlier with Carl and Iris as witnesses, so surely Carl couldn't believe the child's soul was still at risk. Iris watched as Carl thumbed a moist cross on Melissa's forehead, mumbling a few Latin words she couldn't make out.

Finally the doctors returned to claim Melissa's body. "Couldn't even give her a day," Carl said. It was unclear if he was speaking to the defeated doctors or some other presence absent from the room.

That night in bed, Iris held Carl close to her as his body shook, his hands spread open, palms up, as if he could still feel Melissa's weight in them. His labored breath against Iris's chest reminded her not of their present loss, but of some past loss she couldn't name, or possibly a future loss she had yet to experience. "She wore Blue Velvet," she sang into his ear, the words of a pop tune they used to sing aloud in the car back when having a child was just a concept, a dream for the future. But the song made her envision Melissa Rae swathed inappropriately in a tiny blue velvet jumper. Iris could see it so clearly. She ran her fingers through Carl's hair, her own mind—her heart—racing. The room was terribly dark. There was not a speck of light anywhere. She squinted through the darkness, willing a piece of furniture to take shape, until she remembered the crib in the corner, empty and hidden from them. Tiny pricks of color flashed before her eyes, lasting just long enough to remind her of hope.

Eventually, Carl's tears subsided enough so that he drifted into a fitful sleep. When he woke with a start and a moan, his hands groped up and down her body, awkward and lost, as if to reconfirm her substance. "Live, live," he whispered and pressed his hot mouth against hers, half kiss and half resuscitation. For those few impossible hours, their bodies, their physical selves, meant more to him than prayer and proverbs, than all the poems of Lamentations. Was it possible, after all this grief, that their marriage might begin anew, and from the depths of despair might arise a stronger passion and greater intimacy between them?

No. After Melissa's funeral, Carl barely touched Iris for two years.

At first an invisible wall of self-consciousness divided them whenever they lay in bed together, Carl on his side, Iris on hers. Over time Carl's body became the wall, solid and unyielding, a spiritual as well as physical separation. Iris had no idea how to fight this. She learned to live off implication and suggestion. A kind word from him sent a shiver along her spine, a surge of warm gratitude that felt, during those emotionally lean years, akin to love. When she passed him in the hall, she brushed her shoulder or arm against his, as if by accident. Night after night, with Carl turned away from her in bed, she settled for resting her head against his back after he'd fallen asleep. When Carl woke and stepped out of bed to use the bathroom, Iris opened her eyes to narrow slits so she could glimpse his naked body when he returned. So often his penis appeared shriveled and small, as if it, too, meant to frustrate her.

The bed trembled as Carl slipped back beneath the sheets.

After a few months of her covert voyeurism, he started wearing underwear to bed, depriving her of even those quick glimpses of his nakedness.

They had moved past that terrible time, of course, although it had taken them a long while before they'd been willing to risk having another child. Christian had served as their bridge back to the uncertainties of parenting. After he was born and declared healthy, Carl had still treated his new son with a certain degree of suspicion and diffidence. Did he peer into the squalling child's face and see the fleeting image of Melissa Rae? Was Christian's constant crying a reminder of that overwhelming sadness Carl had survived, barely? Iris had protested the name, thinking it was too precious for a minister to name his son Christian, but Carl had been insistent. His grandfather,

Christian Duncan McGregor, had died while fighting a barn fire in Virginia, and Carl had promised his grandmother that he'd name a son after him.

Only weeks before Carl's death, she and Carl had an unusual conversation about Christian. Even then Iris had noticed Carl was acting erratically, although at the time Iris had not associated his odd behavior with anything physical. Carl was in bed propped up by pillows, an open book on his lap, glancing at Iris from over his glasses as she performed her yoga exercises in the center of the room. Privately, Iris regarded yoga as a form of prayer, but she never shared this bit of sacrilege with Carl. Eddie, only months old, was asleep in his crib across the room.

"Christian is a sissified little thing, isn't he?" Carl said from out of nowhere. He began to scribble pencil marks in the book's margins.

"Little thing?" Iris asked, for some reason short of breath.

"I don't think you're breathing right. Yoga is supposed to deepen your breath."

"He's our son."

Carl continued to scribble in the margins, which she saw now was a poetry collection she had saved from a college literature class, Walt Whitman's *Leaves of Grass*. Carl's hand was not altogether steady. "What are you writing?" she asked.

"Have you read any of this? *We two boys together clinging/One the other never leaving.*" The lead of his pencil snapped. He stared at the splintered stub, then at whatever marks he'd made in the book. "*No law less than ourselves owning,*" he muttered.

"I think it sounds lovely. Ourselves owning."

"I suppose it's the poet's gift to make anything sound romantic." He closed the book. "As if that's possible, to own ourselves, or together cling or never leave, for that matter."

She had to concentrate to understand what he'd just said. "Why are you reading poetry?" she asked.

"You don't think I've devoted my life to poetry? What is the Bible then?"

"Okay." Now she was confused. She looked away from his nervous glare. She disliked when he cast judgment upon her and, worse, their sons. She thought of Christian, his hand tucked into hers as they walked up the steps to the church on Sunday mornings, staring into the rafters with his wide, doubtful eyes, afraid to look too long at the stained glass window of a bearded man prostrate on his knees, praying up at a sky that teemed with vengeful angels.

"Maybe we could convince Reed to spend more time with his brother. Toughen him up a little."

"Christian is four! What would you have Reed do, a few sacs in the backyard?"

A corner of Carl's mouth twitched. "Carl?" she said, feeling her breathing, at last, centered in her diaphragm.

"This is the rest of his life we're talking about," he said.

Two weeks later, Carl sat up in bed one night, clutched his skull, and shouted, "My head, my head!" Then, as Iris reached out to him, he slumped like a bag of dust against the pillows and was dead.

*

Iris must have fallen asleep in front of the TV, because when she heard a noise from the kitchen, she fumbled awake, disoriented.

"Christian?" she called.

"Hardly!" The refrigerator door opened and closed, and then Eddie sauntered in the living room, chewing on a Slim Jim and drinking from a bottle of mineral water. He was a somewhat tense boy who was trying hard not to show it, with habitually frowning eyes and a tendency to move his lips almost imperceptibly even when he wasn't speaking. His T-shirt fit a little too snugly around the shoulders, although she'd bought it for him only a couple months ago. Lately Eddie had begun to disconcert her for no obvious reason. She groped around for something meaningful to say, but all that came to her was to ask if Christian had come home yet.

"Why would I know?" Eddie sat down on the lounge chair and stretched his arms over his head in a calculated posturing. "Why would I care?"

His manner troubled her. She was pretty sure he was high; she could smell the lingering scent of pot, even from several feet away. But hadn't he been upstairs all this time? "And what have you been up to?" she asked uncertainly.

He shrugged. "I went out for a little bit," he said, kicking his sneakers off his feet.

"You went out?" What was going on around the house as soon as she closed her eyes? She glanced at the clock. "It's eleven!" she scolded. "You're supposed to be inside by ten."

"No one has to be home by ten, Mom, that's archaic." He looked at her as if she had a tentacle for an arm.

"Old archaic Mom," she said. Sometimes enforcing rules and discipline with her sons did make her feel archaic. She'd only smoked pot twice in her entire life, twice, and she'd gone to college in the early seventies! What a waste! The youth revolution had definitely passed her by. "It's not archaic when things are different—not normal—"

"Can you smell my feet from there?"

"No, not your *feet*."

But he missed her implication. He chewed on the Slim Jim. "That stuff is made out of mechanically separated chicken," she said, not remembering exactly where she'd heard this. "Do you really want to eat that junk?"

Eddie stretched out his legs. "Now you sound like him," Eddie said.

"Who?" Of course they both knew. They didn't even mention Christian's name.

"Why are you still up?" Eddie asked. He contemplated a muscle in his arm. "Don't you work tomorrow?"

"Hmm. I'm not the one with a curfew." She was too embarrassed to admit she was waiting up for Christian, and that she couldn't bear to go to bed until she knew he was safely home from the Intimate Oysters. "Have you fed Stretch?" she asked, trying to steer the conversation in another direction. Stretch was Eddie's pet garter snake. Watching the snake swallow live goldfish out of the tiny stagnant pond in its cage was still too grisly—and too symbolic—for Iris to bear.

Eddie didn't answer. For some time they watched television, Eddie with the remote so they flitted through stations, catching pieces of the world, differing sensibilities—a rightwing bash fest; a black and white Bogart movie with a lot of smoky corridors; several plastic-seeming women selling jewelry; a nature show about kindly bears on the attack. Iris's mind was a little dizzied as they flew through stations. And to think she could remember a time when you could only get three or four channels on the television set, and you had to stand up and actually turn the channel yourself.

When Iris heard Christian's car pull into the driveway, she was so relieved that her smile bordered on radiant. Eddie frowned and shook his head. "Goodnight," he said, picking his shoes off the floor and heading upstairs before she could wish him goodnight.

(3)

Reed didn't start trailing Christian immediately. Although the atmosphere of Barrow's Point had turned sinister, he had no intention of following through on his mother's suggestion. Christian was eighteen, an adult more than capable of looking after himself.

Yet a couple nights after that conversation with Iris, Reed began to have second thoughts. He lay in bed, sleepless again, an unseasonably sultry May heat pressing down around him, making him glad, for once, that he was alone. He remembered the jeering taunts he'd heard leveled at Christian over the years, the sidelong mocking glances he'd sensed, sometimes actually seen, from other men shaking their heads at his brother in a restaurant or at a mall. For some time he kicked around in bed, unable to get comfortable, his mother's words echoing back to him: *You're the police. Be stealthy.*

When he finally drifted off to sleep, he envisioned Christian's prostrate body in a field of tall weeds, his head broken open, blood matting down his Brillo-pad hair, all of him, the death of him, gleaming in moonlight. The image was so powerful, so singularly disturbing, that the next night, when Iris dropped a hint that Christian had gone to a 7:30 movie with friends at the Cineplex, Reed found himself parked in the movie theater's back lot, waiting for the boys to emerge. Once people began flooding out the doors, Reed watched from a safe but not substantial distance while Christian and his two friends, both male, strolled to the friend's car, speaking animatedly and tossing pebbles at one another. His brother seemed happy, Reed saw with mild surprise, or happier than Reed could remember himself feeling since his breakup with Alex. Reed drove behind them for several blocks; parked along the side of the road, out of sight, while they stopped at a convenience store for a twelve pack of beer; followed them to a video store and finally back to the house of one of the boys. He waited until they were safely inside, but still didn't drive away. A light turned on inside the house and someone drew the shades. Reed sat in his car and watched the street drift from twilight to darkness in a few short minutes. He squinted into the darkness as if trying to pinpoint what was almost there, then looked back toward the lighted house where his brother was and felt nostalgic, although for what he couldn't have said.

A girl's scream made Reed nearly jump out of his skin. He pulled away from the curb, and on instinct drove down the street toward the scream, his blood racing. But when he got to the end of the street, two teenage girls were out in front of a house with the porch light on, washing a car and spraying each other with water hoses. Then they wrapped the hoses around themselves and pretended they were in the grip of anacondas. When they saw Reed's car lingering out on the street, they dropped the hoses and dashed inside. The dripping car looked vaguely guilty.

Two nights later, Reed followed Christian again. And then, another night, the same. It was ridiculous, of course, but once started, he couldn't help himself. When he was a boy, he'd invented a game called P.I. He would pick a random person off the street or inside the shopping mall, and then he would follow that person around. Once he'd watched a man in a white shirt and crisp tie scoop up a few bank receipts that people had abandoned at an ATM machine. The man had crossed the street to the park, sat on a bench overlooking a bed of orchids, and cried into the deposit slips. Another time he'd followed a woman around a shoe store. He'd watched her shove one elegant heel under her coat, escape the store without sounding the theft alarm, walk with deliberation to a car several blocks away, where she'd opened the door, shoved the one heel under the front seat, giggled, and darted away thinking she had not been seen.

Reed supposed what he was doing with Christian wasn't so different, other than he had a deeper purpose now, other than the difference between fantasy and reality, which he had learned a long time ago was no difference at all.

One night Reed followed Christian and his friends from a burger joint back to the house where they normally gathered. Only once the boys had parked the car and climbed out, they started darting, three abreast, toward Reed's car on the side of the road. "Damn, busted," Reed muttered before he stepped out of his car to face them.

Christian came to an abrupt halt when he saw Reed. "Wait, wait, he's my brother," Christian said to his friends.

The boys all stared with suspicion at Reed. The tall redhead with Elvis Costello glasses asked, "The cop brother?"

The young Asian man, who wore a white T-shirt with two tears artfully ripped across his chest, set a hand on Christian's shoulder. "You didn't recognize your brother's car?" he asked.

"I don't have my contacts in." Christian looked on the verge of stepping closer to Reed, but then never quite managed it. "What are you doing here?" he asked.

Now that Reed had been unequivocally caught, he felt a little embarrassed. There was something voyeuristic about this whole tailing situation. "Just driving around," he said.

"You've been following us since Roadies," the redhead pointed out.

Longer than that, Reed wanted to say. "Really?" he muttered instead. "I must be bored."

He motioned for Christian to join him on the other side of the car. Christian's friends, taking the hint, started back toward the house. "I feel like an idiot," Christian said.

"Well, that makes two of us."

"Are you chasing Eddie all over town too?"

Christian was glowering at Reed in a way that reminded him of Christian when he was angry as a boy, his face scrunched up and fists clenched. "*What?*" Christian said when he saw Reed break out in a smile.

"Come on. You're really that pissed?"

"*Yes.*" But Christian's face relaxed, his fingers loosened, and he looked, if reluctantly, on the verge of smiling too. "Quit being such a Boy Scout," he said.

"Done. You're on your own." Reed swept a playful arm around Christian's head and ran his knuckles through his brother's bushy hair. "Just be careful, okay? That's all Mom wants."

Christian groaned, trying to smooth down the hair Reed had mussed. "Really? Mom put you up to this?"

At first, Reed told no one about his secret surveillance of Christian. Then one night while working late with Casey, for no particular reason, he confessed the entire story. "Merc, you've got to be kidding me," Casey said. "You're tailing your brother?"

"Well, not anymore." Reed already regretted saying anything. Yet Christian stuck out in Barrow's Point as strongly as if he had a scarlet G printed on his back, and with gay men turning up dead, maybe surveillance was precaution more than misguided. "Nothing wrong with being safe," Reed added.

"So you're going to start wiretapping his phone too?"

"Ha! My side, my side."

By the time they'd returned to the station it was almost dark. Casey's car was in the shop, so Reed gave him a ride home. They stopped at a bank's ATM along the way, and their headlights illuminated, ironically, on the wall facing the alley of the building next door, a spray-painted message: *Christian McGregor is a faggot.*

Reed stepped out of the car and stood in front of the defaced wall, the large block letters growing larger the longer he stared at them. *Christian McGregor is a faggot:* how long had this judgment been muddying up the world, singling out his brother?

Casey shook his head. "Damn kids."

"Right, kids." Reed stalked back to the car, forgetting he'd stopped for some money. Once Casey was inside Reed pulled away from the bank. "We're going in the wrong direction," Casey pointed out.

"Maybe not."

Although it was true, Reed wasn't driving toward their homes. "You remember how we were as teenagers," Casey said. "One side of the brain thinks one thing, the other side does the opposite."

Reed didn't want to think about *back then*, a time when he'd tolerated everything and known nothing. He pulled into the first convenience mart they came across. In the store's small home supply section, he picked up some cleanser, washcloths, and a hard bristle scrub brush. "For Christ's sake, Mercury," Casey said. "You're not going to be able to wipe it away with that."

But Reed had to try. He couldn't very well bulldoze the wall into oblivion. He drove them back to the scene of the crime. For several minutes he stood hunched in the shadows, trying to scrub the words off the wall, aching for his brother, then mad as hell at the perpetrators, the faceless vocal enemy he couldn't silence.

His brother Christian. Once, less than a year after their father had died, when Reed was a teenager and Christian a small boy, Reed had watched Christian faint into a fire. His mother had been in the house tending Eddie, still a baby then, while Christian was assigned to Reed's care. Reed had been burning a heap of fragrant dead leaves in the backyard, daydreaming about nothing much, when Christian moved too close to the flame, inhaled a sulfuric lungful of smoke, and passed out. Reed's response had been so sudden, so automatic, as he yanked Christian out of the flames the child was collapsing into, that Christian wasn't even singed. "What a smoky boy you smell like!" his mother had said later, as she lifted Christian into her arms and carried him into the house, sniffing his shirt and neck and spiky hair. Somehow during the rescue Reed's hand *had* burned, but he kept this a secret from his mother, as he kept the whole incident a secret. His was not a conspicuous burn, but none-theless left a tiny permanent uprising of scar against the knuckles of his right hand that, as an adult, he glanced at from time to time as a welcome reminder of…he couldn't be sure what.

Reed scrubbed the wall until it was dirty with powder and his scarred hand tightened up. "See, I told you," Casey whispered, craning his neck back and forth to make sure no one was around. "You have to think."

"Thought. A foreign visitor." Reed was speaking in the voice of someone he wasn't. He was talking the way he spoke in dreams, in deeply meaning-ful phrases that translated to nothing, or was that meaningless phrases that revealed everything? The world felt surreal, blanketed in terror and the mun-dane. A small patch of thistles grew along the wall's edge, a decaying butterfly speared in one of the thorns.

He drove them back to the same store and this time purchased a can of black spray paint. "Forgot something?" the cashier asked, but he shrugged and didn't trust her smile. Her lips were tinted with black gloss, roughly the same color as the spray paint, and she seemed able to smell the cleanser on him. "Just getting started," he said. "Tracy," he added, reading her nametag.

But she just continued to smile as she handed him the spray paint. "My name's not Tracy," she said.

He didn't have time to delve into that one. They returned yet again to the alley and the scourged wall. Casey's cell phone rang. Reed only half-listened while Casey assured Maggie he would be home soon. They had encountered a delay. "Just business," he told her and hung up. "She's a little on her guard these days," Casey said.

The black spray paint canister rolled back and forth on the dashboard, a rebuke. "What you're thinking of doing now is defacing property," Casey added. "A punishable offense."

"It's defaced already."

"Well, okay, you're redefacing."

They pulled back into the alley for the third time that night. Reed turned off his headlights. "So what do you suggest I do, Case?" he asked.

But the decision had already been made, it seemed. "Hurry up, I guess," Casey said.

In the darkness, with Casey posting vigil, Reed altered the message so it now read *Christ is 4 Faggots*. After he was finished he backed away a step and admired the handiwork, his breath quickening. "Now you're slandering Christ?" Casey whispered.

Reed looked from Casey to the words looming on the wall. Slander?

"Could we hurry up, please?" Casey said. "Our jobs are on the line."

And Casey was probably right about that. Reed knew he, at least, was breaking the law. At the same time he was inwardly convinced he would not be discovered, for the darkness concealed him, and he was right to protect his brother in this way. He didn't care if his new message might offend Christians, or that it scarcely made sense as now written. The Bible seemed remote to him, an ancient document that was just complicating matters. But his mother still attended church every Sunday, and his father had devoted his adult life to God and scripture, so Reed couldn't shake entirely a belief in a higher power, even when that power, if it existed at all, often seemed as angry and unseen as the person who had painted his brother's name across the wall. In the end he sprayed over his own words, blotting out the entire message, so all that remained was a black stinking cloud of pain(t) swirling over the wall like a Hiroshima mushroom cloud.

"We're finished here," Casey said. "This wall isn't saying another word."

Once they were driving away from the scene of their petty crime, Casey leaned his head back against the seat and exhaled. A boyish devilment fired his eyes. "The Badass Cop Mad Graffiti Artist reveals himself at last," he said.

Something about his exuberance rubbed off on Reed, harking back as it did to their younger, less responsible selves. "I'm still wired," Reed said, holding up his hand so Casey could see it trembling.

"You've got some of that crap on your hand."

A streak of black paint was slashed across Reed's wrist. Casey found a smudge of the paint on the sleeve of his police uniform. "Toxic shit," Casey said. "I wasn't even near the damned can."

Neither of them had an explanation. They tried to wipe away the stains with napkins stashed in the glove compartment, but the stains remained in that way stains had a tendency to do.

They drove down streets lit by radiant lamps, and streets that were dark and a little foreboding.

When they arrived at Casey's house, he invited Reed inside for a beer, unwilling, it seemed, to let go of his high just yet. Shamus, Casey and Maggie's golden retriever, emerged from behind a bush and walked over to them almost regally. He licked Reed's hand with a certain obligation.

The front door was locked so Casey had to use his key. Maggie was standing in a corner of the living room, holding a glass of wine in one hand and staring at a painting on the wall. Apparently they'd caught her in a fleeting moment of repose as she stared at the painting, because she didn't seem aware of his and Casey's entrance although they hadn't been quiet about it. When she noticed them she jumped, startled, and then smiled apologetically. "There's a bare spot," she said. Maggie had mild blue eyes Reed knew from experience could flame to violet when aroused. She had a tendency to wear her hair slung over one shoulder and to run her fingers through it when lost in deep thought, which was often enough.

Casey brushed his lips against her cheek, which she extended out to him with a slight pivot of her head. "Right there," she said, motioning to a spot. "It's just bare canvas. It's like that famous painting I can't remember, where a part of some man's arm wasn't painted. Or a leg? Maybe I'm thinking of the Sistine Chapel."

Casey feigned interest by squinting at the painting. Bought in Cancun during their honeymoon, it was a mesmerizing depiction of a serene beach engulfed by a storm-pitched jungle. "What's missing here?" he asked.

Reed saw what was missing, although he had to focus hard to make it out—a sliver of sky that should have been showing through the tiny space between the swaying jungle fronds, but wasn't. Maggie pointed it out again to Casey. "We've had this painting for nearly five years," she said. "How come I'm only noticing it now?"

The men shrugged. "So odd that the artist would miss a spot, on a canvas this size," Maggie continued.

"Or did he just want that piece of sky bare," Reed said. "No color, nothing past that choking jungle of trees."

Maggie pondered this. Casey looked uncomfortable, as he often did when any conversation veered toward art or interpretation of the abstract. He started unbuttoning his shirt, and this seemed to relax him again. "Mercury's staying for a beer. You don't mind, do you?"

"Of course not." In fact, she seemed pleased. Casey and Maggie were nothing if not welcoming.

"Want one?" Casey asked Maggie, but she shook her head and held up her wineglass. Casey stepped into the kitchen. Maggie indicated for Reed to sit down. Casey returned with the beers before they had a chance to make a stab at idle conversation. "I shouldn't ask," Maggie said, "but what is that smell?"

Casey laughed, but Reed was confused. The spray paint, was that what she meant? "It's the smell of a wrong righted," Casey said, nodding at Reed.

He retreated into the bathroom, leaving Maggie and Reed alone again. Reed wanted to unbutton his own shirt a notch or two, already feeling the constriction of the alley, his own disgust and need for vindication. Maggie leaned back against the sofa, holding her wineglass at a dangerous angle. He was reminded of the night he had gone out with Casey and Maggie for celebratory drinks only a week before the wedding. While Casey had been in the bathroom, just as he was now, Maggie, holding her wineglass at a slant, as she was now, had asked, glassy-eyed, "Should I be doing this, Reed? Marrying your best friend?"

Reed had wanted to answer, "No, you shouldn't," but Casey had returned to the table before they could really get the conversation going. And once married, there had seemed no point in resurrecting the question, although Casey and Maggie's marriage had always seemed slightly unreal to Reed, something they were just trying out.

"Sorry we're late!" Casey called from the bathroom. The faucet was running, endlessly running. "Merc and I were engaged in a little urban renewal."

Maggie watched Reed as he sipped his beer, a distant smile on his face. "The boys aren't going to let me in on this one, I suppose," she said.

Reed cocked a roguish eyebrow in her direction, then his face turned serious again. He'd slept with Maggie; it had only been several years ago. He was embarrassed to think of that now—their stark nakedness, his strained attempts to pass as a satisfied lover. It was as if he were remembering incidents from a stranger's life. Despite the passing of time, there remained a slight awkwardness between Reed and Maggie, an unspoken uneasiness they both felt but Casey seemed oblivious to. "Your hands are stained," Maggie said.

Reed glanced down at the streak across his wrist and saw there was now, also, a light smudge of dark paint along the knuckles of his left hand. Missing sky, and now more phantom spray paint. He brushed at one of the spots with his fingers, but of course this helped not at all.

"Merc, come wash your hands!" Casey called from the bathroom.

With a sheepish grin, Reed rose and walked to the bathroom. Casey was shirtless now, his head shoved in the sink under the running faucet. He stood up straight, grabbed a towel, and started drying his dripping hair.

And Reed didn't avert his eyes the way he normally would when in the presence of a shirtless straight man, although Casey seemed oblivious to this as well. "Go ahead, wash your hands," he whispered. "Maggie's a detective at heart. I'd match her against Granger any day."

Reed nodded but didn't move at first. Tiny beads of water glistened on Casey's shoulders and chest. Finally, Reed turned to the sink and started with the pretense of washing his hands. He scrubbed with soap, although his attention was directed more on a couple of strands of Casey's hair that lingered in the sink. Quietly, he picked them up and deposited them in the wastebasket. The bathroom was not large so he expected that Casey would leave, but Casey remained, his back turned to Reed as he gazed out the bathroom window, humming under his breath a hazy tune that could have been most any song.

Reed allowed himself an eyeful of Casey's back through the mirror above the sink, then felt cheap and looked back down at his hands.

The soap and water faded the spray paint stains but didn't remove them entirely. Reed was reaching for a towel on the rack next to the sink when he noticed a calendar hung from a hook above the rack. A few dates had been circled and highlighted.

At first he didn't understand the relevance of having a calendar in the bathroom, but just as the realization came to him, Casey stepped back over and said, "We're trying, Merc."

Ovulation chart, Reed thought. He knew Casey and Maggie planned on having children someday—Casey talked about it often enough—but this diligent charting made the possibility all too real. The calendar cast their marriage in a different light, exposing the blunt sexual reality of it, a side Reed tried to not think much about.

Casey slapped his hand on Reed's shoulder. "How do you feel about being a godfather someday?" he asked, his hand resting, maybe, just a moment too long at the back of Reed's neck.

Before Reed was required to respond, Maggie showed up in the bathroom doorway, still holding her wine, and shaking her head at Casey and Reed. "The party's really been moved into the men's room?" she asked.

Casey dropped his arm from Reed's shoulders, grabbed Reed's beer out of his hand, and took a sip. "Merc wants to be godfather," Casey said.

"Casey!"

"He saw the calendar. It's not a secret, is it?"

Reed's neck twitched where Casey's arm had just been. Maggie was staring intently at Reed. "Put on a shirt, honey," she said lightly to Casey.

Her voice was even, but there was an undercurrent that even Casey noticed. "We have company," she prodded him.

"Merc isn't company." But he shrugged and walked into the bedroom for a T-shirt.

Reed stared down at his beer. He had the uneasy sense that Maggie understood what he was feeling, and he resented her for it. The whole night felt sullied now.

His mood still hadn't improved by the time he was driving home. He was irritated at both Maggie and Casey, although it seemed unfair to be too upset with either one. And what had it meant to find that stupid message about Christian on the alley wall? It seemed an unpleasant harbinger, a warning of some kind, growing louder.

And Anthony was dead—amiable, good-natured, tow-headed Anthony, with his trace of a Southern accent despite ten years lived in the Midwest. Once he'd leaned across the bar at Quench and muttered into Reed's ear, "If you had a brother—"

"I have two brothers," Reed had said.

"You know what I mean." Anthony had smiled and walked to the other end of the bar.

Now that man was dead. When Reed was undressing for bed, loneliness sweeping over him like a current, he phoned Alex on a whim. "We don't have to pretend we've never known each other," he said.

There was a long silence on the other end. "Officer Reed," Alex said.

"Is it a crime to stay in touch?"

He could hear Alex breathing on the other end. "No crime, officer," he said. "No such crime that I know about."

(4)

Reed didn't know that Eddie had been the one who had spray-painted the slur against Christian on the alley wall. Eddie had done this the previous Saturday night with a couple of his friends from the wrestling team when they were celebrating the end of the school year. Danny and Bruce were a year older than Eddie, and he knew they had problems with him because his brother was Christian McGregor, *The Flame Christian McGregor.* Just being related to Christian made Eddie suspect in the eyes of his classmates—guilt by brotherly association—even though Eddie was afforded some respect because his wrestling record for pins far outweighed his losses; how could they not, in some sense, respect his power?

It hadn't been easy for Eddie to escape the house that night. Since his mother had started cracking down on how late he could stay out, Eddie had been forced to go up to his room and pretend to go to sleep. Once Iris had settled into her own room, Eddie opened his bedroom window, climbed out onto the roof, and scuttled down the oak tree to the ground. Then he waited out by the bushes for Danny and Bruce to pick him up. Even with his house only a few feet away, the darkness felt more potent than it normally did, charged with a secretive, killing pulse. Every sound was magnified, both on the edge of familiar and not quite familiar at all. Eddie wanted to stand in the menacing dark and he wanted to back away from it, so when Danny's car pulled up to the curb, Eddie wasn't sure if he was relieved or disappointed.

The boys drove around town for a while, downing several beers and a few shots of whiskey for good measure. Danny and Bruce egged Eddie into the vandalism, roughhousing around and berating Christian until Eddie relented and agreed that Christian disgusted him as much as he did them. His head spinning with drink, Eddie soon found himself standing in the alley, thinking of how much his brother weighed him down, Christian's persecution always coming back at him. He'd had enough, definitely enough. So Eddie took the spray can that Danny handed him and spelled out his brother's name, attaching that name to *faggot* with a zealousness that also left him feeling vaguely sick, digging deep as he was into some personal inner darkness. The boys jumped into their car and crammed themselves into the front seat when a different car pulled up to the bank's ATM machine, headlights sweeping toward them, briefly illuminating them before plunging them back into darkness.

They drove around town some more and quaffed a couple more beers, which had grown lukewarm in the heat. They clapped Eddie on the back and slung their arms around his neck, praising him for acting "criminal." For several minutes Eddie coasted on a wave of giddy comradeship, sitting between his two friends, but when he clapped Danny on the shoulder in return, Danny pulled away with a tense knowing smile on his face.

Soon things began to turn darker. Bruce remembered Greg Averill owned a farm on the edge of town. Averill was a math teacher at their high school who had given Danny and Bruce each a D in geometry, which had nearly affected their eligibility for next year's wrestling squad. "Isn't he maybe queer too?" Danny asked. "Man, they're everywhere. Greg, what a fag name."

Eddie had no real interest in going to Averill's place—he'd gotten a B- in algebra—but he had no way home otherwise, so he rode with them out to the farm. Bruce wanted to piss on the mailbox or maybe bust a window, or they could use the remainder of the spray paint for a message on the lawn that would make Averill think twice before he failed or fucked anyone again. Danny said no, that was uninspired. "That fag killer's raised the stakes," he said. "He's upped the ante, my friend."

How they ended up in the pasture leading to the barn on the edge of Averill's property, Eddie couldn't say. Everything seemed disjointed and moving too fast. Even the pasture felt a little dangerous although it was just a small and open field with nowhere much to hide. Danny and Bruce kept laughing and then shushing each other, and Eddie sensed, maybe, how it was really a nervous laughter. The smell of the spray paint still burned in his nostrils, a conflagration, and his brother's name vibrated in his head, *Christian, Christian*. He was beginning to think Danny and Bruce meant to torch the barn. They were standing beside the barn, in fact, contemplating its enormous wall, when they saw a lamb sleeping on a hump of grass near the door, apparently having been locked out. Danny chortled and staggered over to it, and somehow the animal was in his arms. They carried it about a hundred yards until they were out of the pasture and had stepped into a line of trees. The animal had fully awoken and began to bleat. It was a strange lamb with a shrunken back hoof and a gnarl of black wool on its head. "What the hell?" Bruce said. "This is a goddamned fucking lamb."

Danny shrugged. The animal seemed to mock them now, growing panicked by their agitated movements and the smell of spray paint and alcohol. A hot wind surged past and blew their own drunken breaths back into their faces. The lamb kicked at Danny's arm so that he lost hold and dropped it. Bruce fell on top of the lamb and wrestled it while Danny's hand closed around a stone and struck at the black spot on the animal's head. Bruce chose his own stone and struck at it too. Danny held out his stone to Eddie, an offering. Eddie shook his head no. The blood and violence stunned him.

At last the animal lay broken and still at their feet. Eddie threw up in some brush, the fumes of the spray paint having moved into his brain, poisoning him. A lamb, Christ, they'd murdered a lamb! Dazed, Danny jumped to his feet and jeered at Eddie, an edge of drunken uneasiness in his voice as he stared down at his shirt, flecked with lamb's blood. He said this was *sport*, nothing more, because it was only a goddamned lamb, and they didn't have souls in the first place. All the four-leggeds didn't have souls, everyone knew that. The fear they'd seen in the animal's eyes, the desperate will to live, had been merely a primal bestial thing.

But Bruce was spooked now, with Eddie sick and the cursed lamb dead at their feet. He suggested they get rid of the carcass and then motivate their asses home.

The boys moved further into the trees. Danny lay the dead animal down and kicked some dirt over it. "He wouldn't even take a shot with us," he said, looking squarely at Eddie. "McGregor—*McGreg*or—wouldn't even take a shot."

Back at the car they removed their bloodied shirts before they climbed inside. Eddie removed his, too. His shirt was clean, which made it worthless to him now. He tried to sit in the front again, but Danny shoved him into the backseat.

Bruce drove them back toward town because Danny was "too far gone" and he wouldn't be able to keep the car from weaving into the other lane or off the road altogether. The car was steamy but they didn't bother to open their windows, as if that might expose their crimes somehow. The stink of their sweat and their guilt began to swell in the car, a masculine odor that Eddie, alone in the backseat, thought would make him sick, until he realized that he was breathing the smell in willingly. He couldn't stop himself. His two friends sat hot and restless in the front seat and he wanted in that moment to be sitting up there between them. This was such an unwelcome thought, so *Christian* a thought, that Eddie grabbed the empty paper bag in which they'd been carrying the beers and vomited into it.

"Christ," Danny said. "Quit being such a fuckin' woman. And cut the goddamned vomitus puking. This is my old man's car."

Once in town they stopped in back of Carlson's Automotive to toss their bloodied shirts into a trash dumpster. Bruce had the idea to burn the shirts as a final anarchic protest, and Eddie would have gladly taken part in that ritual. All his vomiting was sobering him up quickly; his own unbloodied shirt now repulsed him. He was bothered that he'd thrown up about the lamb, what had he been thinking? That would cost him in the long run. But Danny had turned sensible by then and said, "No, a flame will attract a cop or," and he looked at Eddie, "this jerk's brother."

Eddie liked Reed in almost equal proportion to how much he hated Christian, but he said nothing in his brother's defense. The boys opened a bag of half-rotted food that was already inside the dumpster, dropped the shirts into the bag, and drove away.

"I hear that cop brother of yours is a faggot, too," Danny said, not bothering to turn and make eye contact with Eddie as he spoke. "That true, Mc-Gregor."

Eddie stared at the strip of raw sunburn on the back of Danny's cleanly shaven neck. Danny could afford to mock because his own brother was straight and intimidating and headed into the Army soon. "Fuck you," Eddie said.

"You wish." The boys in front laughed and shook their heads in understanding, then fell back into silence.

They dropped Eddie off first. They didn't bother to say goodbye, just backed out of the driveway and drove in the opposite direction from where their homes were. Bare-chested, chilled, Eddie climbed up the tree, once nearly losing his grip and falling, before he reached the roof and climbed with stealth through his bedroom window. *Thief, criminal*: the words floated outside of him, yet another accusation. He stepped into the hallway to go to the bathroom and passed Christian's room with a loathing that rose from somewhere deep inside him up into his mouth and tasted like tin. When had loathing taken the taste of tin? He brushed his teeth twice to rid his mouth of the taste. This was his life and he was stuck in the molasses center of it. The animal snorts of Christian's snoring trailed him down the hall to his own room.

*

The challenge between Eddie and Christian had become to ignore the other as much as possible. The other *did not exist*. Yet once school was out for summer break, and with Iris working five days a week and wanting them to stay around the house as much as possible, they found themselves alone together far too often. The house shrank when it was just the two of them, amplifying their dislike of one another. After he'd spray-painted Christian's name on the side of an alley wall, Eddie found speaking to his brother all but impossible. And Christian, sensing things had worsened between them without understanding exactly why, stopped even perfunctory conversation with him.

Sometimes Eddie found himself actually glowering at Christian. He felt little connection to him other than the bond you couldn't help but feel, even if only slightly, for someone who was connected to you by "blood" and that mysterious evocative web called "family history." This hadn't always been the case. Once he and Christian had played together all the time, inventing imaginary worlds that they could mutually rule over and then destroy. But as they grew older, Eddie began to see how different Christian was from the other guys. He didn't fit in; he was teased, taunted, ridiculed, sometimes cuffed on the side of the head or shoved into lockers. Christian's physical weakness and unwillingness to fight back was an embarrassment to Eddie, and a danger to him as well, since everyone at school knew Eddie was Christian's brother and so started looking at Eddie as a misfit as well. To fight against this as best he could, Eddie became good at wrestling, good at sports in general, good at dressing and walking and talking like all the other guys around him. He grew to resent Christian for not being able to do the same, for not being able to *act* normal. And once that resentment started, it was like a strong ocean riptide current inside of him, driven by unseen forces, meaning to drag him under.

Almost everything about Christian aggravated Eddie these days. Start with his finger-in-the-electric-socket hair, as if it, too, had joined in Christian's complete rejection of the conventional. *Even his hair isn't straight,* Eddie laughed to himself, more than once. Christian's mouth was too big, his lips colorless, his breath stale. The freckles sprayed across his forehead, which on a girl might have looked cute, on Christian looked like blemishes. His eyes showed too much white and were perpetually moist, largely from allergies although people often mistook him as on the verge of tears.

If possible, Christian had turned even more aggravating since the murders. Now he was obsessed with watching the news, hunting for whatever scraps of an update on the killings that he could find. Most evenings around dinner time, when he was at home and not working or hanging out with his motley crew of friends, he would park himself on the sofa in front of the television set and lean forward with an anticipation that looked like a bad stage actor's imitation of anticipation. Yet Eddie knew Christian's obsessive concern was genuine, which made it, somehow, even more galling. Once the newscasters on one station had moved on to other news, Christian would flip channels, hoping to catch a lingering update on some other station. When he was satisfied no other reports were forthcoming, he would turn off the TV and leave the room, but for the ten o'clock news he was back on his same spot on the sofa, watching intently and leaning forward, always, like a pincher that had caught a scent.

Eddie wanted to follow what was going on as well—Barrow's Point in the news at last!—but naturally he couldn't sit down on the sofa next to Christian and watch the news reports along with him. So Eddie hovered in the background and strained to hear what he could. The murders were exciting to Eddie—he was almost enjoying the nightmares he'd started having of a man lying under his bed and carving letters into the mattress—but Christian just seemed to grow more and more troubled and outraged as days passed and no suspect was apprehended. Soon his gravity on the matter had trumped Eddie's excitement, making Eddie feel like he was missing something. In no time at all, Christian had staked his personal claim to the murders, the biggest event to ever happen in Barrow's Point, and shouldered Eddie out. To make matters worse, Iris would sit on the sofa and watch the news along with Christian, as if she shared his conviction and sense of urgency. This only alienated Eddie further, forcing him into the periphery of his own family.

He didn't blame his mother, of course. This was Christian's doing, as so much wrong in his life was Christian's doing.

Often Iris would insist that they all eat supper together as a family. She had done this even before the town's outbreak of violence, but now she did it with a devotion that was nearly religious. At these times, Eddie and Christian couldn't avoid sitting across the table from each other, breaking the same bread, bowing their heads in prayer to the same God their father had once served. Eddie imagined his mother was consciously plotting to keep the peace between them by forcing these family meals, not realizing the full extent of their mutual dislike. When she sat at the table and saw two tight-lipped teenage boys staring at one another, she attributed this to the fact they were boys and teenagers and naturally moody. She appointed herself diplomat, the kitchen table negotiator, drawing both into conversations, forever chipping away at their silences, unaware that she was heightening the boys' hatred by forcing them to sit and listen to each other, to tolerate one another, and finally to act cordial, when all they really wanted was distance.

A few days after the murdered lamb incident, they all sat down to a meal of lamb chops, cheese-flavored mashed potatoes, peas, and fresh bread. *Lamb,* Eddie inwardly groaned. It couldn't have been more laughable. He was still jarred by his experience with Danny and Bruce, not because he'd turned against his brother with such vehemence but because his friends had murdered the lamb and he'd done nothing to stop them. He was still checking the *Barrow's Point Gazette* with a gnawing guilt, hunting between the murder headlines for some mention of a slaughtered lamb found on Greg Averill's property. Soon the police would commence a search for a rebel gang of lamb killers. But this never happened. Apparently, he and Danny and Bruce had gotten away with something. As soon as they'd tossed their shirts into the trash dumpster, it was as if they'd cast aside the crime as well.

Only now his mother was serving up lamb chops! She'd broiled three chops with the tacit understanding that two were for Eddie. Christian didn't eat meat. He practiced the traditions of an animal rights group that didn't eat "anything with eyes," which included fish. "I don't eat living tissue," Christian had said once. When Eddie pointed out he didn't eat *living* tissue either, Christian said: "Anything you have to kill first."

He was humane to all sentient creatures, for Christ's sake! It drove Eddie crazy.

So he was a little disgusted when he looked down at the lamb chop on his plate and felt queasy. It seemed nearly alive to him, as had the hamburger patty he'd eaten yesterday, and the blood-red sausage from the day before. Meat's tissue and gristle, its texture, weight, smell…but he loved meat, and he needed to keep eating protein if he wanted to maintain the muscle mass necessary to continue wrestling.

Iris smiled over at Eddie, a little perplexed. "Come on, eat," she said. "Aren't you hungry?"

He stared down at his plate. *For Christ's sake. Only meat.* Finally he looked past the meat although his eyes were still on it, and he cut a spear of lamb and forced himself to swallow.

That night Eddie sneaked to the downstairs bathroom so no one would hear him vomit. But when he leaned over the stool, he couldn't vomit. His stomach clenched, as if a living thing were ready to expel itself from him, a small, shivering beast-embryo. Deliriously, he imagined the meat he'd eaten was taking shape inside him, trying to turn back into a lamb right there in his stomach. His labored breathing was only feeding it oxygen and helping it to form. Small hooves kicked behind his ribcage as the meat fought to reanimate itself. Only the confines of his stomach were holding back the lamb's resurrection. Eddie couldn't vomit no matter how much he wanted to rid himself of the meat, or the meat to rid itself of him. He considered sticking his finger down his throat to induce vomiting, but that seemed bulimic, what a girl would do.

He stood up and slouched back to his bedroom, his stomach still rumbling. The night was turning into a series of animal sounds, not genuine animal sounds but the bestial sounds of what was not animal trying to become so. He lay down on his bed and closed his eyes. A ball of yarn was on the desk, quivering and exhausted, trying to fling itself off.

Eddie jerked awake. Of course there was no ball of yarn on his desk! What a femmie dream, he thought, worried, and stood up. Light-headed, he pulled the sheets off his bed for no special reason, carried them to the basement, and tossed them in the washing machine. He sat beside the machine as it rumbled and shook, a physical manifestation, almost, of what he'd felt inside himself not so long ago. What was it about this night where everything, even the inanimate, was struggling to express itself, as if trying to reach past what was physically possible? He was comforted by this simple domestic task of washing sheets, although even the word, domestic, brought a familiar unpleasant taste to his mouth.

(5)

At first the dead baby birds only distressed Maggie. The terrible symbolism occurred to her later, once she had a chance to think about it.

In late May, she started encountering the abortive bird life everywhere. Tiny broken eggshells scattered about the yard, splashes of yolk dribbling from the cracks. Once she found, nearly on her doorstep, a fractured egg with a half-formed bird embryo inside. Normally she wasn't one of those morbidly squeamish women, but she couldn't bring herself to clean up the mess. All day the broken shell and mutilated half-bird lay out in the sun until Casey returned home and removed it for her.

A couple days later the neighbor's cat, Pearl, an overfed tabby with walrus whiskers, stalked across Maggie's lawn, carrying a small bird in its mouth. The bird was still alive, fluttering and chirping weakly. Horrified, Maggie called for Shamus, thinking the sight of a dog might scare Pearl into dropping the bird, but then remembered Shamus was inside the house. She picked up a couple of small stones and pitched them at Pearl, hoping this would be enough, but Pearl only growled and vanished behind a shrub with her living prey.

Maggie ducked into the house and cried in the shower. She couldn't help herself. Life was so cruel sometimes. Her mind wandered back to that distant Baltimore of her youth when she was a child wearing a pale Easter dress and hunting for eggs in an unseasonable snow. Her knees had been numb from the cold but she had continued to hunt, undaunted, across that stretch of park that had seemed so vast then. As the snow fell more heavily, parents called for their children to return with gathered bounty. Maggie heard her own name called, but her mother's voice sounded so far away, she could easily ignore it. Several of the eggs had innocuous platitudes painted on them: *Happy Easter. Be Good. Mom Loves You. Trust in Jesus.* Maggie found a beguiling blue egg balanced between the branches of a thorny bush, with a message painted in tiny yellow script so it could all fit on the shell: *Ask for the frozen sea within.*

At home, Maggie had shown the egg to her mother. "Someone, I suspect, is beating down the existential door," her mother said, reading the egg once, then putting on her glasses and reading it again. She refused to translate the meaning to Maggie, just sighed and placed the egg in the wastebasket. Later,

Maggie retrieved the egg and kept it under her pillow for a couple of nights, careful not to move her head to the egg's side and crush it. Sometimes she sat with the altered egg in her lap and stared at the mysterious words crafted onto the shell. But what was it saying? Why couldn't she understand? After a week of this, she returned home from school one day, checked under her pillow, and found the egg was not there. She never saw it again nor dared ask her mother about it. The egg and its cryptic message had simply vanished.

She was in college before she learned the words were derivative of a phrase Kafka had once written: *A book should be an axe to break the frozen sea within us.* But hadn't the message on the egg read *Ask*, not *axe*? Had the writer been mistaken, or had Maggie misread it, or possibly was just remembering it incorrectly?

After Maggie finished crying, she stepped out of the shower and dried herself. Then she stood in front of the mirror, arms folded over her stomach, and mouthed the words that by now had become familiar to her: *No baby, no baby.*

The chant was a secret ritual she'd begun after the New Year, right around the time Casey had turned most vocal about starting a family. They'd had long discussions about this—in bed some nights, over wine at a restaurant, once while varnishing a couple of antique chairs that Maggie meant to position on the back porch. "Why now?" she'd asked him when he first proposed she start charting her menstrual cycle. "It's not like my biological clock is running on empty? Why the rush?"

He painted carefully over a slight warp in the chair's back. "Why the wait?"

She couldn't answer him because she didn't know herself, other than the thought of becoming a mother, for years inextricably yoked to a dependent, unnerved her. From where would she draw the patience? She felt no more equipped to become a mother than she'd felt when they'd first married. In many ways she felt less so. Yet in a moment of sentimental weakness, she agreed they should try for a baby. She soon regretted this decision, but it seemed wrong to renege on her promise, and she wasn't underhanded enough to go on the pill behind Casey's back.

So she started willing herself not to become pregnant. She made love to Casey as she always had, Casey a skillful and patient lover, not hasty and predictable in the way so many men were. But after they were finished, she often turned away from him and curled into a tight ball. She could hardly breathe from the weight of an inner ache grounded in nothing she could trace. With Casey's sleeping breath between her shoulder blades, she pulled her hands to her chest and muttered, *No baby*, as if conception could be reduced to this, mind over matter. *Please, no baby* she whispered again, her incantation lulling her to sleep.

Months passed without change. Was it possible that she had willed her body into a temporary state of barrenness? The idea was foolish, and yet a part of her clung to this illusion. What if her mental resistance to the idea of pregnancy was protecting her body somehow and keeping it from fertilizing? The brain was such a susceptible organ; you could talk it into most anything. Sometimes she would take an ordinary aspirin or vitamin tablet and suffuse it with magical powers. "A morning after pill," she would say to herself as she held the tablet in her palm, concentrating until she almost believed the pill was something other than what it was. In that fleeting moment of doubt, she would swallow the pill along with a handful of water.

Maggie told no one else about these private rituals, her own experiment in mind control, a kind of sorcery, a conjured faith in the irrational. She knew how crazy it would sound. In a sense, wasn't she behaving as absurdly as those ancient women she'd read about, who had squatted in the dirt and inserted apricot pits into their vaginas, believing this would prevent an egg from attaching to the uterine wall? And yet she found comfort in her own simple routines. She knew she should feel embarrassed for flirting with such superstitions—and she did—but there was no doubt she also felt oddly protected.

And with Barrow's Point now in the grip of such an unspeakable menace, bringing a child into the world seemed even more wrong. Just the thought of conceiving in this climate of fear and uncertainty made Maggie uneasy.

Nor was working at a daycare center improving her peace of mind about having children. Casey assumed she loved working with children and was good at it. When she'd started at Starcrest Daycare six years ago, fresh out of college and eager, she had been good. But then she'd never planned to work daycare for long. Initially she'd taken it on as a summer job to make money so she could study psychology at Boston University's graduate school in the fall. But that was also the summer Reed had "come out," which had placed an immediate strain on his friendship with Casey. She'd been dating Casey for over a year at that point, so she was the one he'd opened up to about Reed, admitting his discomfort, sympathy, anger, hurt, his passionate desire not to judge, yet his inability to feel comfortable with Reed's "announcement."

When it came to Reed, Maggie's feelings were wildly contradictory. On the one hand, it had been cathartic to share in Casey's surprise and barely suppressed anger, since it echoed Maggie's own hurt when Reed had broken up with her, offering no more explanation than, "We have no future together, Maggie. You must feel it, too." Yet she *had* envisioned a future with Reed, even when she'd sensed a certain detachment in their relationship, a maddening absence that was not present when he spent time with Casey and other members of the college Track team.

After her breakup with Reed, she'd spent a couple miserable weeks in a dazed state, attending classes as if nothing were wrong. She sat in the back of the room, a puzzle to her teachers and classmates—present but absent. Sometimes in *Ethics 102: Knowledge, Values, and the Quest for Meaning*, she would sit by the open window and stare out at the tree with the colliding branches that stretched nearly into the classroom. She daydreamed about climbing out the window, leaving behind the boring lectures and her own unenlightened despair, and lying across one of the branches, among the sprouting leaves, and swaying as the branches swayed. "The wind bloweth where it listeth": On her last date with Reed, they'd gone to a foreign movie that had quoted that very line, although what she remembered most vividly about the film was a grieving father pushing at the slender trunk of a young tree, trying to bend it to his will.

When Maggie wasn't attending classes, she spent a good deal of time flung across the bed in her dorm room, trying to fight past a sense of loss she hadn't felt since her father divorced her mother when Maggie was young. She ate cupcakes and crumb cakes and Trix out of the box yet didn't gain an ounce. Her roommate, Karen, tried to lure her to the dining hall for meals but Maggie refused, unable to bear running into Reed or sitting amid the cheerful clamor and pretending nothing was wrong.

It was while caught in this nether region of grief, anger, and confusion that she'd made the decision to seek out Casey for answers. If Reed was unwilling or unable to clarify matters, maybe his best friend could. She phoned

Casey over Karen's objections, not caring about appearance or consequence, and asked him if he would meet with her so they could talk. Now, tonight. It was urgent and she was tired of creeping around. Casey agreed, although with obvious reluctance. She was waiting at the archway of Old Main, leaning against one of the decorative gargoyle stone carvings, strands of her wind-blown hair catching in the gargoyle's mouth, when Casey arrived. He was wearing a tight-fitting hoodie and looked freshly showered. She was aware he was good-looking but this had meant nothing to her at the time. He was a conduit and nothing more. He smiled at her with a great deal of curiosity, his hands in the hoodie's pockets, a little hesitant at her insistence. They walked along the perimeter of the campus, circling past the meadow and the gardens of the agricultural department, then curling back inward toward the main campus. They passed an open area where a group of guys, slipping and sliding on grass still wet and muddy from the recently melted snow, played an impromptu game of football. The air was vibrant with life, male life, and with the more serene life of blossoming trees and bushes. Maggie breathed deeply, a little dizzied by it all. Finally, she found her voice and asked Casey pointblank about her breakup with Reed.

"He won't tell me anything," she said. "It's like the past eighteen months he wants to erase from his mind. Erase me."

"It only seems that way." Casey's brow was creased, as if he were working out his answer before he spoke. "I don't think even Reed knows where he's at these days."

They spoke in this honest and searching way for the entire long walk, her questions quick and forceful, and his answers slower, more deliberate. By the time Maggie returned to her dorm room it was almost dark and she felt better than she had in weeks.

A few days later, Maggie ran into Casey at the student union. On impulse they walked around the campus together again, in sunlight this time. Soon Casey started showing up in other places where she was at, becoming more and more an active presence in her life. He laughed freely around her now, no longer suspicious and on guard the way he'd been at first. Almost without their noticing, Reed was no longer the focus of their conversations. Still, it wasn't until Casey asked her out for dinner and a movie that their relationship became real, its own separate force. Hesitant at first, she soon yielded to the thrill of being desired again, and ignored the nagging sense in the back of her mind that there was something unseemly about it all.

And so it became common knowledge on campus that Maggie Hastings, only weeks after breaking up with Reed, began dating his best friend.

Despite their shaky history together, Maggie couldn't help but feel an intense loyalty to Reed. This had been especially true when Reed admitted, just days after they'd all graduated from college, that he was gay. While Casey, in his confusion, turned remote and even critical at times, Maggie leapt to Reed's defense, following an instinct as natural as breathing. "Ten years, I've been looking at him the wrong way," Casey confided to Maggie once. "My best friend, and he's this whole other secret person."

"No, I don't think so." Maggie was almost relieved to hear that Reed was gay. His breaking up with her no longer felt like such a personal rejection. "He had this private self that he's letting into the open now," she continued, caught up in her own magnanimity. "It's wrong if we start judging…if we start making this about us."

During this time, Reed, ironically, started seeking out Maggie as a sounding board about Casey, much as she'd first approached Casey as her sounding board about Reed. Soon she couldn't imagine moving away from this charged atmosphere, not while she was the confidante to both her ex-boyfriend and her current one, the tenuous string that bound the two men together. If she left for graduate school in Boston, that string might snap, not to mention place an enormous strain on her relationship with Casey at a time when they were still navigating the waters between them. So she postponed Boston University for a year over her mother's protests. "You may never leave that town if you don't leave now," her mother counseled over the phone. "I've never understood why you felt compelled to go to college in Wisconsin in the first place."

"I'm not staying because I can't live without Wisconsin. I'm in a relationship."

"Isn't this current charmer the best friend of the gay guy you were dating?"

"I'm hanging up now, mother."

"Darling, I'm sorry. Of course I'm kidding. But why can't Reed move—"

"Casey!"

"Yes, Casey. I'm sorry. Reed, the name sticks in my head. Casey can't move to Massachusetts with you, I suppose?"

Maggie was too embarrassed to admit that Reed was as much of a reason for her staying in Barrow's Point as Casey was, too embarrassed to admit that she enjoyed the power she wielded over them both during this unsettled time. She took this power seriously, driven to altruism and self-sacrifice. For several weeks she chipped away at Casey's anger and sense of betrayal, at Reed's stubbornness and fierce pride. Then Reed started hinting at moving to Chicago for "a fresh start." The thought of Reed moving away before anything had been resolved upset Maggie more than she cared to admit. She wasn't sure why she was fighting so hard for resolution between Casey and Reed when she'd never received her own resolution with Reed. Yet she wanted peace for them because it also meant peace for herself. She wanted Casey and Reed to make up so Reed would not leave town. The truth was as simple and inarguable as that.

And so she began her final, fierce attempt to bring the two men together. She insisted that they had to speak one on one, no holds barred. She was sick of playing intermediary. To her sudden insistence, Casey and Reed gradually relented. They agreed to meet at a bar, where the two men talked and drank for some time while Maggie, alone in her apartment, curled up in a chair and puzzled over Virginia Woolf. By the time Casey returned to her very late at night, he and Reed had not only made up, but Casey had convinced Reed to join him in trying out for the Barrow's Point police academy. Maggie was never to know what they'd said to one another that had brought about the reconciliation, since Casey remained maddeningly quiet whenever she tried to drag the whole story out of him. The swiftness of Casey and Reed's turnaround was both pleasing and bittersweet for Maggie, knowing as she did that in bringing the two men together, she had returned herself to the backdrop of their friendship.

A few months after this ordeal, Casey proposed to Maggie. Although analytical by nature, there were also moments when her impulses contradicted reason. She accepted Casey's proposal in a giddy, unthinking rush. She placed graduate school on permanent hold while she planned their wedding, and soon—it had all been a whirlwind, really—she was married. "Congratulations, Mrs. Casey Saunders," her mother said after the ceremony, kissing

Maggie's cheek with a slight but measured reserve that Maggie knew from experience meant resignation. At the wedding reception, her mother drank several martinis and glared ladylike daggers at Maggie's father, seated on the other end of the room with "the new me," although he'd been married to his second wife for over fifteen years, longer than he'd been married to Maggie's mother.

After Maggie and Casey settled into the daily routine of their marriage, Maggie started growing restless. Although she'd loved living in Barrow's Point during her college years, she wasn't sure she wanted to make this her permanent home. But it was the only life Casey had ever known and he showed no desire to live anywhere else, so for the time being she was bound to Barrow's Point.

Starcrest Daycare became, almost by default, Maggie's permanent workplace. She'd always meant to hunt around for a more challenging position, but somehow she never quite did this. Nor was her patience what it had been once. When she'd started at Starcrest, the children had struck her as bright, energetic, and imaginative. She'd adored watching over them, playing their silly games or trying to identify their smeared finger paintings. But over the years some of that charm had worn away. Now the children seemed loud rather than energetic, their clamor disrupting whatever private reverie she might have been drifting into.

One particular child began to trouble her. Anna was a thin Scandinavian beauty who had been one of Maggie's favorites when she'd appeared shy, well behaved, and respectful of her elders. But recently the girl had started to speak with more frankness, revealing a monstrous precocity, an inflexibility of spirit that astonished Maggie.

One bright morning in early June, Maggie watched Anna initiate a game with a couple of boys a year younger than her. Maggie sat in one of the swings built for the older children, swaying from side to side, soothed by the gentle rocking motion that returned her, briefly, to a less complicated state. She couldn't make out what game the children were playing. The boys stalked about looking furtive while Anna crouched behind a sapling. Then she leapt out at them, howling pure as a banshee. The boys wailed and scattered. Anna charged after the smaller boy, Tommy. They dashed around in lopsided circles before Anna cornered him against the chain-link fence that separated the children from the street. Breathing hard, Tommy feinted back and forth as Anna moved closer. When he tried to run around her, she raised her arm and struck him on the side of the head. Maggie stood up from the swing, ready to intervene, but the boy, still in character, collapsed with an exaggerated flourish into the grass. Anna laughed and jumped up and down. "I killed a fag!" she cried.

At first Maggie thought she had misheard. Tommy peered up from the ground. Was the game over?

Anna raised her heel and stomped down on his head.

Instantly Maggie was at Anna's side, pulling her away, while Beth, an ingénue-type uncertain about her own future, tended to Tommy, who had begun to wail.

But once Maggie isolated Anna, she hardly knew what to say. "We were just pretending," Anna offered.

"No you weren't. You hurt him!"

Anna's eyes were quiet with an almost unholy patience, as if Maggie were the one who did not understand.

"What were you pretending then?" Something ugly beat in Maggie's chest.

Anna looked away. "What?" Maggie was insistent. She wanted to hear the girl say it again. But Anna, sensing Maggie was trying to flush her out in some way, grew cautious.

"We were playing Murder," Anna said.

"Okay." Maggie knew she needed to sound reasonable if she meant to get anywhere. "You were playing the killer?"

Anna nodded.

"And who was Tommy playing?"

Anna paused, weighing her words. "The one getting killed!"

Maggie looked away, confused if the child had actually said what she thought she'd heard. "Why do you want to play a game like that?" she asked, a little defeated. "Murder!"

Although she couldn't continue in good conscience, remembering the gruesome games she'd played when young. She and her best friend, Jasmine, had gone through a phase where they couldn't get enough of Drown, holding the other's head underwater—pool, lake, shower, sink, it hardly mattered.

The next day Maggie found Anna sitting alone under a tree, reading a book, so wholesome an image that Maggie approached her almost with suspicion. "What are you reading?" she asked.

Anna showed her the book: *Anne of Green Gables*. Maggie almost sighed with relief. "A book named after you," Maggie laughed.

"No, not me." Anna wiggled one of her loose baby teeth and squinted up at Maggie. "It's an abomination."

The word *abomination* coming from Anna's mouth was startling enough. "The book?" Maggie asked.

The girl's eyes did not waver. "You know," she said.

Maggie shook her head, and then, with the force of a blow to her chest, she understood what Anna was referring to. Homosexuality? Maggie almost said the word aloud but checked herself. Yet Anna had brought it up, hadn't she, by implication? Maggie was caught, somehow unable to say the word aloud in front of a child who was not her own, just as Anna was unwilling to say the word overtly because she was afraid of a scolding or because she was trying to bait Maggie. Was an eight-year-old child capable of such sophisticated manipulation?

"My Mom reads the Bible to me," Anna added.

Her mother was Deanne Gabriel, married to the grandson of one of the founders of Mutual Trust Bank on State Street. Maggie had always found Deanne pleasant and diverting. But what was she saying to Anna, nights, as she soaped her daughter's back in the bathtub, or read her to sleep with the brutal language and images of the Old Testament?

"An abomination," Anna repeated. "I can spell it, too. Do you want to hear?"

"Absolutely not." When Maggie was eight, she'd understood the word only in conjunction with the Abominable Snowman from the Rudolph Christmas cartoon, that claymation figure that stomped and roared until it was defanged, and then it became a somewhat fey monstrosity hanging a many pronged Christmas star atop a giant tree.

Teeth, monsters, abominations, eggs, vicious children, dead birds and dead bodies—all mixed together, the world layered and connected in ways that were too obvious, or else in ways she couldn't quite get at. Unless she was trying to string together connections that didn't actually exist in a random universe. Jasmine had somewhat bleakly come to that conclusion—existence as divine chaos rather than divine order—the last time Maggie had spoken to her. Of course, Jasmine had been enduring a nasty breakup and a nagging bout of mononucleosis at the time.

Maggie rubbed her arms. "Do you like seafood?" she asked Anna.

"I ate lobster on Sunday!" Anna exclaimed with a little more volume than was necessary. "We went to Seymour's Seafood. Daddy picked a lobster and we ate him."

"Yes, but the Bible says eating lobster is also an abomination. So you see, you've committed your own abomination."

Was she really standing there debating abstractions with an eight-year-old? It was just one of those depressingly sunny days, all that warmth and brightness that felt so wonderful against the skin but all the while was aging you prematurely, laying the groundwork for future cancers. She really needed to get a hold of herself. Anna frowned and wiggled her loose tooth again. Once when Maggie was about Anna's age, she'd found a man's incisor in her lunchbox. This discovery had seemed remarkable to her, an early glimpse into the mysterious and the arbitrary. Because of course it was not a tooth she recognized; no men lived with Maggie and her mother. And why had she been so convinced it was a male tooth?

Anna caressed a page of her book in such a way that suggested she meant to rip it out. Then she picked up a stick from under the tree and started poking—how could it be otherwise?—at a dry and abandoned bird's nest lying on the other side of the chain-link fence. "I'm bored," Anna said. "You don't know what you're talking about."

Maggie could all but picture the child's future—Anna Gabriel, one of those tacky blonde women who would appear on partisan TV "news shows" and condemn pretty much everyone who didn't fit into a white, conservative, evangelical world. Soon Anna would be old enough not to believe in evolution. As if to renounce this vision, Maggie walked away without another word, to the jungle gym where Sid Rollins was hanging upside down, imitating a primate. "Once I loved a man who was an abomination," Maggie mumbled aloud, surrounded by children who weren't listening.

"Once," she repeated, and wondered why she should find herself, after all this, hung up on that word.

*

When Deanne Gabriel arrived to pick up Anna the following afternoon, she pulled Maggie aside and, in a somewhat curt but still civil voice, asked Maggie not to involve Anna in discussions *of a moral nature*. "She's just a child," Deanne said.

"I'm not trying to teach her morals." But now Maggie was confused. Because was she? "She stomped on a boy's head a couple days ago," Maggie blurted. "Did you know that?"

Deanne narrowed her eyes. "How could I know if you never told me?"

And it was true that she had never mentioned this to Deanne. "On his head," Maggie repeated, undeterred. "And Anna said something horrible. I had to intervene."

Color rose in Deanne's face and throat. "Child's play is not always attractive," she said. "I hope you're not making assumptions about people you don't really know. She's eight. She picks up things from music and television. The Internet. It's all over the place. Tell me when there's a problem and I can school her on what's right and wrong."

By the time Maggie left the daycare center, she was dispirited and irritable. It was more than her run-in with Deanne Gabriel. Now that she replayed in her mind the initial incident with Anna, she couldn't say with complete assurance what Anna had said. Although what Maggie heard repeatedly in her mind was *I killed a fag. I killed a fag.* But sounds and words were always getting distorted. Only how did the Bible and abomination fit in otherwise?

She confessed the whole embarrassing saga to Casey when he arrived home from work. He listened with a patience that was almost convincing, nodded his head a couple of times, then reminded her they'd agreed to eat at his parents' house tonight as an early toast to Maggie and Casey's fifth wedding anniversary.

"Oh, Casey!" Maggie had forgotten about dinner at the Saunders. "So we're locked in?"

Casey smiled and raised his eyebrows. "You know my mother. There's no exit strategy."

So they drove across town to Phil and Livia Saunders's house. Usually Maggie could overlook Livia's formality around her, but tonight she felt hung on meat hooks from the moment she stepped into the kitchen. Phil pulled Casey aside and poured him some scotch neat, a drink he habitually offered only to his male guests. Once, wanting to make a point of some kind, Maggie had requested her own scotch. Livia had shaken her head in mild disapproval, but Phil had thought Maggie's request a grand joke and, out of sheer perversity, poured her twice as much as she wanted. Maggie disliked scotch but finished the drink without complaint, and went home that night more than a little lightheaded. The next time she and Casey visited, Phil offered her a scotch, but it seemed silly to continue drinking liquor she didn't like for the purpose of vague gender protest. So she declined and returned to her sex, joining Livia in sipping white wine on the sidelines.

Only tonight, when Maggie started to pour herself a glass of wine from the open bottle on the counter, Livia frowned. "You're sure?" she asked.

Maggie was momentarily baffled. "I'm not pregnant *yet*," she said when she understood, annoyed that Casey had broadcast their plans to his parents. What had happened to privacy, discreet waiting?

"He's anxious to start a family, is all," Livia said. "You'll have been married for five years this Friday."

"Yes, five years." The number felt apart from Maggie. Imagine Livia's reaction if she knew what extremes Maggie was going *not* to become pregnant.

As Casey had predicted, the dinner was not a simple informal meal of burgers on a grill, the kind that Maggie might have found relaxing. Instead, Livia had prepared Cornish game hen, brown rice pilaf, Caesar salad, and a couple loaves of Italian bread from a local bakery. Casey's sixteen-year-old sister Cassidy, the only child left at home, joined them, although she was dressed as if she were at an outdoor barbeque—shorts, a halter top, sandals. Maggie envied her the freedom of purposefully defying expectation.

Soon the conversation veered, as conversations in Barrow's Point had a tendency to do these days, to the murders. And instantly talk around the dinner table grew more animated, as if it had received a shot of adrenaline. "The whole thing is too, too wretched," Livia said. "I don't dare let Cassidy out of my sight."

Cassidy picked a shard of ice out of her water glass and moistened her lips with it. "Mom, I hardly think I'm the killer's type!" she said.

"Killers don't have types. They have victims."

Cassidy rose from her chair and began rutting through the refrigerator's vegetable crisper. She returned with a green apple. "I've prepared a feast!" Livia protested.

"But I'm dieting." Cassidy bit too saucily into the apple. "Judy says the killer is probably some repressed closet case. That will be the big twist of the whole thing."

"Is that kind of a stereotype?" Maggie asked. "The whole repressed closet case killer theory?"

"I didn't say that, Judy did!" Cassidy bit again into the apple with the endless effervescence of youth. "But back years ago, when we were twelve or whatever, she said Hitler was probably gay. And now look! She's a visionary."

They all stalled on a response. Phil turned to Casey. "I suppose Mikkelson has placed you on high alert," he said.

"We work a couple of extra hours a week," Casey said. He smiled at Maggie although she couldn't decipher what his smile meant. "Reed's kind of put himself on high alert."

"Of course, Reed." Phil stroked his jaw.

"He's starting to take things a little personally, I mean."

"I imagine it would be difficult not to." Maggie reached for her wineglass. This particular conversation felt unnecessary to her. But then she'd never been comfortable when Phil or Livia talked about Reed. She knew they felt awkwardly about him. They were perplexed that Maggie had been involved with Reed before she'd started dating Casey. To Phil and Livia, Maggie and Casey and Reed were an unwieldy trio they couldn't quite fathom. After Casey and Maggie's wedding, Casey had confessed that Livia had pleaded with him not to rush into marriage with Maggie Hastings "given the circumstances." Of course Maggie had been annoyed when she heard this; while her own mother had been trying to persuade her against marrying Casey, Livia had been trying to dissuade Casey from marriage as well. Not that Maggie could blame either mother for her doubts. Maggie had them herself back then. Actually, those doubts, in various disguises, were creeping up on her again.

"I guess so," Casey said. "It's just he was following Christian around town for a while, sort of spying on him to make sure he was okay."

Maggie was surprised. Was this something Reed wanted broadcast through the gossip underground? And why hadn't Casey mentioned this to her, his wife, but he was telling his parents? "I didn't know that," she said in an almost injured tone.

"He tells me pretty much everything," Casey said.

Maggie felt a pang of jealousy. Casey was right. Reed was much closer to Casey than he was to her. This had always been the case, she realized now, even when she'd been dating Reed, so why should it bother her now? This was yet another reminder of a world Casey and Reed shared that was distinctly their own.

"I need to give Iris a call," Livia said. "We haven't spoken in ages. I can't imagine the stress this horror show must be putting her under."

Maggie had also not spoken to Iris in some time. Despite what had happened between Reed and Maggie, Iris and Maggie had remained friendly over the years, sometimes meeting for coffee or lunch and lingering for hours.

"Those poor boys without a father." Phil sipped his scotch. His plate was already scraped clean. "That's probably part of it."

"Part of what?" Maggie asked.

"Christian, I mean. But I suppose that's his choice."

Maggie frowned and set down her wineglass. The conversation had moved from unnecessary to vaguely ghastly.

"He's called a flamer, Dad," Cassidy said without malice. "At our school there are three types of gay guys: the twinks, the geek gays, and the flamers. The twinks are even kind of popular, but Christian is sort of a flamer. The muscle jocks hate him, but then you have to wonder about some of those jocks. Wasn't Reed a jock in high school?"

Casey turned away and fidgeted with his elbow. "Anyone ready for dessert?" Livia asked.

With difficulty Maggie suppressed a smile. Livia was so serious, so committed to avoiding controversy! She roused Maggie's unconventional spirit. Maggie poured herself a second glass of wine. She couldn't have said why Cassidy's prattle about flamers bothered her less than Phil and Livia's hushed solemnities while discussing the McGregors. She glanced at Casey for silent comfort, but he seemed unaware of any undercurrents shooting across the table. Unless she was "making assumptions" once again that weren't accurate. What if she and Casey ended up like his parents, with Maggie as the politely remote hostess? She couldn't bear it, this steady and relentless encroachment of the "normal," but it seemed to be closing in on her from every direction.

As they drove back home, Maggie was silent, reflective. "Magpie, how are you doing?" Casey asked and set his hand across her knee for comfort. "That wasn't so bad, right?"

She shook her head. Many things felt wrong, but other than the killing fever sweeping through the town, most defied description. "Right?" Casey repeated, and his question seemed to her, in the intimacy of the car, part of the wrong she couldn't name.

(6)

By mid-June even the weather had turned extreme. Rain pummeled the town in driving silver sheets. Occasionally the rain turned to a savage green hail that crushed flowerbeds and knocked the rain gutters from the roofs. Lightning blasted out electricity in scattered neighborhoods. Winds surged, snapping tree branches and upending garbage cans in wait of pick up on the edge of driveways.

With these sudden summer storms as a backdrop, Eddie's own transformation began. Almost overnight he started feeling uncomfortable in his own skin. He itched incessantly. Sometimes he woke imagining bugs were crawling up his legs. Tiny red Army ants, the kind he'd seen on television devouring the carcass of a scorpion.

Hair began to grow on his arms, chest, between his thighs. Fuzz sprouted on his chin and upper lip, along his clenched jaw, repulsing him a little. The fuzz wasn't full or masculine in a way he could feel good about, but thin and wispy, as if his face were unwilling to commit to full stubble. He shaved maybe once or twice a week now, but this only left his chin raw with bits of flesh ripped off, while the most stubborn and puerile hairs remained. One night he woke to a faint whisper like the rustle of corn stalks, and imagined the sound was of hair growing, literally growing over his body. The sound was actually caused by Stretch stirring along the mulch at the bottom of his lamp-heated cage, but still...Eddie ran his fingers down his chest, sending a pleasant chill rippling across his skin.

He began to worry that his breath smelled bad. He brushed his teeth furiously and then stalked around for hours, afraid to exhale in anyone's direction. As for his underarms, they emitted a musky odor no matter how often he showered or tried to disguise the smell with deodorant. It was as if the odor were rising off of his skin from some inner source, from tissue and cells, his whole hormonal being yielding these transgressive smells.

And the sticky persistent heat between his legs, what was he to make of that? Some mornings he woke embarrassed that his bed smelled badly too, an indecent smell like overworked shackled men, like those muscular and half-naked slave men he saw in gladiator movies—hot and sweating and endlessly rowing in the bowels of a great ship on a churning sea, grunting almost more in pleasure than pain. But those oily and desperate men slept on straw or the tortured planks of a ship's floor. They didn't have to worry about waking in the morning with dark heavy stains on their sheets that outlined where their bodies had been. Eddie's sheets were often pooled with such sweat. He started washing his sheets even more frequently, ashamed for his mother to see what his body was up to. Some nights he woke up with his hands down his underwear, jerking himself and moaning. Eddie was disgusted, but unable to dictate where his hands wandered while he slept.

Was it any wonder he lashed himself on the back with a belt every now and then, yet another one of the compulsions he couldn't control? He needed to regain power over his body somehow, corral it. The belt enlivened him, counteracting the wicked lethargy that frequently exhausted him despite his body's hectic pace. On those days when he felt ready to leap out of his skin, the belt calmed him down, grounding him, somehow, in stinging pain.

During this period of indecent growth, with his body in such embarrassing turmoil, Eddie's dislike of Christian swelled to almost unendurable proportions. Where was the solution when you couldn't tolerate your own brother?

When you *could not stand him?* It seemed unjust, a trick of the universe, a sneer from God, that Eddie should be cursed 24/7 with this affliction of brother, his fate always linked to Christian's.

One night when Christian, dressed only in white underwear, passed Eddie's room, Eddie abandoned quiet resentment and trailed Christian to the bathroom. Even Christian's body offended him, its complete repudiation of masculinity. Christian was brushing his teeth with an electric toothbrush, his mouth foaming with paste. When the boys were young they'd eaten toothpaste. They'd also eaten grass, dandelions, and salted worms. There was a time they were willing to put anything into their mouths. "Toothpaste can't save you," Eddie said, lounging in the doorway with arms crossed, a pose that helped him feel like someone different from himself.

And when Christian just continued brushing his teeth, ignoring him, *daring* to ignore him, Eddie added, "Your breath will still reek of cock."

Christian spit into the sink, refilled his brush, and resumed brushing. The mechanical toothbrush groaned and vibrated inside Christian's mouth, agitating Eddie still more. He lifted the toilet seat and began to urinate. *My brother,* he thought, and it was like hearing the words pass through the wall from the darkness outside the house.

After Eddie was finished urinating, he shoved his hands under the sink's running water, deliberately pushing Christian aside. Again his brother refused to engage even after this open rudeness. Eddie stepped away, hands dripping, and wiped them on a towel.

Christian spat toothpaste again, turned off his toothbrush, rinsed it under the faucet, and gargled with a cupped hand of tap water. Finally he glanced at Eddie. "How have your asshole friends been treating you?" he asked.

The question was pointed: Eddie felt his neck turn hot. But there was no way Christian could know about Averill's slaughtered lamb, was there?

Christian had to pass Eddie on his way out of the bathroom. Eddie moved his body just enough so that his elbow jabbed between Christian's ribs. For an instant Christian scowled, then his face turned passive again. He shook his head, walked to his bedroom, and shut the door.

Christian had the gall to shake his head in pity at Eddie? "Faggot," Eddie said to the closed door, and then felt guilty and nearly sad. He fought against it. "Peace be fucking with you, too." He wasn't sure why that phrase had come to mind. It had something to do with church.

With the grace of God that passes all human understanding, keep your hearts and minds in Christ Jesus. These were the words Eddie had grown up with. Now they seemed dead to him, as dead as his father, who must have uttered those very same words over and over again at the end of each church service, although Eddie had never heard him. He had no solid memories of his father, only a couple sketchy images that may or may not have been imaginary, born out of certain apocryphal stories he'd heard about himself as a baby. His father pulled him from under the bed where he'd crawled to poop. His father changed his diaper (was this part of the same memory?) Eddie may or may not have been swung over his father's head, a dizzying jumble of color and light, giving an early and barely formed sense of flight and weightlessness.

He remembered, too, a man who felt like the word father laying a hand across his forehead and holding it there. Then the man lifted the hand away.

Eddie went to bed that night and dreamed his father was talking to him from the other side of the kitchen wall. Only the wall was in the center of the room and not where it belonged. He knew it was his father's voice although his father's voice was unfamiliar to him. The words were mutations, sounds mimicking words.

When he woke, wind was blowing furiously outside the house. He sat upright in bed, thinking *tornado*. But if that was the case, the town's emergency siren would have gone off, and his mother would have already woken up Eddie and Christian to herd them to the basement. Eddie stumbled out of bed and peered out the window. When lightning struck he saw trees lashing back and forth, whipping themselves into a frenzy. Lenore Jackman from next door had left a blouse pinned to a clothesline. The blouse danced and thrashed about, trying to pull free of the grip of the clothespin, which somehow held.

Eddie stepped into the hallway. Outside Christian's room he heard his brother's effortless snoring. Nothing fazed him. "Death knocking," Eddie whispered and tapped on his brother's door. But Christian would never wake to hear it, so Eddie abandoned the ruse before he woke his mother who, like Eddie, was a light sleeper.

Downstairs, Eddie moved through the house like a wraith. Lightning yielded the only illumination. When it flashed, briefly casting the room in dim light, his entire surroundings looked different. This was a new house, a different life he'd stolen into. Why was he here? He could be anyone now. When the lightning flashed another time, he was staring at a wall in the living room. For a moment it looked like the wall in his dreams, slanted and out of place, behind which stood a dead man he would not recognize as his father.

He staggered around the house, enjoying himself even while he was a little spooked by the howling wind outside, and the constant shift between light and darkness, light and darkness, inside. Lightning flashed; whose arm was he wearing? Another flash, and he was looking down at a man's unrecognizable legs with a small bulge in his shorts. He had a wild desire to shout out his own name, only it seemed, suddenly, he might get even that wrong.

Then he had a compulsion to run out into the storm—to dare himself, to step out into the night despite whatever danger might lurk there. He didn't question his own judgment, just walked out the front door and onto the lawn. The rain whipped across his face and shoulders, lashing him, *energizing* him, better than any punitive belt. The wind howled with such primal force it sounded as if it, too, wanted in on the killing action.

But standing out on the lawn wasn't enough. Any loser could do that with the safety of a house so near. It meant nothing. Eddie forced himself out onto the sidewalk, and soon he was jogging down the street. What was he doing? Barefoot, shirtless, wearing only a pair of drawstring shorts, and still feeling the tug of sleep, he ran forward anyway, stomping through puddles, trying not to flinch at the worst thunder and lightning blasts. There was a thrill in being out alone on such a raging night, when nature itself had lost control. *Don't be scared*, he told himself, *nothing to be scared about*. Even a madman wouldn't risk going out for a killing on a night like this.

Unless this was exactly the kind of crazy night that called out to the unbalanced.

You're out here too, dumbshit, he told himself.

But he kept moving forward. An empty garbage can tumbled across the street, making its clamoring and disdainful racket. Eddie pictured arms and legs protruding from the can, as if someone were cramped inside a barrel rolling down a steep hill. A tree branch snapped from the force of the wind and dropped to the ground. Every nerve in Eddie's body felt called back to life, awakened from the grogginess of only a minute ago.

He reached the end of the street. A few flapping shingles on the Butler's roof were picked up by the wind and tossed into the yard. Someone had left a candle burning in one of the upstairs windows—was it a candle or an oddly glowing nightlight meant to ward away danger? *One more block*, he dared himself, and so he continued onward despite how his heart pounded in his chest. He looked up and caught glimpses, between lightning bolts, of the roiling black sky. When he looked back down, he noticed a squashed squirrel lying out in the middle of the road. He paused and stared down at its red garbled insides, feeling a quiet sorrow not quite his own.

Eddie saw the man when he reached the end of the second block. His body froze and he stopped jogging. The man was standing on the other side of the street, his face upturned almost reverentially toward the rain and the wind. His eyes were closed, his head was shaven, and he was shirtless, as Eddie was shirtless, the man's torso strong, fit, and hairless. In the man's hand was a balled-up T-shirt. Still Eddie didn't move, trying to recognize the man, but he looked like no one in particular.

Then the man opened his eyes and looked directly at Eddie. Several seconds passed while the two men stared at one another, only a street separating them although it might as well have been a clogged river, with rainwater and debris sucked down into the storm drains. Eddie didn't look away, a little hypnotized, convinced for a moment he existed only as part of the man's imagination.

The man smiled cautiously and raised his hand in the air.

Eddie turned right and bolted down the street, all but tripping through the puddles. *Turn back, turn back* echoed in his mind, but this only made him run faster. When he reached the end of the block, he turned right again and started back in the direction of his house. Hail dropped from the sky, yet another fury unleashed. A Biblical hail, or nearly, drumming down in a fierce percussion against the cars and house roofs. An angry father's hail; an angry Father's hail? "Stoned, getting stoned," Eddie chanted under his breath. The hail was scaring him, the way it struck at his bare skin, cracked against his skull, and set off a few car alarms. The whole street had gone dark, the night lights and safety lights, all dark, the world swallowed up in it. In a full sprint Eddie ran until he was back in his own yard and veering toward the house.

To his surprise, his mother opened the front door and pulled him inside. Her bathrobe was tied clumsily, and she didn't look at him in anger so much as worry and disapproval. "Eddie, what are you *doing?*" she asked, holding his arm in a pinching grip.

Eddie shook his head. Briefly, he'd wandered out into an anarchic night-scape but now he was back again. Iris tried to snap on the light switch, but of course there was no electricity. She ushered Eddie to the downstairs bath-room, grabbed a towel off the rack, and started drying him as if he were five instead of fifteen. He stood still, shivering and guilty as a chastened dog, and embarrassed that he'd let a man standing in a rainstorm scare him. The entire incident was Eddie's own business, definitely not something his mother needed to know.

"You can't do this kind of thing, Eddie." Iris scrubbed the towel through his waterlogged hair. "Just run outside at night—like *this*. It's dangerous out, and not just the storm—"

Eddie saw the mild alarm in her eyes. It was unsettling—and thrilling— to see he could have such an effect on a parent. Even his mother was starting to question who he was.

(7)

Third body, down so low
Third body drifts to shore...

Reed heard the words in a dream, a drowned muttered calling that rose from the back of some man's throat. "What?" Reed whispered, and turned over.

(8)

When a third man was found dead, this time only a mile from her home, Iris's uneasiness turned to tangible fear. Reed drove by the house to tell her about this newest victim—a college student, early twenties, his body found along some rocks on the edge of the river near the promenade. His skull had been shattered in a way similar to the other victims.

Iris could barely concentrate on Reed over the nervous pounding in her head. The boys were still asleep; she stood alone with Reed in the kitchen in an unnaturally cool patch of sunlight. She contemplated his face, its shifting mix of thoughtfulness, frustration, rage. She offered Reed a cinnamon roll and some coffee, which he declined. "I can't stay," he said. "The brass is calling a news conference. He wants us to look like a united front. I just wanted you to hear from me this time."

"We have to do something," she said, distracted.

Reed looked at her. "*We* do?"

"Yes. Or someone." She was close to wringing her hands together like a harried prairie woman. Instead she untied her bathrobe and retied it again.

"Granger's the detective in this case, Mom," he pointed out. "They don't let me investigate. I just enforce."

She nodded. Maybe she would speak to Arnie, although it was true that they'd been in only sporadic touch since Yvonne, his wife, divorced him two years ago and moved to Tucson with an investment banker. Reed moved to the refrigerator and poured himself a small glass of juice. It unsettled her somewhat, as it always did, to see her son with a gun slung against his hip. What a daunting profession police work was—stalking out crime, moving among the dead and injured, the mad and dysfunctional, the tragic and the careless. *Traffic and death*, she thought.

Someone could literally be forced out of existence. A gun helped but wasn't necessary.

"Why can't they find this man?" she asked Reed. "He can't be that immaterial." Immaterial, was that the word she meant? She fussed around the counter, moving glasses and bowls that weren't out of order. "It's getting so close," she added.

"What is?"

But she shook her head, hearing one of the boys moving in the upstairs bathroom. Christian: she could distinguish Christian from Eddie simply by the sounds he made.

After Reed left she called in sick from work. As soon as she hung up the phone, it rang.

"Iris, you've heard?"

"Hello, Ruth. Yes, Reed just told me." There was an annoying echo on the line.

"It's all over Channel 3. I told Peter we must be hallucinating. The entire town, like some collective nightmare. Maybe if we concentrate hard enough, we'll wake up."

Iris couldn't help but smile. She and Ruth had been friends for more than twenty years, but only recently had Ruth's interests veered toward the inexplicable. Now she couldn't get enough of stories like the one about the family of six that swore they'd seen a statue of the Virgin Mary weeping lemon juice, or the one about people in a Kenyan village who saw a recently deceased child standing beside his own grave.

"I can think of something even more frightening than if it's a nightmare," Iris said. "And that's if it's real."

"Peter, turn the volume down. Oh, Iris, I've always been anti-gun, you know that, but at times like these—"

"Stop!" Iris said. "Let's not add to the collective nightmare."

She hung up the phone when Christian stumbled downstairs in shorts and a mussed T-shirt, hair tangled around his head in its usual mid-morning, cyclonic swirl. He seemed surprised to find her still at home. "Playing hooky," she informed him in such a forced way that he asked her outright if anything was the matter.

She didn't answer at first. Her throat felt sore, as if a piece of sticky bread had lodged in her windpipe. It hurt to look at Christian. He was thin, white, and bruised so easily. There was nothing she could do to alter these simple inflexible truths. She offered to make Christian a couple of waffles, which he accepted and ate heartily, "fuel," he claimed, to get him through another tedious day taking orders at the print shop where he didn't *work*, he *toiled*.

"Phone in sick," she suggested. "Come on. You never miss a day."

He shoveled a large slice of waffle into his mouth, a dribble of syrup on his chin. How impossible it was now to wipe it away for him, when once it would have been so natural. "You want to play hooky together?" he asked and gave her a quizzical look.

Abruptly, she told him a third body had been found. She watched as his face flushed, then his eyes narrowed with a steely hardness. "Gay?" he asked.

In her nervousness, she realized she hadn't asked Reed for specifics. "I don't know," she admitted. "I think, yes, like the others."

"Mom, I need a name. I might—"

He didn't finish the thought but his meaning was clear. They both assumed their spots on the sofa and turned on the TV to the local morning news, Channel 3. According to reports, the most recent murder victim was twenty-two-year-old college graduate Ronald Temple. "Never heard of him," Christian said with no relief in his voice.

The victim's sobbing mother had already been tracked down, cameras trained relentlessly on her as she dabbed her eyes with some throttled tissue and insisted her son had not been gay. "The girls loved him," she said. "He was just a normal boy like anyone. He didn't deserve this."

Christian stared at the crying woman. "A normal boy like anyone?" he said and shook his head. "She doesn't know. She doesn't know a damned thing."

"Her son has been murdered!" Iris cried.

"Yes, her perfectly *normal* son. *He* didn't deserve to die."

How had the tone turned sharp and confrontational between them? Iris fumbled for something more to say, but Christian was already lacing on his sneakers. "You're still going to work?" she asked, almost wishing he was still a child so she could force him to stay home.

"If I don't, the terrorists win," he said with a grim smile. And looking back at the TV, he said, very low as if working out his thoughts aloud, "Time to get proactive."

"What do you mean, proactive?"

Seeing her anxious frown, he said, "Mom, it's daylight! I'll be okay. I'm riding the bike. I promise I won't stop for strangers with hard candy, how's that?"

But she didn't like that set look on his face, which usually meant he was plotting something. "They're getting younger," she blurted. It hadn't occurred to her until that moment. Every dead man a few years younger than the previous one. Maybe it was coincidence and meant nothing, but then again, how could she know? Sometimes what appeared a pattern was actually random, and what seemed random was a pattern not yet deciphered. "Christian," she said, but he was already out the door before she could cast away evil tidings by advising him to be careful.

She wandered back to the kitchen. There was still some leftover batter for waffles. Maybe Eddie would be hungry. She wanted to feed him. Instead she went upstairs. He was still asleep, sprawled on his stomach across the bed, arms and legs akimbo, as if he'd lost his grip from some high place and fallen into that position. She considered waking him. It was eleven o'clock, and he was already sleeping too much. On the other hand, only three nights ago she'd caught him running outside in that battering storm, careless of his own safety, so it was a comfort to see him sleeping now. Iris closed the door and went downstairs.

She fussed out in her garden for a few minutes but returned inside in time for the noon news and Mikkelson's televised press conference. He spoke into an odd gray microphone in front of the court house and reassured the citizens of Barrow's Point that every officer was dedicated to uncovering the identity of this killer, this "cowardly scourge of a man." Mikkelson was flanked by Arnie Granger and several officers, including Reed in a central position—so *handsome*, she thought, and then, in a rush, *so alive.* But her joy dimmed a little when she noticed that Reed seemed the only one who doubted Mikkelson's bravado.

A reporter asked Mikkelson if they had any idea why gay men had been targeted for death, or if the most recent victim had been gay at all. "Our sources indicate that the young man was gay, so we're proceeding on that assumption," Mikkelson said. A different reporter asked why the police trusted these sources over the claims of the victim's own mother. "This isn't the time to go into that," Mikkelson said. "But if he wasn't, then it's a real shocker, isn't it? That you can be murdered for what you are only suspected of being?" His voice shook with indignation. Iris, still watching Reed's face in the background, unable *not* to watch his face, sensed from his expression that he didn't much care for Mikkelson's answer, yet she'd missed what it was Mikkelson had said wrong, just as she'd missed why the bereaved mother had upset Christian. She felt thick-witted and slow, a mental lurch blind to subtext and inference.

At the end of the newscast, Eddie clamored downstairs. She heard him in the kitchen, muttering to himself. He moved toward the stairs leading to the basement before he saw her. "What the hell," he said.

He was wearing a pair of boxers and carrying a couple sheets in his arms. Odd to think that she was in the boys' territory now, almost an intruder in her own home. "It's nearly lunchtime," she said. "Is this how late you normally sleep?"

He looked at her but clearly wasn't going to offer up a thing. Maybe he was a little too much like his father had been in that regard. She felt Eddie was staring at her too warily, as if she were a zoo animal that had stepped outside its cage and was now on the prowl. *Maternal Creepitis*, she thought, and had the silly urge to bend her fingers into claws. "I'm taking a day off," she said. "Do you want me to wash those for you?"

"I'll do them," he said.

Since when had Eddie started doing his own laundry? He turned away to descend into the basement. "Your back!" she cried.

Almost immediately he half turned toward her, so she could no longer see the twin welts along his spine, although she didn't have a particularly good view of his face either. "It's nothing," he said. "Heat rash. Jesus, Mom. Privacy."

*

That night Iris sat on the rug in the center of her bedroom, trying to position her legs into a rough approximation of a lotus squat. Years ago she'd stopped doing her yoga exercises, but it was time, she decided, for her stiffening body, not to mention her increasingly tense soul, to give it another try. Only her legs were no longer nimble, and her joints inflexible and aching. "Shot to hell," she muttered and tried to touch her toes a couple of times. Then she glanced around the room. Something seemed out of place, yet everything was arranged as it had been twenty-nine years ago when Carl was still alive, she'd been pregnant with Reed, and they'd first moved into the house. Now it seemed wrong that she hadn't moved things around after all this time, a lack of preparedness, maybe, or was it a lack of vision? Vision, vigilance, what she needed to be doing, she decided, was paying more attention to things.

And what she noticed in the following days was a town besieged, tension stretched taut and settling over Barrow's Point like a muggy blanket. Once the third body turned up, the town's mood shifted, like Iris's own mood, from caution and disquiet to outrage and borderline panic. There were so many unanswered questions. Had the third victim been gay or not? Who was safe and who was not? Was the killer actually crossing over into murdering students, into murdering *children?* And because no one could answer these questions, locking the house doors no longer seemed enough, not nearly enough. Almost overnight, people started buying pepper spray and investing in expensive alarm systems. Self-defense classes popped up out of nowhere and were in high demand. On her way home from work every evening, Iris drove by a gym with large glass windows, and through them she could see neat rows of men and women in shorts or leotards, punching and kicking and kung fu-ing their invisible assailants.

Safe, safe, safe: Iris sensed these words, too, hanging over the town and whispering through the trees.

One afternoon the mailman placed a piece of the neighbor's mail in Iris's mailbox by mistake. When Iris approached the Jackman's front door to return the letter, she heard the loud and threatening barks of a dog inside the house. In the ten years that Theo and Lenore Jackman had lived next door to Iris, they had never once kept an animal.

The dog stopped barking abruptly and, after peeking through her keyhole, Lenore opened the door for Iris, who handed over the mail. "It was in my box," Iris explained.

Lenore squinted at the envelope and then sighed. "The mailman's probably scared of Rex," she said. "I'm sorry if he scared you."

"Rex is your new dog?"

"Yes. Only he's not a real dog." She invited Iris inside and showed her the contraption—an electronic guard dog alarm that plugged into a wall socket and "barked" as soon as anyone approached the house. "Isn't Rex convincing?" Lenore asked. "He senses movement within a radius of 30 feet. What power lungs, and he's not afraid to use them! I mean, he sounds like he won't take prisoners, doesn't he? We have a gun and now we have Rex, so I figure we're covered."

Guns. Iris returned to her house with a sinking feeling. It probably wasn't just the Jackmans, either. Gun sales were most likely increasing in Barrow's Point and the surrounding area along with the pepper spray. The last thing the town needed, Iris thought, was a bunch of jittery and on edge people with loaded guns at their fingertips. It was especially disturbing knowing that a couple of those people lived next door.

Despite their ten years as neighbors, Iris still didn't feel as if she knew Theo and Lenore all that well. They were a peculiar couple with no children who tended to stay indoors a lot and—or so Iris had discovered over the years—spy on what she and the other neighbors were up to. Seemingly, they preferred winters to summers. Occasionally, after a good snowfall, they would venture into their backyard to build snowmen so they could decapitate them with sticks.

This summer, Theo Jackman would often venture outside long enough to turn on the water sprinkler, then would go back inside and forget about it, leaving the sprinkler running for hours. Sometimes the sprinkler would jerk out of its mannerly rotation, as if it had developed a malevolent will of its own, and shoot streams of water over Iris's bushes and against the side of the house. This, too, seemed a part of what was building out of the fear and the headlines, out of the very fabric of the town, an agitation rising from the earth. Iris could feel it rising.

One weekend afternoon Lenore came over to the house uninvited, which she rarely did, and sat at the kitchen table with Iris for lemonade and a crumb cake. "What do you make of my husband?" she asked Iris abruptly. Blunt scratches ran down both her wrists. "Do you think he's a kind man, or even a perceptive one?"

The question put Iris at a loss. Theo had always treated her with respect, yet he never struck her as especially kind or perceptive, and Lenore had gotten those scratches from somewhere. After a long pause, Lenore said "I see" and stood up without touching her square of crumb cake. "Well, you'd be wrong." She left Iris's house despite Iris's protests. Rex's angry barking greeted Lenore as she unlocked her own front door and stepped back inside the house. "Great," Iris said aloud. "Now my armed neighbors are mad at me."

At the hospital business office where Iris worked, faces started standing out more, mostly men's faces—their darting eyes and tight mouths, perspiring foreheads and firmly set jaws. Always the thought came to her: *Could this be the one the police are looking for? Or this one?* What about the broker in the well-tailored suit who admitted to her, in a low voice so as not to broadcast his shame, that he was actually a little worried about his hospital bill, given that his wife's cancer treatments were so phenomenally high, and he'd just lost considerable money in bad property investments, and didn't want to have to take out a second mortgage on the house. Or what about the young bearded man who waved a neatly Xeroxed copy of the hospital bill in Iris's face, insisting that he couldn't pay his bills, absolutely would not pay. He didn't have insurance, and look at some of the charges. How much was he being charged for that stinking aspirin that had no more cured his headaches than a handful of placebos? How much for that ill-fitting pair of slippers he hadn't even requested? It was all craziness, this hospital, was the world itself going crazy, spinning off its axis, moving toward some grand chaos? At last he took a deep breath, composed himself, and walked meekly out of her office.

Occasionally, young couples from the university would pass by Iris's house on their way from the river promenade, and was it her imagination, or were too many of them tugging at their lover's arms, or yelling or crying, their bodies coiled and tense? The national headlines she scanned from time to time suggested things weren't so different outside of Barrow's Point—besides Iraq, Iraq, Iraq, there were droughts and killer storms, power shortages and power struggles, random attacks on lovers and strangers. A young Kentucky man had been tethered to the fender of a car, his arms bound, mockingly, in a lover's knot, then dragged half a mile until he was dead for trying to make a "pass" at two men in a bar. When Iris first read this story, she sneaked into the backyard and tossed the paper into the Jackman's garbage bin so her boys wouldn't stumble upon it.

And what was she to make of the occasional graffiti she noticed scratched on bathroom stalls or sprayed on cement walls in parking garages. *Nigger, spick, bitch, faggot.* Who was writing this stuff? Iris had the uneasy sense the world was revealing itself in too much detail, prodding her to catch up on what she'd missed. Even her clothes seemed to fit her wrongly these days, hanging loose with unflattering bulges in the hips and shoulders.

One Friday afternoon while she was at work, she wondered about Arnie and the state of the murder investigation. When she glanced up from her desk and the computer screen clotted with unwieldy balances people couldn't afford to pay, there was Arnie, poking his head into her office, his smile jaunty. "Surprise and hello," he said, trying his best to sound offhand.

It was such a pleasure to see him that Iris took her afternoon break early so she could join him at the hospital cafeteria for coffee. But once they were seated at one of the outdoor picnic tables under a gaggle of trees where black butterflies flew about, Iris was somehow bothered that he was dressed in his T-shirt and jeans and not his uniform. "Shouldn't you be at work?" she asked, meaning to sound teasing although there was, perhaps, slight accusation in her voice.

If Arnie sensed the undercurrent in her question, he didn't let on. "Just finished getting the ticker checked out," he said, thumping his fist against his chest a couple of times. "Thought I should at least stop down and see how you're doing." He had a habit of nodding his head as if in agreement or waiting for someone to agree with him. "I have the day off," he added.

A day off from hunting a murderer? She knew she was being unreasonable. Even a police detective deserved some time off. An elderly woman with leathery skin walked toward an empty bench near their table, dragging an IV on a pole alongside her. Who was nursing this woman? The woman belched as she clucked her tongue at the black butterflies.

Iris dragged her attention back to Arnie. Beneath his good humor, she could see the weariness in his face, the hint of melancholy in his eyes. He was probably under a good deal of stress. At least Iris had her sons, always the bedrock that sustained her, but who did Arnie have? His son Ethan was in college in Chicago, and Yvonne had neatly severed herself from him and her twenty-five years lived in Barrow's Point. A wave of sentiment rose up in Iris—forceful, insistent. "We have to talk, Arnie," she said. "Not here, not now, but sometime soon."

Arnie's pleased smile added life to his wrinkles and lightened the dark circles beneath his eyes. Nearby the old woman rattled her pole to try and dislodge one of the butterflies that had come to roost on her IV bag. "I think that's probably a fine idea," Arnie said.

After he left, Iris decided to leave work early, pleading a headache, which was only a mild fabrication. Despite her encouraging conversation with Arnie, a dull pain had begun to press behind her eyes, threatening to break open into something she could only hope would be insight, but now it was just pain. She drove home thinking about Arnie, and when she entered the house and walked upstairs, still thinking about Arnie, she heard an unusual stirring in Christian's room. She entered without knocking and found him sitting on the bed in his underwear beside a slim Thai boy who was also in his underwear.

They weren't doing anything more than holding each other and pecking softly at the other's mouth, but Iris gasped as if someone had set a lighted match to her hair. "Put some clothes on!" she cried, although this was not what she'd meant to say.

"Too hot," Christian said dryly. The boy grabbed for his jeans but Christian remained calm. "Sorry if we scared you," he said.

"No, no, I'm not scared, of course not."

"We thought, you know, you were still at work."

The boy looked embarrassed, in danger of bolting, but Christian's arm around his shoulder stayed him.

"Headache." Iris rubbed her temples for show. She glanced over at Christian's desk, where were spread a couple poster boards and magic markers. They were making posters? Christian must have read the curiosity in her eyes because he said, "Time to be heard, Mom."

Iris shook her head. Christian shrugged and didn't say anything more. Iris sensed she shouldn't pursue it, so she smiled in apology, closed the door, and walked to her own room, unable to banish from her mind the image of Christian with a lover. Of course she knew Christian was gay, but she'd always imagined in a non-practicing way. Actually, she both liked knowing that Christian had sexual needs and feared that this would single him out even more, up his visibility quotient somehow, increase the chance someone might want to harm him. *Time to be heard, Mom.* She didn't like the sound of that at all.

She stepped out of her dress. When had it become so baggy and over-stretched? Last week she'd noticed that the elastic was shot in one of her skirts.

She hadn't dwelled on it then because it hadn't seemed worth further examination, only now, with the boys' muffled voices drifting to her from down the hall, strumming at her own loneliness, it dawned on her that Christian might be responsible. She waited a moment for the thought to settle. She lay the offending dress down on the bed, stepped into a pair of shorts, slipped on a flowered blouse, then lay on top of the bed and stared with longing at her own empty dress. How odd to think she'd dated so infrequently after Carl's death, engrossed as she'd been in making a living and raising her sons on her own. She'd always meant to make more time for a private life, forgetting despite the reminders how easily weeks could turn to years.

She heard the boys laughing down the hall, and wondered if dressing in her clothes was part of some intimate private ritual that Christian and his friend played together, which culminated in the two of them making out on Christian's bed. Of course, Christian was so lean, she was more likely to stretch out *his* clothes, but then again, men's bodies were deceptive. She sat back up. She wanted something; she wanted something badly. What was it? The boys had stopped laughing and all was quiet, although she was pretty sure no one had left the house.

(9)

Iris never considered that Eddie might be wearing her clothes, and he was so cagey and covert about his actions, he gave her no reason to suspect him. Privately, he couldn't believe he had started doing this. The compulsion overtook him when he was alone in the house, usually on one of those lazy meandering afternoons when Christian was working at the copy center and his mother at the hospital. Or that's how Eddie came to think of his own behavior, as yet another compulsion stealing into his blood, a different man's impulses and drives.

Often the compulsion started when he was staring at the TV—music video, hip-hop, new wave, burning down the house—or else rifling through some of his mother's magazines that were spread across the coffee table. So many of the magazines devoted full-page ads to semi-dressed men and women together, their nude tanned limbs entwined, sometimes stretched out over two pages: pouting lips, mysterious heavy-lidded eyes, erotic underclothes. Eddie couldn't stop staring at the photographs, of the men as well as the women, even when they began to depress him—all that effortless and unattainable beauty. He knew he wasn't much to look at, nothing like Reed, who both men and women had fallen in love with on a whim. Even Reed didn't resemble the men in the ads. Magazine beauty was an illusion, Eddie knew this, but that didn't make it any less depressing. Maybe that was why it was depressing in the first place.

Some days Eddie resisted the compulsion by escaping the house or hunting down a friend to shoot some hoops, anything to kill a couple of hours. Other days the belt was enough. But there were days when he couldn't resist, when the compulsion grew so strong it propelled him up the stairs to his mother's bedroom. He'd open the closet door and face the closet's interior, a private desire urging him to touch one of the dresses; at least do that much; he was alone; would he stop shutting down? A battle between fear of discovery and the need to wear a dress would compete for control of his thoughts, his movements. When the compulsion would win out, his fear and guilt would fall away, and there was only this *moment*, this fleeting, transitory moment in which he would try on a dress and complete that picture of himself.

Once he'd pulled a dress from its hanger, it would become the one he would step into, which was easier than slipping it over his head and trying to wrestle it first over his shoulders. He would step out of his shoes, slip on his jeans, and remove his shirt. As he'd tug the dress up over his hips, his excitement would build to a heady crescendo, adding to the fever in his blood. He'd unzip the dress as best he could and stand before the mirror, gazing at himself with suspicion. He wouldn't know how to feel about this person in the mirror, for (s)he looked grotesque and malformed. His ugliness was not hidden nor his true self revealed. He'd simply created some monstrous sad sack in a dress. Sometimes, if he were feeling especially bold—or especially driven—he'd thrust his feet deep into a pair of his mother's pumps until his feet hummed from the pain. He wouldn't walk around in the shoes and the dress, because that struck him as ornamental, too obvious and womanly. He'd merely stand in front of the mirror, staring at his absurd reflection, trying to grasp what he was feeling and how it related to who he was. When he'd stared at himself in the mirror long enough, the thrill gradually diminished to embarrassment and disgust. The clothes just hung on him, restricted him. A metallic taste rose in the back of his throat. This was all ridiculous, beyond what even Christian would do. If Danny ever found out about this, or his brothers or his mother... but he would kill himself before any of that happened. Besides, no one would find out, because he was never doing this again. He had little desire to see that pathetic, slovenly creature he'd created in a dress. Now that he knew she existed, he could bury her and her slovenly softness in the deep soil at the back of his mind.

Only the next time would come, and he would find himself alone in the house with the compulsion again swelling to life. He meant to kick past the barriers to some other existence, apparently, even if against his will. The more his actions scared and disgusted him, the stronger his compulsion grew.

And what about his father? He could hide his activities from his mother, brothers, friends, but his father was dead and saw everything. But maybe his father couldn't see, after all. The dead were hard to figure out. Were they omniscient witnesses to human folly, or were they dust and bones without consciousness, and so not to be feared?

One afternoon, after he'd thrown on a dress but still felt lethargic, he painted his mouth with some of his mother's melancholy lipstick. What the hell? Look at him, the bought red lips. How far was he willing to push himself, to spiral deeper into this behavior that was not who he was? For a moment his impulse was to devour the lipstick, swallow it whole so he could no longer use it as an instrument in his own undoing.

His cell phone rang. Startled, he fumbled for the phone in the pocket of his jeans and saw on his caller ID: *Danny Sternes*. Eddie yanked the dress off before he answered; he couldn't talk to Danny while wearing a fucking dress!

"Hey!" Eddie said into the phone. He moved out of his mother's room, away from the heap of discarded clothes —the confusion of pants and T-shirt, dress and provoking heels.

"McGregor," Danny drawled. "What the hell you up to?"

"Nothing."

Danny said nothing was about right. The whole fucking town was doing nothing right now. How did Eddie feel about a little wake-up jolt? Danny couldn't go into specifics on the phone, except that "hallucinogens" might be involved.

"Really?" Eddie rubbed his hand across his mouth, blotting away the lipstick that tainted his words, making his voice sound soft and breathy.

"Did you hear what I said? Could you manage some sort of human reaction?"

But Eddie couldn't get hold of himself. Maybe he was no longer wearing a dress, but he was still talking to Danny while stripped down to his underwear with his testicles hanging out. Idly, he ran his fingers over his bare chest and then stopped himself. He was always doing this. His fingers were still red from the lipstick, and now there were light crimson marks across his chest like some pathetic imitation of primal war paint.

"You coming or not?" Danny asked, and Eddie said yes, yes, he'd come, of course he'd come. "Fifteen minutes," Danny said and hung up.

During that fifteen minutes, Eddie managed to smooth out his mother's dress and hang it back in the closet; put the heels back on the shoe horns; scrub the lipstick off his mouth, hands and chest; shower to clean himself of what he could; and toss on a pair of jeans and a fresh T-shirt. "Close enough," he said into the mirror, at the reflection straining to turn back into Eddie McGregor.

He was disappointed to see that Danny wasn't alone. Danny's brother was driving the car, a beefy eighteen-year-old known as "Soldier" because of his military buzz cut, his fondness for wearing fatigues, and his very vocal plan to join the Army. Soldier had served as captain of the wrestling squad this past winter, had barely graduated in May, and would head off to boot camp in the fall. His ambition was to someday fight in Iraq, as two of his cousins had done before him. One cousin had already returned with a missing arm and a steel plate for a hip, but this hadn't deterred Soldier's plan.

Danny and Soldier's cousin, Tess, occupied the back seat. She was a lean tomboy of a girl, a year older than Eddie, with hair cut in a stylish short crop. The boys grunted greeting in Eddie's direction; Tess smiled and snapped her strawberry gum as Eddie climbed into the back seat beside her. She was holding in her lap a brown paper bag.

They drove to an old deserted house outside town. The duplex had been partially burned in a fire five years earlier. The owner of the property, an elderly widowed man named Tarleton, had planned to rebuild without ever quite mustering the incentive to do it, and so the house remained, one side neglected but intact, the other scorched and gutted from within. Normally the police kept frequent tabs on the place since it was a magnet for kids and truants and the occasional shady dealings, but with the police on "psycho patrol," Danny said they'd have the dump to themselves.

They walked into the unburned side of the house, which was largely empty except for one hard-backed chair and a small collapsed sofa that the previous occupants had left behind. A couple of the windows were broken, glass lying in prisms and small shards on the floor. They found a grungy blanket lying abandoned across the sofa. "Someone's been here!" Danny said, lifting up the spotted blanket and tossing it aside. "This wasn't here last week."

Danny opened up cans of beer and passed them around. Tess declined. She set the paper bag on the floor, walked into the kitchen and returned with a jar of peanut butter. "Maybe some bum spent the night," she said and unscrewed the lid. The jar was almost full and there were finger marks in the peanut butter, as if someone had scooped it out with his hands. "I'm going to hurl," Tess said and set the peanut butter aside. "This place gives me the creeps. We could find anything out here."

She didn't say *a dead body*, but they knew what she meant. And it was true, the dead bodies that kept turning up were somewhat exciting for all of them—the unknown, the stealthy approach of the sinister. The house seemed to connect them to that danger. Danny and Soldier claimed the sofa and started lighting up. Eddie tried not to notice that Danny's sleeveless T-shirt showed off his arms to good advantage.

They passed the joint around. Tess picked up the paper bag and withdrew from it a bottle of rum, a liter of cola, and a clear plastic cup. She began to mix herself a sloppy rum and Coke. Danny smirked with a little too much energy. "That shit's what you mix when you want to pretend you're drinking," he said.

"Really? That remark is what you say when you want to pretend you're talking."

A couple of hollow minutes passed in silence. Now that Eddie was here, away from the Christian-infested house of charades called home, he felt weird and vulnerable. Only an hour ago he'd been someone else entirely, and now couldn't shake the fear he'd left some incriminating piece of evidence on himself. He kept wiping his mouth, which felt sticky and a little sluttish. What if his lips were still red?

Danny handed Eddie the joint, so of course Eddie inhaled, although he feared for a second that he'd leave a light lipstick smear on the joint.

Soldier pulled a bottle of Jim Beam from Tess's bag and started drinking it straight from the bottle, looking with mild contempt at Danny's and Eddie's beers. When Tess went back out to the car for her cell phone, Soldier, who sat like a kingpin on his side of the sofa, waved Eddie to his side. "She might appreciate a little roughing up, you know," Soldier said.

Eddie smiled dim-wittedly. Roughing up?

"For Christ's sake, McGregor," Danny said, rolling up another joint. "He's trying to pimp her out to you."

Soldier smacked Danny on the side of the head, one of those "playful" male swats with enough aggression behind it to make anyone wonder. "Asswipe," Danny laughed, then his expression shifted to quiet embarrassment, a look Eddie lived with on a daily basis. He was almost pleased that Soldier had caused Danny to feel similar pain.

"She'd slit her throat before she sucked your dick, bro," Soldier said. "She doesn't eat cheese." He whooped with laughter. Cheese? And Tess was Danny's cousin, so what was all this about sucking his dick? Once again Eddie felt the reality of his own ignorance pulling at him, but this time he didn't let on.

Tess returned, tugged on Eddie's shirt, and asked him to go upstairs with her. Maybe he'd rather stay downstairs with Danny and Soldier, but he also realized the points he'd score for disappearing for a while with a girl, so he agreed, basking in the conspiratorial wink Soldier gave him as he turned away.

The stairs were dusty and creaked, as stairs in abandoned houses often did. The second floor featured a bedroom with a bare mattress lying in a corner and an iron bed with sagging bedsprings. Under the bedsprings they found a discarded pack of cigarettes with one crushed cigarette inside and an empty soda bottle with a few ashes floating in the slush at the bottom. A scorch mark stretched across one wall like a black glove reaching out.

"I hate hanging out with the boys," Tess said, "but apparently it's going to be my fate in life." She ran a nervous hand through her hair. Eddie noticed tiny pellet-like mouse droppings in a far corner, at the same moment that Tess said, "Vermin!" with girlish disgust. "I can just see it. At night the rodentia emerge out of the walls and stake their claim to this deathtrap."

"Is rodentia a word?"

Tess snapped her gum. "You're cute and serious," she said. "Do you know what I hate more than hanging out with the swinging cocks downstairs? Hanging with the swinging cocks *here*, in this place. Guys like this fire pit because it's lost all sense of order, but disorder isn't all it's cracked up to be either. Plus I hate picking shit out of my hair!" She shook her head to rid her hair from what wasn't there. "All this crap floating around. Dust mites, bits of ash. Have you seen a dust mite under a microscope?"

Eddie admitted he hadn't.

"They're like tiny crabs with spider legs," she said. "And our skin." She held her arm in front of his face. "We shed little pieces of ourselves every day. Tiny microbes of Tess and Eddie floating around, making other people sneeze or break out in hives."

Sometimes there was absolutely nothing to say. From downstairs, Eddie heard laughter and explosions of breath.

One of the bedroom windows looked out over a section of roof. Tess tried to open the window but it stuck, so Eddie put some muscle behind it and the window, with an angry protest, finally yielded. Tess stepped out onto the roof and sat down on the worn shingles, facing out toward an overgrowth of trees. The sky was clouding over, promising yet another afternoon storm. After a small interval where Eddie waited for her to invite him onto the roof, which she didn't, he stepped out on his own accord. He sat down near her while still keeping a reasonable distance, and looked out at the trees as well.

"This house was burned by lovers," Tess said, sipping her rum and Coke.

He nodded as if he understood, but he didn't really. "They set it on fire?"

"Yes, but not in the way you think." She flicked away a purple fly that had crashed into her face. "No gasoline and a match, nothing obvious like that. This couple was young and living together, seeing if they could make the two of them work. Only, apparently, they couldn't. The guy didn't stop sleeping with her, he just stopped fucking her. I mean, there he was in bed beside her every night, yet he wouldn't touch her. His thoughts were elsewhere."

"How could you know all this?" Eddie asked.

Tess shrugged. "My aunt's a hairdresser," she said. "She hears things."

Eddie was trying to sit with his weight leaned manfully forward. "You said they burned the house down," Eddie prodded because she had lost the arc of her story, it seemed.

"Yes. One night the woman woke to a strange sound coming from the living room. A crackling whisper she should recognize, although when you first wake up, everything you hear sounds like something you should know. She woke up the so-called lover, thinking, maybe, someone had broken into the house. He was the one who first understood the intruder was fire. By the time they made it out to the living room, one corner was already in flames."

Beyond the trees lay a marshy pond. Once the pond had been drained in search of a missing child, but all the police found in the murky sludge was a slit-open deer's carcass. This was back during a time when people felt the need to hide what they killed.

"They never figured out how the fire really started," Tess continued. "No bad wiring, no papers too close to a heater. Spontaneous combustion, that's my guess. Don't you think, maybe, with so much pent-up tension in that side of the house, it just, you know, one night, ignited."

Eddie had heard stories about spontaneous combustion. Once a man had been running along a beach with his dog, surf washing over his feet, gulls circling overhead, feeling the heady rush of exercise and a cool breeze striking his face. The next moment, he was on fire. A young woman gathering shells witnessed the incident, a blaze that had come from nowhere, she'd said, a flame that had come, seemingly, from within.

How the dog must have circled and whimpered over the sudden ash heap that only minutes ago had been its owner. Eddie wanted to adopt that dog, but how did you adopt what only existed in a story?

"The bastard." Tess moved closer to Eddie and held his hand. He stared, disbelieving. "Wouldn't even touch her."

Eddie stood up. "Maybe we should go back down," he said.

Tess sighed. "Be still my heart," she said.

Danny was giving Soldier the Heimlich maneuver. Or that's what it looked like when Eddie and Tess entered the living room, Danny standing behind Soldier with his arms around Soldier's chest, squeezing with some force, although he was really only trying to make Soldier pass out. There was a trick to it, Danny explained, requiring Soldier to hyperventilate while Danny squeezed him with the correct amount of pressure. Only he wasn't squeezing Soldier's chest hard enough, or else Soldier wasn't hyperventilating in the way he needed to, or else Soldier was intentionally resisting passing out although he would never admit that. Tess fished a cigarette from a pack Soldier had left on the sofa and lit it with his lighter shaped like the handle of a knife. "I have their blood flowing through my veins," Tess drawled to Eddie.

"Could be worse." Eddie lapsed back into silence. Supposedly one of his great-great uncles, when fighting in some Irish war, had lopped off a man's hands. Was part of that violence, that propensity toward brutality, still genetically coded within him, somehow?

And then, too, there was *Christian.*

Danny and Soldier decided to switch places, Soldier now standing behind with his arms around Danny's chest. "If you kill him," Tess deadpanned, "they won't let you fly to Iraq and kill evildoers."

But no one paid much attention to Tess. Eddie watched, rapt, as Danny gulped down several deep breaths. When Danny nodded, Soldier squeezed his chest from behind. It looked like a Heimlich maneuver but was different, which was how things were most of the time. The intent wasn't to save a life, but to walk the edge of no life. After several seconds, Danny's face turned an odd color, and he slumped to the floor. Tess giggled and hiccupped. Eddie stared down at Danny, lying motionless with only his eyelids fluttering. Soldier couldn't stop laughing. "Now *that's* a corpse!" he said.

"Get used to it." Tess was looking around for the lighter she'd already misplaced.

"Is he all right?" Eddie wanted badly to kneel down and touch Danny's throat for a pulse.

As if on cue, Danny's eyes opened. He focused first on Eddie, looking at him without sarcasm or judgment. "McGregor," he muttered.

Soldier helped Danny to his feet. Danny smiled but looked groggy and pale. "Fucking hit a wall," he said. "Then nothing."

"Thanks, Plato." Soldier stared at the red spot in the center of Danny's forehead.

Danny sat on the sofa for a minute. "Let me try putting McGregor out," he said.

Eddie said no fucking way but Danny insisted, and Soldier admitted he wouldn't mind watching that one, since Danny had failed so miserably putting *him* down. Soon Eddie saw there was no way out, and he'd learned from experience that it was better to give into these things and get it over with quickly... and then again, he wasn't sure he wanted to resist.

Which was how he ended up with Danny's arms wrapped around him from behind, Danny muttering, "Breathe harder, McGregor, Jesus." For a queasy moment Eddie was afraid he would grow hard, right there in front of everyone. Then dizziness struck him, or he struck it. He slumped to the floor, still conscious, and then again, not. A wall of membrane separated him from the world. His friends were leaning over him, yet they weren't his friends. They were wearing flesh to conceal who they really were.

Gradually substance—or was it essence?—returned to their faces. Tess was shaking his shoulder. "You were out too long," she said. "We could see your tongue."

"Leave it to McGregor to take the whole game too damned serious," Danny said.

But he looked at Eddie almost with understanding. They had both shared this area of breathless nothingness, gone and come back again, and now Eddie sensed a frank intimacy between them. He hoped for his own sake that Danny couldn't.

"I won't press charges," Eddie said. But the afternoon was different now. Eddie felt lightweight and out of place, his chest still sore from where Danny had squeezed him. Resurrection hadn't felt at all the way he'd imagined it would.

(10)

We have to do something: and so his mother's words began to haunt Reed. He lived with the murders by day, carried them to bed with him at night. He dreamed of boxes and dark caverns; he dreamed of dead men's voices, beg-ging forgiveness and trying to explain themselves. But when Reed woke up, he couldn't remember what it was that any of the dead men had told him.

We have to do something: Iris's words urged him toward action although there was little he could realistically do. He wasn't a detective on the case; he wasn't a detective, period. He was a lowly officer, a foot soldier, a conduit be-tween the police department and the community. Yet he felt the town's mount-ing anxiety, and worse, his mother's private anxiety, seeping into his head, shadowing his heart, until soon the murders felt like a personal assault.

Reed's feelings of uselessness only increased when Alex felt compelled to take matters into his own hands and write a guest editorial for the *Barrow's Point Gazette* that was critical of the police department's slow and "passive" re-action to the murders, a lack of urgency he implied was due to the victims hav-ing been gay. Alex was quick to reassure Reed that his editorial was critical of the police department's "upper brass," in particular Mikkelson and Granger, and not the "rank and file" cops. Still, Reed couldn't help but feel indicted as well, just another cog in the police department's sluggish wheel. At the urg-ing of the university's gay and lesbian alliance, Alex also helped organize a memorial vigil-protest for the murder victims. The intent, Alex said, was not only to honor and pay tribute to the dead men, but also to publicly apply pres-sure to the police department's accountability on the case. Alex didn't neces-sarily expect a large turnout for the vigil since a lot of the faculty and students were gone for the summer, but it was a "symbolic gesture" if nothing else, a chance to demonstrate resolve and solidarity. Somehow Christian had become involved in planning the vigil as well, although he didn't start college until the fall term, while Reed was stuck in his uniform, caught in the middle between the personal concern he shared with Alex and Christian, and his duty to the police department and his job.

Frustrated, Reed asked for a private meeting with Arnie to discuss the murder investigation. Arnie agreed to this although it wasn't commonplace for an officer to ask for an update from a detective. The air conditioner in Arnie's office was down, so he switched on his desk's rotary fan. The blades rattled as they spun, chopping up the sticky air and blowing it unevenly around the room. Arnie closed the window blinds, sealing off natural light in favor of a cooler darkness. Then he turned on a desk lamp.

"I'm not sure what it is you expect I can tell you, Reed." Arnie heaved his weight into the revolving chair behind his desk. "We haven't got much of anything new."

"Three people are dead."

Arnie dragged his gaze from Reed to an Aztec stone ashtray on the desk. A pipe balanced on the tray gave off the faintly nostalgic smell of a bygone era. Arnie picked up the pipe and placed the tip in his mouth, chewing on it rather than lighting it. He admitted that they had uncovered new evidence, a couple discreet carpet fibers found on the shirt of the third victim, fibers that had survived the river and did not match any carpeting in the victim's apartment. Even this potential piece of evidence had led them nowhere. The fibers were from a brand of carpeting sold widely in the area, and they didn't have a suspect to try and link the fibers to.

"You don't have anyone even under surveillance?"

"We need a suspect first," Arnie said. "You know that, Reed."

"Have you thought about increasing patrol? Keeping up a more active presence until the bastard is caught."

Arnie leaned back in his swivel chair, then instantly thought better of it and sat forward with elbows propped on the desk. His arms were bulky and the hair on his forearms looked dusted with talcum powder. "You'll have to talk to Mikkelson about that," Arnie said. "But we've already got most men working longer shifts than usual. We can only expect so much from them, especially during the summer."

Reed's knee bounced up and down; he stopped so as not to betray himself any further. "But men die in the summer too," he said carefully.

"We're trying here, Reed. We're doing the best that we can."

"I didn't say you weren't trying."

But not trying hard enough reverberated between them. He remembered Arnie and his father going on fishing trips together, or spending late Sunday afternoons in grease-spotted white T-shirts over a hissing outdoor grill. He felt a strong connection to Arnie as a friend of the family, even as he also felt a growing annoyance that Arnie couldn't seem to muster an appropriate amount of energy and *steam* behind the investigation—in short, that all of Alex's accusations of inadequacy were true.

"There are ways of increasing vigil without shaking down the department," Arnie said a bit defensively. "Community policing, for one." He stood up, now balancing the paperweight in his hand. His shirt was misbuttoned, exposing a strip of hirsute stomach, completing the portrait of his inadequacy. "Don't get too close to this," he said. "You'll get sucked in and that won't be good for anyone."

Arnie was right about that much: Reed knew he was getting drawn more and more into the labyrinth of the murders. First one man, then two, now three. Reed still thought about Zach Solomon from time to time, the first mysterious victim that no one had known well. Solomon remained a sealed book, an untold story. Reed had seen the book's ending in the form of a corpse with one eye dragging upward, but he couldn't get to the pages that would explain the narrative of Solomon's life, to what circumstances had led him to meet up, face to face, with the man who would destroy him.

Sometimes Reed thought about Anthony, too, and with a greater emotional force. The back of a man's neck in the grocery line would trigger a memory of how Anthony used to brush his shoulder-length hair away from his neck, exposing skin that was surprisingly bronzed. The smell of lime in Reed's drink became the pleasant tangy scent of Anthony's breath when he leaned over the bar that night and whispered in Reed's ear, *If you had a brother...* Once, when Reed and Alex were climbing into bed, Alex had turned briefly into Anthony. This had not been a dream because Reed had been fully awake. Yet there was Anthony beside him, naked and alive, his skin warm and lungs expelling breath. For a delirious moment, Reed had felt the improbable joy of a miracle—Lazarus, cloaked in the raiments of the dead, sitting up in his cave and calling Christ's name. Reed leaned over Anthony to whisper, "And what then?" But Anthony frowned, and in an instant Anthony was Alex again, frowning too. Reed tried not to show his disappointment, his sense of loss, not just for Anthony but also for a world operating outside of physical laws. He wanted spirit, life beyond this oppressive gravity.

The college boy rarely crossed Reed's mind. Let him haunt someone else. Reed had enough dead men tapping at his heart.

After his unproductive talk with Arnie, Reed confided everything to Alex that night, expecting to find a sympathetic ear. To his surprise, Alex was now, of all times, even-handed. "They just don't have the same stake in this as you do," he said.

"And what happened to giving the brass hell for not getting involved enough?"

"I'm on your side," Alex said calmly. "Just stating a fact. They don't have the kind of stake in this that you do."

"So only gay people should have a stake in finding the murderer of gay men?"

Reed was sitting on one end of the sofa with a computer in his lap while Alex was sitting on the opposite end of the sofa with pillows behind his back, nursing a glass of pinot noir, dividing his attention between the TV and proofing the final draft of the editorial he planned on sending to the paper tomorrow. For a college literature professor, Alex was much more TV-minded than one would imagine. Tonight he had settled on a cable show with several vivacious men who advised heterosexuals on the finer points of fashion and interior design. "Why are you watching this gay minstrel show?" Reed asked.

Alex mock winced and changed the channel. A man was roaming a wintry European street. There was snow, ice, a whore with fur wrapped around her throat pounding on the door of a closed bar. A sign in Polish read *Zamknięty Dla Biznesu*.

"And community policing," Reed continued. "How's that going to work? We all have our faces buried in our cell phones, jerking around on our iPods and BlackBerrys." He stared down at the computer in his lap. *A blind man never knows what he's done*: Reed couldn't remember where he'd heard this before. He removed the computer from his lap.

"Actually, though, it's worked well in the past," Alex said. "Community policing, I mean. You just need a group of people who really give a damn."

"Good luck with that." Reed was tired of arguing, tired of the feeling he didn't quite belong anywhere—not with the police and their labored investigation, not with Alex and the fledgling protest movement.

"To be fair, I imagine Mikkelsen and Granger are in a little over their heads," Alex said. "It's not like you guys have had a lot of experience with murder investigations."

"Then maybe they should bring someone in from the outside to oversee the case."

"Got it right here in the editorial!" Alex waved his paper in the air and then slapped it back down on the coffee table. "Not that anyone will really do it." He refilled his wineglass. "At least the boogie man's gotten your attention this way."

Already Reed could feel the impermanence of what he and Alex had resurrected. "Admit it, Reed," Alex said, his voice caught between seriousness and a playful jousting. "You wouldn't be as invested if this lunatic wasn't so out of reach. Always the allure of the unattainable with you."

Alex seemed to regret what he'd said as soon as the words were out of his mouth, but it was of course too late to retract anything. "Guess that's why I ended up back with you," Reed said, and they both fell silent.

*

When Reed took the time to think about it, his relationship with Alex had been tenuous from the start. They were supposed to have met two years before they actually had. A college friend of Reed's had mentioned that there was a young gay professor moving to Barrow's Point to begin teaching in the literature department at the university. The man was coming off a rocky relationship and so might be a little gun-shy at first, the friend said, but if Reed was interested, maybe they would care to meet?

Reed, who at the time hadn't been "out" for all that long, was already feeling the lack of his choices in Barrow's Point, so he'd called Alex and they'd talked on the phone for some time before agreeing to meet at Quench on a Friday night. Only while Reed showed up at the appointed time, Alex did not. Reed sat at the bar, nursing a beer, and when an hour passed and he realized he was being stood up, he switched to whiskey on the rocks.

(Was it that night that Anthony had leaned across the bar and whispered into Reed's ear: "If you had a brother…" Reed couldn't be sure, although it felt as if it may have been the same night, a comfort to him as he'd walked out of the bar, unexpectedly alone.)

Reed's pride kept him from phoning Alex the next day, and Alex never called Reed with an apology or explanation. After a few days, Reed let the

matter go and forgot about Alex, although he was disappointed in the outcome, having enjoyed his phone conversation with Alex even more than he'd
expected.

Two years later, Reed and Casey were dispatched to a house only a few
blocks from the college campus. A man had called about a break-in. Very little
had been stolen, but his things had been messed with, drawers turned over
and emptied. The man met them at the door, a lean attractive man a few years
older than Reed, his arm in a black sling. Instantly Reed identified with this
man although he couldn't have said why, other than the appeal of the sling.

It was when Reed and Casey were taking down the man's statement and
he gave his name—Alex Caldwell—that Reed realized who this man was. He
narrowed his eyes but remained quiet, allowing Casey to ask the questions.
No, Alex said, nothing much had been stolen other than a laptop computer and
a little money he'd left out on the coffee table. No, he didn't have any "enemies,"
although he had a jealous ex-lover who "could get out of control," but the lover
had just moved out of town. And yes, he was a professor and occasionally did
encounter a disgruntled student, but poor grades hardly seemed adequate mo-
tivation for theft, for breaking and entering, did it?

Reed waited until Casey stepped out of the room before he said, simply,
"We were supposed to meet a couple years ago." And when Alex just looked at
him blankly, Reed said, "We had a date set up at Quench."

Apparently the memory returned to Alex then, because he flushed and
turned his eyes away. "Oh, man," he said, but Casey returned before either
one of them could say more.

That night, Alex called Reed. "Let me explain," Alex said. "Can we meet
at Quench in an hour?"

"You've got to be kidding me."

"Think about it," Alex said. "I'll be there, and if you don't show, we'll call
it square."

A part of Reed wanted to dismiss the call, chalk it up to missed signals
and ships passing and karmic payback. But he drove to Quench more out of
curiosity than for any other reason. And there sat Alex in his black sling, sipping a martini and eying the door when Reed entered.

They went to a side table to talk, where Alex spent an hour explaining
himself: his ex-lover Randy had shown up in town two days after Alex's phone

conversation with Reed, and by the Friday of their scheduled date, Randy had managed to "spin my head back around" and convince Alex that they were worth another shot. "No excuses," Alex told Reed several times that night. "No excuses *but…*" He'd known he should have called to cancel but he would have felt like a shithead backing out of their date, so he'd taken the cowardly shithead route by letting it slide. "Obviously I made a mistake," he said and ordered them another round.

Alex glided over Reed's questions about his second breakup with Randy and Randy's subsequent move to Minneapolis. Instead, Alex started asking Reed questions about how it felt to be the only gay man on a small city police force, showing an almost penetrating interest in him, a clear absorption that Reed had wanted to resist but could not.

"And what happened to your arm?" Reed asked, looking Alex straight in the eye. It occurred to Reed that maybe Randy had been responsible in some way.

But if Alex picked up on Reed's suspicion, he didn't let on. "It disagreed with what my legs were up to," Alex said with a ghost of a smile.

Within a week, Reed and Alex began to sleep together. The first few months of their relationship were harmonious enough, although it stuck in the back of Reed's mind how Alex initially had stood him up with such abruptness. And although that had been years ago, and Alex had explained his situation and apologized, the memory still gnawed at Reed at unexpected moments, chipping away at his trust. So when the night came that Alex whispered he loved Reed, and Reed kissed Alex with a hunger and a need that was palpable, Reed wasn't able to say the words in return. What was it that was holding him back? Certainly there was more to it than having been stood up years ago. When they were apart, Reed longed for Alex's company, his conversation, the steadying presence of his body in bed every night, which had made more baffling Reed's lingering sense that he was with the wrong person.

After eighteen months together, the fights began—the disagreements, the doubts, the second-guessing. "You don't love me," Alex accused him more than once. And even when Reed argued this wasn't true—he did love Alex in a sense—they both felt the deficiency of that love, how it was blocked and cast in shadow. Finally, with neither one of them able to change, they broke up and made an attempt to move on with their lives.

A separation Reed had honored until the night he'd found out that Casey and Maggie were trying to have a baby, when his peculiar hurt and loneliness at the news led him to call Alex on impulse and start the whole wheel revolving again.

*

June passed into the first heady dog days of July. And with the change in months, the storms ended and a brutal heat wave descended on the town.

The heat wave coincided with the publication of Alex's editorial in the *Barrow's Point Gazette:* blunt, eloquent, critical without being excessive, a piece the police department actively resented but that much of the town privately conceded was accurate. With the town's faith in the police department now openly shaken, a rumor—random, outlandish—circulated through Barrow's Point with the increased heat: what if the killer were a police officer or an ex-officer? Could the lack of evidence in the case suggest a perpetrator who knew what he was doing? And "it was possible" the blows to the side of the third victim's head had been made with a nightstick, or so the coroner had said when asked the question directly.

Was it possible, then, that the blue wall of silence was responsible for the police department's lethargy in the case? They knew the killer was "one of their own" and were trying to protect him and the department's reputation?

The rumor never gained enough traction to become anything more than a conspiracy theory, and was soon replaced by other, equally farfetched scenarios: all three bodies had been arranged ritualistically, suggesting a link to devil worship; a married man had been having a clandestine affair with the third victim, had murdered the college boy when he'd threatened to reveal their affair, and then disposed of the body in a way that would mislead police into supposing the boy was part of the gay killing spree. And while Reed didn't believe a police officer was responsible for the murders, the idea of a homicidal police officer no longer struck him as so implausible. Any police force, even those in cities and small towns, was subject to flashes of hostility, irrational prejudice, the reflexive use of violence. In extreme cases, suspects were beaten, choked with clubs, and shot to death. Reed had heard all the stories. In the pursuit of order, lawlessness commonly erupted.

The publication of Alex's editorial also marked the beginning of Reed's estrangement from the police force. All his fellow officers knew Alex was Reed's boyfriend, so when Alex criticized Mikkelson and Granger, he was, by extension, also criticizing every man or woman in uniform. If Reed was truly on their side, they reasoned, he would have talked Alex out of publishing his "hit piece." And so their uneasiness with Reed began to mount as their resentment of Alex grew.

When Mikkelson announced another increase in street patrol, meaning that all the day officers were required to work one night of overtime on a rotating basis, that uneasiness turned to barely suppressed anger. Few of the officers took into account that the increase in patrol was largely a response to the town's growing dissatisfaction with the police's handling of the murder investigation. In the officers' eyes, Reed was responsible, since it was no secret that he'd been lobbying for just such an increase. Granger had a sentimental soft spot for Reed, everyone knew that, and Granger had pull with Mikkelson, who made all the final decisions. And so Reed, although he was one of the youngest officers on the squad, was manipulating the strings of policy and altering their work schedules to suit his personal sense of right and wrong— his *boyfriend's* personal sense of right and wrong. This growing bitterness was not lost on Reed. The murders had drawn an unseen line in the sand, it seemed, and apparently he was standing on the opposite side from the rest of the officers.

Two days after the publication of Alex's editorial, the vigil for the dead men was held in Court Square in front of the police department. Reed and Casey were two of six officers assigned to ensure the gathering remained peaceful, although no one realistically expected otherwise. Officers J.T. Rivera and Hannah Adair patrolled the southern perimeter of the square while Mitch Sternes and Ken Blanchard patrolled the northern perimeter. Reed and Casey trafficked inside the square where the people would gather.

The evening was humid and sticky with a trace of melancholy in the air. When people started to file into the square, most were dressed in as little as was possible to still remain decent. Some of the young men peeled off their T-shirts and tied them around their heads like bandanas, guerilla style, while many of the young women wore cagey halter tops and short shorts that tele-graphed their impatience with the formality of clothes. As the crowd gathered, milling around and greeting one another, Reed was pleased to see a healthy mix of people in attendance—young and old, gay and straight—and that it wasn't comprised only of the college faction that hadn't left town for the sum-mer. Even the older people wore shorts and T-shirts, unafraid to show their liver spots and varicose veins, pale legs and grainy skin. Many people also carried obligatory protest signs, expressing their dissatisfaction with not par-ticularly clever slogans:

Death to Homophobia

Homo Hate, 3. Cops, 0.

Police=Stone Wall

One cryptic sign, clutched in both hands by a woman with a crew cut, read: *We're Only Who You Think We're Not.*

A microphone had been set up in the square close to the police station, and around the microphone were mounted a couple of sign holders with enlarged photographs of Zach Solomon and Anthony Tull. On the other side of the mi-crophone was another placard with a charcoal drawing of the third victim, Ronald Temple. Apparently, Ronald's mother had refused to release a photo-graph of her son to organizers of the vigil. Reed wasn't convinced the pictures of the victims were a good idea—it seemed, almost, a brashly sentimental dis-play—but Alex and the other organizers insisted it was necessary to remind people of the individual lives lost to the murders. So there Zach and Anthony were, looking out with unwitting smiles at the crowd, neither man aware that he was dead. Only the drawing of Ronald managed to escape an eerie pathos. In fact, the sketchy Ronald looked impatient to get on with things.

Christian, along with a tanned boy wearing stonewashed dungarees, and a girl whose face was peeling although not from sunburn, moved through the crowd, each carrying a box piled high with small, fervent candles. People reached into these boxes, claimed their candles, and held them with the ap-propriate degree of reverence. A few in the crowd had brought their own can-dles from home—some removed from candle holders, some used and already burned down to half their normal size—and these people eyed the smaller, more conforming candles a bit enviously but nonetheless seemed committed to sticking with their family candles.

A couple of news reporters and photographers were also present, but they already looked bored and ready to call it a day.

As Reed stood on the edge of the crowd and waited for the show to start, so to speak, he noticed several people staring at him and his police uniform with temperate reproach. He tried not to let it bother him: vague anonymous disapproval was the least of his concerns. Still, his uniform had rarely felt so heavy and hot, so constraining and frankly subversive. It might as well have been a straitjacket. When Iris arrived in the square with her friend Ruth, she spotted Reed and walked over to him while Ruth staked out a spot for them on the outskirts of the crowd. "Where's Eddie?" Reed joked.

Iris rolled her eyes. "A tractor couldn't have dragged him here," she said as she looked around at the gathering. She wiped her forehead with tissue. "I hope this was a good idea."

"It's only a vigil, Mom."

She nodded although she wasn't looking at him. Her eyes were fixed on Christian milling about with his box of candles. "I don't think I know half of these people," she said.

A women's studies professor stepped up to the microphone and welcomed everyone to the vigil, so Iris whispered goodbye to Reed and returned to Ruth's side. The professor, who was cooling herself with what looked like a genuine Japanese fan, introduced Alex, who went up to the microphone to read his editorial to the crowd. The editorial sounded less harsh and more measured than it had read on paper—Reed wondered if Alex was softening the tone for his benefit—but when Reed glanced over at Casey, and then across the square at Mitch Sternes and Ken Blanchard, they all appeared tight-lipped with their eyes cast slightly downward, as if each word out of Alex's mouth was a torment they were forced to privately endure.

I don't think I know half of these people: again his mother's words reverberated with Reed, gaining force the longer he thought about them. A suspicious dread began to tease at the back of his mind. Anyone could be in this crowd, including the killer. Of course, it seemed unlikely that a man who had killed three people would show up at a place with such an active police presence, but then again, maybe a truly narcissistic killer would get a perverse thrill, even feel a dark pleasure from showing up here for just that reason—to hide in plain sight, to mix with a crowd that was celebrating the memory of his victims, to hold a candle in mock tribute to lives he had snuffed out. What power that would give him, to remain so publicly invisible. *I am here*, he must have thought, *I am right here, among you, beside you, too close for you to see.* And the more Reed tried to shake his rising paranoia the more persistent it became, until it no longer felt like paranoia so much as possibility.

But a far-fetched possibility impossible to prove. The crowd was not particularly large, but it wasn't small either, roughly 200-250 people. Alex finished at the microphone and the women's studies professor took over again, asking not only the police but the entire Barrow's Point community to look upon the murders not as *other*, not as something that was only happening to *them*, but rather to see it as an attack on all, an attack on community. Reed was no longer paying much attention to the vigil itself. Instead he was scanning the crowd, the sweating and glistening crowd, trying to root out any suspicious behavior, any crack in the camouflage or chink in the armor, whatever would help shift his perception just enough for him to spot the monster among them. Yet Reed saw nothing that struck him as out of the ordinary. If the killer was truly present, he'd cloaked himself enough in normalcy to escape detection.

As the sun slipped behind the courthouse and a red-tinged twilight moved in, people started lighting their candles and passing their Bics back and forth. The crowd grew hushed and expectant, as if in wait of something larger to descend. The photographs of Zach and Anthony and the sketch of Ronald grew more obscure in the waning light. Christian broke away from the crowd long enough to jog over to Reed and hand him a candle from the bottom of the box. For some reason Reed remembered Christian back when he was a child and had nearly fainted into the fire. It didn't seem as distant a memory as it once had. Reed smiled at Christian, squeezed his brother's shoulder, and accepted the candle. Christian held a lighter to the candle's wick until Reed had a fumbling flame, then he hustled back to his friends.

It wasn't long before Reed felt a heat like flame in his chest.

It was only after he was holding the candle that he noticed the tanned boy with the dungarees and the girl with the peeling face were approaching the other officers, Casey included, and offering them candles. But all of them gave terse shakes of their heads, continued to look straight ahead, and refused to engage.

A photographer from the *Barrow's Point Gazette* snapped a picture of Reed, and when he turned to look at her, she snapped another.

*

The next morning everyone at the police department seemed in a bad mood, a defensive mood. An article about the vigil was printed on the front page of the paper along with a photograph of Reed holding a candle. The caption beneath the photograph read: *Officer Reed McGregor honors the slain.* The photograph only increased the department's lingering tension. Even Casey was a grim presence in the car as he and Reed patrolled around town. "You have to be careful," he told Reed. "That picture in the paper. The image is powerful, Merc."

"All I did was hold a candle." Actually, the more Reed thought about it, the more it bothered him that Casey had shrugged off the tanned boy's offer of a candle.

"It makes it look like you agree with them."

"*Them?*"

"Be careful about pissing people off, that's all I'm saying."

"Who am I pissing off?"

Casey drove for a moment in silence. "In general, I mean," he said.

Back at the station, as if to highlight Casey's point, Reed found a porno magazine stashed in his locker. The magazine was open to a centerfold of a strongly built Latino man lying on a fur rug with his hands locked in steel cuffs, stroking between his legs with a rhapsodic expression on his face. The photograph, cast in a dreamy light, gave the naked man's beard stubble and closely-shaven head an oddly spiritual glow. Someone had circled the model's penis with black magic marker and scribbled a cryptic message between the man's thighs: *suckmydick.com.*

Reed didn't mention the magazine to Casey or Alex. He brought it home and placed it in a drawer beside his bed as a reminder. Only a member of the police force could have raided his locker, probably someone blowing off steam about the vigil, Alex, the candle, who could judge? Reed mentally thumbed through faces and suspects, all of them his co-workers and "friends": Norm Jamison, Ken Blanchard, J.T. Rivera. Mitch Sternes was the most likely culprit, a man with a red face and rust-colored hair, with an adolescent's love of the anarchic, ill-timed practical joke. He was an uncle to one of Eddie's friends, but this had never bonded Reed and Mitch in any way. Even before this summer, Mitch had never liked Reed much, or Reed Mitch, but they'd been able to overlook that. That was another thing the murders had done. What had been tolerated once was growing harder and harder to ignore. Not so long ago, people often forgot that Reed was gay. Even Casey had seemed to forget, or act as if he did. Now, in the charged atmosphere of the town, this was becoming impossible.

When Reed walked into the break room at the station the next day, Casey was sitting with Mitch, their voices loud and brashly joking. When they spotted Reed, their laughter stopped and there was an awkward pause. Reed walked over to the vending machine to buy his soda. For the first time in years, in his life actually, it occurred to Reed that he didn't really know what Casey said about him to other men when he wasn't around.

"Merc, we're hitting the court after work," Casey said. "Want to come?"

Reed opened his soda and took a couple of deep measured gulps. "You sure?"

"What do you mean am I sure? I wouldn't ask if I wasn't sure."

They went to a court only a few blocks from the station—Reed, Casey, Mitch, Ken, and Gary Baylor, whose ferret-like eyes always photographed red in pictures. A college student was shooting free throws at one of the hoops, clearly killing time, so they recruited him to play so they would have an even six. The young man agreed to this but looked a little wary, as if he could smell the police on them although they were no longer in uniform. Mitch suggested that he, Casey and Ken, who was older and balding and out of shape, should take on Reed, Gary, and the "college boy." No one protested, although Reed was growing tired of how Mitch always paired himself with Casey in basketball games. Casey was the best far court shooter and everyone knew it.

A coin toss determined that Casey's team was shirts and Reed's team skins. Reed and the college boy removed their shirts and tossed them to the sidelines. "I hate this skin shit," Gary said and removed his shirt, staring with contempt at his beer gut. "No one get a hard-on."

The friendly game quickly turned more competitive. Mitch and Casey were a formidable pair, with Mitch playing excellent defense, blocking Reed while Casey shot from the outside. Casey and Mitch charged recklessly as they dribbled, shouted to one another, whooped each time the ball sank through the hoop, their masculine energy fast taking control of the game. Ken was barely part of the team, a good-natured third wheel who Mitch and Casey largely ignored. When Ken found himself holding the ball, his tendency was to shoot quickly and without aim, as if fearing the ball would be taken from him. "What can I say?" he apologized sheepishly. "I bowl."

Gradually, Casey and Mitch's aggressive teamwork began to irritate Reed. They both thought they had the game won, especially Mitch, with his smug and surly grin. But Casey, too, seemed self-satisfied and overly confident in a way that ignited the fight in Reed. Gary was a routine player without the fire or energy to contribute much, but the college student was a lean and scrappy player, the best dribbler on the court, dodging and feinting his way around Casey while maintaining expert control of the ball. Frequently he spun the ball to Reed, who charged around Mitch for a lay-up. Reed preferred this style of play, quick and fast from the inside, approaching the basket from a side angle. Together, Reed and the college student started to gain on Casey and Mitch's lead. Mitch was breathing hard and labored now, his T-shirt shadowed with sweat. He swore when Reed stole the ball twice from him. Even Casey was looking at Reed with surprise and annoyance. Reed took a dark pleasure in this.

Soon Reed and the college student's more consistent and methodical play, with Gary's steady if unspectacular assists, closed the gap within two points.

When Casey missed a long shot, his game play turned more haphazard under the pressure, the college student caught the rebound and passed it on to Reed, who saw his opportunity, *bring this mother to a tie*. The basket loomed, in reach, waiting. Reed dribbled in for another lay-up, a shot he could make in his sleep.

Something struck him in the back with such force he lost the ball and was slammed, face first, into the chain-link fence. His vision blurred as his knees buckled under him and he fell to the ground. "Foul!" the college student yelled.

"For Christ's sake, Sternes!" Casey said. "What the hell was that?"

Their bodies swayed over Reed. Mitch was already holding out a perspiring hand to help him to his feet. Reed didn't accept his hand. A dark, angry rage—he'd felt it at his back a moment before Mitch had slammed into him. "An accident," Mitch said. "Don't know my own strength."

"You fucking checked him." Casey helped Reed to his feet. "Lighten up. Jesus."

"Keep reminding yourself, Saunders," Mitch said.

"You guys should start a prison league," the college student said. Everyone felt too strange to finish the game, so the boy fished his shirt from the pile and walked off. Quietly, Reed picked up his own shirt and followed after the young man, feeling he owed him something. Reed caught up to him and they walked side by side for a few seconds.

"Sorry about that," Reed said. "We don't usually play gladiator style."

The young man nodded and began to dribble the basketball somewhat arbitrarily, his hair glittering with sweat. Reed still couldn't tell if the young man knew he was a cop. "What's your name?" he asked.

"Kip," the young man said.

"Reed. You play great offense. Do you belong to a team?"

"No," Kip said. "Not really."

The two men walked for a few seconds more, unsure what else to say to one another. Reed felt an odd desire to protect Kip although he wasn't sure from what. Still, when they parted company at the end of the lot, it was Kip who peered over his shoulder and called to Reed, "Watch your back!"

(11)

One sticky July night Maggie woke to find she was paralyzed from the waist down. She felt instantly the absence of feeling—her legs heavy and numb, empty shells lacking all sensation. She sat up in bed, a jack-in-the-box springing upright on its coil, and meant to cry out, but all that came from her throat was a dry croaking. Surely this paralysis, this lack of voice, was part of some convincing nightmare. But this was no dream; she was coldly, jarringly awake.

In those first confused moments of consciousness, she imagined it was Reed lying beside her. The bed felt narrow and constrained, so much like Reed's bed back in Osborn dorm on the hill facing a plunge of woods leading down to the river. *Reed, help me,* she thought, but her tongue, more swift than her mind, managed to whisper "Casey."

She reached for her legs and touched only fur. She recoiled—her own legs!—but in the next instant reality shifted into place as Shamus, lying across her with his full body weight, woke and stretched his limbs.

"Oh, you precious thing!" Maggie said in a flood of gratitude. With Shamus lying on top of them, her legs had merely fallen asleep. She opened her arms, so Shamus moved obediently into her embrace. His magnificent heart pounded in his ribcage, steadying her.

"Magpie?" Casey murmured, and she told him to go back to sleep, it was nothing. "What's he doing in bed with us?" Casey whispered.

"He loves you," Maggie said, still groggy. But Shamus had jumped off the bed and disappeared from the room. She patted at her knees, grateful for the pinpricks of pain as her legs returned to life, so much more welcome than the horror of no feeling at all.

*

In the days following that peculiar incident, Maggie grew increasingly nervous, but a personal nervousness that stemmed from more than the tension surrounding the town. What it was that was bothering her she couldn't pinpoint; it would not, apparently, be named.

But her body started reacting to the tension. She lost her appetite. A hard little pain tightened in her stomach. Her hands went numb at odd moments, and there was a distant ringing in her ears. One day she and Casey went grocery shopping, and while they were unloading the food, spreading it out on the kitchen's granite countertop, Maggie's hands buzzed and she dropped, of all things, a carton of eggs. Several of the eggs shattered and ran yolk at their feet. Maggie stared down at the mess, stuck in this moment that felt echoing and ancient. "911," Casey said, and he grabbed some paper towels and bent down to clean up.

Maggie's eyes brimmed with tears. Casey dumped the yolk-drenched paper towels into the garbage can and then ran his hand along Maggie's shoulder blades. "Come on, Magpie," he said. "It's only a carton of eggs."

She nodded, unable to express how it was more than the eggs, or at least, more than these eggs. The secrets she was keeping from him—her silly and primitive anti-pregnancy rituals most of all—were dividing her from him. And the more she tried to pretend everything was fine, the more she felt that odd pain in her stomach and back, and the more her hands buzzed with sensation.

As the days passed, she also noticed a difference in Casey. Mostly he seemed to be paying too much attention to her, often with a small puzzled smile on his face. "You're sure you're fine?" he asked once, and she smiled and nodded because he needed her to smile and nod, although this was not the truth, and what was more, Casey seemed to know it.

"There's a smokiness in your eyes," he said.

"What? A *smokiness*?"

She thought about what Casey had said as she brushed her hair that night and stared at herself in the mirror. Was it true her eyes were smoky— *smoky?*—hinting at some inner fire? Casey lay half-naked on the bed, his hands folded under his neck, watching her. *Quit studying me*, she wanted to say, for the more he looked the more deeply he was driving her back into herself.

Impulsively she said, "I'm sorry."

"For what?"

She ran the brush through her hair. She couldn't begin to reveal her small deceptions, how she wasn't being truthful with him although it felt necessary that she not reveal too much. How could she explain that she had agreed to try and get pregnant but was now having second thoughts and hadn't bothered to tell him? In a sense, wasn't she leading him on?

"Please don't watch me," she said, her hair crackling beneath the brush. The air conditioner grunted and wheezed but the room still felt stifling.

"Magpie, I want to look at you. It's not watching." Maggie continued to brush her hair and didn't say a word. "Fine, if you don't want me to look," and Casey turned so he was facing the other side of the room.

She knew she had hurt him but didn't know how to alter that. She waited for a couple of minutes, sitting at the mirror with her snapping hair, brush stationary in her hand, looking in the mirror at Casey turned away from her (*who's watching whom?*) and she was disquieted. She almost didn't dare turn around in case her marriage really had turned into something she hadn't known it to be.

Eventually she did turn around, rose, turned off the light by the bed, and slipped under the sheets next to Casey. He was still awake, probably awaiting some overture from her, but everything seemed too convoluted now, and silence was best.

*

The next morning Maggie was at Starcrest Daycare, supervising the Sladek twins as they cut out of construction paper a crude red sun with narrow yellow eyes, when Beth, arriving late for work from a doctor's appointment, told Maggie the police had arrested a man in connection with the murders.

"What?" Maggie held an open can of paste to her chest. She almost didn't dare to hope. She plied Beth with questions, but Beth, maddeningly nonchalant, knew nothing more.

When Maggie had a spare moment, she ducked into the lounge area and turned on the television set. The police had arrested a 35-year-old man on drug charges and had questioned him about his possible involvement in the murders, but had already determined that he was not involved. And just like that Maggie's brief hope for justice and clarity was shoved back into the quagmire of not knowing, of that horrible waiting. A blunt ache pressed between her ribs, and the familiar tingling in her hands returned.

"Wishful thinking," Casey told her when he returned home from work that night. "There was never any real evidence against the guy. The department's jumpy now that we're apparently to blame for murder."

Was it her imagination, or was Casey making it a point not to look at her directly? "We're all jumpy," Maggie said, as close to an apology as she could manage.

Despite the lingering tension between them, Maggie and Casey went ahead with their evening plans to dine out, a first celebration of their upcoming summer vacation to New York for two weeks of city life with a couple of college friends. For tonight's "kickoff dinner," as Casey called it, he changed into the button-down white linen shirt she'd recently bought for him as an anniversary gift. The shirt suited him and suggested their hopes for the evening.

They were in the middle of wine and seafood at a restaurant along The Promenade, sitting outside in an area cooled by several large oscillating fans, and speaking openly to one another if not exactly candidly, when Reed called Casey and invited them to have a couple of drinks with him and Alex at Alex's summer cabin on the lake a few miles outside town. Casey and Maggie accepted the invitation, although on the drive to the lake, Casey didn't seem thrilled at the prospect of spending time with Alex. The two men had never quite gotten along even before Alex had written his editorial and organized the vigil.

The beginning of the gathering was civil enough. Reed and Alex had placed a couple foldable wooden chairs along the beach and laid out a couple of blankets in the sand. On one of the blankets was a pitcher of mojitos, a few paper cups, and an ice chest. She and Casey sat in the chairs while Reed and Alex lounged on the empty blanket. They were both casually dressed in shorts and T-shirts and looked like they had sunstroke. "I feel like a fucking gentleman," Casey said, running a finger under the moist collar of his dress shirt. He kicked off his shoes, peeled away his socks, and settled his feet in the sand. The shoes looked odd next to the chair, without his feet in them. "We came straight from dinner," he explained.

Maggie accepted the mojito Alex handed to her in a paper cup. "Thank you, sir," Casey said, possibly a little too jovially, when Alex poured him a mojito. Casey and Reed exchanged smiles. "A lousy, miserable day, right Merc?" he said.

Reed looked, Maggie thought, almost sad. He, too, must have been elated with the thought the murders were about to end, only to discover that this was not the case, that the streets ran as dark with blood as ever. She felt a small pang of inadequacy, wanting to comfort him but having no idea what to say. Besides, there was a complicit understanding between them all to keep the mood light, and so ignore all talk of murder and work-related policing. Instead, they talked about travel, mutual friends, Casey and Maggie's vacation plans.

But after the second drink, Casey and Reed started taking over the gathering a bit. Maggie was convinced they were unaware of this and couldn't help themselves. Casey laughed and joked, recalling stupid antics from when he and Reed were kids, and gradually drew Reed out of his mild funk. They jogged along the beach for a while, then returned and pulled a couple beers from the ice chest. There was something about Casey and Reed's energy together that was headlong and a little intoxicating, Maggie thought, even when it excluded everyone else.

Alex retreated into the cabin momentarily, so Maggie joined Casey and Reed in a stroll to the dock. It was such a peculiar evening. The setting sun tinged everything with a startling light. Casey reached for her hand and she accepted his, although mindful of Reed beside them. They sat on the dock with their drinks, settled their feet in the water, and stared out at the placid lake. Maggie thought of the three of them as children, sitting on a dock and splashing their feet together. But of course she had not known Casey and Reed when they were kids. She was the late entry in the tangle that had become the three of them.

They noticed an empty rowboat drifting out onto the lake. Apparently, the boat had become unmoored from a nearby dock. An old couple on shore, both wearing sun visors against the glare of the setting sun, were surveying the listing craft and pointing. "I guess the boat got away from them," Maggie said.

Casey watched the boat for a moment. Then he stood up and set his beer down. "I suppose we could go get it for them," he said.

"We don't have a boat," Reed reminded him.

Casey removed his shirt and tossed it at Reed. Maggie's heart rose up in her chest and then fell back again. "What, you can't swim?"

Now Casey was removing his shoes. A slow smile crept over Reed's face, a liberating and joyous smile. Reed hurried to his feet and removed his own shirt. It was unfair, Maggie often thought, how men had this liberty and women did not. "Come on, Magpie," Casey said and grabbed hold of her arm.

"You have to be kidding," she said, only half-resistant.

Casey released her arm and jumped, cannonball style, into the water. Maggie mock-shrieked, instantly regretting the girlish sound of her scream, as a wave of water broke over the dock and across the front of her dress. Then Reed dove in after Casey, and they began swimming away. Maggie watched them go. The boat seemed further out in the water now, but this didn't deter them. She splashed her feet some more in the cool water. Watching their muscular strokes as they gained on the boat made her feel not envious so much as excluded, even though she'd been invited to join them, hadn't she? Without thinking, she pushed off the dock and dropped into the water fully clothed. She laughed, filled with a fleeting, nameless thrill. She swam underwater for a bit, dress billowing around her, unencumbered and light. Then she curled into a ball and floated for a few seconds, *an embryo*, she thought in sudden alarm and pushed her way back to the surface. Casey and Reed, more distant from her now, had not noticed that she'd taken the plunge, in a sense, along with them. She swam around for a minute longer, gliding her arms back and forth, although her delirious sense of release was already deserting her. Her dress was growing heavy, dragging at her legs.

She boosted herself back onto the dock and picked up the men's shirts and shoes in her wet arms, trying to keep them as dry as possible. Somewhat dreamily she returned to shore, reluctant to leave behind such freedom and lack of restraint. Alex had gathered up some logs from a stack beside the cabin, and along with a little dry brush, was building a bonfire. "Don't ask," she said, wringing the moisture from her skirt, the water anointing her bare feet. "It was impulse."

But he didn't return her smile. He was peering out over the darkening lake. They could hear the sound of Reed and Casey calling out. Already they'd reached the runaway boat and were now hanging off it, diving underwater, wrestling each other, caught in some boyhood remembered, apparently in no hurry to return to shore. Finally Alex turned, and with one sweep of his eyes over her, made her complicit in his vision. "They're a magnificent pair," he said.

Maggie sat down on her wooden chair but did not lean back into it. Ducks flitted across the surface of the water, then landed and began paddling about. Their calls were sharp, piercing—were they male or female? She looked at

Alex, his smooth firm jaw and striking profile. "They've been best friends since they were kids," she pointed out.

"Yes, I'm sure that's part of it." He rose with his almost empty mojito and asked if she'd like a refill. She nodded, although she'd left her paper cup on the dock. The pitcher was empty, so Alex went inside yet again to mix some more, leaving her to contemplate the two men in the water. How strange to watch her husband in the water with Reed, her ex-boyfriend. She raised Reed's shirt to her face, and for an instant she felt connected to his body again, his scent, then pulled away in surprise and embarrassment.

Alex returned with another pitcher of mojitos at the same point that Casey and Reed were swimming back to shore with the old couple's boat in toll. They reached shallow water and emerged dripping from the lake to deliver the boat to the old couple wearing the sun visors. "We must look terribly ridiculous to you," Maggie said to Alex.

She handed Alex Reed's clothes; he set them down on the blanket beside the ice chest. "No, not terribly," he said and bent down to light the bonfire.

Reed and Casey walked over. There was, Maggie couldn't help but think, a pagan quality about them. "Welcome back," Alex said and kissed Reed on the mouth. Maggie noticed—couldn't help but notice—how Casey averted his eyes to the sand. She handed Casey his shirt and shoes. He looked down at her as if he recognized something unusual but couldn't quite place that she, too, was wet. For all the times he followed her with his eyes, he sometimes missed the most obvious details. "We were starting to think you two were going to swim off into the sunset," Alex said.

The bluntness of the remark made them all uncomfortable. Some magic was about to be released from a bottle, Maggie thought, or was that some poison? "You could have joined us," Casey said with a kink in his eyebrow.

"No, I think you and Merc are more of a spectator sport." There was something about Alex's dryness—his clothes, his humor—that made them all feel foolish. And Alex never called Reed Merc. Reed gave Alex a dubious look and then walked back over to the elderly couple, who were now having difficulty tethering the boat to the dock.

While Reed was away, no one spoke. Casey was trying to make eye contact with her but she felt odd now about making eye contact with him. Alex stirred his finger in his drink and made no effort to counteract the baffling silence.

Reed returned with the elderly couple. "Could you pour them a couple of drinks?" Reed asked Alex.

Casey and Maggie offered the old couple their chairs and sat down on the blanket with the ice chest. The elderly couple were still wearing their sun visors, although it was now nearly dark. The man had a weathered face, the kind found in framed, black-and-white, Depression-era photographs that hung in museums.

While Alex poured the old couple their drinks, Reed mouthed "sorry" to Casey, who shrugged, picked up a stick next to the bonfire, and started poking it into the sand. "A bonfire during a heat wave," the old woman said with delight. She had one prominent tooth missing in her yellow smile. "How perfect. So unnecessary."

The old man looked at Casey and Reed and Maggie—their still wet selves—with curiosity. "Fire as dryer, not heater," he observed.

The old woman tugged her husband's arm. "The fire reminds us of something," she said.

"What's that?" Reed asked.

"Oh, I don't know."

Alex handed mojitos to the old couple, then sat on the blanket and motioned for Reed to join him. They all devoted their attention to the remainder of the sunset and also to the fire, the disappearing sun competing with the more furious fire, the steady snapping flame. The side of Maggie that faced the fire was already dry, but she could feel dampness still lingering on her back.

When she focused back on the others, she found they had started talking again, and the conversation had turned, of all things, into a discussion about police brutality. "I'm speaking in general," Alex said, his legs crossed in a way that struck Maggie as deliberately casual. "Maybe I'm expecting too much from you guys. Maybe I'm expecting too much thinking the police will get fired up about the murders of gay men, when the police themselves have a history of not treating the gay population particularly well."

Casey leaned forward, his body taut, the posture of someone preparing for battle. Maggie had appreciated Alex's guest editorial in the paper—it had been an indictment of homophobia as much as indictment of the police, hadn't it?—but she knew Casey was eager to argue about it. Maggie had meant to attend the vigil, but she'd known that would cause additional friction between her and Casey, so she had, regretfully, stayed away. Now that seemed a cowardly choice. Embers from the fire snapped in the air, interrupting her thoughts. Maggie had the sudden urge to grab at one, those hot bursts of color and heat. When she was a girl, she'd believed if she caught an ember from a fire it would turn into a butterfly. All the embers had done, naturally, was scorch her palms. She looked down at her hands. No, that had been in the past, she couldn't keep waiting for signs.

"My brother was a sheriff," the elderly man said. "You couldn't buy your way out of trouble in Kingston, Nebraska, let me tell you."

"Alzheimer's," the woman said. "The one thief he couldn't subdue."

"I wonder how often the police are themselves violent toward gays," Alex said, steering them a little mercilessly back on topic. "One of my old professors at NYU was in the city back in '69 during Stonewall. There he was in the streets with his lover, getting clubbed and shackled by the police. He said the cops were itching to kill if there had been a way to get away with it, if there hadn't been such a crowd around as witnesses."

Maggie tried to picture the teeming streets of the West Village on that legendary night, but all she envisioned in her mind's eye was a man in a dark uniform beating Reed with a police baton, over and over, unrelenting. She saw Reed, with a bad sixties mop-top haircut, collapse onto a sidewalk, shielding his head with his broken fingers.

"That's one man's story from a long time ago," Reed said.

"True, but it's not like the police aren't still clubbing and shooting their way to authority. You see the videos all the time. Black men get it the worst."

After a careful pause, Casey said, "We only hear about the extreme cases."

Casey was leaning too close to the fire, Maggie thought distractedly, but he did nothing to pull himself back. She glanced over at Reed, who also seemed excluded from the conversation. His eyes were on Casey. "Wasn't some Muslim protester tasered several times just last month?" Maggie said.

"By the police?" Casey looked at her with something resembling betrayal.

"I think so." She stammered, she wasn't at all sure why she'd mentioned this. "Maybe they were just security guards of some sort."

"I'm not so sure it is just extreme cases," Alex said. "I wonder if the shooting and clubbing isn't even more commonplace than we hear about. And cops have never been big on civil disobedience."

"Hey, didn't we just jump into the fucking lake with our clothes on?" Casey protested.

"Your clothes half on." Despite the humor in Alex's voice, Maggie noticed his eyes were unsmiling. Embarrassed, Casey glanced down at his shirt that he was holding, but he couldn't put it on without looking like he was caving to Alex's will.

"What a marvelous sight that was, your plunge!" the old woman said to Casey. "But why bother with clothes at all! Weren't you tempted to go the full Monty?"

"Don't think that didn't occur to us," Casey said, trying to make a joke of it, although his eyes were still on Alex.

"I don't think jumping into a lake in your jeans counts as civil disobedience," Alex pointed out.

"All right, all right, we get it," Reed said. "Casey, myself, all police everywhere, one big mass of blue skin."

"Exactly," Casey said. "Some people can't see past the blue skin."

Blue skin? The underlying tension of the night was fast overtaking them. "Tag team," Alex said quietly and left it at that.

Maggie felt a little sorry for Alex, although he was, in many ways, the instigator against her own husband. Now she wanted to leave but of course could not request this without placing too much attention to the strain, so she and Casey remained and finished their drinks with the rest of them, listening to the old couple chronicle their recent bird-watching excursion through Arizona's Sonoran Desert.

But once they were in the car driving home, Casey allowed his anger freer rein. "He hates me," Casey said.

And why would that be? It hovered on the tip of her tongue, hot and sharp. "Alex is just opinionated," she said instead. She rolled down her window so she could feel the breeze in her hair. "You know how college professors get."

They drove past dark trees and shimmering water. "What does Merc see in him?" Casey asked.

Maggie rested her head back against the seat. Love was unwieldy and stubborn and there was no use trying to reason with it. "To Alex we're all chest-beating, minority-clubbing Neanderthals," Casey continued. "Now half the town thinks so too."

She squeezed the hand Casey was not using for driving. It was a simple gesture that made her feel better, whether he felt the same or not. There was more to what Alex had been saying, but she didn't have the desire to pursue it any further.

When they reached the outskirts of town, they stopped for a red light at a wide deserted intersection. A car with flashing taillights was pulled over on the opposite side of the road. Someone was standing out beside the car's open hood, staring into the car's coiled interior. Casey rolled down his window. "Everything okay?" he called out.

A man's voice came to them, just a voice from out of the darkness: "Transmission's dead!" He started crossing the highway toward them.

A sudden fear swooped down at Maggie with the force of a startled bird flying into her face—this shapeless, featureless man, his uninvited approach. "No, Casey!" she whispered. And when she saw the traffic light turn green, she said, "Go! Go!"

Galvanized by her urgency, Casey called out the window "Good luck!" and then drove on. Maggie leaned back in her seat but somehow didn't feel much better. "He just had car trouble, Magpie," Casey said.

By the time they'd arrived home, Casey was more relaxed while Maggie had grown tense. She was embarrassed the man on the side of the road had frightened her so. When they entered the house, Shamus was asleep in the hallway by the door, stretched out and luxuriant. He lifted his head and Maggie leaned down to stroke him, remembering her recent paralysis fears: the inability to move; the heavy weight on the soul; the utter dependence on others. Fear had so many different faces; she had to be careful. They didn't turn on the lights, as if in deference to Shamus. Quietly they moved upstairs. Yet they also didn't turn on the lights in the bedroom. While Casey turned on the fan, Maggie ran a brush through her hair, made somewhat coarse from the bonfire's heat. But the brush was too reminiscent of last night, so she set it down.

Casey sat on the bed and removed his shoes. Had the big toe on his left foot always curved inward? They removed their clothes, Casey hurriedly and

Maggie more tentative, uncertain. Her fingers were clumsy. It was odd she should feel so naked in front of her own husband. "Did you lock the door?" she asked. "You never know what a criminal mind—"

"Relax. Shamus is on night patrol." Casey kissed her throat, her eyelids. She clung to him, wanting to forget. Why was forgetting so difficult for her? "We're fine," Casey said. "Honey, don't worry. Whoever this lunatic is, he's not coming after us. He's only killing gays."

Her spine stiffened, but it took a moment for her mind to catch up. Casey lowered her down on the bed, running his hands over her breasts and collarbone. She found herself on the precipice, too, of yielding. But a persistent annoyance grew stronger. He looked down at her with dreamy and slightly narrowed eyes, his desire open and raw, disconcerting her a little. "Only killing gays," she repeated. "But your best friend is gay, there's nothing only about it."

He frowned, not too deeply. "I mean no one's breaking in and coming after us," he said.

"We don't know that for sure." Of course Casey was right, he'd spoken without rancor or malice, and yet... She sat up, puzzled by a hot flush of anger.

"You're not serious," he said. "Magpie? Come on, you're not really mad."

His disbelief only fueled her anger. "It's when you talk that way," she said, fumbling a little. "Like—everyone else."

Casey swore and stood up, naked before her, embarrassingly aroused in spite of himself. "I've known Reed a hell of a lot longer than you have." He groped in the dark for his pants.

There it was, the crack in his eternal patience at last! "Yes, I know," she said. "How can I forget, you two make it so plain." She had to get hold of herself! Yet she couldn't quite let it go. "Only gays getting killed, don't worry, Magpie, only them," she said.

"Great. You two drinking together from the same trough again." He shook out his pants so they snapped in the air like a whip before he shoved his legs into them.

Maggie wasn't quite sure what he'd meant by that. "And walking in front of him shirtless at every opportunity," she continued, undeterred, words spilling from her mouth in a ruinous, cleansing flush. "What's that about?" She stammered, wanting to say more, but she had nothing more. And yet *it* was there, somehow, in their bedroom, she could feel it, that persistent *it*, even from Casey, as he put the linen shirt—her gift to him—carelessly back on. "Your implications," she said at last. "You don't hear the way you sound sometimes, is all."

By now Casey's hands had clenched into fists. She almost wished he would hit her, some clear wrongdoing she could hold against him. Instead he picked up one of his discarded shoes and lobbed it at her. The shoe deflected off her knee, striking her funny bone. She laughed outright at the ridiculousness of it all.

"I'll tell you who the real killer is here." Of course his head must have been swirling as dangerously as her own. "You! Every good moment between us you're out to spoil."

She stopped laughing and her head cleared for an instant. "We shouldn't be parents, Casey," she blurted. And once she had spoken the words outright, the months of subterfuge and quiet deception fell away to free her. "Not yet," she added, to soften it.

For a moment his face looked twisted and she wanted to reach out to him. "The heart of the heart of the matter," he said, moving toward her and picking up the tossed shoe from the floor. Then he left the room, walked downstairs, and mumbled something incomprehensible to Shamus, unless he was talking to himself. The front door opened and slammed shut. After an interval, the car pulled out of the driveway and she was utterly alone.

She wandered downstairs, maybe for the comfort of Shamus, but the dog was no longer lying in the hallway. Her chest and collarbone burned from where Casey had kissed her. She double-checked to make sure the doors were locked, then went into the bathroom, moistened her fingertips under running water, and wiped at her shoulders and throat. A confusing twist of emotions rose inside her. Before she had a chance to beat them back, an ugly truth glared her in the face: she was jealous, but not because of Reed's feeling for her husband. No, she was jealous of Casey, of his effortless ability to elicit feelings from Reed that she never could. Her very body, her *sex*, had worked against her and always would.

Only wasn't jealousy the province of lovers? She paced back and forth, willing herself to root deeper. She wasn't always sure she was in love with Casey. A chill ran down her spine at the thought; she fought against it. Of course she loved Casey. She was just angry and lashing out. But a greater truth had presented itself, and too swiftly for her to ignore. What if she'd taken the remnants of her feeling for Reed—lingering, unresolved—and transferred them onto his best friend? A horrifying thought, this, how she might have built the entire foundation of her marriage on something so misguided. Was this obvious to family and friends—not just Reed's true feelings for Casey, but her own fierce loyalty to Reed, and all that implied?

She sat on the edge of the bathtub, frightened now, and by so much more than the murders and strange men with car trouble. Her eyes fell on the ovulation chart, and a final sickening thought came to her: When was the last time she'd had her period?

(12)

—It's the way you were talking, like you were confronting him—

—But I thought you were onboard about confronting the police, I thought you agreed they weren't trying hard enough to find this killer, that it showed their lack of priorities…

For nearly an hour Reed and Alex argued on the beach beside the waning, spitting bonfire. Casey and Maggie and the old couple had long gone, so they were free to attack at will. They interrupted each other; they backtracked; they poked and prodded and called each other out, with Alex finally going for the jugular:

—Admit what you're really mad about, that I had the audacity to challenge *him*. Why not just say it? I don't know why I let myself get sucked back into this old dance, except for whatever few more scraps of you I can manage to horde for myself.

Eventually they calmed down, but spending the night with Alex was impossible now, so after Reed helped Alex put out the bonfire and carry the blankets and chairs into the cabin, he drove back to town alone. He'd drunk three mojitos and a couple of beers and supposed he shouldn't be driving, but at that moment he didn't care. He hated when Alex threw Casey up in his face, which he'd started doing with increasing frequency.

At the intersection leading back into town, a car with blinking lights was parked on the side of the road. Reed drove through the intersection, then on impulse made a U-turn and drove back. He pulled up behind the stalled vehicle. What was he thinking, exactly, when he stepped out into the night and approached the flashing car? Maybe he wasn't thinking much at all. But no one was inside the dirt-streaked car. There was clutter in the back seat but Reed couldn't decipher what. A couple of minutes passed as he waited around in the hot and empty night, hoping to spot something revealing, then he lost patience, returned to his own car, and drove off.

At first, when Reed pulled up in front of the house he rented, he didn't notice anything out of the ordinary. He was walking across the lawn toward the front door when he heard someone call his name. His blood froze: was this how it had been for the others, sabotaged from behind, a voice calling from out of the darkness at your back, offering up the final, reassuring sound of your own name?

Disorienting, then, when he turned around and noticed Casey's car parked on the street. Reed walked over and leaned his head toward the open window, where Casey sat in the darkness with an open bottle of Jack Daniel's. "Imagine meeting you here," Casey quipped.

Despite that he'd been drinking, he didn't sound drunk. Still, there was something completely wrong about Casey sitting with such deliberate nonchalance in his car outside Reed's house so early in the morning. "Everything okay?" Reed asked, and when Casey shrugged, he invited Casey into the house.

"No, come sit in here for a few minutes," Casey said. "I won't stay long."

Reed circled over to the passenger side. As soon as he was inside and had shut the door, he felt ill at ease. The car was stuffy, so Casey closed his window and turned on the air conditioning. "I didn't know if you'd be coming back tonight," Casey said.

"You drove all the way over thinking I wasn't going to be here?"

Casey shrugged again. Despite that he was wearing the same clothes as he had been earlier in the evening, he looked more rumbled now, in a faint state of disarray. "I didn't really think it through," he said. "I just wanted to have a word with you."

Have a word with you: the phrase sounded vaguely chastising. Reed couldn't fully pinpoint what was different about Casey other than his more reflective tone of voice, other than the way he eyed Reed with such forthrightness.

"Go on. Have some." Casey held up the bottle of Jack Daniel's. Against his better judgment Reed took the bottle, drank from it, and handed it back to Casey, who ran his finger over the mouth of the bottle. "So what brings you back to your own house tonight?" he asked.

"Alex and I had a fight." What was the point of denying it?

"Must have been something in those mojitos. What was your fight about?"

Reed just shook his head.

"Great. Should I feel guilty?" There was gravity to Casey's words, a weight to them. "So we ended up here for the same reason, then."

Except that I live here, Reed thought. And what was Casey implying? He and Maggie had fought over Alex? Or over Casey? Or himself? Lately, Reed had been meaning to have a frank and serious conversation with Casey, but now that Casey had something on his mind and was ready to throw down the gauntlet, Reed was tongue-tied. He'd always imagined himself as the instigator of such a conversation, and so in control. But here Casey was in the literal and figurative driver's seat, looking at Reed with such disquieting focus, the whiskey a lubricant to his tongue, assisting him in finding his voice. Where most men's speech grew sloppy and cheap the more they drank, Casey's, apparently, was finding clarity, depth, resonance.

"That's why I drove over here. To talk about you and me." Casey stared out the windshield into the silent street. They knew this street like the backs of their hands. "And Maggie."

There was always Maggie between them. Reed supposed he was really responsible for that, if he bothered to trace the years.

"Revelation number one. I'm not sure she loves me anymore." Casey said this without a trace of self-pity. "And revelation number two? She sure as hell doesn't want to have a baby with me, after all these months of pretending."

Already Reed felt as if he was hearing too much.

Casey exhaled. The light from the street lamp fell across one side of his face, and it was that side, the lit side, that looked most melancholy. "She loved you once," he said. "Sometimes I think she still does."

All the wind felt punched out of Reed's lungs. Casey held out the bottle, and again Reed drank, unhesitatingly this time. "Why is that so preposterous?" Casey asked, and the bottle seemed to tremble as Reed passed it back to Casey. "You were her first real love. Those pesky first loves can fuck people up. Tell me if you've heard all this before."

They were on the brink of something—a startling admission, a reckoning. "How well do you remember your first love?" Casey added.

Reed was silent. Was Casey really serious with this question? "I don't remember much," Casey continued. "Janie Latchman. Strange that I can remember her name but not her face. The junior prom." He shook his head, his eyes still fixed on Reed but his gaze drawn inward, as if he was struggling to reconstruct the puzzle of Janie's features in his mind. "All I remember is that I could hardly breathe when I was next to her. Yet when she moved to Florida, I was pretty much over her in a week. I guess she didn't fuck me up at all."

For a moment there was no sound other than the steady hum of the air conditioning. "She wasn't Maggie," Reed said. He was surprised that his voice sounded a little bitter.

"That's right. Magpie. Even our fight was about you."

There was an edge to Casey's voice now, a slightly goading quality beneath the world-weary pondering. "All this death and killing and Alex is out there in the forefront, bullhorn in one hand and poison pen in the other, and you're right there beside him most of the time. How could she not notice?" Reed couldn't tell if it was admiration or judgment in Casey's voice. Of course he should know the difference. "But then I realized she's sort of idealized you long before now. Before you came back, and I was sitting here wondering if I should stay or go, and drinking this excellent Jack, I tried to trace back to when it first started. And the thing is, I couldn't. That's because she's always been like that, ever since I've known her, quietly in your corner."

Reed knew there was some truth to what Casey said. He'd always suspected, always felt, that he was still bound to Maggie, and not only because of Casey but also because of his own shaky past with her. "You two have a certain simpatico," Casey said. "You see the same things, I mean. I'm just the blind man stumbling down the side of the road."

Reed was at a loss over what to say, but apparently his silence was not a deterrent to Casey. "Who the hell knows what she's thinking half the time," Casey said. "Maybe you can tell me. She doesn't even like the way I act around you."

"She said that?"

"No." Casey looked away, and Reed knew he wasn't getting the full story. "Not exactly."

"She's not the judge of our friendship. Who handed her the gavel?"

If Casey sensed Reed's irritation with Maggie, he didn't let on. "I'm glad you don't see it that way," he said. "So you and Maggie disagree on something." He spun the steering wheel a couple of times in his hands, going nowhere, of course. "You know, other than my family, you're my most long-lasting friend. I've known you far longer than I've known Maggie."

Reed let his mind drift back to his boyhood self before he and Casey had become friends. He could barely remember those years. "We didn't like each other at first," Reed said. "You bloodied my fucking nose because Pam Larson wanted me to feel her breast."

"You didn't have to do it," Casey laughed. A muscle shuddered in his jaw. "Were we twelve then? Thirteen? Your dad died not so long after that. I remember I used to look up at him in the pulpit every Sunday, wearing that white robe you know makes ministers feel queer as hell. When my parents told me that Pastor McGregor had passed away, I tell you, I was a little freaked out. I only remembered later that he was your father." Casey smiled a bit, remembering this past grief not his own. "I couldn't imagine it. That size of loss. Somehow I had to become your friend. It's like I made a conscious decision."

Casey had never shared with Reed the actual thinking process that had led him to Reed's door several days after Carl's death. "The lure of death, even at thirteen," Reed said.

"You think that was it?" Casey moved his shoulder in a way that caused his collarbone to crackle slightly. "Maybe I just wanted to help you. Who the hell knows why? I just did."

Casey's voice had taken on a reminiscent quality, leading Reed back over the years to that crushing, spiritless afternoon when Casey showed up at the

McGregor's doorstep wearing a light olive-colored backpack. With hair flopping in his eyes and feet shuffling nervously, he'd said: "Can you come with me? Right now? Your Mom, will she let you come?"

Casey had asked in such a way—kind yet firm, insistent—that made refusal impossible. Reed's grandmother, who'd been staying with them for a couple of weeks to "help out," had gone grocery shopping and taken Christian along with her. Iris was lying on the hammock in the back yard with baby Eddie settled on her chest, a quilt pulled over them both although it was summer and too hot for a quilt. Iris had scared Reed a little, how remote she seemed, how listless, staring up into the snare of the tree branches as if even the baby wasn't real to her. But when Reed said Casey Saunders had invited him to "go somewhere," she'd smiled vaguely, and didn't even ask the boys' destination. "Of course you should go, honey," she said. "Go somewhere—anywhere—away from here."

Although he was only thirteen, Casey was already riding around town on a mini bike. Reed climbed onto the back of it, clutching at the seat although Casey had instructed him to "hold onto my hips." They rode outside town a couple of miles, Casey's backpack shivering against Reed's chest, as if alive. Reed leaned into it. Casey veered onto a dirt path that angled into a stretch of woods. Once the path became too rocky to drive along, Casey parked the bike and they continued on foot. They didn't say much during the hike, the two boys trudging forward like grim soldiers, winding deeper into the modest woods with no particular destination in mind. Finally they had stopped at an outcropping of rock, sat down in one of the patches of sunlight, and tried to establish some level of comfort with one another. "I'm real sorry about your dad," Casey said, his brow puckered in a serious frown.

Reed nodded, unable to manage even a whisper of thanks. His father's death was still an inexorable weight he carried inside his chest.

With death having been acknowledged, the boys didn't feel a need to mention it again. Casey withdrew from his backpack a magazine with slick pages. On the cover a nude woman in heels, biting down on a whip, observed them with disdain. "Look at those mammaries," Casey said and clapped Reed on the back. The woman was meant to cheer Reed up, although he was more cheered by the sun on his face, the trees murmuring overhead, and the smell of Casey's bubble gum breath in his face.

"Nothing like starting the caretaking early, I guess," Casey said now, pulling Reed from his reverie. "Do you think that's how I first got involved with Maggie? I thought I could give her everything you couldn't."

The observation stung a little, but Reed overlooked it.

"No, maybe it's time I start considering what's really going on. Facing the truth head on." He held a hand rather dramatically to his own face. "Maybe I was just some cheap cement for Maggie's heart. I plugged up the hole you left, but maybe it would have been better to let her heart bleed itself to health again, instead of sealing it off early with our cheap cement knockoff of a marriage."

"For Christ's sake, Casey. Cheap cement?" Reed laughed in frustration. Something was slipping away from them. He rubbed his arms, which were growing chilled. "Maggie and I dated for only a year. Count it. One."

"Eighteen months. People have married in less time. Look at Maggie and me." He trailed off. "It's like I'm disappointing her somehow. Just in general instead of anything specific, which is worse. That starts messing with your head after a while. You start to doubt yourself."

Reed suggested that Maggie was just rethinking having children right now. "Whatever is going on with her, it's probably less about you than you think."

"Truly alarming thought there, Reed. My wife's in some turmoil and it has nothing to do with me." Casey took another drink, only this time held the liquor in his mouth as if he meant to gargle with it. Then he swallowed and looked out, again, over the deserted street. Not even a dog howled. "So here we are, the three of us," Casey said. "One big incoherent knot."

Reed wanted to keep the conversation focused on light, memory, connection, pulling each other from the precipice of grief, incoherent knots be damned. "If you need a place to spend the night, you're welcome to crash on the sofa," Reed said.

"Apparently you're the only person I can rely on these days. Always dependably there." Casey stretched his arms in the cramped car. The bottle was still in his hand, yet they didn't pass it between them this time. "I'm afraid of losing her," Casey admitted. "That's it in a nutshell."

Reed nodded. He had nothing to say about loss.

"Or maybe just drifting apart. The slow death. You and me too."

"That won't happen."

"You don't think so? But it's already started, hasn't it? Sometimes all of life feels like moving toward and then away from people."

Reed had no idea what he was talking about…and then again, he did. This summer in particular, he'd felt a force trying to separate them, a surreptitious wedge prying them apart. Neither one of them could explain it; they could only feel it, like an ominous shadow spreading around them, *between* them, and where there was shadow was also darkness and cold. The cold: it had found them again after all this time. Reed could feel it taking over the car, a palpable presence they couldn't escape. It was a part of the air and so they were forced to breathe until the cold had moved inside of them, frosting their hearts against the other.

Maybe the cold had turned Reed anxious and light-headed, or the alcohol had caught up with him, or Casey's confessional had turned him sentimental. He made the mistake of looking at Casey's collarbone—that fucking, once-broken collarbone—and then looking up at Casey's face, at his eyes staring somewhat ruefully back at Reed. Before Reed knew what he was doing, he'd shoved his body forward and pressed his mouth against Casey's.

Startled, Casey moaned at the base of his throat. For several endless seconds it was only breath and tongue and heat, shouldering out the past cold that shrieked all around them.

Then Casey turned his head, his hand on Reed's chest, pushing him away, quietly but firmly. "What are you doing?" he whispered.

Reed shook his head. He didn't know.

Then, louder: "Man, *what are you doing?*" The meditative Casey was gone, replaced now by this other Casey that Reed had glimpsed at the police station in the company of Mitch and other men on the force—the harder, more sardonic Casey.

Reed was trying to remember someone or something, although the memory wouldn't come to him. The cold had tricked him into thinking they had moved forward into the past. "Sorry," Reed whispered. "I just thought—"

"You thought what?"

In that moment, with their defenses stripped away, Reed saw an open look of disgust pass across Casey's face.

Casey wiped his mouth—twice—with the back of his hand.

Reed could feel the cold-hot adrenaline still surging through him. A few more seconds crawled past them. Finally, Casey sighed and turned off the air conditioning. "I shouldn't be here," he said. "Maggie was right." His accusatory tone was gone now and replaced by something worse, a chill and severe detachment.

"I wasn't thinking. Casey. You can still crash on the sofa. It's the alcohol."

Casey's laugh was strained. "No, I don't think so," he said. "I need to get home. I was stupid to leave in the first place. Maggie and I are going to goddamn New York on Sunday."

"You shouldn't drive then. You're a cop. You've been drinking."

"Yes, I fucking well have. We all have. "

"Come on in and—"

"Christ, Reed, would you let it go?" He capped the bottle of Jack Daniel's and set it on the car's floor. "Good night then," he said.

There was nothing left for Reed to say. The damage had been done. He stepped out of the car, slammed the door, and watched as Casey pulled away and the car moved down the street.

He cursed aloud on his way back to his house. Inside, a deafening silence filled the room, a harsh and unforgiving silence he must have transported with him from the car. The taste of Casey still lingered in Reed's mouth; he tried to wipe it away out of spite. "None of it true," he whispered. He tore at his own shirt, ripping it off almost, and lay across the sofa. The unlocked front door was an invitation for any fag killer who might want to slip inside and bash his skull in his sleep. Why not? Let him come. "Let him come!" Reed said aloud. "Hysterical."

He lay on the sofa for some time, shuddering as if in a deep fever. How swiftly and surreally it had all ended! In one hasty and misjudged moment, he'd broken the decade-long spell between him and Casey, whatever the spell had been, and caused this emotional tearing. Already he could feel Casey's back turning against him. Only it wasn't the cold that had divided them. Reed had done that himself. He *was* the cold.

(13)

The past, the past, the past! How was it that just as Iris resolved to pay more attention to the details of her day-to-day existence, the past began to sneak up on her, demanding equal time?

And the past—her past—was Carl. She started thinking about him more often than was necessary, particularly when she was feeling on edge, which was often enough these days. Sometimes she quite literally felt his presence near her, though she never imagined anything as crude as a ghostly vision. When she caught herself worrying about Christian or Eddie—and she was worrying about Eddie more often now than she had been only weeks ago—she was struck by how much he resembled Carl in unapparent ways: the slightly coiled set of his shoulders; the hint of tension in his face; the way his eyes drifted mildly to the side when he was speaking, as if he didn't trust full eye contact.

Eddie, the son that most baffled her, her increasingly harried and mysterious son, her baby.

Maybe it was the summer's mounting heat wave, not to mention the anticipation of death in the air that heightened everything and called Carl back to her. At night, when she lay alone in bed, hot and with the sheets sticking to her arms and legs, a fierce longing overtook her of a sort she hadn't felt in a decade. Sometimes when she stepped into a room, she imagined she smelled traces of his cologne. *My darling little heartthrob, my heart is throbbing for you, my dear:* sometimes he whispered those words to her while she slept, words he'd actually said to her, jokingly, in the first years of their marriage. Or he would say something more unaccountable, words he'd never spoken in real life: *We are a mystery to ourselves. We know not where the other heart soars.* She tossed and turned and awoke in the night muttering heartsick into her pillow. A pillow! This was what she had to comfort her these days, a patchwork of feathers and goose down.

Since that day when the two of them had shared coffee together in the hospital, Iris started spending more time with Arnie Granger. What began as friendship and commiseration turned within a week to a gentle but no less exciting form of flirtation. She hesitated calling it a romance. Because of their long and platonic history together, it seemed unlikely they would fall madly in love. Yet this did not deter them from seeking out each other's company and exploring what they could offer to one another.

When Iris thought about it, she'd known Arnie for thirty years, far longer than she'd known Carl. For a dozen of those years, Arnie, Yvonne, Carl and Iris had been each other's closest friends, through countless dinners and barbecues, camping trips and nights out on the town. Naturally, Arnie had been closer to Carl while Iris had gravitated to Yvonne. The women had confided openly to each other during their long friendship, including their occasional frustrations with married life. From Yvonne, Iris learned that Arnie was sometimes too mild-mannered; he was sloppy around the house; he lacked a certain forcefulness of character. "A forcefulness of character?" Iris asked, and Yvonne shrugged, unable to clarify what she meant. "Maybe I just mean a certain drive," she said.

In turn, Iris confided to Yvonne how Carl could be so inflexible at home, so frustratingly withdrawn at times, almost cold.

"Really?" Yvonne looked surprised to hear it, and perhaps she didn't believe Iris fully. People in Barrow's Point had loved Carl—his steadiness and friendliness, the sense of a spiritual community he'd so effortlessly fostered. "Well, he's a minister. Maybe he walks more comfortably with God than with the rest of us."

Iris knew this was sentimental. Carl had walked with God no more comfortably than he'd walked with anyone else. She didn't expect others to know this or to understand. Carl had *performed* the role of minister quite well. It was only as a husband and father, possibly even as a man of private faith, where he'd struggled. And yet this didn't strike Iris as having always been true of Carl, but something that had evolved (devolved?) over time.

In the year following Carl's death, Arnie and Yvonne had rallied behind Iris, checking on her constantly and offering to babysit the boys if she needed "alone time." Arnie stopped by every now and then to toss a football around with Reed or play catch with Christian, who always seemed skeptical of the flying ball and Arnie's fatherly attention to him. And because Arnie and Yvonne were so kind, Iris didn't have the heart to explain that their company made her uneasy. When the three of them were together, Carl's absence loomed so large that Iris could scarcely bear it. When she was alone with Yvonne, she could almost imagine they were widows together, but when Arnie entered the picture with his clumsy and good-natured maleness, Iris's tongue gummed up and she felt adrift. She and Yvonne might as well have lived on different planets.

Years later, when rumors began to float around about Yvonne and an investment banker in town, Iris was at first shocked and disbelieving. She remained unconvinced even when Yvonne stopped returning her phone calls with any regularity. When they did manage to get together, Yvonne was distracted and a touch irritable, not really present in the friendship the way she'd normally been. Once, rather impulsively, Iris asked Yvonne if everything was okay between her and Arnie. Yvonne looked at Iris with a frank air of bewilderment. "Oh Iris, what a straitjacket I'm in" was all she would say on the matter.

By the time Arnie and Yvonne's son Ethan graduated from high school, it was clear to Iris that the rumors about Yvonne were true. Yet she was surprised by how suddenly Yvonne announced her divorce from Arnie and moved to Arizona where the banker had taken a new job. Yvonne cut herself off from her past with the swiftness of an amputation, as if Arnie and everyone in her old life were diseased limbs threatening infection. A few months later, Iris had an urge to write Yvonne a long, probing, old-fashioned letter asking, among other things, about the state of their friendship. But writing such a letter proved difficult. Something inward blocked Iris from doing so. Instead, she sent Yvonne a kindly but measured email in which she updated Yvonne on her life and then asked Yvonne for an update in return. After a week she received Yvonne's hasty reply: *Very happy these days. Sun and cactus and plenty of sangria. I even have a tan!* The reply was so offhand, so throwaway that Iris never answered back, metaphorically stuffing that friendship into a bottle and tossing it into the restless sea of memory.

With Yvonne in Arizona and Ethan attending college in Chicago, Arnie found himself living alone for the first time in over twenty years. After work at the police station, he returned home to an empty house. Iris knew, of course, that there were different kinds of empty houses. There were the empty houses that people chose for themselves, private spaces that offered nourishing silence and healing respite from the vagaries of the outside world. And then there were the empty houses that people did not ask for and did not want, that came to them through bad choices, unlucky circumstances, or the cruelty of others.

These were the empty houses that were always waiting to lure someone in and then snap shut like a steel trap.

In many ways, Arnie was not the sort of man Iris normally found attractive. He was somewhat doughy-looking these days, and given his high position in the police department, less commanding than one would expect. Sometimes he cracked jokes that weren't quite funny. Yet the more time Iris spent with him, the more her heart warmed to his jokes, which struck her now as amusing in a casual, quirky way. Despite his flaws he was a kind man, if somewhat *awkwardly* kind, and as she'd aged she'd learned the value of kindness over charisma.

Even the boys had begun to pick up on Iris's changed demeanor. "Mom, what are you *up* to?" Christian teased her one night when she walked into the kitchen dressed somewhat stylishly to meet Arnie for dinner on The Promenade. A T-shirt was spread out on the living room table, a T-shirt Iris was pretty sure was not Christian's own, although he was spraying letters onto it with spray paint. The TV was turned on in the background. Always there was the news, always the wait for some new development about the murders, which never seemed to come.

"I don't know what you mean," Iris answered, feigning coyness.

"You've been out kind of late these days."

"You're not putting me on a curfew, are you?" She felt almost like a teenager again—that silly delicious rush of secret and clandestine plans.

"Do I have to?" he asked and raised his eyebrows. Iris laughed but said nothing more. Let her sons graze on unsatisfied curiosity for a while. From where Iris was standing, she couldn't make out what Christian was writing on the shirt. "What are you doing?" she asked.

"Trial run," he said. Then: "Mom, you're not fooling anyone. We know you're hanging out with *Arnie Granger.*"

"Oh." She felt her aura of mystery desert her with a *pop,* as if with the wave of a magician's spellbinding hand. She didn't know what to make of the way Christian said Arnie's name with just the faintest hint of disapproval. "Does that bother you?"

He shrugged. "It doesn't *bother* me," he said.

"Arnie's a very nice man."

"Sure. Nice man. Lousy detective."

"Christian! When did you become such a cynic?"

But Christian didn't back down. "You know it's true, Mom. If the cops were doing a better job—"

"Your brother's a cop!"

"It's not Reed's fault. He's trying—"

"Everyone's trying! You can't believe anyone is happy with this, the way things are?" She tried to keep her voice level but without much success. It was so unusual for her to even disagree with Christian, much less to feel angry at him.

Christian looked down at his handiwork on the table. "If he was doing a better job," Christian said, "we wouldn't need *these*."

A warning bell went off in Iris's heart. Christian held up the T-shirt he'd been laboring over: *VIGILANT,* it read. "Just a sample," he said.

"What's that for?" Iris asked. Now that she could read the T-shirt, it seemed menacing, in collusion with Christian against her.

Christian explained a new idea that a university professor ("not Professor Caldwell," he said) had come up with: a volunteer self-policing watch group. So far they had 20-30 people connected with the college, mostly students, who had already committed to helping out. Two groups of three people each would go out for several hours at night to drive and walk around town and offer additional patrol, another set of eyes. They would wear the red *VIGILANT* T-shirts to identify who they were. They would escort people home upon request and phone the police if they saw anything suspicious. "Stay vigilant" was how Christian phrased it.

"No!" Iris cut him off, surprised at the vehemence in her voice.

Christian lowered the T-shirt but didn't say a word.

"I mean—" She paused, weighing her words. "I mean, why do you have to be a part? It sounds dangerous. And vigilant, like vigilante—"

"Mom, I *am* a part of it. Haven't you noticed what people are getting their heads bashed in? And it's not vigilante at all. The opposite, actually. More like vigil."

Tears rose in Iris's eyes but she fought them back. Christian's high profile role in the vigil had been nerve-racking enough, but this was much worse, almost a direct challenge to the killer. "Please, Christian, don't," she said. "Let the police handle it."

"They're not handling it, Mom. That's the point. And I'm not going to be out there alone. There will always be at least three of us."

"So three to put in harm's way instead of one? Fabulous idea! Don't make yourself so visible—"

As soon as the words were out of her mouth, she knew she'd made a mistake. She could see it in the momentary deflated expression on Christian's face, followed by the familiar hardening resolve. "I like being visible," he said before he left the room with the T-shirt, the hand-sprayed *VIGILANT* staring back at Iris.

The dust-up with Christian all but ruined her dinner with Arnie. She told him about having an argument with Christian but left out details about what they'd been arguing over, wanting to both protect her son's plans from Arnie and Arnie from her son's judgments. Yet Arnie seemed able to read between the lines of what she wasn't saying. "I'm sorry, Iris," he said. "Everyone wants our asses all of a sudden. Notably mine."

She reached out and held Arnie's hand. It seemed wrong that he was receiving the brunt of the town's anxiety, this lonely and deserted man.

After their dinner at The Promenade, Iris and Arnie returned to his house to share a bottle of wine. It had just turned dark and so was not very late, and yet she felt, almost against her will, nervous that she wasn't at home with the boys. She called her landline number, mostly to make sure that Eddie was at home to pick up, and after she'd spoken briefly to him, she felt somewhat better. "Take it easy," Arnie said. "Your boys can fend for themselves." Arnie opened the liquor cabinet that had belonged to Yvonne's family. She had left the cabinet behind in her mad dash to the desert and a new life. "Red or white?"

Iris chose red because she knew that was Arnie's preference. She looked around a bit self-consciously at Arnie's untidy rooms. She felt odd holding his hand inside the house, almost as if she were messing around with Yvonne's husband behind Yvonne's back. Not that Yvonne would have minded. Still, Iris was relieved when they took the wine, a couple of wine glasses, and a blanket and headed outside. The crickets were calling, and the sound calmed Iris somewhat. Arnie shook the blanket and laid it out a little unevenly, so Iris smoothed it down in a way that she hoped wouldn't appear fussy. Arnie poured Iris a glass of wine and then filled a glass for himself, and they lay down on the blanket together as if mesmerized. It was one of those starless nights where the sky looked vast and a little wild, a blank indifferent slate on which anyone in the world could write.

Although Iris felt a little sticky—the damned humidity!—nonetheless she curled up beside Arnie, wrapped her arms around him, and felt a measure of peace settle around her, beating back even further the tensions of the day. It was more than the simple comfort of having another human being lying beside her. Or maybe there wasn't more to it at all.

"Look at us, Iris," Arnie said as she rested her head against his shoulder. "You ever think we'd end up together like this?"

She raised her head off his shoulder. "Are we together?" she asked. She sounded almost coquettish. In another minute she'd be batting her lashes and tossing off a fiddle-dee-dee.

He shrugged and gave her a slow smile. They had no clear word for what they'd so readily become to each other. "Well, dating," he amended.

"Are we dating?"

Arnie poured a little more wine into her glass to avoid answering the question. They had to keep brushing away at the mosquitoes that wanted a piece of them. Why, Iris wondered idly, were there so many mosquitoes when the insects supposedly thrived in moist weather? The female mosquitoes were the ones that stung, Iris remembered reading once, forever seeking out a blood meal for the development of their eggs. "It's not just Christian who's different these days," she said absently. "It's Eddie too."

"Welcome to fifteen."

"Yes, but..." Iris floundered. Even to Arnie she couldn't quite articulate her full concern: that Eddie had become like an alien son, a pod son, pretending he was someone he was not. He looked and sounded like her son, and yet there was some ineffable quality, something intangible, that was not Eddie at all. Catching him running outside that night during the storm had opened her eyes in that regard. He was secretive and jaded, touchy, quick to anger. Some nights she heard him moving around the house, and was nearly afraid to investigate to see what he was up to. She could imagine herself going downstairs and finding him in the process of doing almost anything. Standing silently out in the backyard and calling down the mother ship, for example. Or talking to the TV like in that movie with the little girl who got sucked into the television set and became an annoying and echoing voice from which the family could not escape. One night Iris dreamed she woke up to find Eddie tiptoeing around in her room. She lay still in her cave of a bed and pretended not to notice, although she was afraid she might have left some dirty clothes lying around somewhere.

"Reed's yet another enigma," Arnie said. "If you figure out how I can get on his good side again, let me know. I hate thinking I let your kids down."

A teenage girl and a small boy stepped out the back of the house next door. The girl grabbed a spade from the porch, turned on her flashlight, and began to hurry across the lawn. The boy followed, carrying a small box. The girl stopped under a willow tree, handed the flashlight to the boy, and began to dig. "Is that for Peepee?" the boy asked.

"No, it's for our next mob hit." The girl dug a little ferociously, absolutely attacking the dirt. "Hold the flashlight down!" she said and adjusted the boy's hand just so.

"A funeral?" Arnie whispered to Iris.

"I guess they're burying Peepee," Iris whispered back. She pictured in the small box the stiff downy body of a parakeet or canary. Once when Eddie was five, he'd found a baby sparrow that Iris had allowed him to keep in a cardboard box out in the garage. Eddie named the sparrow Burp. "Honey, don't you mean Chirp?" Iris asked, but Eddie said no, he meant Burp. Three days later, Burp died, and so Iris, along with Eddie and Christian, buried Burp in the back yard under the largest oak tree. Burp's had been a rather ceremonial burial, actually. Iris had a distinct memory of reading a passage from Psalms, for God's sake.

Arnie ran the fingers of one hand along her skull as if giving her a scalp massage. Iris wondered if this was something he'd done with Yvonne over the years, before those years had ended. Eventually, he started talking about Carl. "You couldn't always tell what was on his mind either, that's for sure," Arnie said softly, spilling a bit of wine on his shirt. Iris gamely pretended not to notice.

"Yes, I know." Fifteen years after his death, and if anything, he had turned more mysterious to Iris, more troublingly complicated. Sometimes it frightened her to think she had been married to a man for so long and yet had not known or understood him. But she only understood this in retrospect. "He had two sides," she muttered to Arnie. "The man he was in church is not the man he was at home."

Arnie asked her what she meant but she didn't elaborate. Already she felt she'd said too much. Carl had never liked it when she'd try to analyze and probe, which was probably why she wasn't very good at it. Two sides: even that sounded inaccurate, banal, not at all what she meant to think. She drummed her fingers on Arnie's chest, a little impatient with herself and with Carl too. Even in death he wasn't quite getting through to her.

"Put him in!" the girl said. The boy shook his head and said the hole wasn't big enough. "We're not burying Dumbo!" the girl said, and when the boy sniffled and said it wasn't *big* enough, she snatched the box right from out of the child's hands. "Be a little man!" she said.

Iris wanted to shout out some reassurance to the boy—the girl's gruffness was already grating on her—but of course the whole ill-tempered funeral was none of her business. Tomorrow was the anniversary of Carl's death! The memory came to Iris in a rush. How could she have nearly forgotten?

"I remember a time when I was alone with Carl," Arnie said, still speaking low as if he didn't want the children next door to hear. "Okay, there were three of us if you count the bottle of bourbon. This was not long after that little girl of yours died, when Carl was—not himself. I said what I could, but you know, he was the minister, not me. Finally I just sat there and let him rest his head on my shoulder and cry."

Carl's head on Arnie's shoulder—was Arnie speaking figuratively or literally? Iris moved her head from Carl's shoulder to his chest. "And once he started," Arnie said, "he couldn't stop. It was like some valve had been turned on inside him and he had to let it all out."

She was silenced, remembering the way Carl had been with her in bed during those first long nights after Melissa's death. Until this moment she'd thought Carl had shown that part of himself only to her—that vulnerable, broken side. "Then he started talking," Arnie said. "It just kind of washed out of him."

"Really?" She wouldn't describe conversation as something that normally had "washed out" of Carl. The girl pounded at the dirt with the spade, sealing up the hole. The door to the house opened and a tall woman in unseasonal red slacks stepped onto the porch. "What are you doing out there?" she said, and she motioned for the children to come inside, the way mothers were beckoning their children to safety all over town.

The girl hefted the spade onto her shoulder and stalked back toward the house. The boy glanced over toward Iris and Arnie and Iris waved, but she couldn't tell if the child saw her or not. He simply walked back to his mother, the door was closed behind them, and, like that, Iris and Arnie were alone again, unearthing the unstill past.

"To tell you the truth, I didn't even understand some of what he was saying," Arnie said. "I understood the words but they didn't string together right, you know? They didn't make sense exactly. But some stuff I do remember. What I remember most is how he kept saying he loved me. *I love you Arnie*, he kept saying, just like that. *I love you, Arnie.*"

Iris wasn't sure how to react. She couldn't admit that she felt betrayed that Carl had opened himself emotionally to Carl when it had seemed so difficult for him to do the same with her. For a full minute she and Arnie lay together, sipping at their wine, her head on his chest, discerning the rhythm of his heartbeat, their minds flung back to that mysterious night twenty-five years ago. It was as if they were standing in Arnie's garage right now, watching as Carl sobbed away his grief on the younger Arnie's shoulder.

Love. It was one of those words Carl had had a great deal of difficulty saying.

Then Arnie kissed Iris, a long soft kiss made tart by memory. Both Carl and Yvonne were part of the kiss, but this was understandably not something Iris wanted to linger on. When they were finished, Arnie just stared at Iris for quite some time. Then he picked up the wine bottle and sat up with a bit of difficulty. "Let's go inside before the mosquitoes drive us crazy," he said.

*

After work the next day, Iris stopped at a flower shop, bought a half dozen roses, and drove out to Greensmith Cemetery to visit Carl's grave, as she did every year on the anniversary of his death. Once the boys had accompanied her in this ritual, but those days were long past.

It was a somewhat rambling graveyard spread out over a stretch of gently sloping ground. Iris parked in front of the wrought iron gate and then sat inside the car for a moment, contemplating the crows that blanketed one of the trees at the cemetery's entrance. Yet when she stepped into the cemetery, her disquiet had nothing to do with crows. Normally she passed the other tombstones without a second thought, but this afternoon she was conscious of the graves, how each was a human story she was passing, a testament to another life lost. And how deeply her roots ran in this town, that she should recognize so many of the names on the gravestones. There was Marion Porter, who'd died at 94-years-old before she'd ever finished that science fiction novel about dragons that she'd started writing at age fifty. She'd served as the organist at the church for nearly five decades before her fingers became too stiff and gnarled with rheumatism to move across the keys with any grace. The gravestone of Tommy Holicky looked more weathered than it should have, as if in reflection of a man who'd never found his footing in life and had drunk himself to death. Connie DeWitt's story wrenched at Iris's heart, this young mother who had died from a particularly virulent strain of cancer, leaving behind two sets of devastated twins. On and on the stories ran, the graves a reminder of the closed chapters in the town's past narratives.

For some reason Sally Gardenia came to mind, the woman whose husband had accidentally shoved her through a plate glass window. Two years ago this had been one of the most violent occurrences to have happened in Barrow's Point, but now the incident seemed minor, almost commonplace. Iris considered going to pay her respects at Sally's grave, although she hadn't known Sally well so there seemed no particular reason for doing this. Sally's grave was on the far north corner of the graveyard, if Iris wasn't mistaken, requiring a small climb up a modest incline.

When Iris peered in that direction, she saw a man with a camera standing at the top of the slope, photographing a wilting tree with a split trunk that gave the impression it was not one whole tree but two half-trees. As far as Iris could tell, he was the only other person in the cemetery other than herself. She decided against seeking out Sally's grave.

Carl's grave was located near the center of the cemetery. Iris walked to it, the scorching heat pressing down around her. The ground was so dry it was splitting open in spots. The grass was the color of vaguely burnt sepia. Iris could feel the sun singeing the roots of her hair. A large stone obelisk marked Carl's grave, one paid for by the church to honor a man that had served the Barrow's Point religious community for thirteen years. She had no recollection of having agreed to the obelisk as Carl's grave marker, but apparently she had because there it was. Iris had always found the stone a little imposing, a little too monolithic for Barrow's Point. She could all but hear Strauss's *Thus Spoke Zarathustra* every time she approached his grave.

Next to Carl's grave was Melissa's much smaller one, her life in this world merely hours long. She had existed without consciousness, had died before she had a chance to think, sense, react, process. Iris had not even been able to breastfeed her. And from such experiences one was asked to believe in a pattern to the universe, one was asked to blindly worship at the altar of meaning? *Everything happens for a reason*: how she'd resented the people who had mouthed this lie, over and over, to comfort her.

Iris kneeled beside the grave and leaned the roses against the obelisk. A couple other small floral bouquets had already been set down beside his grave, apparently from mindful parishioners, although they had all quickly wilted in the heat. Still, her heart flushed with gratitude. She couldn't help but wonder who had taken the time…the man who had been photographing the beleaguered tree was moving toward her. Was he taking a picture of her? Sunlight spilled down from all sides and yet she felt an unaccountable chill. "I wish you wouldn't do that!" she called out to him.

The man hesitated for a moment but still held the camera in front of his face. Was he staring at her through the camera lens, pondering this diminished view of her? Finally, he lowered the camera. "I'm sorry," he said. "It's just you make a wonderful picture."

"I've taken maybe two good pictures my entire life," she said with a small laugh.

"I doubt that." He approached her with a careful steady stride. Her body tensed, a natural if embarrassing instinct given the shadow hanging over the town. And here she'd left her purse with the mace back in the car! What good was it to buy mace if she was always forgetting to carry it with her? The man seemed to notice her hesitation because he paused while there were still several feet separating them. "I get a little camera happy at times, I suppose," he added.

He appeared harmless, blond and Nordic-seeming with a ruddy complexion and a soft aristocratic precision to his mouth. The more she looked at him, the more she seemed to almost remember something. "Can't imagine why you'd want to take a picture of *me*," she said.

The glare of the overbearing sun was in his eyes, giving him a perpetual squint. "That's quite a grave marker, isn't it?" and they both regarded the rising, implacable stone with Carl's name etched in large Latin-style letters that looked almost blurred from the heat. Carl had even spoken some Latin. He'd taught Iris a few phrases once but she'd long since forgotten them. *Ab Astern*: she still remembered that. "My husband," she said as if the man had requested an explanation.

He moved his fingers along the camera strap around his neck. Somehow, he was now standing next to her although she hadn't been conscious that he'd moved. "And what about the little one there?"

Iris didn't know whether to appreciate the man's curiosity about her life or feel he was being invasive somehow, upsetting the quiet ceremony of her visit. "My daughter," Iris said and trailed off. Everything she said to this man felt clumsy and unnatural.

"My mother's grave is off on the far end." The man pointed toward where he'd been. "Strange blighted tree. The trunk is split and growing in two different directions."

"Your mother?" Iris said before intuition took hold. "Was your mother Sally Gardenia?"

The man looked at her with a kind of perplexed surprise. "Yes," he said. "Timothy Gardenia. You knew my mother?"

Iris paused, unsure how to answer. Timothy looked crestfallen. Sweat glistened above his upper lip. "I see," he said. "You know *of* her."

Iris was embarrassed but couldn't stop herself from speaking: "I was just thinking about her. Only minutes ago."

"Isn't that a little odd, to be thinking of someone you barely knew?"

Iris couldn't admit, of course, why she'd been thinking of Sally. "I suppose it's natural for people to think of her now, though," Timothy said, wiping at his upper lip with a bit of tissue. "Given what's going on in this town these days, it's kind of nostalgic to think back to an old-fashioned wife murder."

"But I thought she wasn't murdered," Iris said. "I thought the whole point was that it was an accident."

"Why, because that's what dear old dad said? He killed her all right. In the heat of the moment, maybe, but still with *intent*, Mrs. McGregor. I've never had a shred of doubt."

Iris felt the back of her neck turning damp with sweat. "Oh, I'm sorry then," she said.

"Yes, the old man was a powder keg waiting to go off. It runs in our family, unfortunately. How do you unlearn that sort of thing? He even dishonored my mother by killing her in a stupid way."

Again, Iris wasn't sure how to respond. "Well, it was nice chatting with you," she said.

Timothy's face puckered into a frown. "I'm sorry, am I bothering you?"

Was it her imagination, or was there a chill in his voice now? Or maybe hurt, stung vanity, or just the expected shortness that comes from not a particularly welcome recall? "No," Iris said. "I just thought you were leaving—you know, before—"

"Oh, I was, yes." His voice had gone level and tranquil again. "But you sidetracked me. The Humble Woman of God kneeling before the giant Obelisk of Death, not to mention all this talk about my mother, who wasn't a saint herself if you want the truth."

The Humble Woman of God? Obelisk of Death? There was something wrong with this conversation, and yet they were both sinking deeper into it. Here they were, out in the open in the brutal sun, the air so heavy and oppressive it nearly hurt to breathe, and yet neither one of them could quite pull away. "The preacher's wife," Timothy continued. "I'm afraid I don't remember your husband at all. We weren't exactly a churchgoing family."

"I guess we lived in the same town for years and just missed each other."

"Yet here we are now." His eyes wandered back toward his mother's grave. "So tell me if my mother is dancing with the angels as we speak, Mrs. McGregor. I figure I can ask you, being a preacher's wife. You must believe in God and an afterlife and all that."

"Yes, I suppose." She glanced down at her hands. She was holding them in a strange manner, as if she was prepared to start rutting around in the dry dirt.

"You suppose? Hardly a ringing endorsement from a preacher's wife."

"I can't say I know what does or doesn't happen after we die. It's arrogant to pretend we can." She was conscious of the little cross she was wearing on a modest chain around her neck. She felt foolish wearing it now, a false expression of faith.

"You could say what you *believe*. You seem to be equivocating on even that much."

Was she? Equivocating? It was true that her religious beliefs had been so much more defined when Carl was still alive. After losing both Carl and Melissa, nothing had seemed as clear-cut. Their deaths had brought into focus the mass hypothetical grayness of the world, where it seemed both one thing and then another. She attended church most Sundays but more for the familiar rituals—the hymns, the organ music, the liturgy readings, the socializing with friends afterward—than for any theological certainty. "And what do you believe?" she found herself asking Timothy Gardenia. "I suppose you believe in nothing."

Timothy chuckled a little grimly. "Why? Do I look like someone who believes in nothing?"

"I don't know." She met his eyes. "Sometimes you talk as if you *want* to believe in nothing."

"See, then you've misjudged me. I admit I don't believe in God or heaven or any of that other religious superstition. At least not in the traditional sense. But that doesn't mean I don't believe in anything. And I'm certainly not a man who *wants* to believe in nothing."

"Now you're beating around the bush."

There was a bit of a smile in his eyes now. The camera hung from his throat, the lens pointed at Iris like a mechanical eye. "All right," he said. "What I really believe in, Mrs. McGregor, is consciousness. I sit up some nights and I wrestle with it. Our bodies die, sure, but our consciousness? What happens to that? Did my mother's essence really just disappear? Nullified? And doesn't our energy, or whatever, have to go somewhere? I'm a bit of a biomedical ethicist at heart, you know, science and spirituality converging…"

Timothy trailed off before crouching down beside her. It was too smooth a movement for her to feel any lingering apprehension. "I suppose that's why I wanted to take a picture of you, Mrs. McGregor," he said. "Because, kneeling here, you looked comforted but also like you had a great deal on your mind. You're carrying a heavy weight on your shoulders, and yet something about you gives off a great deal of light. The exact opposite of my parents, I'm sorry to say."

Never had a stranger spoken to Iris so unaccountably, with such bluntness. Or was he a stranger if she knew him in an offhand way? Iris nodded although she wasn't sure she agreed at all with what he was saying. Timothy coughed, his eyes misted over, and his breath rattled. "Are you all right?" Iris asked.

Timothy nodded and wiped tears from his eyes. Then he removed an inhaler from his pocket and breathed into it. "The pollen and the heat, it'll kill me yet," he said and tucked the inhaler back into his pocket.

For a moment they just looked at each other. They didn't move. Iris had the quite mad sense that he was on the verge of kissing her, or on the verge of touching her in some way. And if he did that, she was not at all sure how she would respond. Any reaction seemed possible.

From the road she heard the stabilizing sound of another car approaching, its wheels grinding in the gravel as it pulled to a stop in front of the cemetery. She glanced over her shoulder and saw Arnie emerge with difficulty from the car, a few flowers in his hand.

Timothy stood up and brushed at his knees although they'd never touched the ground. "It was nice chatting with you, too, Mrs. McGregor," he said. "Good to hear not everyone has forgotten." Then he wandered off. Iris watched him go, surprised by her urge to call him back.

(14)

The brother. Eddie kept hearing the words echo at the back of his mind, a constant in his life that he couldn't extinguish.

Or escape. Even when Christian wasn't in the house, Eddie imagined how it was possessed by him. His smell, the rank fruity odor of his protest sweat! It was a long hot summer and everyone was sweating, but it was Christian's smell that Eddie could not bear, the piquant stink of him like an overripe melon that was quickly taking over the entire house but that no one else seemed to notice.

Eddie opened the windows to try and circulate the air. He closed his bedroom door even during the day to keep the smell out. But it was pervasive and doors were not enough. Doors, walls, locks, none of them enough.

When he complained to his mother that the house smelled *weird*, she laughed until she realized he was serious. "Honey, what are you talking about?" she asked. "The house smells fine." Then she looked at him with an anxious frown. "What smell, can you describe it?"

"It smells like——" But of course he couldn't really say what he meant. He couldn't say the house smelled like rotting fag brother.

It was bad enough that Christian was stinking up the house, but he was also part of that *VIGILANT* group that was wearing defiant red T-shirts around town and trying to patrol the streets like they could do something the cops couldn't. It was just another way Christian was hogging the limelight and making the crime spree all about him. First he'd participated in the vigil outside the police station, although fortunately Christian was not one of the people featured on the TV news report about the gathering, so Eddie didn't have to relive that embarrassment. It didn't bother him that his mother and Reed had been at the vigil. Mothers were supposed to act civic-minded, and Reed was a cop so had no choice but to work where assigned. Even the newspaper photo of Reed holding a candle seemed minor in comparison to the unending embarrassment of Christian's "loud and proud" behavior.

And as the days passed, the sun broiled hot in the sky, a throbbing white ball of airborne fire, an eye, almost, gazing down at Eddie with fiery impatience.

When he could, Eddie spent as much time as possible away from the house, from Christian and his mother's closet. More and more he found himself going over to Danny's house. Bruce was away because his overreacting mother had sent him to live with his father in Ohio for the summer, far away from the Barrow's Point murders. This meant Eddie spent more time with Danny than he normally would have. But even at Danny's house he was uncomfortable, since he had a sense that even when he was invited over he wasn't entirely welcome. Danny's behavior ran hot and cold, mercurial, impossible to predict. Eddie suspected Danny's father, Ticker, didn't think much of him either. Eddie was Reed's brother and Ticker's brother was Mitch Sternes.

One night Danny invited Eddie to stop over and watch an Ultimate Fighting match with him before they drove around town with Soldier. When Eddie arrived, he found that Danny's father and uncle and a few other guys were out in the backyard, cooking burgers and getting boisterously drunk. Eddie sat in the "family room" with Danny in front of the TV set—Danny, who looked bored out of his skull, who looked as if he were trying to ignore the noise of the men outside. He wore one of his signature sleeveless muscle T-shirts and a pair of torn jeans. Two beers were already standing out on the end table. Danny opened them and handed one to Eddie, who looked at it almost with doubt. "Your old man's outside," Eddie reminded him.

Danny sneered just so. "For Christ's sake, McGregor," he said.

Before Eddie had a chance to get comfortable with his beer, Ticker and Mitch Sternes entered the kitchen, their voices rough and a little callous. Then the two men stepped into the room and looked at the two boys slouched on the sofa. Mitch stared at Eddie until Eddie turned away. Was it because he wasn't supposed to be drinking beer in the house? Mitch was a police officer, after all. Yet neither one of the men seemed to care about the beer bottles the boys held openly in their hands. "Where's your mother?" Ticker asked Danny, who shrugged and stared at the TV with a forced nonchalance.

Ticker was a little bulldog of a man, compact and hard with a bum leg he'd ruined years ago in a car accident. He'd also suffered a head injury that had left a small piece of his brain soft and brown and dead. Or that was the case if Eddie could believe what Tess told him. Since the accident there was always something off about Ticker. "Hey, your father asked you a question," Mitch said in his cop voice, his eyes still focused on Eddie.

"Upstairs," Danny said. Ticker walked off as if he'd already forgotten what question he'd asked. Mitch shook his head and followed his brother back outside.

For a minute Danny sat with an odd twist of pain on his face. Eddie knew enough to let Danny break the silence. "He's an asshole," Danny said at last.

"One thing I'll never be is an asshole cop. That's something we got in common, McGregor. Our relatives are fucking *pigs*."

They clicked their beer bottles together although Reed was the least of Eddie's worries. "But yours is a candle-hugging queer, too," Danny added with heat in his eyes. "So I guess I lucked out."

He said this with a partial smile and without the same sarcasm he would have used if Bruce or Soldier were in the room, almost as if he were teasing Eddie for a reaction. Eddie gave what he hoped was a contemptuous look but didn't say anything. What could he say? He was caught in the gay brother trap and there wasn't a damned thing he could do about it. Even chewing off a limb wouldn't free him.

The boys stared at the TV set. Eddie couldn't help but enjoy Ultimate Fighting. Two shirtless men were always grappling, squeezing each other, bashing one another in the face. Of course Christian hated the show, calling it "Brutality Theater" that played like a human cock fight, tapping into the audience's blood lust and instinct to destroy. Christian's dislike made Eddie's devotion to the show almost fanatical. He'd have to remember to buy an Ultimate Fighting T-shirt that he could wear around when Christian was wearing his *VIGILANT* shirt.

"Not that this is going to be any kind of contest," Danny said. "Diego can't lose against McQueen. I mean, the fuck. Diego's Dominican."

For the hell of it, Eddie said he liked the looks of McQueen. "You would," Danny said before Eddie could catch his own error. "You realize Diego is un-de-feated," Danny said, shoving a few Corn Nuts into his mouth. "You're voting against Diego? Care to make a wager?"

Eddie shook Danny's hand to seal the bet although they'd never made clear what they were betting. They watched the fight in relative silence. It didn't take long for Diego to choke out McQueen and claim the victory. They heard Ticker and a couple other men yelling out someone's name in the backyard. "You lose again," Danny said

"Whatever." Eddie liked the sound of his voice tonight, terse and hard, no confusion. The lamp gleamed soberly between them.

"You owe me. Time to pay up."

"No money," Eddie said, although that wasn't exactly true. He got paid a few dollars a week allowance for taking out the garbage and keeping his room clean, which he rarely did, but he usually got the money anyway.

"Cheap bastard," Danny said. "Okay, for the rest of the night you're my slave. You do what I tell you to."

A TV commercial came on for Ambien. All the TV drugs were riddled with side effects, it seemed: nausea, dizziness, drowsiness, headaches. Yet people were dutifully swallowing these pills all over the world. Eddie knew vaguely that Danny's mother was on several medications, which was maybe why she spent so much of her life up in the bedroom. Eddie wasn't even sure how he knew this. Maybe Tess had told him this, too.

"Polish off that beer," Danny said. "Jesus, my grandmother drinks faster than you."

At first Eddie had no intention of playing along with Danny, so why was it that he picked up the bottle on cue and slanted it into his mouth, drinking fast, feeling his throat undulate. When he was finished, he set the bottle down on the coffee table and let out what he hoped would pass as a manly belch.

"Now go get us two more," Danny said.

Eddie nodded. This seemed easy enough. But when he was out in the kitchen, scanning the refrigerator, Alberta Sternes stumbled down the stairs and into the room, her hair a tangled, unwashed mess, wearing a pair of pale underwear and a blouse that was barely buttoned. She looked at Eddie in alarm. "Who are you?" she asked.

"Eddie," Eddie said, although he'd met Mrs. Sternes several times before. "Danny's friend," Eddie reminded her. He tried not to stare. Her underpants embarrassed him.

"Oh yes, hello, Edward." She squinted out the window at the men gathered around the unvarnished outdoor bar. "Terrible, awful men," she said. "They have reduced the world to rot. Promise you won't grow up to be one."

While Danny's father often seemed absent due to his little piece of fogged brain, Danny's mother struck Eddie as somewhat crazy. There was the sense that she might say anything, a wildly disconcerting trait in a mother. Iris could always be trusted to say the sensible motherly thing, Eddie thought with a grudging affection. Eddie opened a drawer, found a bottle opener, and opened the beer bottles. "You boys aren't *drinking?*" she said in the same tone she might have used if they were engaging in a satanic ritual.

Eddie smiled dumbly, unsure what to say. "Just bring them out here, Mc-Gregor!" Danny called.

And because he was accustomed to answering to Danny, Eddie picked up the beer bottles and carried them into the living room, where he handed one to Danny and sat back down beside him. Mrs. Sternes followed him out into the room. "Daniel, you're not old enough to be drinking," she said.

Danny bumped his beer bottle against Eddie's and drank long and hard. There was an even more unusual tension between Mrs. Sternes and Danny than there had been between Danny and his father. "Ticker only has half a brain because he drank," she reminded them. "Drove that car right into a wall."

"Yeah?" Danny said, and he seemed to look right at his own mother's crotch. "What's your excuse?"

Mrs. Sternes stood very still for a moment. Just when Eddie thought she was going to break into tears, she sat down in the nearby lounge chair and fixed her gaze on Danny until even he, audacious and unflinching Danny, was forced to turn away. "I gave birth to you," she said.

"Christ," Danny muttered.

"You don't remember but I do. I'm you mother. Unless, of course, someone switched you at birth. They do that sometimes. Nurses get mixed up, or some strung-out mother takes a different baby. And like that—"she snapped her fingers "—you're living with the wrong family."

Danny stared at the TV where a different pair of men were punching and beating and cleaving to the other. "Like animals," Mrs. Sternes said about the men on the television screen. "No, worse, like a species we have never known before. But how much you want to bet they were babies once, too. Maybe the stolen ones."

She stood and wandered back into the kitchen. Eddie didn't know what to say. The whole pitch of the night felt so strange and disorienting. "Sorry," Eddie said, but Danny only scowled at him. "What are you sorry about?" Danny said. "You're the slave, not me." He lifted his arm over his head. "Smell my pit."

"The fuck?" Eddie laughed, thinking it a good joke, yet another audacious joke, but Danny only smiled in that gently nasty way. "I own you," he reminded Eddie.

Out in the kitchen they heard Mrs. Sternes breaking ice from the ice trays. "I want a real drink," she said. Was she talking to them still? "None of this beer urine the men drink."

Eddie waited for Danny to signal the end of his joke, but Danny just sat there unmoving, his arm raised in the air, his armpit exposed with its whorl of hair. Eddie felt suddenly immobile, that familiar sense that he was teetering on the edge of his own humiliation. And yet he couldn't turn away even while he couldn't actually do what Danny was asking, and so he could move neither forward nor back, caught in a limbo state.

From the kitchen came the sound of liquid poured into a glass. "Sometimes I feel like I was stolen," Mrs. Sternes said. "One life right into another."

There was a kind of fierce solemnity in Danny's face as he wiggled his arm a little and made mock sniffing sounds, something Eddie recognized as Danny *demanding* that he pay his debt in full, even with Mrs. Sternes out in the kitchen, only steps away. Or maybe *because* she was only steps away.

Eddie grabbed hold of Danny's arm, leaned forward for a quick sniff, and then pulled away and sat back. Danny shook his head. "Come on, McGregor," he said. "You have to do it for real."

Eddie's heart rattled around in his chest. He was teetering ever closer to that edge. "My head is on fire," Mrs. Sternes said. "But I think it's a dry fire."

What kind of fool was he, Eddie asked himself later, that he leaned forward a second time. Only this time Danny grabbed the back of Eddie's head and pushed Eddie's face straight into his armpit, holding Eddie's face there... and so he was forced, wasn't he, to slavishly inhale Danny's scent, his musky boy-man soapy sweat smell? Eddie tried to pull his head away but Danny's grip was firm and a little cruel.

After several seconds, Danny released Eddie, who nearly forgot to pull his head away. The wanton smell of Danny was all around him now, antithetical to the smell of Christian, the smell of *brother*. It was like a dangerous musk injected into the air, a smell that would suffocate Eddie if he wasn't careful.

"Now show me your cock," Danny said mildly.

Since when had Eddie fallen asleep, when had he started dreaming? The smell of Danny was now stuck inside his nostrils, rendering him an automaton. "You don't have a say, McGregor," Danny said. "Don't bet if you aren't man enough to pay up."

And Eddie was too confused by now, too lost in the strange tilt of the night, to remember the exact nature of his bet with Danny. Had he really agreed to slavery? He heard Mrs. Sternes ascending back upstairs, muttering to herself, and out at the backyard bar, the loud male voices continued, oblivious to the drama unfolding within. It seemed that Danny was in control now, as somehow he was always in control, but more so this time because he was pushing things so far, dangerously far, discovery only steps away. Eddie was like a solipsist that Danny controlled with his eyes, or worse, with the entirety of his body.

Without his will or conscious intent, Eddie's hand moved down into his lap. It was a compulsion similar to when he'd sneak into his mother's closet, but different too, because that compulsion was controlled by some inner pull he didn't understand, while this compulsion was driven by Danny, the puppet master, the wizard behind the curtain. Eddie opened his fly and pulled himself out for Danny's inspection, his penis pointing in the dim light.

Danny regarded him with a still, unknowable expression. Then he said: "Christ, McGregor, you're getting a bone." He took a final swig of his beer and shook his head. "You're such a faggot."

*

The rest of the night Eddie passed through as if in a dream. The scene in Danny's living room had in itself been a dream, such a cruel and jarring humiliation that the only way Eddie could deal with it was to fall back into detached numbness. A bubble surrounded him now and no one could touch him. The night was simply something to survive.

He had no desire now to cruise around town with Soldier's posse, but he'd already committed to it and didn't know how to back out without drawing more attention to himself, so when Soldier's car pulled up in front of the house,

Eddie passively joined Danny in the backseat of Soldier's car where Tess was also sitting. Soldier was driving, and next to him sat a girl with long red hair and a tattoo of a unicorn across her left shoulder. Eddie could never remember her name but did remember she had a thing for unicorns. Once she'd told them all what a unicorn represented, a mythological blend of horse and bearded goat, a wild woodland creature that symbolized purity and chastity and could only be tamed by the caress of a virgin's hand.

And the horn! The horn, she'd decided, was maybe too Freudian to bother with.

Eddie's initial fear that Danny would tell everyone what had happened in the living room began to fade when Danny gave no indication he planned on telling anyone, possibly because he'd have to reveal his own complicity in the scene, even if it had all been a lark for him, his most audacious joke yet. How far could he make Eddie go, just how *gay* could he force Eddie to act? But now that it was all over, Danny seemed to have already half-forgotten the incident.

Eddie could not forget. It was like an invisible mist of poison that encircled him. Tess was sitting in between Eddie and Danny, unaware of the poison, her head against Eddie's shoulder. At first he was afraid of Tess sitting too close and smelling Danny on him. She was high, they all were except for Danny and Eddie, who were only slightly buzzed off their beers.

They hadn't driven far when Soldier pulled off the main road and turned onto one of the pot-holed, badly lit streets that cut through the warehouse district. They were going to meet up with the Pickering brothers, two more of Soldier's friends, who'd been out of high school for a couple of years and shared a dumpy apartment near the warehouse where they both worked. But just as Soldier was driving along a particularly rough and deserted section of road, there was a sharp puncturing sound as one of the back tires blew out. They sputtered to a stop on the side of the road.

"The hell?" Soldier said. He wasn't in a good mood to begin with, and now here the world was, rubbing salt into the wound.

"It's just a flat," Tess said. "Go out and change the tire."

But Soldier shook his head and they all understood what that meant. "You drive around without a *spare?*" Tess asked.

Soldier muttered something and called one of the Pickering brothers on his cell phone, telling them they were on Hyde Street near the Balsom Warehouses and to meet them there with a spare tire. "It's going to be a few," Soldier said after he'd hung up.

They all sat still inside the car and didn't say a word. Balsom Warehouses: something in the name reverberated with a tantalizing menace. "Wasn't a body found around here?" Unicorn Girl asked. She spoke more out of curiosity than anxiety.

Soldier turned off the car headlights and plunged them into darkness. "Turn them back on!" Tess said, and her voice was a little raw.

But Soldier said he didn't want to risk draining the battery. Besides, he wasn't going to give any lowlife killer the satisfaction of scaring them. He'd love for someone to try and mess with them right about now. Just give him an excuse to go all Third World on someone's ass!

Still, Eddie couldn't help but notice how they remained sitting in the car with their doors locked. No one stepped outside to wait. The outer darkness pressed up against the car, giving Eddie a welcome jolt that almost, almost helped him forget his shame at Danny's hands.

"I'll bet every one of them knew the killer," Unicorn Girl said and sneezed. The car was turning stuffy but no one dared to ask Soldier to turn on the air conditioning. "That's why it was so easy to off them without a fight."

"But they couldn't have," Tess said. "It would be too easy to connect them back to one guy."

"Probably thought they were going to get their dicks sucked," Danny said.

Eddie inwardly flinched and waited for Danny to take some potshot at him, but Danny didn't say anything more. None of them did. Outside the darkness pressed harder up against the car, as if it meant to intimidate them, to trick and deceive, confuse and exhilarate them. *Dominate* them, Eddie thought, a darkness this hushed and aching and devoid of light.

"I think I have to go to the bathroom," Tess moaned. She asked Unicorn Girl to come with her, but Unicorn Girl just clutched Soldier's arm and said, "*I* don't have to go."

Tess turned to Eddie and tugged on his arm. Sitting around in the car with the doors locked was making things too simple, so Eddie agreed. Besides, sitting in an enclosed space with Danny felt almost more dangerous than stepping out into this swirl of black night.

Once Eddie and Tess were outside and moving away from the car, the darkness felt even more wrong, somehow, tainted by criminal secrets. There was a hint of scrappy moon in the sky and their eyes had adjusted somewhat to the dark, so it wasn't like they couldn't see at all. Yet their steps forward were hesitant and shambling, the ground itself unsteady beneath their feet. "I'm afraid I'll trip," Tess whispered and grabbed hold of Eddie's arm.

They moved toward a clump of bushes that looked pale, sharp and lunar, like shrubs from a different planet's moon. Tess stepped behind the nearest bush, and Eddie heard the sound of her tugging on her shorts, followed by her peeing, which only made his stomach clench tighter. "I'm probably pissing on the scene of the crime," she said. "Now I'll get haunted by a ghost in a feather boa."

Eddie couldn't believe he was standing near an empty lot at the Balsom Warehouses, close to the scene of a murder, listening to a girl pee after showing his cock to her cousin. It was all part of the surreal daze that had overtaken him since he'd exposed himself to Danny. Eddie knew he was expected at home by now, but home felt impossibly out of reach.

When Tess had finished her business, she said, "Come back here for a minute."

"Why?"

"You moron! See if they'll notice we've *disappeared*, that's why."

Eddie stepped gingerly behind the bush, worried that he might stand in her puddle of urine. Tess sidled up next to him and they waited, but there wasn't a trace of sound or movement from the car. "We could be getting bludgeoned to death and they wouldn't notice," she sighed.

"They can't see us."

"Or maybe they're the ones getting it right now. Wouldn't that be the weirdest? To go back and find them all slaughtered and sacrificed."

Eddie rapped his knuckles on Tess's forehead. He meant this as a silly playful gesture, but Tess must have supposed he was coming on to her. In an instant she had slipped her arms around his waist and pulled him close, the both of them sticky and nervous and alive. "Haven't you done *anything* before?" she asked.

Tess pulled his face to hers and kissed him, loosening up the kiss with her tongue. Eddie went along with it because it wasn't real, any more than the rest of the night was real. But after a few seconds of kissing, a car with its head-lights turned on high pulled up behind Soldier's car, and there was a mutual blasting of horns. "Great," Tess said. "*Now* they show up."

*

Once they were back on the road with the Pickering brothers following be-hind them, the energy in Soldier's car was heightened. They entered the main part of town again, "civilization" as Tess called it, but the uneasiness they'd felt out at the warehouses still lingered and turned them restless. Tess kept pulling Eddie's face to hers and giving him soft pecks on the mouth, trying to recreate their few clumsy seconds behind the alien shrubs, and Eddie let her do this so Danny could see that he was kissing a girl! In the front seat, Soldier had his arm around Unicorn Girl, and occasionally he took his eyes from the road long enough to shove his tongue down her throat, which left Danny as the loner misfit in the car. But Danny didn't seem to be paying much atten-tion to Eddie or Tess or anyone in the car, for that matter. It was only when Tess looked at Eddie and said, "You have to do it like you mean it" that Danny made eye contact with Eddie and said with an ironic smile, "Yeah, McGregor, put some *conviction* into it." And then he just looked out the car window as the night flashed past them.

The Pickering brothers kept weaving back and forth on the road and flick-ing their lights on high so a fierce glare would blind everyone in Soldier's car. But Soldier was too preoccupied to care much about what his friends were up to. The pall he'd been lost to earlier in the night had now given way to impatience and anger. He was already having doubts about joining the Army. Didn't he have a right to want to keep all his limbs? Now he wasn't sure he wanted to risk trouncing through the city of Fallujah or maybe up into the mountains of Kabul wearing a ballistic vest and camouflage uniform that his cousin said, on hot days, made you feel you were scorching alive inside a sec-ond skin, and all the while not knowing whether a bullet would shoot from one of those distant hills and spatter your brains across the Persian desert.

"I mean, come on," Soldier said and cranked up the music. "I don't hate Muslims that bad, do I?" He pronounced Muslims *Moos-lums*. "That I'll risk getting killed to shoot a few towelheads?"

Tess leaned forward and smacked Soldier on the back of his head. "You have the brain of a schnauzer," she said. "You're not going over to kill Muslims. You're going over to kill terrorist *operatives*." She giggled at her own use of the word operatives. "Is my breath okay?" she whispered to Eddie.

Soldier told Tess to fuck off, but affectionately, since he had a bit of a soft spot, he'd often confess to his friends, for his liberal and hectoring cousin. In the end, Soldier said, there was nothing he could do. He was stuck, the military mechanism was in full motion, and once the military had its hooks in you, there was no way to escape other than running away, and he wasn't one of those cowardly runaway types. He was *owned* now and had to do what he was ordered to do. It just sucked if you were getting ordered to go take a bullet. "But maybe it won't be so bad," he said to Unicorn Girl. "Right?" He drank from an open bottle of tequila Eddie was just noticing now. "I wonder what the women are like over there."

"You can't see them," Unicorn Girl said. "They wear those robes."

"*Hijab*," Tess said. "God, you guys!"

With all the talk about war and bombs, explosions and bullets, it wasn't that much of a surprise when they drove past the park and the basketball courts and something fell from the sky and struck the car's windshield. Unicorn Girl let out a horsey snort, Soldier cursed under his breath as he veered the car to the right, and those in back grabbed hold of something, instinctively cringing: *What is it? What has happened?*

"Now what the fuck?" Soldier said after he'd braked to a stop. He was feeling around on himself as if he thought, maybe, he'd been prematurely shot.

They all spilled from the car, their hearts surging, feeling a vague repetition to the night. The windshield was not broken but was laced with several spider-vein cracks. The Pickering brothers had driven right past when Soldier pulled over. Now they braked to a stop in front of Soldier's car and herded out to survey the damage, two lanky tattooed guys, one with a flat top haircut and the other with rock star hair.

"What the fuck was that?" Soldier said. A baseball? A rock? First the Army, then a flat, now someone had thrown a fucking *baseball rock* at them? "It didn't just fall out of the goddamn sky," he said.

"It was a baseball," said the least tattooed Pickering brother, the one with the rock star hair. He'd caught a glimpse of it, white and shimmering like ice, dropping with speed and velocity, coming from the park and the basketball courts. They all looked in that direction and caught a glimpse of a couple of boys darting into the park.

"Don't!" Unicorn Girl said, trying to hold Soldier back, but he paid no more attention to her than he would the buzz of a mosquito. He pushed past Unicorn Girl and hurried toward the courts. After a moment the others followed, a kind of dread settling around them.

The park was dark at night with very little illumination. They looked around but nothing stood out except for two men down at the end of the basketball court. One had a basketball in his left hand, and he was leaning close to the other with his right hand rested on the back of the guy's neck. Eddie's first thought was that he was whispering into his friend's ear, maybe a secret play although there were only the two of them on the court. "No, it's not them," Tess said. "The other ones were kids."

The two men laughed, broke away from each other, and the guy with the basketball tossed it to the other one. "Hey!" Soldier shouted at them, moving forward, jogging toward them now. The posse followed, obedient as oxen. Unicorn Girl called out, "Hon, let's go, I want to leave, I feel sick," and Tess muttered under her breath, "It's wasn't *them*."

But it hardly seemed to matter anymore who was who or what, specifically, had been done. Eddie felt the pull to follow but also to stay where he was, some reluctance getting the better of him. Tess turned to Eddie and her eyes were—the word just popped into his head—beseeching. "Don't let them do anything stupid," she said.

As if he, Eddie, could stop them or held any power over any of them. He was the youngest and the least... what? Tentatively, he stepped forward on the edge of Soldier's posse. The two young men playing basketball turned around, and Eddie, a little forlornly, pictured himself and the others through the eyes of the strangers: a motley ragtag lot, hostile and itching for a fight. The young man without the basketball was tanned and fit with a floppy haircut, his friend with the basketball a little shorter and broader with a well-trimmed wedge of hair on his chin. Both wore T-shirts with the local college logo on them.

"What's so goddamn funny?" asked Soldier. "Don't suppose you two know anything about that goddamn baseball?"

The young man with the floppy hair glanced at his friend and then looked back at Soldier, trying to disguise his apprehension. "Baseball?" he said.

Soldier repeated the word *baseball,* mocking the floppy hair, and the more heavily tattooed Pickering brother with the flattop haircut laughed along with Soldier in a kind of jeering pantomime. "It came from fucking somewhere," the flattop Pickering said. "You two are the only ones around that I can see."

Eddie's mind was still lingering in a fog, so he just kept watching as Soldier and his posse threw a few more accusations around, stepping closer to the young men, crowding them, and Danny a part of the posse too but lesser than, yet the same malevolence hung over his face. Soldier started to yell about his goddamn *windshield,* and there were more denials from the college kids. Unicorn Girl walked over to Soldier and whispered "baby, baby," trying to talk him away from the edge, and whatever direction Soldier turned was the direction the rest of them would follow. But Soldier pulled his arm away; Unicorn Girl was passive and reasonable and *female.* He turned back to the boys in the college T-shirts and asked who was going to pay for his goddamn car's goddamn broken windshield. Someone was going to pay for it. They weren't just going to let some idiot, baseball-hurling cumstains get off scot-free.

"We're just shooting a few," the shorter one said, but his words curdled. Soldier had gone silent, which was even more intimidating than when he was shouting. Eddie knew this faceoff was on the verge of spiraling out of control, and though he felt a little sick to his stomach, he just stood there in dumb and paralyzed wonder.

As they all stood in dumb and paralyzed wonder, waiting for Soldier's next move. "Open season these days," he said with deliberate calm. "Open season."

The shorter one hurled the basketball at Soldier's face. In a second he was bolting out of the court, running with the speed of an animal in danger. Soldier and the Pickering brothers swore, pushed past the floppy hair, who looked as stunned as they were, and took off after the shorter one. Danny looked ready to follow Soldier, but then he lunged at the floppy hair. But the young man was on his guard and hit Danny in the face, if only half-heartedly. Still, it was enough to unleash Danny's inner beast. The two started brawling, and in a moment they were on the ground, wrestling around and slugging at the other. Wrestling was Danny's specialty, of course, but the floppy hair had the size and age advantage, and soon it was Danny who was in the headlock. Tess and Unicorn Girl continued to shout for Danny to stop, for both of them to stop. Then Tess turned on Eddie with a small vehemence. "Do something!" she cried.

"Jesus," Danny grunted, trying to break free of the floppy hair's hold on him. "*McGregor!*" he panted.

Danny's call for help was like a shot of adrenaline to Eddie. Danny was asking for him, *needing* him. Was it really him, Eddie McGregor, who pushed past Tess and charged forward? Was it really Eddie McGregor cuffing the floppy hair in the head and around the face until he dropped away from Danny? Together, Danny and Eddie punched and kicked at the young man, his chest and head and face, Eddie trying not to hit too hard, unsure even what he was doing, really, everything rushing at him in a blur. How was it possible that he could feel such elation even as he felt this familiar swirl of sickness? But he wasn't going to be sick again, no, this was not another night of the goddamn stoned lamb, and so he kept at it, even when he heard Tess, so close and yet so distant, yelling, "Stop!" and yelling, "Don't *kill* him!"

(15)

When Reed heard the news the next morning—a young college student attacked and beaten at West End Park—he was furious with himself. "Blinded again," he muttered as he phoned Will Brackett, a police officer on the night shift who had taken the young man's statement. According to Brackett, the victim claimed he'd been confronted by several guys and attacked by two of them but was unable to offer much in the way of useful description. Because the young man had been "worked over" pretty badly—a concussion, a couple cracked ribs, several bruises and contusions—he'd been held overnight at the hospital for observation. "This wasn't part of the killing spree, Reed," Brackett felt compelled to remind him. "This was—something else."

And yet when Reed hung up the phone, he couldn't shake a deeper sense that they *were* connected, just not in the obvious way. He drove to the hospital to speak to the young man before the doctors discharged him. He didn't know what he'd say, exactly, or even if he was violating some departmental rule by interrogating a victim on his own without proper authorization. But authorization was too much of an inconvenience right now, just another wall he had to try and fight his way around.

Reed wasn't expecting to recognize the victim—Kip, the "College Boy" who had played basketball with Reed and the other officers only weeks ago. Kip was sitting up in the hospital bed, wearing the requisite dingy hospital robe and picking at a sliver of flaky fish that was on a tray set before him. One side of his face was bruised and swollen while the other side looked very much like the young man Reed remembered from the park. They both were uncomfortable when they recognized the other. Reed pulled up a chair beside the bed and smiled at Kip, who didn't quite smile back. "Another rough game, I see," Reed said.

"I remember you." Yet Kip seemed unable to quite place him.

The basketball court, Reed reminded him. About a month ago. The Gladiator Smackdown.

"Right," Kip said with a puzzled frown.

Even now Reed was reluctant to acknowledge the true reason for his visit, but he had no real choice. He'd been hiding long enough. "True confession," Reed said. "I'm a cop."

Kip's face didn't register any emotion at this revelation. "You were all cops," he said, a statement more than a question. "I thought I'd seen one of you before."

Already Reed could feel Kip turning inward, closing himself off from further interrogation. "You don't remember anything more about the guys who did this to you?" Reed asked, pushing ahead despite Kip's obvious reluctance. It could have been Christian or Eddie lying in that bed.

"It was dark," Kip said.

He picked up the tray and reached over to set it on a stand beside the bed, but he moved with such stiffness that Reed could picture the constricting bandages wrapped around the boy's ribs under the robe. He took the tray from Kip's hands and set it down, which only made Kip look at him with greater suspicion. "Did they say anything to you?" Reed asked, and Kip shrugged. "There must be some reason they attacked you."

Kip narrowed his eyes in a way that made Reed miss the young man he'd seen on the basketball court. He and Kip had been on the verge of a fumbling friendship after that basketball game, but now they were standing on the opposite side of the same unspoken divide that was separating Reed from so many people these days. "They were kids, mostly," Kip said. "Stupid idiots, but I'm not going to make a federal case over it."

Reed stared down at the burn scar on his hand. Useless for him to try to reach out and save Kip from this fire. "You don't think they attacked you because...they thought you were..." Why was Kip making it so difficult for him to state the obvious?

"What?" Kip's eyes flashed.

Reed exhaled, fighting against his own frustration at Kip's rising resistance against him. "All right, they were kids," Reed said. "That's a start. How old?"

"I don't know. Younger than me. Teenagers."

"How many were there?"

"Five or six, I guess."

"What did they look like?"

"I don't remember. Jesus."

"You don't remember anything?"

Kip just stared, stony-faced, off into space. "I think someone had a tattoo," he said.

"Where?" Kip was silent. "On his arm? His shoulder? Neck?

"I don't know."

"What kind of tattoo?"

"I don't know."

"Were you alone out there?"

Kip swallowed, and Reed felt an ache in his own throat. "At the basket-ball court," Reed pressed on. "Were you out there shooting baskets alone on a Saturday night?"

"A friend was with me. He got away. I said, I already talked to that other cop and told him everything."

"What's your friend's name? Maybe he'll remember more than you do."

At this point Kip looked on the verge of tears, or maybe on the verge of confessing something. But then he just shook his head and began to fiddle with a stray thread on his robe. "I don't know him," he muttered at last. "But it wasn't what you're thinking."

The conversation continued on for a few more minutes—stubborn, circu-lar—but Reed soon saw it was useless. Somehow *he* had become the enemy in Kip's eyes, *he* was the one to push away. How could Reed fight against any of this when the victim himself was indifferent to the crime, when he seemed to want to brush it all aside as an inconvenience?

In the following days, as the noise about the attack quickly died down as just some ugly teenaged skirmish, Reed couldn't help but feel this was another victory for the killer. He couldn't have said why, exactly, other than how the town itself was seemingly growing accustomed to the violence, as if it was all to be expected, wasn't it? As if in comparison to the extremity of murder, a young man's bashing wasn't anything to get too upset about.

*

"And so begins the obsessive descent."

Twice Alex said this to Reed, laughing yet not, as he struggled to define the conundrum that had become Reed McGregor. "You never mentioned you were thinking about switching over to the night shift," Alex said when Reed first mentioned the possibility. "How often are we going to see each other if you're working nights?"

Reed was too self-conscious to admit to Alex that Casey was part of the reason he was considering the switch. After he'd thrown himself at Casey only last week, Reed knew how difficult it was going to be to work with Casey once he and Maggie returned from New York. Reed still couldn't forget the momentary look of disgust that had crossed Casey's face as he'd wiped his mouth clean. A reflexive reaction rising out of Casey's deepest self, beyond thought, really, almost cellular. Only no, not cellular. More like a subconscious instinct that was base, primal, learned. Could instinct be learned? Even Reed's memory of the snowstorm was now corrupted by this new image of Casey, a funhouse reflection he hadn't much noticed until now.

At first, the possibility of working the night shift made sense to Reed. It would spare him and Casey any more unnecessary awkwardness while also allowing Reed to patrol the streets when violence was most likely to occur. After all, it had been a ragtag handful of college students from that *VIGI-LANT* group and not the police who had first found Kip in the park, struggling to stand up. But the more Reed thought about it, the more a transfer to the night shift seemed a reactionary move against Casey, an unspoken ceding of some ground, a tacit agreement of wrongdoing. When Reed thought about it in these terms, a stubbornness he'd inherited from his father kicked in. *He* wasn't going to back down, *he* wasn't going to pull away. Whatever his future was with Casey, he would face it head-on. He had nothing to feel guilty about.

With his mind now made up, Reed told Alex of his decision, hoping to calm any fears that Alex might have about their relationship. But Alex only nodded in a rueful way, muttered an offhand "good," and seemed not to want to discuss the matter any further.

With his private life in such a baffling tangle, Reed tried to refocus his attention on the killer who, omniscient and unseen, had still not been caught. Nearly seven weeks had passed since the last murder victim had been found and the police had no fresh leads, which only increased Reed's conviction that the town was being lulled into a false state of complacency, softened up for the next kill.

At those times when Reed was saddled to the desk with paperwork rather than patrolling the streets, he daydreamed about what the killer might look like. Occasionally, he sketched faces that loosely matched up with theories he or the police force had formed about the case. But what any of them knew about the man was vague and required conjecture, leaps of analysis. His method of killing—bashing the victim's head—suggested that the killer was a man of at least moderate strength and a somewhat primitive mind, for why else the appeal of bludgeoning? A rock, a baseball bat, a police baton, whatever was used, still conjured images of stoning, that historical method for killing the heretical and the perverted. Did the man lust for the violence of the act, long to stand beside his victims and experience their moments of death, or even to share in them? Shooting was too impersonal, after all, and bullets could be traced. Stabbing was more personal but too messy. Strangling was possibly the most intimate murder of all, requiring sustained one-on-one contact, and it was clean, but suffocation required time, and a lithe or athletic victim might easily escape before the act was completed.

Reed suspected the man would be inward-drawn, someone who spent too much time in the swirling morass of his own interior, so his outward appearance would reflect that. He wouldn't necessarily be dirty, unwashed, or brazenly neglectful, which would violate his external need for order. Yet some smaller physical trait might point to his inner disorder. His hair would be grown out in some ridiculous way, for example, or his jaw would be lightly spliced from where he'd shaved with a dull razor and hadn't noticed that he was cutting himself. His face might seem flushed, demonstrating how he was burning in his own hatred.

But how could Reed draw any of this and make it concrete? First he sketched a man's wide face, narrow eyes and a grimace for a mouth. How about a messy haircut that stuck out in random animal clumps? It was all conjecture, of course. Because the killer's victims were young, Reed imagined the man was young himself, no more than thirty-five, but what if he was actually in his forties? Who said the man was murdering his own shadow? Reed envisioned the culprit as a man who wore a uniform—was stuck in a life emblematic of a uniform—only this man could just as easily have been a teacher or an innocuous businessman, engaged in some other profession that required no uniform but nonetheless fit like a strait jacket. Instead of feverish eyes, what if the killer possessed cold, expressionless ones, which would suggest he was freezing in his own hatred rather than burning in it. The fires of hell were hot or they were cold; not even the ascetics had figured that one out. Reed couldn't rid himself of the maddening thought that this man was eluding him out of spite. He gave his sketch a Mephisto beard and menacing eyebrows for the hell of it, then took a marker and etched a large X across the jeering face.

"You realize what you're doing?" Alex asked Reed one night in bed. "You're creating a man inside your head." Alex tapped Reed's forehead, then used that finger to brush away a stray lock of hair that had dropped across Reed's brow. "Only instead of a demon lover, you've created the demon nemesis. The phantom menace."

"I've already got myself a demon lover." Reed kissed Alex, who only half-appreciated the joke.

"I guess it's almost like being in a threesome," Alex added.

"Don't start."

Alex kissed Reed's shoulder. "You're not going to tell me what happened between you and Casey, are you?"

Reed's attempt at a smile faded. He hadn't said a word to Alex about *that night*, but when it came to Casey, Alex's instincts were keen. "Traded one case for another," Alex muttered. "Well, I suppose this new threesome you've got going would nearly be sexy if it wasn't for the fact you're creating a man to hate."

"He already exists. I'm trying to put a *face* on him. There's a difference."

"The Great Protector. At least you've stopped tailing Christian all over town."

Later, they began to make love. After a few minutes Alex turned overheated and insistent. Maybe he only wanted to battle against the shadow of the other man he insisted lingered inside Reed's head. His movements seemed too forceful and quick, as if their lovemaking were now under a time constraint. One of the things Reed most appreciated about sex was the build-up—just lying pressed together, breathing, kissing mouth and throat and chest, setting each other gradually on fire—so he tried to slow Alex down. They moved around in bed, increasingly insistent, one against the other, unable to find their normal rhythm, their former simpatico, with Alex moving his mouth lower down Reed's body, and Reed trying to build up a mood first. In time they reached a compromise, and although the lovemaking was not precisely what either one had wanted, it was still good enough, welcome enough.

After Alex had fallen asleep, Reed lay awake for some time and listened to a teasing trace of breeze rustle through the trees outside the house. He couldn't shake his loneliness for Casey, for the friendship they'd had for so many years that was now ended. Or if not ended, then significantly altered. And though he was lying in bed beside Alex, it felt to Reed as if his body was still in shock at the suddenness of his estrangement from Casey. And what about Alex? He watched the way a vein in the side of Alex's neck pulsed with each breath. The loneliness for Casey spread outward, sweeping up Alex in its muddy waters. They were ex-lovers who had fallen back into sleeping together out of habit and need. Ever since he'd told Alex that he'd been thinking of working on the night shift, he'd felt Alex pulling further away from him, a pulling that had begun the night they'd invited Casey and Maggie out to the lake. Or maybe it had started even before then, with the writing of Alex's defiant editorial.

Reed fell into a light sleep with his face buried in Alex's shoulder. He dreamed he was lying on a bed of coals. A man holding a stick of firewood stalked over and stirred the coals, forcing the glowing ones to the surface so Reed's back would scorch.

In the morning, Reed still felt unsettled. His back was actually hot. When Alex woke he leaned over Reed with one elbow, just gazing down at him with a sleepy, drugged smile on his face. "I don't think it's just gay men he hates," Reed blurted, trying to get at something.

"So we're back to him? The shadow? Talk about sleeping with the enemy."

"Suppose the guy hates—I don't know. Our life force, our life source, just everything. Hell, the society that allows us to exist, the God that created us. It's in his blood, his *soul*, this hate." Reed stopped before any more words condemned him. He sounded over-the-top in a groggy morning way. "At some point we're going to have to talk about why we're just going through the motions like this," he added.

Alex reached over to the nightstand, popped a couple of breath mints into his mouth, and kissed Reed slowly, the way Reed preferred. Then he stood and slipped on his underwear. "Anyone ever mention you have a serious side, Officer Reed?" he said.

Reed took a deep breath. He wished he'd chewed on a mint before Alex had kissed him.

Alex leaned over the desk to open the window. "Don't," Reed said, and Alex turned to him, puzzled, but stepped away from the desk. Reed couldn't bear the smell of wilting flowers and trailing vines, part of the anesthesia blanketing the town, part of what was distracting all of them from finding the killer.

But how did you battle a killer who was a wraith, an enemy whose face existed only in your head? Where was the retribution for that? How did you deliver retribution to a ghost?

After Alex had left to return to the lakeside cabin and pack his bags for a four day faculty retreat, Reed climbed out of bed, walked into the bathroom, and swallowed a couple of aspirin. He was thinking too much about retribution lately. The world moved so swiftly except when it came to justice, and then it was like Sisyphus pushing his boulder up the mountain. Not that retribution and justice were the same thing, but that was often misunderstood.

Retribution, that fire inside of him to even scores, to right wrongs both real and imagined. His father had instilled in him a hearty fear of divine retribution, although the possibility of paternal retribution had been far more real to Reed. He remembered a time when he'd gotten into a fight after school and come home with a bloody nose and a bruised hand, his knuckles scraped and swollen. His father had been in the front yard wearing a multi-colored sweater that blended with the autumn leaves he was raking up and stuffing into a large black garbage bag. Something about Reed's demeanor must have tipped Carl off because he'd squinted at Reed and noticed the wounded hand almost instantly.

When he'd asked for an explanation, Reed remained silent, not in defiance as much as fear of self-incrimination. "You were in a fight?" his father asked. "A fight you started?"

Reed turned away, feeling his father inside his head, fingering his thoughts, rutting about for the truth. He wiped a small trickle of blood from his nose.

Carl took Reed into the bathroom and ordered him to rinse his injured nose and hand with warm water while Carl retrieved a bandage and some salve from the medicine cabinet. When Reed was through washing and drying the offending hand, his father dabbed a stinging ointment onto the abrasions. "Hurts, doesn't it?" his father said. "You're lucky the pain is immediate. Someday you will fight the pain that comes years too late."

Reed nodded, embarrassed by the physical intimacy of his father grasping his hand. His father smelled like damp earth. A purple leaf stuck to an elbow of his sweater. "This hand has drawn first blood," Carl said.

First blood? Had Reed started the fight? He couldn't remember. The boy Reed tried to pull his hand away but his father's grip was unyielding. "Retribution," Carl continued. "Don't go down that path. Where the end is violence and misery. Where the clash of enemy sabers is not enough. Where you will want more. Where soon will come the blood in the dust. Don't end up in that pit of despair, Reed."

Reed wasn't convinced he was still speaking to his father. The voice was his but the words were far different. "Do you understand?" his father asked, wrapping the bandage around Reed's hand too tightly, causing a pain that Reed nevertheless did not resist. "Do you?"

"Yes." Reed's fingers swelled with blood.

Later, Iris was shocked when she noticed Reed's bandaged hand. "Reed, you've bandaged yourself way too tight."

Reed pressed his lips together. "You'll cut off your circulation," she said as she undid the bandage and refastened it into a loose and more comfortable fit. Maybe, just maybe Reed missed the tighter bandage. His father had been silent as he sat in the lounger near the window, jotting notes for a sermon.

Reed had other, less strict memories of his father—sitting around a television watching the Green Bay Packers on a Sunday afternoon, or resting his hand on Reed's shoulder when they passed in the hallway some mornings. But the memories of his father's rigid side were the ones that came to Reed with more clarity these days. Iris was partially to blame for this. She'd confided to Reed that she was thinking too much about Carl these days, "almost like he's still here, like after all these years, *now* he has to get something off his chest."

A minister's son. It was rare for Reed to think of himself in this way. "The son of a preacher man," Reed said aloud to the bathroom mirror as he shaved. He missed his father at that moment, but from a distance. He glanced down at his mildly scarred hand, the hand he was looking at too often these days. Then it came to him: the boy he'd been fighting that long ago day had been Casey. Their infamous fight over Pam Larson, the both of them posturing as her boyfriend although they were only twelve, already feeling the masculine pull toward territory and competition.

A few months after that strange incident with his father, Carl had died and Casey had shown up at Reed's doorstep, offering to take him for a ride.

Five years later, a blizzard had forged their friendship into myth. Ten years later and they'd shared another woman, in a sense. Fifteen years later, and they were still caught up in it. Or were they at last reaching its protracted end?

By the time he went into work, Reed was feeling stronger if not necessarily better. It was Friday and his last day working without Casey. The mood in the police station was still somewhat raw and embarrassed, especially since those *VIGILANT* volunteers had found Kip and called the police. Until then the cops had scoffed at the idea of volunteers driving around town in red shirts to protect the town from bashers and murderers, but now there lingered the gnawing sense this group of upstarts had usurped them, arriving at a crime scene before they had. As Reed entered his cubicle, the first thing he noticed was a small manila envelope on his desk, with his name and the police station's address written in a bold hand. He didn't recognize the handwriting or the deliberate, upright block letters. He opened the envelope and removed a clipped-out newspaper photo of himself holding the candle at the vigil. Across the photo, in the same upright block letters, was written in black marker: *Look in, not out.*

He squinted down at the photo. What the hell? Hannah Adair's laughter at the coffee machine down the hall only heightened the sense of absurdity. Reed studied the envelope more carefully this time, but there was nothing distinguishing about it other than the fact it had a smudged and unrecognizable postmark, and that it was addressed not just to the police station in general but specifically to him. The letters looked as if they had been written by a man's hand, although it seemed silly to imagine this. *Look in, not out.* The words didn't sound threatening so much as philosophical.

At the end of the day he brought the newspaper picture and the envelope home with him and placed them in the drawer where he'd stashed away the porn magazine he'd found in his work locker last month. The drawer was beginning to accumulate a certain weight. All these cryptic and indecipherable messages, a hint of mystery both tantalizing and taunting. After a moment, Reed took the news photo right back out of the drawer and decided to take it with him when he went out to Alex's cabin to spend the weekend with Eddie.

Reed had agreed to this arrangement partly as a favor to Iris. "Something is wrong with Eddie," she'd confided to Reed. "Maybe you can reach him."

But from the moment Reed picked Eddie up and drove him out to the cabin, he knew Iris had not been exaggerating about Eddie's mood. It was no longer that Eddie was just angry, frustrated or resentful. Now there was a bruised quality he carried around that was evident but hard to understand.

All weekend Reed tried to break down Eddie's wall. This was harder than Reed had anticipated because Eddie said very little, and when he did talk, most of what he said had an ironic or sarcastic spin, as if to ward off any real connection. But at least he had Eddie's full attention at the cabin. They ate like bachelors, heating up frozen pizza and grilling burgers and hotdogs to accompany the nacho chips and watermelon, although Eddie ate less of the hotdogs and burgers than Reed would have thought. They stayed up and watched the late night comics. Reed could have done without the lantern-jawed one who cracked a couple of crude gay jokes that sent Eddie into a spasm of canned laughter. "It's not *that* funny," Reed said with a hesitant smile, but Eddie said, "It *is*!" and continued to laugh like some hired plant in a studio audience. During a commercial break, Reed turned the channel and stopped on some boxing match, thinking Eddie would appreciate the slugfest, but after a few seconds Eddie stood up, wiped clean of all that crazy laughter. "Bed," he muttered and walked off.

Despite the isolation of the cabin, Reed didn't sleep well that night. He lay in bed for some time, a small lamp burning at his side, and stared at the mysterious news photo. Who would bother to send him something so cryptic? It probably wasn't worth puzzling about, and yet he couldn't seem to set the photo aside. He felt as if he were staring at only a version of himself.

In the morning, Reed and Eddie took a hike in the woods. Something about the trees and the silence seemed to relax Eddie. Then again, a few minutes later, when they ran across a young deer standing on wobbly legs just a few yards down the path from them, Eddie looked uncomfortable again. In the afternoon, Reed took Eddie out on a canoe into the middle of the lake. They lay their oars aside, peeled off their T-shirts, dove into the water and swam around. Then they lifted themselves back into the boat and continued to row around the lake. Eddie rowed hard, too hard really, as if the goal were pure strength and muscle, the release of energy. Again they didn't talk a lot, but out in the middle of the lake, it didn't seem they needed to. A quiet unforced camaraderie was building between them, one born of the solitude and the shared momentum of their arms rowing. Reed wished he could focus more on this and less on the memory of how he and Casey had swum out into this very lake a couple weeks ago to retrieve the old couple's boat. He and Casey had wrestled a bit in the water, putting each other in mock headlocks and dunking one another underwater, just goofing around as they'd often done. Only now Reed was beginning to question his own memory. Wasn't there that moment when Casey came up from behind and slung his arm around Reed's neck a little too gruffly? When Reed tried to break free, Casey pushed his head underwater, and hadn't he held Reed there for a couple seconds too long? Or was he misremembering the entire incident?

As soon as Reed and Eddie reached shore again and had docked the boat, the silence between them inched toward awkward again. "Your back is sunburned," Reed said, noticing just now the gleaming and painful red. "You didn't put on sunblock?"

"I'm not a girl," Eddie said. Once inside the cabin, Reed caught Eddie standing in front of the bathroom mirror, trying to examine his sunburn from behind. "Put some lotion on it," Reed said, hating the paternalistic sound of his voice. He squeezed some lotion into his palm and started to rub it on his brother's back, but Eddie just winced and pulled away. "I can do it," he insisted, but watching him try to slap lotion on his own back was comical. "All right, all right, do it," Eddie finally conceded.

When Reed rubbed the lotion into Eddie's shoulders and back, he felt the tension in his brother's muscles, Eddie's whole body rigid and suffocated. "It's okay to breathe, you know," Reed said.

Later, after Reed stepped out of the shower and was drying his hair with a fresh towel, he walked into the living room and saw Eddie sitting on the sofa, staring at a framed picture of Reed and Alex. He glanced up at Reed. "You guys don't look that happy," he said.

The remark was so unexpected that Reed felt a little winded by it. "Jesus, Ed," he said.

"I'm just saying."

Reed sat on a chair next to the sofa and took the photograph from Eddie's hands. It was a picture of Reed and Alex before their first breakup, when they were still struggling to survive, so of course it was no reflection of who they were now. Reed was about to answer with the pithy response—*Yes, of course we're happy*—but he couldn't quite bring himself to say it. "Where is this coming from?" Reed asked before he added, "We have our moments."

Eddie nodded. His face was starting to look sunburned too. "Quid pro quo, then," Reed said. "What's on your mind these days?"

Eddie was squeezing one of his wrists with his opposite hand as if checking for his own pulse. "Do you two live together?" Eddie asked.

"No, not technically." Reed ran the towel through his hair just to keep his hands busy.

After a pause, Eddie asked, "Can I move in with you? At your place in town?"

At first Reed thought Eddie was joking, but it soon became apparent he wasn't. "Ed, you know you can't," Reed said. "For one thing, there's no way Mom would agree to it."

"Forget it." Eddie shook his head. "*He* thinks he owns the place."

"Who? Christian?"

But Eddie didn't say any more. His eyes were fixed on Reed in a way that wasn't pleasant. "And quit staring at me like that," Reed said, trying to make light of it.

"I'm staring because you're staring."

Was he? "I'm a cop, I'm supposed to stare," Reed said.

"A cop," Eddie repeated. "I keep forgetting."

Sometimes Reed wished he could forget. Certainly he'd never planned on becoming a cop. He'd had no leaning in that direction until Casey had talked him into it several years ago. Now here he was, caught in this place of murder, violence, and transgression.

"You can come over and camp out with me more often," Reed said. "Will that help?"

Eddie's lips moved although he didn't really say anything.

*

When Reed drove Eddie back home on Sunday night, he had to admit to himself that he hadn't been as successful in reaching Eddie as he'd hoped. A wall had come down briefly between them, but soon Eddie had built it back up again. As soon as Reed pulled into the driveway, Eddie said goodbye, climbed out of the car, and slouched into the house, ignoring Christian who was stepping out the door at the same moment Eddie was stepping in. They made it a point not to touch each other.

Christian, wearing his red *VIGILANT* T-shirt, leaned his head into Reed's open window. "You couldn't just drop him off on the side of the road somewhere?" Christian asked.

Reed glanced back at the house, the very same house in which he'd grown up. "Lighten up on him a little, okay," Reed said.

"Lighten up on *him?*" Christian was incredulous.

"He's having a rough go of it." Reed remembered back to when Eddie was four and would hide from his mother or brothers in the clothes hamper, burying himself in the family's dirty clothes. Where was that boy hiding now? "Come on," Reed urged Christian. "You can't be vigilant inside the house too?"

There was a long pause before Christian sighed. "I don't know how good I am at this turning the other cheek crap," he said.

After his chat with Christian, instead of returning to his own house, Reed drove all the way back out to the cabin, wanting one more night at the lake alone to mull things over—his brothers, Alex, Casey. Tomorrow he and Casey would be working together again.

You guys don't look that happy.

Reed had just settled back in the cabin and had mixed himself a scotch when the phone rang. Not Reed's cell phone but Alex's landline. Reed answered the phone instead of letting the answering machine take the call.

"Alexander?" a man's slightly exasperated voice said.

"Who's this?" Reed asked.

There was a pause. "I get it," the man on the other end said. "So I'm talking to my mirror image now?"

Reed wasn't in the mood for any more riddles—his life was becoming increasingly complicated by riddles—so he was tempted to just hang up, but some instinct dissuaded him from doing this even before the man asked, "Reed, right? You're Reed?"

"Who is this?" Reed asked again. He didn't know what he was thinking other than this man's voice had put him instantly on his guard.

"I love the sound of your voice, Reed," the man said. "Listen, maybe we should talk for a few minutes, just you and me. Screw Alexander."

Reed didn't know why this man calling Alex Alexander should bother him so much. Maybe it was just the proprietary way he said the name. "Come on Reed, talk to me," the man said. "Jesus."

'I don't know you."

"That's why people talk, right? To get to know each other. And how do you know you don't know me? Come on, I thought you were a cop."

How did this man know so much about him? Reed had the vague sense he was being toyed with, yet he lost all interest in hanging up. "I can tell you're drunk," Reed said.

The man laughed with a refreshing vigor. "Two gin and tonics and a gimlet with lime, is all," he said. "Moderation, Reed."

It came to Reed then who he was speaking to—the ex-lover! "Randy," he said.

"For Christ's sake, you know me by what I *drink?*"

"Alex isn't here. I can leave him a message."

"I like a nightcap or three before bed, it's true. I'm a little British in that regard. Don't tell me you're too cop to have a drink before bed."

Reed glanced at the glass of scotch he was still holding in his other hand. "Listen," Randy continued. "I called to talk to Alexander, but since the bastard isn't there...Where is he, by the way?"

"A faculty retreat."

"Ah yes, the faculty is always in retreat. I've been curious about you, Reed. Alexander talks about you pretty favorably most of the time."

A small heat passed through Reed's blood, and then it was gone. But Randy must have taken note of Reed's momentary hesitation. "Oh, man," Randy said. "So he hasn't mentioned we still talk? Well, don't worry. It's all very innocent. We're as platonic as two Baptist newlyweds. I don't read a thing into most of what he says."

"I'm surprised he gets the chance to say much of anything."

"Ha! Put down your sword, officer! No, Alexander and I, we were the proverbial wheel that just kept spinning round and round. I drove him *crazy*, Reed. He drove me crazy. Do you see? I couldn't help myself. He brought things out in me. Awful things. Violent things. My heart, you know. I'm that organ of fire type. I think maybe you drive him a little crazy too, but in a different way. What are you? Fire? Air? Water? Tell me you're not an Earth, I can't stand those grounded types."

Outside, Reed could hear the sound of the lake's ceaseless lapping. "I'm not talking to you about *us*." He sipped his scotch. He would never drink this same scotch ever again.

"Well, there's the difference between you two, I suppose." Randy said. "Aren't you on the hunt for a madman or some such melodramatic thing?" Reed heard the sound of melancholy music playing in the background, a bluesy funky sound that reminded Reed of a whole other life impossible for him to reach.

"I have to go," Reed said. And yet he stood there, not going. "I'll tell Alexander you called."

"Yes, you do that, Reed." There was a quicksilver flash of anger in Randy's voice, rising out of nothing. "But you don't know what the hell he's thinking any more than any of us know what the hell any other person is thinking. For all you know, he isn't really on a faculty retreat. It's early August, for Christ's sake. Wake up, Reed. For all you know, Alexander is here with me right now. What if he's in my shower, only a few feet away, and what if I'm just waiting until he's done and then we'll fuck—"

Reed hung up the phone with one decisive move of his hand. What had taken him so long? A few seconds later the phone started ringing again. Reed decided not to answer at the same moment his hand reached for the receiver. "I'm sorry, Reed," Randy said. "Really, this is stupid. I shouldn't be talking to you like this. It isn't decent, is it, for Lover #1 to talk to Lover #2 in this way—"

Reed hung up a second time. When the phone started ringing yet again, he unplugged the phone and stepped outside with his scotch to sit on the porch for a while. The sound of Randy's voice battered around inside his head, not helping him make sense of things. The sky flashed with lightning, and a minute later, when a spotty rain dropped over the lake, Reed couldn't help but wish that it was snow.

(16)

Maggie was strolling down the Coney Island boardwalk amid the carnival atmosphere of snack shops, game booths, and food on sticks, when her mind went dark and she paused. Casey and the friends they were visiting, Trevor and Amy, moved ahead of her, unseeing. Then all sensation returned to her in a dizzying rush: the smell of meat and redolent spices; the sight of vendors hawking their goods; the feel of the briny ocean air against her face; the noise of people passing on all sides. She dashed off the boardwalk behind a balloon tent with her hand clapped over her mouth, sure that she was going to be sick. For a moment she stood hunched over with her hair in her eyes, and coughed and dry heaved as the unfamiliar scene contracted and then expanded around her, contracted and expanded, relentlessly beating to the rhythm of a vast cosmic pulse. "Senorita?" a bejeweled woman called out from a nearby fortune teller's booth ("$10.00 for Mama Gonzales to tell it all!"), but Maggie ignored her, if indeed the woman was calling to her at all.

After a moment the wave of nausea passed, and Maggie stood up. Of course she wasn't sick: she was pregnant. This wasn't intuition so much as certainty. Something foreign, something *other* was there inside her, quietly making its presence known.

Eventually, Casey found her behind the tent. "Magpie?" he asked and she turned to him, drawing a breath. "I think I have a touch of food poisoning," she said.

The next day she begged off joining Casey, Trevor, and Amy in their outing to Ellis Island to visit the Immigration Museum, although the museum had been Maggie's idea in the first place. Once she was alone, blessedly alone, she went out and bought a home pregnancy kit. She returned to the apartment and shut herself in the bathroom as if still in danger of discovery. The bathroom was tiny and narrow, more the size of a broom closet than a bathroom. She had to step in sideways before she could close the door, and then had to squat down carefully over the toilet seat to pee on the stick. Another wave of claustrophobia hit her but she pushed through the ritual, if only to confirm what she already knew, what her body already knew. Still, when she held the stick up to the light, she willed it *not* to turn blue, desperately pinning her hopes once again on the power of mind over matter. But there it was, confirming her worst suspicions: blue. Her eyes misted over with frustrated tears. *Stupid fool*, she argued with herself. She should have started on the pill months ago instead of playing those ridiculous mind games with herself. Or no, she should have simply been honest with Casey from the start.

She put the pregnancy kit into a paper bag and carried it to a dumpster down at the end of the block, and disposed of the pregnancy kit there so it could not be traced back to her.

For the rest of their time in New York, Maggie acted as if nothing were the matter, or tried to, but inwardly she was worried and perplexed. A baby! As with so many things, pregnancy was coming at the worst possible time. Her body felt hot, languid, a vessel of deceit and slow trickery that had turned against her. There were too many babies in the world anyway, filling up strollers and buggies, and she didn't even particularly want a baby, and yet here she was, giving her assist to the overpopulation of the world. She thought it best not to tell Casey she was pregnant until they had returned to Barrow's Point and she'd had her first check-up with the doctor. It wasn't difficult continuing the subterfuge since Casey's attention was focused where Maggie wished hers was, on New York City and enjoying the company of their friends, who had, after all, taken time off from their work schedules to show Maggie and Casey around the city.

Maggie felt the familiar strain with Casey only at night, in Trevor and Amy's cramped living room, on the rickety rollout sofa bed that felt at any moment as if it would spring up on itself and trap them inside like two unaware insects caught inside a Venus flytrap. The tight quarters became an excuse to avoid intimacy with one another. This was just as well, Maggie supposed, since the thought of Casey's hands caressing her naked stomach unnerved her. What if he should somehow feel what she was hiding?

And so for several nights they lay together on the unsteady sofa bed, and whispered a little idle chitchat to one another before they drifted off into their own private sleep. Occasionally, one or the other of them would forget, and his or her arms or hands, in sleep, would fold around the other. One night Maggie awoke to the feel of Casey's arm wrapped around her stomach. For a brief moment she almost reared up like an unbridled horse. Casey was asleep, his steadying breath in her ear, and so she relaxed and adjusted herself just enough so that his hands were nearer her hips than her stomach. Beneath the window she heard the sound of sirens passing, so many sirens in this city, police and firefighter sirens, but the sound of them did not have the menacing and personal reverberation of sirens back in Barrow's Point.

On their final night in New York City, after a late dinner, Trevor and Amy went to bed while Casey decided on a final nightcap. Maggie waited up with him because she didn't have much of a choice, although she was ready for bed and for returning to Barrow's Point, despite all its problems, so she could begin the difficult task of sorting things out. Casey poured himself a drink and then held up the bottle. "You sure you don't want any?" he asked.

"No, thanks," she said, trying not to sound suspicious.

Casey set down the bottle and looked at her. There it was again, that scrutiny, as if he were trying to fathom her. She didn't like it; she didn't want to be fathomed. She went into the tiny bathroom and changed into a thin baggy T-shirt for sleeping, nothing provocative, but when she emerged Casey had that certain gleam in his eye. She turned away from it, folded her clothes and set them down on a chair. Casey came up from behind, lifted her, and fell with her down on the sofa bed, causing it to shake to its limits. "Casey!" she whispered, her hands grabbing protectively at her stomach.

"Come on, baby, let's wrestle," Casey said into her ear. It was something they had done from time to time in the early days of their marriage, a playful jousting, a twisting together of limbs, not wrestling so much as an intimate and impromptu game of *Twister.* Maggie used to find the goofy sparring arousing, but not now, with Trevor and Amy in the next room, not to mention her pregnant state. "Stop it!" she snapped, her words a steamy hiss.

"Right." Casey rolled off of her and turned his back away to sleep. No other words of recrimination, nothing but the abrupt seizing up of his body. Maggie turned off the light and lay down beside him. She touched his back in apology but of course he didn't respond. It was just another night of the sort they'd been having too much lately.

*

Once they'd returned to Barrow's Point, Maggie still put off going to the doctor. Even now, she stalled. Casey and Maggie both went back to work. All the children's faces at the daycare center seemed intensified to Maggie now, intensely personal. Was it her imagination, or were they looking at her with a guarded wariness? Most evenings she returned home from work tired and preoccupied. Soon she would have a child she couldn't leave behind once 5:30 rolled around. When Casey came home from work, he, too, looked preoccupied and deep in thought. "How is Reed?" she asked, almost randomly, but Casey didn't answer her. For the first time it occurred to her that Casey had his own secrets. She felt a stirring of curiosity but was too absorbed in her own worries to give this more thought.

Even the house had started feeling wrong to her, no longer a place she returned to for safety and solace. She felt a bit like a monstrosity walking the rooms where she and Casey had lived their five years of married life. Sometimes the house seemed smaller to her, as if it were shrinking. A dollhouse, she could all but envision it, she and Casey as plastic figurines moved around the rooms by a rude child's hands. Occasionally, Shamus came up and rested his head in her lap, and this alone saved her from feeling like a total fraud.

One late afternoon when Casey was still at work and Maggie was standing on a chair in the living room with a wrench in hand, trying to fix the temperamental air conditioner, her clothes sticking to her like a second skin, Livia dropped by to give Maggie some mail she'd picked up for them while they were away in New York. "Is everything all right?" Livia asked pointedly, amused at the sight of Maggie sporting a wrench.

"Yes, of course," Maggie said. Always, always she felt Livia's subtle disapproval of her...a passing glance, a delicately arched eyebrow, a meaningful sigh. Maggie couldn't help but wonder just how much Casey was confiding to his parents about the recent strain of their marriage. "Yes, of course," Maggie said again.

"You don't seem like yourself."

"Really? Who do I seem like?" Maggie was surprised by her own irritation. Her house was hot and she was sweating and Livia was so briskly composed, never a hair out of place.

If Livia noticed Maggie's annoyance, she didn't let on. "Don't you think you should leave that ghastly thing for Casey to fix?" she asked.

"You know me. I love a ghastly challenge." On top of everything else, Maggie was starting to feel guilty about having stood on a chair in her newly pregnant state. Where were her protective maternal instincts?

"Well, good luck," Livia said and gave Maggie a stiff hug on her way out the door. "I just hope you know what you're doing."

"I'm sure I don't, but thank you." After Livia had gone, Maggie hurried to the bathroom and checked her face in the mirror. *Did* she look different, and if so, in what way? But all she saw was the flushed face of Maggie Hastings staring back at her.

After a few more days, Maggie couldn't delay her checkup any longer, so she scheduled an appointment with her gynecologist. But Dr. Mooney was on vacation, so Dr. Bowen stood in for her, listened to Maggie's story, and gave Maggie a blood test. When Maggie returned to his office a couple days later, Dr. Bowen had his cell phone open on his desk and was texting a message. He didn't even glance up at Maggie when he spoke. "You're not pregnant," he said.

She stared at him with frank disbelief. "What?"

His cell phone signaled a text message. He glanced down, pressed a few buttons, and then focused back on her. "You're not pregnant, Maggie," he repeated.

"But I took a home pregnancy test."

"False positive." His gaze was mildly disinterested, which seemed right for a man with such icy hands. "You must know," he said, "that those store bought kits aren't infallible."

"They're mostly accurate, though, aren't they?" She wasn't some schoolgirl novice who didn't know how to read a pregnancy test. And yet how could she argue with a doctor's diagnosis, even one as distracted as Dr. Bowen. "I missed my last period," she offered.

"Nerves. Stress. Women miss a month or two all the time. Doesn't mean they're pregnant." His cell phone dinged with another message. Maggie wanted to grab the phone and hurl it out the window.

"Are you sure?" The light was spilling wrongly through his window. She had no patience with it.

Dr. Bowen chuckled, either at her question or the new text message that had popped into his bin. "I'm sure," he said. "I'm sorry."

She stood up. This whole shameful meeting appeared to be over before it had really begun. She wanted to call out Dr. Bowen on his rudeness, but really, what good would it do? He would dismiss her as just another woman upset that her phantom pregnancy hadn't panned out.

After she'd left Dr. Bowen's office, Maggie stopped in the bathroom and patted some water over her face. A pregnant woman—a genuinely pregnant woman with the rounded stomach to prove it—emerged from one of the stalls, ran her hands under the faucet, and offered Maggie an offhand smile as she walked out the door. Maggie dried her own hands, then felt a delayed twist of pain in her chest. She ducked into a stall and cried a little. But this was good news, wasn't it? She hadn't wanted to get pregnant in the first place. And yet she couldn't shake the feeling that she'd been betrayed, that her body had deceived her and trumped her at her own deceptive game. After all the months she'd spent trying to trick her body into not getting pregnant, it was as if her body had now tricked her into believing she was pregnant. And what was that intrusive feeling inside of her over the past couple of weeks, if not a baby? Eventually she stood up, wet her hands again under the faucet, dried them and pondered her reflection in the mirror. There were always mirrors, and this was not a particularly flattering one.

False positive: her life was ever sinking into the false.

When Maggie stepped off the elevator at the ground floor, she took a small detour down a hall where she knew there were water faucets. Her throat felt dry and prickly. She drank some of the fountain's surprisingly cool water, and when she turned back the way she'd come, she noticed a woman's small purse lying on the floor next to the door leading into the chapel. Maggie picked up the purse. It was shiny and black, a stylish little number, but when she opened the purse, hoping to find some identification inside, all she found was a store receipt, a dollar bill crumbled into a ball, and a half-eaten slice of pound cake wrapped in a napkin and tucked neatly away in one of the purse's folds.

Maggie looked around, hoping to see someone dashing down the hall to reclaim it, but the hall was empty. Maggie opened the door of the chapel. No one was inside here, either. Or she thought no one was inside, but just when she was ready to leave again, she heard a stirring and Iris sat up on one of the pews. "For goodness sake," Iris said, embarrassed. "What time is it?"

She glanced at her watch and then smiled over at Maggie. "I think I fell asleep for a minute," she confessed. She clutched at her back. "It's not the most comfortable place for a nap."

Maggie hadn't seen Iris in months. Since the day Reed had first introduced Maggie to his mother, Iris had liked Maggie instinctively, and this had not changed when Reed and Maggie broke up. "Reed broke up with you, I didn't," Iris had told her once, and the two women had maintained a friendship since that day. Maggie walked over and sat down beside Iris. "You nap in the chapel?" Maggie laughed. It was not the sort of chapel that inspired reverence or sleep. The room was somewhat stuffy and smelled remotely of Pine-Sol. The statue of Jesus in the pulpit suggested a jacked-up Easy Rider sort of hippie rather than the Son of God.

"Don't tell!" But Iris was smiling too. "I'm on break. This is one of the only places where you can at least lie down and stretch out." Iris smoothed her rumpled hair. "And what are *you* doing here?"

"Is this yours?" Maggie asked, holding out the purse, although she knew it wasn't even before Iris shook her head. "Someone dropped it, I guess," Maggie said, staring back down at it. Suddenly it felt an encumbrance to have found a nameless woman's purse.

"I hope you're not sick," Iris said, prodding a little.

"It's nothing." Maggie reconsidered; she was lying again. "I had a pregnancy scare," she said. "But the damn stick turned blue, and I thought, you know, since I'd missed a month—"

"Maggie, you're pregnant?" Iris grabbed Maggie's arm.

"No, no. False positive. Dr. Texting said so. Apparently everything's fine."

"Oh." Her hand still held Maggie's arm and she didn't seem to know quite what to do with it now. "You weren't trying to get pregnant?"

"Yes, we were. Sort of. Or Casey wanted to." Maggie paused. How to clear the thicket enough so Iris could see? "It's too complicated to get into. I'm sorry."

"Well, as long as you're fine." Iris patted Maggie's arm and then withdrew her hand.

"It's all just stress, I suppose. Not that I have more reason to feel stressed than anyone else." She slung her hair over one shoulder and ran a hand idly through it, as she had a tendency to do. "The thing is, when I first thought I might be pregnant, I panicked a little. The timing is all wrong. But now that I know I'm not, I feel kind of..." She shook her head, at a loss.

"How *is* Casey?" Iris asked.

"He's fine. We've had better days."

"It's this awful heat, I think," Iris said. "These terrible murders, and then that young man in the park. Everything feels wrong, doesn't it? Or distorted or something."

Maggie wasn't convinced she could blame all her problems on this irrational summer of murder and heat. She wondered if the problem was really the opposite of what Iris described: the murders and the heat and the anxiety they aroused were melting away the façade of her life, forcing her to take a long hard look at truth, to see past the distortions of the everyday.

"What's going on between Reed and Casey these days?" Iris asked. "Something's wrong there too, I think, but Reed has decided to clam up about it."

"Casey isn't saying much either." Maggie didn't mention the fight she'd had with Casey over Reed just before she and Casey had left for New York. Was it possible that had caused the tension between Reed and Casey? "I guess it's another secret between the boys," Maggie said and leaned forward so far that the forgotten purse almost slid out of her lap. "Do you ever wonder if Reed and Casey have grown too close as friends? If maybe that isn't part of the problem now." She trailed off, her eyes blazing, giving her face a luminous quality. "Reed doesn't stop by anymore. I'm afraid I'll become the collateral damage in whatever is going on between Merc and Case." Maggie and Iris sat for a moment, feeling the precariousness of time and memory. "I'm sorry," Maggie said. "I sound like an idiot, I know—"

Maggie stopped in mid-sentence and leaned back in the pew as if in pain. "Maggie?" Iris asked, but Maggie waved her concern off with a quick motion of her hand. "I'm fine, it's nothing," she said, unable to admit what it was that had startled her so, coming now of all times—the dark cheating flow of menstrual blood.

(17)

Iris didn't discover that Eddie was responsible for her overstretched clothes entirely by accident. First there was her general suspicion, mounting steadily over the summer, that Eddie was withholding something from her. And though she couldn't have said how she knew, she understood something major was bothering him, far beyond the fact she'd placed him under "house arrest."

The "house arrest" business had seemed necessary at the time. She'd been out with Arnie on a Saturday night, and when they left the downtown restaurant where they'd eaten, they heard a car alarm going off down the street. A moment passed before Arnie recognized his own car alarm. Just as they reached his car, three young people, two male and one female, wearing the *VIGILANT* T-shirts and looking appropriately watchful, rounded the street corner and hurried over. "Is everything okay?" the girl asked them, and Arnie said everything was fine, his car alarm was touchy and went off at the slightest provocation.

One of the young men Iris recognized as the Thai boy she'd found with Christian up in Christian's room earlier in the summer. "Hello," Iris said, and the young man smiled a little before he looked away.

"They're becoming pretty ubiquish these days," Arnie said after he and Iris had driven off.

Iris nodded although she was pretty sure Arnie meant ubiquitous. Something about the car alarm, the red T-shirts and earnest young people seemed to warn Iris. She cut the evening short, much to Arnie's disappointment, so that she could return home to the boys. Only both Eddie and Christian were not at home. Christian was an adult now, ready to start college in the fall, and so, despite her misgivings, she didn't have much say in his comings and goings. Eddie was a different story. She sat in the living room and waited for his return, growing anxious when his eleven o'clock weekend curfew came and went. Didn't he understand the risk of staying out so late when three men, all older and more self-possessed than he, had been murdered? Or didn't he feel in any personal danger, the murders as remote to him as war casualties overseas? She would have to discipline him for such flagrant violation of the rules. The last thing she wanted was a confrontation between them, but what choice did she have? She was his mother.

Iris lay down on the sofa and then sat up again when she heard a car pull into the driveway. But it was Christian returning home, not Eddie. "What's this, an all-nighter?" he asked when he saw her sitting on the sofa, doing nothing. She supposed she'd look more natural if she had a book open in her lap.

"Your brother isn't home yet."

Christian's face showed no interest as soon as he realized she was waiting up for Eddie. She'd seen that look on Eddie's face often enough whenever she mentioned Christian. "Would it kill either one of you to at least pretend you care?" she said.

"He's fine, Mom," Christian said and then, unruffled, went upstairs to his room.

She grabbed a book from a nearby shelf—*Crime and Punishment,* what kind of a joke was this?—opened it, spread it across her lap, and lay again on the sofa. This time she drifted off. Carl nudged her feet aside to clear room to sit down. He was nattily dressed in one of those white linen shirts she'd always loved to see him wear. The shirt was a little rumpled, actually, but she decided not to mention it. "So, love," he said. "How are you hanging?"

Love? Carl never called her love. Darling or honeybunch, sure, but not love. And hanging? Maybe something was being lost in translation from the afterlife. "Oh, Carl," she said. "Our boys are in trouble."

She wasn't sure what she meant by this other than she hadn't meant what it seemed. Carl adjusted the glasses he was wearing, the ones that gave him a remote scholarly air. "Don't wear yourself out," he said.

"Eddie isn't a baby anymore. You should see him."

Carl was playing with one of her toes. She didn't remember him as such a foot fetishist. "You too, love," he said. "But I'm leaving. Now wake up and go deliver our son."

When Iris opened her eyes, her feet were slanted off the sofa in an awkward manner. Her toes felt tingly and numb. Outside she heard an odd rustling sound in the oak next to the house. Her heart fluttered as she sat up, but when she glanced out the window, she couldn't believe what she thought she saw in the tree. "Eddie?" she said and limped outside on her numb feet. And sure enough, there was Eddie, balanced on a branch as he jumped down onto the roof.

"Eddie, what are you *doing?*" she called out, shocked, not caring if she woke the neighbors. And when Eddie looked down at her, swaying, she cried, "Get down from there!"

He crossed the roof and climbed into the house through his bedroom window. Iris darted back into the house and glanced at the clock on the wall: 2:13 a.m.! What a terrible, murderous time to stumble home, she thought, still cloudy from sleep. "Look at the time!" she scolded him as Eddie came down the stairs, one shoulder leaning against the wall for support.

He didn't say anything, just weaved past her into the kitchen. In a stab of revelation, she realized that Eddie had been doing this all summer and possibly longer, pretending to go to sleep in his room and then sneaking outside at all hours. "You're grounded for two weeks," Iris said.

Eddie didn't bother to turn on the kitchen light and neither did Iris, finding it easier to speak in the concealing darkness. Instead, he went to the freezer, broke some ice out of the ice tray, then went to the sink and started rubbing the ice over his hands. Ice? It was another strange thing for him to be doing at 2:13 in the murderous morning. After a few seconds, he wiped his icy hands on one of her clean dishtowels. In the dark his hands looked troubled. She shivered; she was standing in a cold spot. Was this also Carl? But no, Eddie had left the refrigerator door open. He turned and rummaged in the freezer for an ice cream bar.

"House arrest," she continued. "Two weeks. I mean it. You're fifteen. You can't just drift home anytime you please. It's not safe—"

"For some people," Eddie muttered.

"For *you,*" she said, and when he looked away, she added, "For anyone."

Eddie opened the wrapper of the ice cream bar with his teeth. Iris could sense how flustered he was. She could smell him too. He smelled the way some people did after they'd been running at a dead sprint. "Where have you been?" she asked.

"'Night," was all he said and walked past her on his way upstairs.

And the next day, when Iris heard about a college boy attacked and beaten in the park, she felt at once horrified and vindicated. "That could have been you," she said to Eddie, "running around at all hours! You have to be more careful, this town isn't safe anymore. How many times do I need to say it?" Although now that she thought about it, she'd said this far more often to Christian.

Eddie just looked at her with eyes that begged for her silence. "I know, Mom, I know," he said, so low it was nearly a whisper.

In the first days of his "house arrest," Iris tried to make sense of his unusual behavior. He was too silent; he sealed himself off in his room; sometimes he laughed a little bitterly at nothing; often he seemed lost inside himself, so that when she addressed him, he looked at her with a momentary, blinking caution, as if she'd forced him out into an unwelcome light. Well, hadn't she, even when he was first born? She still had the scars from her C-section, her labor with Eddie so difficult, so preternaturally brutal, that after 32 hours of labor she'd been pleading for her own death, anything that would put an end to such irreducible pain. The next moment, weak from the epidural that was doing her no good, she said she must see it through, she couldn't risk losing another one. Then she fainted. When she regained consciousness, Carl was yelling for the doctors to "cut it out of her. Open her up. Take the damned thing out."

Although later, Carl denied he'd ever said this. "You were delirious from the pain," he told her, and Iris had pretended to believe him, although the memory was too clear for her to have any doubt.

The damned thing, Eddie, cut out of her and suffocated in his own umbilical cord. The doctors had all but thrown him against the wall to force him to start breathing.

Had he been marked from the start for a difficult and struggling life?

Because she saw how, even at fifteen, he carried himself a little clumsily, as if he couldn't quite find a gait that suited him. On a wrestling mat he moved swiftly, decisively, even a little savagely, but once he stepped back into real life and the real world, his body fell back into its subtle hunch. True that he didn't draw much attention to himself, but she was becoming aware of the effort this required for him to blend in.

On a sultry Tuesday afternoon in early August, rather than eat lunch at the hospital cafeteria, Iris returned home to check on Eddie and to make sure he was obeying his "house arrest." Even to herself she had to admit this was only part of the reason. What she also wanted was to walk into the house unannounced and catch her sons—both of them—unaware. Eddie's increasingly strange behavior had opened a trapdoor of curiosity about the secret lives of her sons, how they lived those parts of their lives that they kept hidden from her.

Christian was not at home but Eddie was, posting vigil in front of the TV set, paying scant attention to the soap opera woman with multiple personalities as she morphed from a crisp, judgmental woman into a bellicose boy with clenched fists. At least he'd stopped hiding out in his room for days. "I didn't know you watched the soaps," Iris said.

Eddie stared down at his hands, which in the daylight were once again the hands of a boy. She went to the kitchen and fixed a sandwich and a tossed salad. When she was a girl, she'd become attached to a soap opera her mother watched that occasionally presented episodes "live." Most of the plots had revolved around a central murder investigation. Her most vivid memory was not of the show itself but of a commercial she'd seen for one particular storyline. "A killer is on the loose," a male's disembodied voice announced, "and one of these people will be his next victim." The camera had shown each potential victim in close-up, all staring ahead without expression. All the potential victims had been major characters except for one, the rich family's peculiar uncle, who had not been on the show all that long and was a supporting player. The commercial had thrilled Iris even though the likely victim had been obvious, even to a child.

She'd been so young back then, when murder was more a plot device than anything real.

Once Iris sat at the kitchen table to eat, she couldn't enjoy the meal since Eddie was now staring at her from across the living room, as if waiting to see what she might turn into. A harridan, a depressed woman on a crying jag, a plate hurler? At least he was maintaining a level of eye contact, which surely was a step forward. His stare wasn't bored or laconic or even exasperated so much as openly willful, demanding and maybe pleading. Her swift exit was what he seemed to want; that was *all* he seemed to want.

She didn't rush herself. "So what grand plans do you have for today?" she asked.

Iris waited him out until he said, "Not that much, since I'm on *house arrest.*"

"You can invite someone over," Iris said. "What about Danny? Or Tess? Are you two still hanging out?"

He didn't answer, and she saw that she'd said the wrong thing. Talking to Eddie had become like picking her way through a field of concealed landmines.

When she was finished eating, she rinsed her plate and silverware in the kitchen sink and scrubbed down the counter. Finally, although she wanted to linger, she knew she must return to work. She said goodbye to Eddie and stood in the doorway until he offered a negligible reply.

And so she had learned nothing of value. Once she was driving back to the hospital, she wondered if Eddie's defiant stare hadn't been laced also with anticipation. But why anticipation, and for what? With a spontaneity that thrilled her, Iris turned the car around and drove back to the house.

She parked on the side street where Eddie could not spot her car. She regarded her house and backyard, for a moment picturing herself creeping beneath the oaks and spreading elms, a stealthy figure struggling for invisibility amid all this daylight. Then she found herself approaching the house in very much the same way as she'd imagined. *What silliness*, she thought, and yet something propelled her forward. If Eddie questioned her return, she'd make up an off-the-cuff excuse. She sneaked in through the back door, passing through the kitchen first and then peering into the living room, her heart pounding, unaccustomed to such subterfuge. The TV was still on, but Eddie was no longer riveted to the sofa.

Iris removed her shoes and climbed the stairs. When she saw a shadow in her bedroom through the half open door, she paused, knowing with a sure intuition that the only way she could pass through the trapdoor was to remain still. And there she saw what she had returned for: Eddie standing barefoot in front of her closet mirror, wearing the lemon-colored sundress she'd bought just last week at a vintage shop, the price tag still dangling off the collar. At Eddie's feet his own clothes lay tossed in a resigned heap. Her breath boiled in her chest but she didn't move. Fortunately, Eddie's back was turned and he was unaware of her presence. What immediately struck her was how Eddie didn't appear to be pretending anything, as she'd imagined Christian doing when she suspected he was the guilty party. Where was the inner life, the sense of drama and masquerade, the brief, daring parade before the mirror as he enacted his private fantasy? Eddie just stood motionless, his strong back stretching the material to its limits, a rugged schoolmarm cursed with a boy's troubled gaze, miserably mesmerized by his/her own reflection.

After a moment a light panic overtook Iris. She mustn't be here, she mustn't be seen. She hastened back down the stairs, still holding her shoes, and stepped out the back door in the shade of the porch and the deeply rooted elm tree that the Jackman's sprinkler was inadvertently watering. She felt dizzy and displaced. Her hands actually shook. When she'd imagined Christian was responsible, she hadn't felt this stirred. This worried her, too, her own wrongful assumptions. She glanced around. Was Lenore Jackman peering at her from behind her neatly hung curtains, as she was prone to do? Iris put her shoes on and hurried across the backyard like a guilty child. Of course she had no intention of letting on to Eddie that she knew what he was doing. That much was clear to her.

Once in the car she didn't immediately drive away. Now she understood why Eddie avoided her and Christian and tried not to share meals with them. Now she saw—at least in part—what was eating away at him, digesting him, an emotional parasite he carried that was his burden alone. She saw, and yet it would be difficult from now on to look at Eddie in the same way, possessing as she did this secret knowledge that only increased her love for him, if not her understanding.

How, over all this time, couldn't she have seen? "Eddie, Eddie," she kept saying aloud.

That night she removed her yellow dress from the closet. She held it up to herself. The dress felt counterfeit, not hers at all. She slipped it back on a hanger and placed it in the very back, out of Eddie's immediate reach. But no, that was selfish of her, and if he noticed the dress hanging in a different place than it had been, he might suspect she was on to him. She moved the dress back to the front.

Soon after her discovery of Eddie's secret, in the middle of his "house arrest," Iris arranged for him to spend the weekend with Reed out at Alex's lakeside cabin. The house arrest business was starting to feel ill-timed and counterproductive. If he was out in the country with Reed, he could have a change of scenery, and she wouldn't have to worry about his safety or what he was doing at night.

"Look, Arnie," she asked him one afternoon when Eddie was away with Reed. "I'm not wrong, am I? Didn't I have to be firm? Punish him in a way that he couldn't ignore?"

Arnie was sitting on a lawn chair in her backyard, nursing a bottle of root beer while Iris pulled weeds from her garden. It was a modest garden with carrots and lettuce heads and the stubborn muskmelon, but she tended to it zealously on weekends, enjoying the feel, the *smell*, of plants flourishing. Arnie smiled at her question and made the closest thing to moon eyes she'd ever seen from him. "Being a single parent is a chore," he offered.

"That's a non-answer, Arnie." Iris tugged at a weed, or what she thought was a weed, but suddenly she was holding in her hand a vegetable root of some sort. It was not a root of anything she remembered planting. "For heaven's sake," she said, staring at it. Eventually she tossed the indecipherable root to the side. Three inexplicable murders; an unprecedented heat wave; a troubled son who was wearing her clothing; a dead husband trying to get her attention… the uncanny root was the least of the mysteries and not worth another thought.

More and more these days, when feeling harried and undone, Iris found herself visiting the church, mostly at odd hours when the building was empty. The day she'd run into Maggie at the hospital chapel had not been an anomaly. Silence in a church was not quite like a silence anywhere else, speaking to Iris in ways that sermons and recitation of liturgy never could. Words, *discourse,* could only take her so far.

One afternoon she stopped by the church on her way home from work. When she'd first started doing this periodically during the summer, she'd felt a little reluctant to enter the church alone, as if she expected to run across a desecrated altar or a blood-soaked message left on one of the walls. A couple of weeks ago she'd stepped into the nave in time to see a man hurrying through the door in the front that led back to the church offices. The sight of him had disconcerted Iris somewhat, although there'd been nothing unusual or threatening about the man. The town's suspicious climate had turned many solitary figures into something off-kilter and a touch menacing, particularly those spotted as quick, fleeting movements out of the corner of the eye.

Today there were no such fleeting figures inside the church. The air, however, felt even more stuffy and uncirculated than usual. Iris sat in a pew next to an open window and contemplated the church's vaulted ceiling, the mahogany balcony, the stain glass window of the frightened men on their knees, the one that had scared Christian so much as a child. Fresh flowers stood radiant and blooming from vases in the front. Iris had the uneasy sense they'd been left behind after a funeral. Her mind swept back to when she'd spoken to Timothy Gardenia at Carl's grave. What was it he'd said about consciousness and the unlearning of family violence? She couldn't remember now, or even why she'd thought it important in the first place. Iris touched a hymnal, picked it up and set it on her lap, liking the feel of it, the hopeful and steadying weight. She opened it to the first hymn and read a few lines: *Rock of ages, cleft for me/ Let me hide myself in thee*…The words burrowed into her, their rhythm and cadence. She could almost hear the old rustic echo of the organ from the home-town church back in her childhood, its jarring and vibrating chords: *let the water and the blood/From thy wounded side which flowed*…

For some time Iris sat and allowed the silence to penetrate. The hymnal in her lap called back more memories. Once she and Carl had arrived at the church early on a rainy Sunday morning and found several hymnals scattered across the church lawn. They'd carried the hymnals inside and tried to dry them out with paper towels in front of a heating grate, but the books were permanently warped, so finally Carl had disposed of them. Iris glanced up at the pulpit where he used to stand, speaking to the congregation from that position of authority, raising his hand, slashing a cross into the air. This was the same man she'd lain beside in bed every night for so many years, so long ago.

What, she wondered, would Carl have made of this overheated summer and its sinister undertow, the paranoia and darkness metastasizing through the town like a black cancerous spread? A beast was attacking them all: that was how Carl would have seen things. He would have conceptualized the danger in Barrow's Point as an external force, a spiritual evil that multiplied and spread over entire families and communities and possessed them. From the pulpit he would have spoken of nothing less than the epic battle between good and evil for each individual soul in Barrow's Point. But Iris couldn't embrace such an apocalyptic vision. She didn't see the town's violence as an outside force attacking them, but the result of something awakened from within. Possibly, after all, the real danger wasn't external, but internal, the violence peeling away at the town's seeming serenity, its friendly complacency, and exposing the darker layers lying beneath.

The silence around Iris—inside her—deepened. She lifted the hymnal from her lap and placed it back in the hymnal rack. Then she stared at her knuckles, a little red from having gripped the hymnal so tightly. For some reason she remembered the time Reed had to wear a bandage around his hand because he'd bruised his knuckles in a school fight. Eddie's knuckles had looked much the same way on the night he'd returned home so late. "Was Eddie in a fight?" she said aloud.

(18)

The silences in the police cruiser between Reed and Casey were of a different sort—uneasy, clumsy, challenging, casting a pall over every conversation they attempted.

Once Casey returned to work, both Reed and Casey pretended their transgressive night in the car outside Reed's house had never happened. "Someone's sunburned" was the first thing Casey said to Reed, with a casual laugh that nonetheless sounded insincere. "Spent the weekend at the lake," Reed answered, and that shallow exchange had set the tone between them and served as their bridge back to one another.

But Reed could sense how the bridge was shaky and uncertain and in danger of buckling under the weight of everything they left unsaid. Talking to Casey had been effortless before, but now that ease was gone and there was work involved. As a result, they frequently fell into lengthy silences. Sometimes they tried to beat back the silence with levity, but the jokes and lightheartedness lacked conviction, more performed than felt. Their occasional conversations sounded self-conscious and idle now, exactly what they once had not been. Caution had set in, and neither of them knew how to wrest himself free of it.

When Reed and Casey were at the police station, they tended to keep their distance. Casey stopped barging into Reed's cubicle at the slightest provocation, or lounging on Reed's desk and peering over his shoulder as he filled out paperwork. Reed tried to make the best of it. He'd convinced himself he wasn't solely to blame. There had been *some* reciprocation on Casey's part, however fleeting.

Or at least that's how he remembered it.

Days passed and then a week, and yet little changed between them. They continued to avoid talking about anything personal. Reed didn't mention to Casey how he and Alex were breaking up again. There was a formality to their breakup this time, lacking the anger and hurt that had marked their first separation. Reed's phone conversation with Randy on his last night out at the lake was only seemingly the catalyst.

"I'm not seeing him behind your back, you know," Alex had said when Reed mentioned Randy's late night phone call. They had this conversation while doing dishes at Reed's kitchen sink, Alex's arms slick to the elbows with soap.

"I know." But Reed didn't know, really. He wiped his eye with his fist where a little soap had crept in. He was drying, for Christ's sake. "You're still in touch with him, though. You talk on the phone. Confide in him."

"You have your confidant. I'm not allowed mine?"

"Mine isn't my ex."

"No, not exactly." But the remark lacked the sting it once might have had. "Randy's living in Minneapolis now," Alex reminded Reed. "Every now and then he drifts into town. He does have some roots here, you know. *History.*"

"It's just strange you never mentioned you were back in touch."

But neither of them felt up to examining the issue with any more depth than this. They'd been preparing so long for the possibility of another breakup that they didn't have the inclination to fight against it. When Alex made the quiet decision to fly out east to visit family before the new school semester began, Reed knew it was the end, despite Alex's attempt to try and make it sound as if he just wanted a break from the tension of the town. There were no recriminations or accusations between them, not even a clear final goodbye. Alex packed, Reed drove him to the airport, and they hugged for only slightly longer than normal before Alex disappeared into the terminal and Reed drove away, allowing himself only a brief nostalgic glance back in the rearview mirror. His life was retreating from him, bringing with it this solitude.

That night Reed dreamed he was about to eat a burger with no meat inside. He squirted ketchup between the buns and started to eat anyway. The buns were soft and downy. He woke up half-asphyxiated in Alex's pillow. *The world, the world,* Reed thought in one of those late night stupors. Yet the dream had left him feeling oddly buoyant.

As skilled as Reed had become over the past several days at controlling how he acted around Casey, he still hadn't fully tamed his eyes. His eyes strayed from him at will, as if they, his damned *eyes,* couldn't make a clean break from Casey. Reed noticed small things: a faint, almost silver indentation in Casey's bottom lip; the worry lines across Casey's forehead; the dark circles running beneath his eyes. He saw how Casey's legs, when riding shotgun, were turned at a slight angle toward the door. Everything between them these days felt on the verge of turning symbolic.

Even Casey's face had started to appear different to Reed. It was heavier now, fuller, more shadowed and reflective. Something was bothering him, something more than the distance dividing the two of them, yet Reed felt as if he'd lost the right to ask what the matter was.

As it turned out, Reed learned more from Maggie than he did from Casey. One weekend in mid-August, with an empty weekend ahead of him, Reed decided to stop at Drake's Tavern before he drove to Quench or maybe headed off to the Twin Cities to catch up with a couple of college friends. Drake's Tavern was a place Reed and Casey used to frequent, in fact was where they had gone years ago to mend their friendship back when Casey had first convinced Reed to join the police force. Maybe it was nostalgia that brought Reed to Drake's, or maybe just some instinct he didn't care to analyze, only follow.

Once he was sitting at the bar, he noticed Maggie at a back booth with a couple of her friends from work. He didn't approach her, only smiled and nodded. His estrangement from Casey seemed to include her as well.

The bartender was Scott Oates, whom Reed knew casually. "There he is, the wayward son," Scott said with a wry smile.

Reed wasn't sure what he'd done—or hadn't done—to earn that title. He drank his first Guinness rather quickly, and when he ordered a second, Scott said, "How about we make this one a Black Velvet. Put some hair on your chest."

He poured Reed another Guinness and topped it off with champagne. Maggie's friends stood up and left without fanfare. Maggie carried her drink, still half full, up to the bar. "Of all the gin joints in the world," she said and sat on the empty stool beside him.

For whatever reasons she had decided to stay, he was glad for the company. She peered, puzzled, at his drink. "Black Velvet," Scott said. "Women love a man who drinks a Black Velvet. Not that this one's interested in a woman's viewpoint." Scott laughed and gave Reed a friendly swat on the shoulder. Then he left to serve another customer.

Scott's words silenced them at first. Reed sipped his drink and looked at Maggie. He'd made love to this woman once. The memory rattled around at the back of his mind along with other guilty, unwelcome memories. Just how much did she know about the reason for his estrangement from Casey? "Why are you boring yourself with me tonight?" he asked.

"Casey went to the Boundary Waters for the weekend. You remember. You used to do that with him at the end of the summer. He didn't tell you?"

"Nope." All he knew was that Casey had received permission to leave work at noon.

Even now, Reed couldn't help but feel a flash of jealousy that Casey had gone with someone else on the Boundary Waters trip they used to do together, sometimes with a handful of friends, sometimes just the two of them. Those weekend trips of hiking, fishing, canoeing, drinking, and quiet reflection were part of a past that was swiftly becoming irretrievable. Reed stared at the bar as if he could see in its polished surface the person Casey had gone to the Boundary Waters with. "He and Sam left just a few hours ago," Maggie said, reading Reed's thoughts.

He nodded. Sam, Casey's brother, who lived in Minneapolis with his wife and their son Trey. "How is Sam?" Reed asked.

Maybe it was the drink that emboldened Maggie or maybe it was something more. "What's going on between you two?" she asked. "It's not like you guys to be so—remote."

"Ask him."

"Maybe he won't tell me a thing."

Reed whistled through his teeth. "Small talk be damned," he said. The bottles behind the bar looked as if they'd been stacked in haste. "It's not like Casey and I haven't fought before. Remember I told him I was gay and he nearly disowned me. He would have too, I seem to remember, if you hadn't managed to tape us back together again."

"That was different." Although offhand, Maggie couldn't have said how.

"Why are you two fighting?" Reed asked. "That's a better question."

Maggie sighed. It was getting confusing, who was mad at whom. "Our seven year itch was premature," she laughed, and then stopped because it sounded glib. "Casey and I will get past this," she added with a confidence she was far from feeling. He had started sleeping down on the sofa, for one thing. Not every night, but often enough.

"You're lucky then." Reed raised his glass to his lips and found it empty. They ordered another round of drinks. They were in no hurry. Normally, Maggie made her own plans on the weekends when Casey went off to the Boundary Waters with the guys, but this year nothing much had appealed to her, so she'd decided, in the end, to stay in Barrow's Point.

Finally, Maggie stood and announced she was ready to go home. She hadn't fed Shamus and it was getting late.

Reed had lost all sense of time in the comfort of their conversation, the easy give and take. "All right," he said. "Good talking to you."

She looked at him with a touch of mischief in her eyes. "Don't act like you're staying here," she said. "You're driving me home."

She explained that she had ridden over to Drake's with her friends. They, of course, were long gone, and she certainly didn't intend to walk across town alone at this hour. Was he going to force her to ride the bus?

Reed and Maggie drove through the streets without saying much, simply enjoying the presence of the other. Once they arrived at her house, Maggie invited him inside for a final drink and to say hello to Shamus. Reed agreed because there was no reason not to, because his head was light with drink, and because a part of him wanted to enjoy a little more time with her even in Casey's absence—*especially* in Casey's absence. It was obvious to them both that a door had opened between them, at least somewhat, after all these years, even if for only one night.

Reed sat on the sofa while Maggie went into the kitchen for a bottle of wine. Shamus romped into the living room to greet Reed, who gave him the requisite belly rub. Then Reed looked over at the wall to the painting that he, Casey, and Maggie had stared at with such intensity last spring when Maggie had first noticed a sliver of bare canvas. Reed squinted but could not make out the bare spot now. Shamus headed back into the kitchen when he heard Maggie shaking food into his bowl.

Maggie returned with the wine bottle and two glasses. "What happened to you and Casey getting pregnant?" he asked. There seemed no time left for indirection.

She poured Reed a glass of wine and handed it to him, then sat down on the other end of the sofa with her own glass. "That didn't take long," she said.

Reed nodded, willing to accept her non-answer, but then she continued on her own. "Actually, last month I thought I might *be* pregnant," she admitted. "But the tests came back negative. I never mentioned it to Casey." She wasn't sure why she wanted Reed to know this. "I didn't tell many people. Iris was the first."

"You didn't tell your husband but you told my mother?"

"I ran into her at the right moment. We've always been able to talk, Iris and I."

"She thinks you're great, you know."

"Good. That makes one of you." Instantly Maggie was alarmed that she'd spoken aloud. But Reed just smiled and mock-stabbed his heart. He studied her through his inky lashes. Maggie couldn't help but feel a thrill, his eyes focused on her in such a sustained way. Sometimes Reed reminded her of a man in a painting she'd once seen—the lashes, the coloring and complexion. "Let's not talk about babies anymore, please," she said.

"Okay. What do you want to talk about?" Nothing immediately occurred to either of them. "How about the time we went to that Halloween party dressed as inkblots?"

Maggie laughed. "People were trying to interpret us all night."

"And no one guessed a gay guy dating a straight woman." Now it was Reed's turn to look surprised by what he'd said aloud. Yet he followed the thread of the thought. "You know, we might have been perfect for each other. All I needed was different wiring."

"Oh yes. I know." Of course, the whole wiring thing was an insurmountable problem.

Exactly where the time went, neither of them could say. They continued to talk and drink the wine, and before they knew it they were lying on the sofa together but in head-toe fashion. Shamus had spread himself out on the far side of the room, oblivious to the incongruity of Reed lying beside her. "What am I doing here?" Reed asked.

She didn't care why he was here. The why didn't matter. They were together and she was glad. There was comfort in this physical contact, this innocent intimacy. She had no way of knowing that Reed felt the room was undermining him with all its small reminders of Casey—a shirt draped across the corner chair, his shoes lying haphazardly under the coffee table. Casey's presence was in the room, part of the air, maybe part of the intimacy that was happening between Reed and Maggie. Reed started massaging her bare foot, his face deep in thought. "I remember this one little spot," he said, smiling, and pressed his thumbs into the sole of her foot, as he once had, to make her blood jump.

She clutched his legs. It was so hopelessly wrong to want this. Yet his touch felt wonderful. Her heart leapt forward to grasp at this unexpected happiness.

"Man, why am I here?" Reed said again, this time to the heavens.

Because Casey isn't, she might have said but didn't. "You're here to reconnect with an old friend," she said.

"An old friend," he repeated, still playing with her foot. "This has been the most wretched summer of my life, old friend."

"It's almost over."

"The bullshit with Casey. Alex, the murders. It's like we're a bunch of hick cops knocking our heads against a stone wall trying to find the bastard who started it all." Reed shook his head, pondering this. "Sometimes I think we're all guilty."

His feet had a spicy smell, as if he'd been walking barefoot in desert sand after a rainstorm. She was probably romanticizing it. "Of what?" she asked.

"Of creating him. The killer. Every one of us. The whole town." He stared toward the ceiling. It was better than continuing to stare at Casey's things lying around the room.

Maggie ran her hand along Reed's ankle, the powerful bend of it. "I suppose, in a sense," she said, although she wasn't exactly sure what he was getting at.

"Actually, it's not even just this town. It's everywhere. A monster in our own image. Dr. Frankenstein, every one of us."

"Well, not everyone. Not you, of course."

He raised his head off the arm of the sofa. "Why not me?"

She was growing confused. "Not me, then," she said a little defensively.

"Maybe not you." He smiled and laid his head back. "I suppose it's not good for any of us to look too far past the River Jordan." He had no idea what he meant by this. He felt drunkish, less lonely than he had been but more vulnerable. No, he felt more than this, a little as if his recent life had gutted him, slit him open from neck to groin, and Maggie had found him in a bar and brought him home and stitched him back together with her kindness and her reason, at least as much as she was able, and now he was indebted to her. Again. Much in the same way he'd been in her debt after she'd helped broker his friendship with Casey many years ago. It was difficult suspecting that he was loved by someone in a way he could not return, and yet how could he complain? How could anyone complain about being loved? Yet at times he thought it was terrible, to be loved so undeservedly.

Then he wondered if he loved Casey in a similar way.

The drinks weren't helping his clarity. His eyes were turning heavy, so he closed them for a few seconds that became minutes. White spots swirled in front of him that reminded him of places he couldn't get back to.

Maggie caressed his ankles as she had many years ago, as if from memory. Then she closed her eyes too, still clutching Reed's feet. She and Reed were lying in a rowboat, gently rocked back and forth. The boat lurched. When she opened her eyes, Casey was sitting in the chair across from the sofa, a glass of whiskey in his hand, staring at them.

Casey? But of course she was still asleep. She closed her eyes again, waiting for the mirage of husband to pass. She opened her eyes a second time. He was still there. How strange, this apparition of him. Yet apparently he was no apparition. "Casey?" she said groggily.

He mock-saluted her. His expression was both stony and reproachful.

"What—I thought you and Sam were spending the weekend up north."

"Liz called. Her mother's sick. She's flying out to Montana in the morning. Sam had to come back to take care of Trey."

Reed stirred and opened his eyes. "Hello, pal," Casey said, looking at Reed with that same expression of calm reproach. "Sleeping in my bed?"

"What time is it?" Reed asked, staring at Maggie's feet in his hands.

"Time," Casey said with a contemptuous flick of his hand.

He fixed his gaze back on Maggie. She was aware now how it must look, with her and Reed draped across the sofa, embracing the other's legs. The open wine bottle on the coffee table. But surely Casey couldn't think that anything had really happened between them? "You should have called and told me you were coming back," she said, a hint of reproach creeping into her own voice. How long had he been sitting there in silence, watching them sleep?

"I tried. Your cell phone's off."

"Is it?" But she rarely turned off the phone.

Casey pointed to the answering machine for their landline phone on the end table beside the sofa. The machine was blinking one message. He pressed the button, and they all listened to Casey's voice explain that he and Sam were turning around and heading home. "Guess you weren't checking messages," he said when they'd finished listening to his recorded self.

"I guess not," she said, growing annoyed. How had he entered the house without her or Reed hearing, or Shamus? But Shamus knew the sound of Casey approaching the house and would not bark over that. No, she would not feel guilty. She'd done nothing wrong, because what, under the circumstances, could be done?

Or was Casey angry because he suspected what she might have done if the circumstances permitted?

"Look at you two," Casey said and sipped his whiskey. "Where have I been?"

She could hardly bear Casey's gaze on her, so she looked over at Reed, who was looking at Casey. Even now they couldn't break free of it. Yet still, still, she and Reed remained where they were. All three sat unmoving, waiting.

Finally, Reed broke the spell, pulling his feet away from her and sitting up. Maggie was disappointed; she couldn't help herself. She looked combatively at Casey. "You know what we should have?" Casey asked Maggie. "A three-some. You'd both love that, I'll bet."

Maggie tried to match his stare but could not. Never, never had she heard Casey say something so openly rude, not even in his worst moments. She turned to Reed. "Maybe you should go," she whispered.

Reed didn't answer for a moment. A part of him wanted to fly in the face of Casey's jealousy—was that what it was, simple jealousy?—but of course Maggie was right. Apparently he'd become fuel to their marital fire. He stood up and started looking around for his socks and boots. *Threesome:* it was a word that kept finding its way back to him.

"Don't go," Casey insisted. "Jesus, Maggie, why are you kicking him to the curb? A little foreplay, it's a start." He stood and held his arms wide as if to scoop them both up in a rollicking embrace.

Maggie looked at Casey almost with loathing. "Please stop," she said, and she stood as well. With all of them standing, everything felt too emphatic. Plus they were sobering up fast, which, strangely, wasn't helping matters.

Reed had found his shoes and one sock but couldn't find the other sock. Where had it gone to? And where was Shamus—had Shamus made off with his sock? The room felt wrong, tilted and off balance, but the alcohol alone wasn't to blame. Reed knew he had to leave; he shouldn't be here, didn't want to be here, at least anymore; this was all none of his business. And yet... He stopped searching for the recalcitrant sock when Casey turned to him and said, "Apparently, the only way I'm getting back into bed with her is if you're there, too. I mean, *really* there."

Maggie made a small embarrassed moan in the back of her throat. Reed didn't think through what he was doing, he simply acted. He stepped away from Casey and stood next to Maggie. It must have been the symbolism of Reed and Maggie standing side by side that made Casey's face curdle the way it did. "Touché, then!" he said. "Nothing left for us here."

Casey ran his hand along his collarbone. Reed tried to ignore this. He couldn't keep mythologizing the damn collarbone. He shook his head, feeling them careening toward some moment years in the making. He'd only meant to keep them all grounded in reason. At least, that's all he thought he'd meant. "Christ, Magpie, wake up!" Casey said. "He wants *me*. Don't you see that?" His voice was cool, hard and steady, each word a blow.

Reed and Maggie stood unmoving. Maggie's breathing had grown rapid, and her eyes had flamed to violet. Her hand itched to slap him, but she had never slapped anyone in her life. "Look at you, all agitated," Casey said with an unnatural smile. "Maggie the Cat! Maggie the Cat ready to jump off her hot tin roof."

This time Reed stepped in front of Maggie so he was now standing between them and face to face with Casey. "You're getting good at this," Reed said.

Tiny veins stood out in Casey's forehead, but he didn't say anything more. Maggie placed a hand on Reed's arm, possibly in solidarity or maybe just to steady herself. Then she went out into the kitchen for her car keys. Where had she left them? She started digging around in her purse. It was too much; she wouldn't listen; it was as if she were arguing with a perversion of Casey, one she'd helped create.

But of course Casey followed her into the kitchen. He couldn't let her leave with any shred of dignity. "Magpie, where are you going?" he asked, now almost placating.

The car keys, why couldn't she find them? To make such an exhibition of leaving, and then not be able to follow through on it, was intolerable. "Come on, stop it," Casey said.

But she was determined not to be appeased. He wasn't the only one who could charge out of a room in the middle of a fight! "Jesus, Magpie, do you want me to leave?" he said. "I'll leave. The house, you two can have it."

He grabbed at her purse, and for a moment they tugged at it. Then Casey had the purse in his hands. "Stop!" he said.

"Leaving now!" Reed called from the living room. "Keep the damn sock!"

Maggie pushed past Casey without a word, returned to the living room, and followed Reed out the door. He was walking toward his car, carrying his shoes and the lone sock. "I'm sorry," Maggie apologized when she caught up. She wanted to say more but nothing came to her, words like a hot stinging paste stuck in her throat.

Reed sat down on the car seat with his legs stretched outside, slipped on his sock and the accompanying shoe, then pushed his bare foot into the other shoe. "Talk about stepping back in time," he said.

Maggie's every nerve felt on fire, quivering with insult and injury. Casey was standing at the front door, looking out at them, at *her*, there was no escaping it. Almost, *almost*, she asked Reed if she could go with him, but where were the words for such an impossible need? "It's all…*wrong*" was what escaped the censor of her tongue.

"Not your fault." Reed squeezed her hand. Again she felt the bold electric leaping of her heart. "But how about I stay away from now on."

He smiled to reassure her, then slung his legs inside the car and shut the door. In a moment he was driving away, leaving Maggie with nothing but to go inside and return to the accident of her life. Only no, not an accident. More like a mirage she had willfully chosen years ago. What a girl she'd been then, committing her life to a foolish daydream!

Casey was no longer standing at the door, perhaps to make it easier for her to come inside. But returning to him had never been more difficult. For some time she stood out on the lawn, staring at the house which no longer felt like her home. Had it ever? She rubbed her arms and shivered in the heat. Despite the blur of her tears, she'd never more clearly seen that her marriage was doomed.

(19)

"Swear on it! We don't say a word. Not a fucking word. To anyone."

*

House arrest! At first Eddie couldn't believe his mother was serious. A criminal, was that what he was now? *Well, aren't you?* an inner voice prodded, and Eddie winced and tried to block out that voice. To protect himself against any more of his mother's questions and lectures—against *scrutiny*—he sealed himself off inside the cell of his room, away from the larger prison of the house. Alone in his self-imposed solitary confinement, he passed the time by listening to music on his iPod and watching Stretch slither around in the mulch of its cage. Hiding away from the world had become preferable to participating in it.

For the first three days of his "house arrest," Eddie reigned supreme over his own exile. He ignored his mother when she tapped on his door, stuck her head inside, and invited him—was there a trace of apology in her voice?—to come downstairs for supper. He wasn't sure what he would do if she demanded that he come downstairs. How far was he willing to push his isolation, his stubborn desire to challenge her? But she never insisted. Usually she brought a plate of food to him, and once she had gone back downstairs, he would eat but with little appreciation or gratitude. It was only slop for the condemned man. It would not feed his spirit. After he was finished eating, he would open his bedroom door long enough to set the plate on the floor with a quick snaky movement of his arm, then close the door and resume his banishment.

He never allowed himself to feel *too* guilty when he heard his mother climb back up the stairs and pause outside his bedroom door. He could picture her crestfallen glance at the plate before she bent down, picked the plate up, and returned downstairs. None of this gave him much pleasure, and yet he couldn't seem to stop himself from wanting to hurt his mother or distance himself from her. Once it was Christian who picked up the plate outside the door. "Lame-itude!" he said, clearly intending for Eddie to hear —*the brother*, of all people, standing in red T-shirted judgment of him!—but Eddie didn't shout anything in return. His solitude, the purposeful suppression of his voice, was the main source of his power now.

Gladly he would leave this house, turn around and not come back, if he could figure out a way to do it, if it would help him to feel better again, clear his head of the swampy thoughts that were overtaking him more and more these days. "A prison break," he muttered to himself and stared down at his wrists, which he had crossed as if shackled. There were his knuckles, still somewhat bruised and raw from the fighting.

He left his room only to use the bathroom down the hall, and he did this only when he had no choice. First he would cock his ear to the door and exit when he was convinced no one was around. As soon as he'd finished with his business, he would hurry back to his room. One night when Iris and Christian were asleep, Eddie crept out to the bathroom and saw his empty plate still on the floor, gleaming wickedly at him, a victim to his folly.

He never phoned or texted his friends, nothing that would break his austere sense of isolation. When Iris and Christian were at work and he was alone in the house, he still wouldn't leave his room except to go to the bathroom, not even to go downstairs and fix a sandwich. This wasn't just some cheap stunt! He didn't shower or brush his teeth, and he started turning off his bedroom fan so his room would turn hot and he'd have to sweat it out—*broil a little,* he told himself. Maybe his sweat would flush out some of the poison that ran, slow-moving and dark, through his blood like cyanide.

His main battle was against boredom. He had no access to the Internet or video games because the family computer was downstairs and his own rules forbid him to go there. Sometimes he spent long stretches of afternoon staring out the window. Once the window had been his escape route, but now it was useless to him other than the view it offered, which wasn't much. He could see his own backyard and an elbow of the Jackman's yard, the part with the old-fashioned clothesline that was always sporting jeans, shirts, blouses, flowery pillowcases and wrinkled sheets. Further off, he could make out a section of Clinton Street where a car would occasionally pass. Once he stared for several minutes at Mrs. Jackman peeking through her curtains at Iris and Arnie as they grilled steaks under Eddie's window. He continued to stare even when it appeared Mrs. Jackman had spotted him and was scowling up at him.

The boredom and lack of activity eventually turned him lethargic, and then, unbidden, more thoughtful. During the day he could manage to keep himself from thinking too deeply or remembering too much, but at night he couldn't drive the thoughts away. Once his eyes were closed, images flooded into his head like rubbish from a breaking dam—the fevered, jittery, guilt-laced memories of a convict. He saw the young man they'd beaten lying on the ground in the park, curled away from the blows and the kicks Eddie and Danny had rained down upon him. He heard again the young man's soft grunts each time a fist or a vengeful foot caught him in the head, chest, or ribs. Soon these nightly memories turned so persistent that Eddie had a hard time sleeping at all. If he closed his eyes he was *back there,* reliving that night of violence and misunderstanding and mesmerization at Danny's hands. Because wasn't that why he'd joined in the beating in the first place—because Danny had commanded it?

Or was there more to it? Eddie's memory of the attack was spotty. He didn't know for how long he and Danny had been lost in attack mode. There had been an indeterminate dark period of kicking and punching and stomping that felt like a very long time although probably had lasted only seconds. "Don't kill him!" Tess had shouted at them, her words weak and ineffectual against the dark tide that had washed over him. The next thing Eddie remembered was Tess pulling him away by his hair, and Unicorn Girl doing the same to Danny. On the opposite end of the park they heard voices, and so they simply scattered, all of them running in a blind rush away from the young man lying sick and concussed on the ground. They ran back to the car and met up with Soldier and his friends, who had abandoned their own chase. They all piled into their respective cars and drove off. Sobbing, shaking, Tess recoiled from Eddie when he sat too close, while Danny, still flushed with adrenaline, lay his hand on Eddie's shoulder in a rare motion of bonding. "McGregor and I beat the *snot* out of that crumb!" Danny bragged, his breath salty and sharp.

Soldier said that their douchebag had given them the slip. "The fuck smashed me in the face with a basketball and he's still roaming the earth," and Soldier shook his head and felt around at his nose to make sure nothing was broken.

"Sick, all of you!" Tess's mouth hung open as if she were about to pant.

Danny told her to shut the fuck up and quit pissing on them all the time. Tess said Danny was a primate, worse than a primate, a jelly-spined subspecies that had crawled on its belly from out of the primordial seas. Danny started to argue but Soldier took up for Tess, as he often did, and soon Soldier and Danny were arguing back and forth. The car veered dangerously close to a parked van when Soldier turned away from the wheel and smacked Danny on the side of the head. Unicorn Girl steered the car until Soldier was facing front again. "Another word out of your sorry cunt mouth and you walk home," Soldier said to Danny.

Danny glared at Soldier while Soldier glared back through the rearview mirror. *They hate each other*, Eddie thought. *They're not so different.* All of them were quiet for a while—raw, stung, and complicit.

Soldier made everyone swear an oath of silence. He couldn't risk any "legal bullshit" interfering with his Army plans. And they had promised, even Tess, all of them conscious of the dark tapestry of violence that ensnared them.

"One of us goes down, we all do," Soldier said. "Flushed into the sewer together."

Eddie tried to make amends with Tess, but when he placed his hand on hers to offer comfort, as he imagined a man would, she jerked her hand away. Her eyes were cold and hard; there was no forgiveness in them. "You're the worst," she whispered, and when he just looked at her, tongue-tied, she mouthed her final condemnation: "Coward!"

Now, lying sleepless in bed on his third night of exile, Tess's words began to haunt Eddie as much as the memory of the beaten college student. *Coward*: it was yet another label that hung over him, ready to stick.

The brother, dead in his cell
Waiting, thus, the raptures of hell

Eddie climbed out of bed and walked around his dark bedroom, prowling and restless. Then he lay back down on the bed and crossed his arms over his chest. *Don't kill him! Don't kill him!* A violent chill swept through his body. He sat up again, grabbed his belt, and lashed his bare back a few times, then in disgust tossed the belt across the room. The belt was no good, an empty punishing gesture. Yet again he lay down, his back stinging. Maybe it was right that his body should feel its own pain. In truth, he hardly felt like himself anymore, body and soul taken over by some angry spirit, *the other*, he thought, twisting him up and clogging his mind, forcing him to become who he wasn't.

He missed himself.

All night Eddie tossed in bed, biting into his pillow and wrestling with these thoughts, in the grip of an emotional convulsion. "I'm sorry, I'm sorry," he kept muttering. But the young man they'd beaten wouldn't leave Eddie alone! He was crouched inside Eddie, holding Eddie's heart in his hands, squeezing it back to life. Eddie rested his open hand against his chest. He couldn't shake the thought that his father was watching him and was disappointed.

By the next morning, Eddie, while spent and exhausted, was also more clear-headed. He couldn't—wouldn't!—go on like this. The thought hung over him, simple and pure. "Done," he muttered and changed into a fresh pair of clothes. Then he ventured sheepishly out of his cell of a room, even though Iris and Christian were at work and no one was around to witness his return to civilian life. Once downstairs he smelled his own funk and was ashamed. He took a hasty shower, his first in several days. The water pounded against his chest and liberated him. There came the fumbling, not terribly welcome realization that maybe his mother's punishment wasn't so unfair after all. Maybe it was necessary, possibly even earned, after what they'd done.

What *he'd* done. To please Danny.

Coward.

Don't kill him.

After his shower, Eddie tried phoning Tess. He knew she probably didn't want to talk to him yet, but he wanted to make the effort. Finally, after he'd phoned several times in several minutes without leaving a message, she answered. "Stop calling!" she said.

Eddie said he just wanted to make sure she was okay.

"I don't want to talk to you." There was an icy and tremulous lilt to her voice.

"That guy, you know, he's all right," Eddie said. "Just so you know. We didn't really hurt him that bad."

"You mean, *other* than the concussion and the broken ribs?"

Broken ribs? Eddie didn't remember hearing anything about broken ribs. Maybe Tess was exaggerating just to twist the knife. "You haven't said anything?" he asked.

Tess's laugh sounded scalding. "So *that's* why you called," she said.

"That's not why I called." But Eddie couldn't remember now why he *had* called, other than he didn't want her to hate him, which seemed like wishful thinking now.

"God!" Tess said. "I can't believe I let you hear me pee!" He heard her set the phone down for a moment and then pick it back up again. "I have to cover for your asses but I don't have to talk to any of you Neanderthals. At least not you."

After she'd hung up, Eddie knew he'd lost her. There was no point in trying to explain and justify himself because what explanation and justification was there? Danny had called out for Eddie's help, and so Eddie had given it.

As if on cue, Danny phoned Eddie not long after Eddie had spoken to Tess. But Eddie had no strong inclination to speak to Danny now. Yet Danny was persistent as always, so Eddie answered one of the calls because he didn't know how to avoid it any longer.

"Where the hell you been?" Danny asked.

"Nowhere." Eddie explained how he was under house arrest.

"Then you should have time to pick up your phone, right?"

Just the sound of Danny's voice put Eddie on edge, but not on edge in any way he'd felt with Danny before. At first Danny didn't seem to notice Eddie's remoteness. He told Eddie that the "asshole" they'd "pummeled" had apparently not turned them in. The guy must not remember what had happened, or else he hadn't gotten a good enough look to identify anyone.

Eddie pictured himself removing his penis from his underpants, all at Danny's Svengali bidding. But now Danny's voice only sounded scratchy and faintly aggravating, not capable of wielding such power. "Speak up, McGregor," Danny said.

"How could he not remember?" They had stood in a faceoff, staring at each other for a couple of minutes before all hell had broken loose.

"Take the damn gift horse, McGregor," Danny said. "Maybe we kicked the shit memory right out of him."

Danny laughed. Eventually, Danny stopped when he realized Eddie wasn't laughing with him. "You got something on your *mind*, McGregor?" he asked. It was as if he could sense his own weakening hold on Eddie, right there over the phone.

"Gotta run," Eddie said and hung up. He stared at the cell phone in his hand, expecting Danny to call back, but Danny did not call back. And while Eddie was relieved to hear he'd apparently gotten away with another crime, it also seemed strange that the victim wasn't telling the cops all he knew. A piece of the puzzle was missing somewhere.

Over the next few days, Eddie slowly indoctrinated himself back into his home life. What choice did he have, really? He still didn't talk much to either his mother or brother, but he also didn't spend all his time in his bedroom or creeping to the bathroom like a thief. A couple of times, when he was alone in the house, Eddie revisited his mother's closet, but here, too, some mesmerized spell was breaking. Now it felt as if he were donning his mother's clothes more out of routine. The compulsion he'd once felt had appeared out of nowhere only months ago, and now, just as quickly, was fading.

After a week of Eddie's "house arrest," Iris shifted course and allowed him to spend a weekend with Reed out at the lake. The cabin belonged to Reed's boyfriend, and while there Eddie couldn't help but notice evidence of his brother's relationship with Alex, hints of their everyday life together—several framed pictures of the two of them together; a pair of Alex's sneakers next to a pair of Reed's near the cabin's entrance; a note on a desk that read *Buckets of my tears,* apparently written by Alex since it wasn't Reed's handwriting. But these details didn't bother Eddie in the way they would have if Christian had been involved. While at the cabin, Eddie made one final attempt to escape his home life by asking to move in with Reed. If he had to live with a brother, why couldn't it be Reed? But Reed turned him down and so Eddie ended up back in his mother's house all the same. This upset him less over the passage of time. Maybe escape wasn't what he should be seeking now, after all.

In those final days of his "house arrest," Eddie yielded to whatever calm and reconciling force had settled around him. He couldn't explain and so didn't try to understand his own changing behavior. Now, when Christian returned home from work or walked around in one of those red *VIGILANT* T-shirts, Eddie no longer pointedly walked away, nor did he try to crowd Christian out of hallways or the bathroom. He no longer avoided any glass or fork his brother touched. Even the stink of *brother,* which for most of the summer he couldn't escape, now vanished from the house. He still didn't feel toward Christian what he knew he should feel for a brother, what he had, in fact, in his younger days, truly felt. But Christian was his brother, and there was not a damn thing he could do about it, now or ever. What was the point of fighting what irreducibly was?

As for Danny...when he started to call Eddie again, Eddie didn't pick up his phone. He'd have to talk to Danny when school started again, but now wasn't the time. On the last night of Eddie's "house arrest" (before his "full pardon," as Iris put it), Danny, apparently out of frustration, started leaving messages on their landline phone. After the second message, a little more harsh and demanding than the first, Iris asked Eddie, "Don't you want to talk to him?"

Iris and Eddie were sitting on the sofa together, watching *Se7en* on TV. It wasn't really his mother's type of movie—he had the feeling she was watching for his benefit—but Eddie loved movie mysteries. They were always so twisted, so intricately plotted. Murders by alphabet! A murder for each of the deadly sins! Ten people on an island getting picked off one by one according to a grisly nursery rhyme! Movie murders weren't like the murders in Barrow's Point, which just sort of happened and then hung in the background, leaving everyone astonished and feeling like idiots for not knowing what was going on.

"I don't know," Eddie said. "Not really."

Iris didn't ask any more questions. Absently she fingered the childish barrette she wore in her hair. A few minutes later, when Danny started leaving a third message, Iris made her let-me-handle-this face, went to the phone and picked up. "I'm sorry, Danny, Eddie can't come to the phone right now," she said.

Eddie heard Danny's muttering on the other end. "No, really, he can't," Iris said. Then there was a long pause while Danny spoke again. Iris blushed. "Don't call back," she said and hung up.

Almost instantly the phone rang again. Iris looked down at the number, sighed, unplugged the landline and the answering machine, and sat back down on the sofa.

For a few seconds they just stared at the TV. Two men walked through a clammy, darkly lit corridor. "What did he want?" Eddie couldn't help but ask. He felt actual heat in his chest.

"It doesn't matter." Iris removed the barrette from her hair and tossed it down on the coffee table. They stared back at the TV again. "I'm not sure about your pal Danny," Iris said.

There was a time—only a couple weeks ago, actually—when Eddie would have taken these words as an insult and leapt to Danny's defense, but now he felt little loyalty. Danny was fading away from him in a way he couldn't explain. Iris said goodnight and went off to bed. Eddie sat alone for a while. The movie was only on the third victim, representing sloth. He didn't have the energy to sit out the movie until the end when the head of the young detective's wife was served to him in a box. Eddie turned off the TV and waited. But what was he waiting for? His mind drifted to the man he'd seen on the street corner the night he'd run out into the storm. Why did he now wish he'd met this man, even though, at the time, Eddie had run away as soon as the man made a friendly gesture? A different compulsion started tugging at Eddie now, one he didn't recognize at first and didn't especially care to acknowledge. But it was there inside of him, some motion or movement born from his days of self-exile. Eventually, he followed it, as he'd followed other compulsions in the past, and it led him upstairs to Christian's bedroom. Eddie paused outside the partially open bedroom door. Even now he wasn't sure why he was here. There was Christian, his brother, with that pale skinny body Eddie had loathed once but now seemed harmless enough. He was packing up the first of his boxes in preparation for when he moved out of the house and into a college dorm room for the fall semester, even though he was only moving across town to the Barrow University campus. When Christian noticed Eddie, his face settled into its customary lines—part suspicion, part dismissal. "What do you want?" he asked.

Eddie stood in the doorway with the posture of someone who was waiting to be granted permission to enter. But no, maybe it was better if he didn't enter.

"Eddie?" Christian said.

His name coming from his brother's mouth was what untied his tongue, the words coming to him unbidden: "Sorry."

Christian looked, frankly, dumbfounded.

As did Eddie, who tasted the unending dust in his mouth. "We all are," he said for greater absolution. And when Christian looked at him, still uncomprehending, Eddie shook his head and walked away, right past his mother's bedroom, unaware that she was on the opposite side of the door, listening too.

(20)

The next afternoon, Iris took off from work to drive to the other side of town to speak to Ticker and Alberta Sternes. It wasn't just Danny's perverse behavior from the evening before that was on her mind, although naturally it was that too. The boy was falling out of line and something needed to be done. But some hunch was propelling her forward, a hunch similar to the one she'd felt when she'd returned home and caught Eddie wearing her dress. Eddie's apology to Christian last night was part of that hunch, part of her suspicion. His cryptic addition at the end of the apology, *"We all are,"* was what had given Iris pause. Somehow—she was sure of it—Danny was part of that *we*.

The day was humid and overcast. Iris drove over the bridge and through the industrial side of town, where she passed several men unloading skinned cow carcasses from the back of a large truck. Iris tried to remain unseeing. But no, she had spent too much of her life looking away, and the ravaged animals seemed to her, right now, significant. For a moment she felt almost a moral obligation to bear witness to their brutal ends, but she'd already driven past the warehouse and so she simply pressed onward. She drove out of town and turned onto the thin stretch of pavement, cursed with several potholes, which led to the Sternes's place.

After she'd pulled up into the driveway and parked the car, she hesitated about going inside. She glanced at the house. It needed a new paint job and rain gutters along the roof were badly in need of repair, but otherwise it could have been anyone's house. Yet there was something a little unsettling about it that went beyond the borderline physical neglect. A dog with matted and patchwork-seeming fur was lying on the porch and staring back at the car. She kept waiting for it to start barking but it never did.

Quit playing defense and put the fucking faggot on the phone! That was what Danny had said to her last night before she'd hung up on him. The level of contempt in his voice, not to mention his brazenness and the barely suppressed anger in his voice, was what had caused her to hang up. Now here she was with a fire at her back.

Eventually, Iris left the car and started walking toward the house. She still imagined a vague meaty stench in the air. She tugged at her blouse, sticking to her skin like cheap glue. From somewhere out back she heard the sound of heavy pounding, hammer against wood, but Iris didn't dwell on this. She kept her eye on the inscrutable dog. "Hi, boy," she said as she stepped onto the porch. The dog was a mongrel sort with a narrow face like a coyote. The dog stopped chewing on the knotted red dishtowel between its paws long enough to growl at her, a somewhat lackluster growl, yet Iris felt suddenly quite unwelcome.

The front door was open but the screen door latched shut. Through the screen Iris could see Alberta Sternes lying across the sofa on her back, one arm flung across her face. Her other hand was holding a glass to her chest. The TV was turned on to a soap opera, the one Iris had caught Eddie watching only a week ago, but this did nothing to make the scene feel more inviting. Iris knocked on the screen door, saying Alberta's name, and when she didn't respond, Iris tapped again, a little more insistently this time. "Alberta?" she said again.

Finally, Alberta looked up from the sofa with a jerk of her head. She rose and moved to the door, disheveled as usual, wearing a man's T-shirt over a pair of underwear. A ragged dishtowel similar to the one on which the dog was chewing was slung over her shoulder. Or was it only half of a dishtowel? She squinted through the screen door at Iris. "May I help you?"

"It's Iris McGregor," Iris said. "I called and asked if I could speak to you and Ticker."

Alberta's face relaxed. "Yes, of course," she said. "You should probably come inside," and she opened the screen door even as she looked self-consciously around the room.

Iris noticed the inside of the house was similar to the outside, unruly but not terribly so. The slight meaty smell outside was replaced inside by the quite distinct smell of grease and pork chops, despite the three fans in the living room all humming and rattling at full blast.

Alberta did not offer Iris a seat, just peered at her while clutching the glass so loosely it looked in danger of slipping from her fingers. Iris recognized that it was vodka inside the glass but she cast no judgment on Alberta for this, remembering how it had been for her that first year after Carl's death. "I'd like to speak to both you and your husband if I may," Iris reminded her.

"You may indeed. Only Ticker isn't here right now."

The hammering sound out back drifted into them from the open windows. Something was being constructed, something large and hulking. "Okay, maybe the two of us can speak then," Iris said.

"The dream I was having!" Alberta exclaimed. "I was a girl again and living in Belle Plaine and there was a nuclear explosion of some sort. It was night and I was alone. I saw the nuclear snowfall through the kitchen door and it was really very pretty, but at the same time, I knew it would burn me alive.

Then I saw the refrigerator had defrosted itself. The puddle on the floor looked like what was left of a vast ocean."

"Is your son at home?" Iris was sick enough of her own dreams. "Danny, I mean."

"Daniel? I don't know." Alberta looked around, baffled. "Daniel!" she called and passed from room to room, lost in her own home. "I don't think he's here," she said when she'd returned. She didn't hear, or was ignoring, the pounding from outside. "What has he done now?"

Iris recounted Danny's numerous phone messages, his final nasty conversation with her.

Alberta sipped at the remaining sluggish liquid in the bottom of her glass. "I can't do a thing with him these days," she admitted. "With either one of the boys. Although they're not exactly boys anymore, are they?"

"But someone has to do something. They can't just—*harass* people—"

Alberta sat down on the sofa but still didn't offer Iris a seat. She couldn't shake the thought that Alberta was treating her circumspectly. "Something's happened between Danny and Eddie," Iris blurted. "Something..." She could hardly bear to finish the sentence. She wasn't even sure what it was she wanted to say.

Only it seemed that Alberta knew what Iris was trying to say even if Iris didn't. "Then you know?" Alberta asked in a half-whisper.

Iris just looked at her.

"It's true," Alberta said. "They beat up that boy in the park. A whole pack of them did."

Iris drew in a breath, the bluntness of the remark catching her off-guard. At the same time she wasn't surprised, as if she'd suspected this in some unacknowledged part of herself. "How long have you known?" Iris asked, trying to sound calm.

"Nothing stays buried in *this* house." Alberta ran a hand through her snarled hair. "Iris, sometimes I pretend they're not even my boys. I think, maybe, when they were babies, when my back was turned, someone took my boys and gave me different babies. Two different times they did this, in two different years. Two babies all filled with poison so they would match their daddies and uncles. Have you ever had that feeling?"

The incessant pounding and building outside stopped and was followed by an expansive silence. "No, never," Iris said.

Alberta fingered the rim of her glass. The glass looked as if it had been sloppily kissed. "Well, you have three sweet gay boys," Alberta said. "I wish I had a sweet gay boy. I would love him to death. But maybe Edward isn't gay? Daniel swears he is, but, you know, Edward doesn't *act* like he is."

With difficulty Iris ignored the comment. "What are we going to do about this?" she asked.

"Do?" Alberta said. "Why, nothing, I guess."

Iris shook her head. Her brain was starting to feel fizzy. "We can't rat out our own children, you see," Alberta added.

Before Iris could answer, a door banged open and shut in the kitchen, and then Ticker Sternes limped into the room. His face glimmered with sweat and he held a hammer in his hand. His face was twisted into a scowl that only altered somewhat when he saw Iris. She couldn't fault him, with her own smile so stiffly held in place. She turned to Alberta. "I thought he wasn't home," Iris couldn't resist saying.

But Alberta looked befuddled at the sight of him. "Ticker, what are you doing here?"

He ignored Alberta and kept his eyes focused on Iris. "Hello," he said.

"Ticker, Iris knows," Alberta said.

Ticker narrowed his eyes and only now looked, rather severely, at his wife. "Knows *what?*"

Alberta smiled at Iris. "Isn't he a dreary liar? And he used to lie so well!"

"Standing right here." Then Ticker glanced down at himself as if to make sure.

For the first time Iris realized there were others out in the kitchen. She couldn't tell how many. She heard only the sound of water swallowed down male throats. Or at least she assumed it was water. She had a sense that the conversation was not taking place only inside this room. "I think," Iris said, lowering her voice, "we have to turn them in."

But she said this tentatively, because did she really want to turn Eddie in, her own son?

Ticker must have noticed Iris's hesitation because his smile was indulgent. "When I was eighteen, I put a firecracker in a teacher's mailbox and blew the damn thing up," he said. "For that the Coast Guard went AWOL on me. I was branded fuckup and so before you—"he floundered a bit as if stuck in his own sentence—"I stand wrecked."

"But we can't just—overlook this."

Glasses were set down on the kitchen counter and she heard the sound of feet shuffling about. None of the people in the kitchen were speaking, that was the odd thing. "Not sure what else we can do, Mrs. McGregor," Ticker said. "What's done is lost at sea."

Lost at sea? Since his accident, Ticker frequently had a problem finding the right words to express what he meant. Certain words and phrases stumbled into his sentences and stuck out like bulls with their horns caught in a rose shrub.

"A lot of boys will get into trouble if we speak up now," Ticker continued. "So what's our point?"

And in truth, Iris wasn't sure what the point was. Was silence the answer after all, a carefully considered collusion between her and Eddie and the entire Sternes family? After a moment of feeling seduced, lured to the simplicity of silence, her conscience reared up. No, wasn't silence part of the problem here? Silence, hiding, tape over the mouth to gag them all? "My son's a police officer," she reminded them.

Ticker laughed, a bleak laugh. "My brother too," he said. "So what? You think they give a shit some guys jumped a whacker?"

Iris felt as if the earth were shifting beneath her feet. "I think," Iris said, "my son would care." She felt no blaze of moral superiority saying this. Rather, it was as if she were feeling her way through this moral quandary, trying to find the position that made the most sense.

Ticker's eyes had gone dark. "You can't say anything, Rose," he said.

"Iris," Alberta corrected him. "Her name is Iris—"

"Shut the fuck up!" Ticker snapped at his wife. "She can't go running her mouth off, no matter what name she is."

Ticker's voice was so forceful that Iris didn't even notice at first when the other men stepped into the living room. But then the room was filled with men, men's bodies and their odors and their sweat-spotted T-shirts, and they seemed to crowd the room although there were really only four of them: Ticker and his sons, and a man with a crew cut and one arm. Two of them were smoking, Danny and the man with one arm. Soldier had a dirty blue bandana tied too tightly around his scalp, and beads of sweat ran from beneath the kerchief. They were all looking at her with the same troubled expression, their eyes at once challenging and discrediting her. They had come in from out back, hot and irritated and uneasy now with her presence in the room, her *conscience* in the room, like a hovering aura that cast off a glare.

Even now Iris did not back down. "I'm sorry," she said, "but I think there's only one thing that *can* be done."

Ticker turned to Danny, who stood off from the rest of them—Danny and his slick T-shirt with no sleeves, an undefined arrogance about him. Iris didn't like him, she realized now. She never had. "Mrs. McGregor there says you've left phone messages around," he said.

Danny shrugged. He didn't bother to look at Iris at all. Ashes from his cigarette fell in a wan drift to the floor.

"Maybe if you apologized," Ticker said, "we can just move ahead and let this dirty laundry wash itself."

"No, that's not necessary," Iris said. "I mean…it isn't about that anymore."

But there was a hard little pressure squeezing at her temple. She didn't know how to extricate herself from the situation. The front door loomed out of reach. It would seem such a deliberate act, to leave now.

"He won't pick up his damn phone," Danny said.

"He doesn't have to pick up his damn phone if he doesn't want to!" Iris said, surprising herself.

"Tell Iris you're sorry, Daniel," Alberta said. Iris had nearly forgotten about her and couldn't help but feel comforted, even in a small way, by another woman's presence in the room.

"Say it," Ticker said.

Danny muttered his apology. "Done," Ticker said. "There, you see? We're all clean now."

The older son, the one they called Soldier, stared at Iris in a way she considered, almost, voracious. There was an appetite behind his sneer, only not a sexual one. "She knows?" he said finally. "Who the fuck told her?"

So they had been eavesdropping on her conversation from the kitchen, after all. Iris glanced over at Alberta, who was holding the partial dishtowel in her hands now and staring at it as if wondering where the other half had gone to. Perhaps she'd already forgotten her role in leading Iris to the truth.

"She's not going to say anything, is she?" Soldier asked, speaking as if Iris wasn't in the room with them while staring as if she were the only one present.

"Mrs. McGregor knows what is." Ticker picked something from his teeth. A bit of detritus, possibly, or a seed of some sort. He shuffled into the kitchen, and there was a loud banging sound that made them all wince. Had Ticker swung the hammer at something? Then she heard the screen door slam shut behind him as he stepped back outside. A heavy silence followed. Everyone felt strange now that Ticker had left so clumsily. The man with one arm backed away and followed Ticker outside.

Soldier and Danny made no move to follow their father. They looked sinister at that moment, sinister yet also a bit clownish, their contempt for Iris so evident it was somewhat insulting. She knew not to confront them or acknowledge their disrespect in any way. Iris turned to Alberta, who was still staring down at the dishtowel in that odd manner. "Thank you for your time," Iris said.

But when Iris turned to leave, Soldier stood in front of her with his arm against the door, blocking her exit. His body was so close Iris could feel the heat radiating off him, could see how his eyes, bright and yet so empty, repudiated her. "Excuse me, I'm leaving now," she said, struggling to remain polite although her voice had taken on an edge of its own.

Soldier didn't move out of her way. What was it about his coiled-inward aggression that sparked such recognition in her? "Don't be in a hurry, Mrs. McGregor," he said. There was veiled insinuation mixed in with the deferential (if mocking) *Mrs. McGregor*. Quite deliberately he moved his eyes up and down her body, not in a lascivious way but nonetheless in a way that was meant, perhaps, to badger and disconcert her. "Did *he* tell you?" Soldier asked in a mock conspiratorial way.

Iris met his eyes. She had come out here not expecting to even see Soldier. How had he become the major obstacle in front of her now? "No, *he* didn't," she said.

Soldier nodded with a false thoughtfulness and leaned down as if to whisper in her ear, but then he didn't whisper at all. "We're good about all this, then?" and he put a finger to his mouth and pantomimed *sssh*.

Iris didn't answer. Why should she? This was madness, such open rudeness out of this young man who, as a boy, she remembered now, had come to her door once to sell "band candy." Iris had even bought a box before discovering he wasn't in band. The thought of either of Alberta's boys playing a trumpet or a saxophone, how had she ever fallen for it?

Her silence caused Soldier to bristle in some unseen way. "You don't want to be sorry about all this," he said in a calm way, his mouth large and moist, the mouth of a zoo animal standing too close to the bars of its cage during feeding time. Iris didn't flinch but gazed back into his face as if to reach his inner self. What did he represent to her other than some monstrous reflection of what path her life might have veered if he'd been her own son? Soldier shook his head, trying to rid himself of her reproachful stare. It nearly excited her, the thought that she'd made him uncomfortable.

Thinking they'd reached a detente of sorts, Iris reached around him for the door knob, but Soldier adjusted his weight so she was again unsuccessful. Did he really mean to detain her? "Alberta," Iris said, glancing over at her, who had looked up from the frayed cloth and was staring, somewhat disbelievingly, at her own boys.

"Frederick, Iris has to leave now," Alberta said, wringing the dishtowel in her hands.

Danny, the avid witness, was leaning against the wall, the cigarette reduced nearly to a stub between his lips. His expression was blank, neither sympathetic nor reproachful.

"You see, Mrs. McG, I'm leaving for boot camp next month," Soldier said to Iris. "Have you heard? Can't jeopardize that, you know, with any shit on the record."

"Maybe you should consider that next time before you beat someone up," she said.

"Maybe I don't," Soldier said. "Maybe my idiot brother and your dipshit son do."

Danny cursed under his breath, the blank expression wiped clean from his face, but Iris's eyes were fixed on Soldier. The animal scent was rising off him, a smell like hot wet fur, almost, while her blood ran cold inside her veins. She was wrong to have come out here alone, wrong to have tried to see through to Soldier's humanity when it was humanity itself, she thought a little wildly, that he could scarcely endure. In one swift and startling moment, as if part of some ghastly vision, Iris saw the life ahead for Soldier: the alcohol and the brutality, the numbing inarticulate depressions, the boot to the throat of any man or woman who dared challenge him. She saw the misery of his heart shrunk and hardened to the size and weight of a small river stone, the way he would leap to violence to defend himself, and the cold ruinous life he would live as a result, angry and insular, crying out in the night with a gun to his head. The military wouldn't save him. The things he would see and do over there would only hasten him down the path of his own destruction. In a rush, her heart lurched out to him. "You poor soul," she said before she could stop herself.

And she saw how his face shuddered for a moment—fleeting, but there!—as if he, too, saw the ragged pieces of his future reflected in her face. Or maybe what he saw was her pity for him, an awful mother-like pity. He grabbed hold of her wrist, twisting it hard enough for Iris to cry out, more in shock and indignation than pain.

Alberta jumped out of her chair and lunged at Soldier, swatting his shoulders, arms, and head with the ravaged dish towel. "What have you done with him?" she cried, showing her teeth. "Give him back! I want Freddy back!" Then, with a burst of passion, she turned on Iris. "Get out! You, *you* can leave, why are you still standing there? Run! *Run!*"

The fury in Alberta's voice shocked and galvanized them. Soldier backed away from his mother's assault, from the seer's truth in Iris's eyes. Iris seized the opportunity and hurried out the door. At least the growling dog with the mouth full of towel was no longer on the porch. She speed-walked toward her car, breathing a sigh of relief that she was out in the open again, away from that house of shameless men, but it wasn't until she was at her car and fumbling with the door that she realized Danny had followed her out of the house. He stood in the middle of the yard and watched her with a laconic, almost clinical eye, again impossible to read, as if his face meant to offer up as little clue as possible to his own future. She climbed into the car and shut the door, but when she turned the key in the ignition, there was only a feeble sputtering sound. She tried a second time, and for a disbelieving moment feared someone had tampered with her car. "Dead!" Danny called out.

When the engine turned over on the third try, Iris released a breath and backed out of the driveway. On an impulse she opened her car window, stuck out her arm and flipped Danny the bird as she straightened the car onto the road and drove away. It was only when she'd reached city limits, passing again those ugly warehouses with the evil stench in the air, that tears rushed to her eyes and she pulled to the side of the road and cried out in anger.

*

Iris intended to phone Reed and Arnie as soon as she got home and tell them everything she'd learned. Only once she walked into her house, she didn't—couldn't—call. Instead she poured herself a glass of white wine and went to sit in the backyard. Theo Jackman was running his rogue sprinkler again. How much of the earth's water was he planning to waste with that ever-straining, ever-revolving contraption? Still, watching the water shoot forward in choppy arcs was hypnotic, the water glittering like airborne diamonds. Lenore was out in her yard, on the opposite side of the bushes, clipping at undergrowth with a garden shears. She was wearing a pair of white gloves too elegant for garden work. Iris was almost irritated to see her, but she couldn't very well begrudge Lenore access to her own yard.

Iris turned away from Lenore. The behavior of Soldier and Danny, even Ticker for that matter, had shaken her more than she cared to admit. And that odd pitying connection she'd felt for Soldier, where had that come from? Yet despite her anger and confusion, or maybe because of it, she couldn't decide if Ticker and Alberta had a point. Their thoughts were now meshed with her own, complicating matters. Did she really want to risk Eddie to this exposure and the kind of judgment it would bring? If Soldier was to be believed, then Eddie and Danny were guilty of the actual beating. She couldn't fathom it. Never had she imagined Eddie capable of such aggression. No, not aggression, already she was softening it. Violence: the word reared forward to slap her in the face. All summer she had feared violence would come to one of her sons; it had never occurred to her that one of her sons would commit the violence. Could Eddie end up in jail even though he was still a minor? And hadn't Reed mentioned that the victim himself was not saying all that he knew? If the victim wanted to forget and move on, perhaps there was no point in dragging the whole hateful incident back into the spotlight.

But keeping silent about it also seemed wrong. Terribly wrong, and weak-willed, kowtowing to convenience and the path of least resistance.

After a few minutes, Eddie joined her out in the backyard. He was bare-foot, in shorts, and held a bottle of grape soda in his hand. Grape soda! It har-kened back to the boy he'd once been before the moody adolescent had begun to intrude, the one who, despite her numerous protests, came home smelling like beer and pot. "Why aren't you at work?" he asked.

Eddie had been abstract and lost inside himself for so many months that Iris was surprised he even noticed she was upset. Had he come outside to check on her? Now, when she most wanted privacy and space to think, her son had turned observant? She didn't even know what to say to him. Where were the words for this? There was so much about him that she knew and he didn't know she knew. It made her feel indecently omnipotent. "I don't want you hanging out with Danny Sternes anymore," Iris said, "or that creepy brother of his."

Eddie sat down in the grass beside her. There was so much of Carl in his pensive expression that Iris had to turn away. "Why?" he asked.

Why? There was always the why. "Never mind," she said. She wasn't talk-ing like herself, decisive and even somewhat brusque. "Just do it, please."

She was expecting a fight, so when Eddie agreed, she looked at him with suspicion. The past few days he'd been almost too quiet and reflective, as if no longer quite inhabiting his body. "That's it?" she asked. "Just like that?"

There was hesitation in Eddie's eyes, maybe even regret, but he didn't re-tract what he'd said. A rustle from the bushes reminded Iris of Lenore, who had stopped clipping the hedges but still hadn't gone inside. "This is a private conversation, Lenore!" Iris called out.

She caught sight of Lenore's flustered face between two of the trimmed bushes. "Well, I never!" Lenore muttered. She dropped the sheers with a clatter onto the ground and went into her house through the back door, still clutching a couple pieces of shrubbery in her hands.

Iris turned back to Eddie. "Thank you," she said and couldn't help but smile. How nostalgic she was feeling, suddenly, for only a few days ago when the bulk of what she was worried about was getting Eddie to eat or to come out of his room, or wondering whether he was still messing around in her closet.

She didn't know how to reconcile these two sides of him, the boy who was secretly trying on her clothes with the boy who would rashly join in the beating of a young man. A picture popped into Iris's mind: Eddie wearing one of her dresses and hitting a man over the head with her purse. She burst out laughing; she couldn't help herself. It almost frightened her, how unreasonably funny the image struck her.

"Mom," Eddie said with a goofy affection. "You seem—weird."

Even the way he said "weird" sounded playful and boyish. Or was his light grape mustache only giving her that impression? "Yes, well, it's going around, isn't it?" she said and took another sip of the wine.

By the time she climbed into bed that night, her nerves had calmed some, although things still felt gray and unresolved. Eddie, Christian, Reed—the names of her sons swirled inside her head, entwining together like a helix molecule. She almost wished that Carl would return to her in a dream and give her another nudge, but Carl had stopped coming since that night he'd held her feet in his lap. No, she was past expecting guidance from The Great Beyond. The fact Soldier had grabbed her with such force, his inward disgust manifesting itself outward in physical form, was what worried her now and rooted her to reality. "The unleashing of the furies," Iris said, perhaps to Carl's nonpresence in the room.

(21)

At first, in her confusion, Iris thought the police had come in the night for Eddie.

For what other reasonable explanation was there, as she opened her eyes to the loud, revving sound of engines, of cars pulling into her driveway—the noise, the sheer *force* of the noise rising up at her. She groped awake, her heart accelerating, her mind leaping on instinct to Eddie. He was in danger! She knew this deeply, without reason. *They* had come for him, *they, they, they.* As she was feeling her way out of bed—*wake up!* her mind cried out—several headlights were turned on full blast, flooding the room with a harsh light.

Iris grabbed for a T-shirt on the corner chair, one Arnie had left behind and that fit her like a tent. She slipped it on, unable to think, only to react, to scurry for movement, operating more on a sensory level than an analytical one. But why would the police storm the house for a fifteen-year-old boy at (her eyes glanced at the clock) 1:25 a.m.? How had Reed, Arnie, Casey, any of them allowed for it?

Eddie was already standing out in the hall. There was something about the way he held his body, tense and guarded, and the knowing look on his face that suggested he knew something she did not. Iris didn't have time to ask questions. "Go back to your room!" she demanded as she hurried downstairs, trying to *hear*, trying to make sense of the voices that had begun to shout in between blasts of the car horns. But why wouldn't the police come to her door instead of shouting from the street? Once she was standing in the living room bright with the unnaturally aggressive light, her mind slipped into place and she understood that whoever was outside was not the police. There was a mocking, chaotic sound to the shouting, punctuated with brutish laughter and drunken catcalls.

And then she knew, at last, who was outside.

For a moment she did nothing, unable to grasp a course of action, her mind cluttered and uncertain. All she could think was *we are under siege*. Eddie had followed her downstairs after all, and they stood together, astounded by the glare and the taunting jeers. Eddie's and Christian's names were called out here and there, and rising up like a seismic wave to engulf them, Iris heard: *faggot, faggot, faggot.*

When she glanced over at Eddie, their eyes momentarily locked, his humiliation and shame so palpable that a fire tore through her heart. "Stay here!" she ordered again. "Promise." And she stood and she waited, ignoring the jeering outside, until he had nodded and his lips moved for what, in the heat of the moment, passed for agreement.

Damn them, damn them: Iris felt an impotent rage swell inside her, even worse than what she'd felt yesterday after her encounter with the Sternes men. The danger had come to her doorstep at last, as she'd always feared it would, only in the alarming, unexpected form of people she knew.

She opened the door and stepped onto the front steps. How many cars were there? Two? Three? And weren't they parked on the lawn instead of the driveway? She squinted but couldn't see past the malevolent yellow glare, almost theatrical, her front yard lit up and exposed as some garish carnival sideshow. Iris waved her arms toward the light, no, toward the jeering voices beyond the light. She wasn't even sure what words she shouted. An uproar of laughter greeted her, the shouts and catcalls of men, or mostly men, because wasn't that also the high-pitched hyena cackle of a woman? A shadow darted out into the middle of the lawn and away from the blinding headlights, a gremlin crouched low to the ground. Iris stepped down onto the grass.

She heard it then, an ominous whistling drone followed by a sputtering red light that shot toward her like a missile. She froze; she knew this moment. Then an explosion went off not two feet away with such a deafening force that the air rocked as if upended and she dropped to the ground in shock. Two more explosions followed, ripping at the air and shaking the earth, a heaving force meant to punish, perhaps to destroy. Glass shattered in one of the living room windows at the same moment a pressure popped in one of Iris's ears and her hearing went numb, followed by a vague ringing. She crawled toward one of her shrubs. She could scarcely catch her breath, the explosion and the demon lights too overwhelming, as if she had stepped out of her immaculate home and into a war zone.

From the corner of her eye she saw a flash of motion. Naked except for the pair of boxers he was wearing, Christian ran past her, brandishing a baseball bat in his hands. She grabbed at him and called out, but couldn't prevent him from running toward the light. Iris felt more than heard another swelling of drunken laughter, and for an instant had the quite mad sense that was Eddie's voice heckling from behind the headlights. She tried to climb to her feet but her legs collapsed back out from under her. A dog started to bark, and there was a shadow of someone else running across her lawn. A man grabbed hold of Christian and held him back—was that Theo Jackman?—while pointing something at the glare of headlights. Reality swooped back in a heaving rush and Iris cried out, "Don't shoot!"

Through her ringing ears she heard curses, car doors slamming, tires grinding as the cars backed out of her driveway in full throttle retreat. The cars spun off into the night as quickly as they'd come, until the mocking sound of car horns grew more distant and then disappeared.

For a paralyzing few seconds, there was silence except for the barking of dogs. A dog was barking down the street and a different dog was barking nearby. Lenore hurried over to where Iris was still crouched on the ground. Lenore wore a silly baby doll nightie, and there were a couple of silver slashes of zinc under her eyes. "Unconscionable!" she muttered as she helped Iris to her feet. But it was no use, Iris couldn't stand yet on her own volition, her legs still noodle-y and foreign-seeming, certainly not her own. With Lenore's help, Iris inched her way toward the front steps and sat down.

Theo walked over to her in his slippers and bathrobe, a surreal soldier with lumbago and a gun in his hand. Christian followed Theo, and he too seemed shell-shocked, unable to fully grasp what had happened. The dog down the street had stopped barking, but the other dog kept at it. "Just a sec," Lenore said, and she hurried over to her house, went inside, and after a moment, the barking ceased.

The silent night settled back in, disturbingly, around them. "You all right now, Iris?" Theo asked, or at least that's what she thought he asked through that dull ringing still in her ears.

Iris shook her head. All right? She looked out over her yard, ravaged and attacked, the well-mowed lawn churned up and the large ominous spray-painted letters on the grass, red tainted letters visible in the moonlight, forming a clear message: R.I.P. So there it was—terse, declarative, confrontational, a final jeering reminder. To Iris it felt as if the threat had been blasted into her lawn by a force larger than them all, spelled out by the halitosis of the earth.

Lenore returned and handed Iris, of all things, a glass of lemonade. "God-damn idiots!" Theo said and glared back at the road where the cars had disappeared. "Do you know who those punks were, Iris?"

"Maybe," she managed to say and took an obligatory sip of the somewhat tart lemonade. But of course she did know. She'd known since that moment when she'd met Eddie's eyes, the tacit understanding that happens between mother and son when they know what has come for them just outside the door.

Eddie. Iris turned and saw him through the open door, standing in the same position he'd been when she'd stepped outside. She wanted to go to him but was still not physically capable of it. Adrenaline coursed through their blood, Iris could feel it, not just in her but in the others as well, a glow like radium running just beneath their skin. The air still felt disturbed by small echoing ripples. Iris's throat closed up with tears and her hands trembled. Such violence—never had she experienced such violence, such *personal* violence, right in her own yard.

"Everyone's fine now, Iris," Lenore said. Iris nodded and clutched at Lenore's hand with a warm rush of gratitude toward her voyeuristic neighbors who had exasperated her only hours ago, and yet who had rushed outside so unheedingly, even in the midst of explosions, to protect her and the boys. How was it possible they'd lived side by side for so many years and yet always seemed slightly at odds with one another, that they had never quite become friends?

Theo paced back and forth, still wired and not fully satisfied with the outcome. Finally, he glanced at the gun in his hand and shoved it in the pocket of his bathrobe. "Hell, Iris, it's not even loaded," he said. "Just wanted to scare the bastards."

"You did that all right." Christian seemed unembarrassed that he was standing outside in plain view in his pin-striped boxers. He sounded almost admiring of Theo and the gun, Christian of all people, an admiration that felt to Iris distinctly male and apart from her. "Assheads!" and Christian cleared his throat as if he meant to spit but then thought better of it.

"Assheads who knew from explosives," Theo added. "Those were more than just bottle rockets they were using."

"Should we call the police?" Lenore asked.

"No!" Iris said. Now wasn't the time. In the morning she would speak to Reed and tell him what she knew, everything she should have told him yesterday. Enough with the silences, the obstructing secrets, the lack of faith in each other, the lack of faith, period. Enough of blood and savagery and the veiled sinister threats, the nasty whispered asides, the straining to hear and to understand what was said between the lines. The danger she'd felt closing in around her and the boys over the past months was now visible, had taken on a concrete human shape, and so was made flesh and weak as anyone. Relief and a stunned dark thankfulness passed through her, that she knew now whom she was fighting. It had taken the blinding headlights, the blaring horns and marauding explosives, the jeering message on her lawn to make her path, at last, clear to her.

Lights had snapped on in a few of the houses down the street. A handful of the neighbors were gathered out on their lawns or on the street corner, in robes and nighties and shorts and various other forms of nightwear, Therese Daniels with a butcher knife clutched in her hand. They stared over at the Mc-Gregor and Jackman houses like witnesses to the pillaging of a village.

Theo glanced through Iris's open front door, just now noticing Eddie, who still had not moved. "You boys better take your mother back inside," Theo said. "They won't be coming back tonight. I'll sit up just in case." Then he turned and shouted at their wraith-like neighbors: "Go back to bed, you gawkers!"

(22)

His fault. Somehow, again, all of this was his fault.

For they had come for him. His name they'd called out, his name they'd ridiculed. Even when they were taunting Christian and Iris, he was the reason for it.

The vortex, the figurehead, the source. *Flushed into the sewer together.*

Eddie lay awake in bed for the rest of the night, unable to sleep. He wanted to fight someone and he wanted to hide, and it was all a clot inside him. When the first explosion had gone off near his mother, a wild anger and panic had flooded through him, and yet his body had simply *frozen.* He hadn't stayed inside because he'd promised Iris that he would. He'd stayed inside because his feet had rooted to the ground as if encased in cement. And though he'd wanted to run outside and help his mother, his body had turned off and not allowed it.

Even Christian had run outside! Theo and Lenore Jackman too, all of them ready to face the firing squad together. Eddie alone had remained in the safety of the house, standing in place like a statue hewn out of marble.

Coward.

And why had they come for him in the first place? He couldn't figure out what it was he'd done wrong. But maybe they didn't need a reason other than that he was Eddie McGregor?

The shadow of tree branches writhed across the ceiling. It was time. But he wasn't sure for what. He closed his eyes. A man was under his bed again, punching at the mattress, the same man, Eddie was sure, he'd glimpsed out in the storm back in June.

When Eddie opened his eyes again, it was morning. A young and fresh sun was pushing its way into his window. Eddie heard a small knock on his door, then Iris entered, dressed in shorts and a blouse he remembered, embarrassingly, having worn once. A button had dropped off when he'd been putting the damn thing on, but now it looked okay, all the buttons in their appropriate places. Iris sat down on the side of his bed in so purposeful a way that Eddie understood, through this simple act alone, that she knew everything. The beating in the park, his coerced silence: she knew. Maybe she didn't know about the lamb. He prayed she was at least spared that much.

Yet, knowing everything, still she leaned forward and kissed his cheek. Eddie felt nothing redemptive in his mother's kindness. His body tightened and he looked away. "I'll call Reed over," Iris said, undeterred. "We'll explain how they bullied you into this."

She sounded calm, but her eyes snapped with energy, an avid sharpness. There was something naked about his mother's face that surprised him. And how could he explain that they hadn't bullied him into anything, at least not the night in the park. His participation in the beating had been much more complicated than that, rooted less in fear than the simple and ugly desire to conform to his friends. But you couldn't say this kind of thing to your mother. You had to spare a mother what you could, even now, when she was flushed with a commitment to make things right. But sometimes things could not be made right so easily. Eddie sensed his mother's determination battling with her uncertainty, the two forces struggling against each other for supremacy. A battle, a fight, warring factions—he couldn't seem to grasp the world outside of wrestling terms. Domination or submission, strong or weak, top or bottom, pin or be pinned. He knew the world was more than he was seeing, but now he could only see in black and white, except for the dazzling heated blue of his mother's eyes, there in the room with him.

She brushed a flake of something from the corner of his eye. Again his body tensed. "We'll tell Reed before Arnie," she said. "They can help, but only if you tell *everything*."

He nodded because he didn't want to disappoint her any more than he already had.

So this was how it was going to end, with himself as a nark? Iris went downstairs while Eddie took a quick shower. He thought he was ready for the confessional he knew was coming next, his Hail Mary to the truth, but as soon as he was standing in the living room again, *the scene of the crime*, he paused. The broken window gaped at him. Through it he saw out to the front lawn, where Iris with the water hose and Lenore with her garden shears were trying to rid the grass of the damning, spray-painted letters.

When he saw a police cruiser coming down the street, Eddie grabbed his backpack that he'd left out in the living room. Then he hurried out the back door, jumped on his bicycle, and rode off onto Clinton Street. He couldn't face Reed, not yet.

Coward.

He rode downtown to the Court Square for no particular reason. The bankers and executives, the well-suited and well-heeled, moved gracefully through glass doors, as if this wasn't a town plagued by murder and late night attacks. The religious hippie lady was out in full force, holding her punctured cup out to passersby. Eddie sat on a bench near where the vigil had taken place, the vigil he'd so decisively avoided. It was probably not a great idea to be sitting so close to police headquarters. Eddie's phone rang. He knew it was his mother even before he answered. "Eddie, where are you?" Iris asked.

"I had to go out for a while." It was as close to the truth as he could manage. Actually, it was as close to the truth as he knew. "Don't worry about me."

"Honey, Reed's here. He has to get back to work soon."

"I'll be home later," he said. "Bye Mom."

He turned off his phone and looked around the square. It was still early and yet everyone was sweating, at least everyone that he could see. No, this wasn't where he should be. He rode off to the section of The Promenade farthest away from his house. There he found a well-shaded area and lay down for a nap, using his backpack as a pillow. But he didn't exactly sleep. It was more as if his mind drifted away, his body resting for a battle he couldn't yet name.

Finally, when he sat up again, it was past noon. A barge pushed its way down the river. Then he dug up some gritty change from the bottom of his backpack and bought a hotdog from a vendor along the main walkway. After he'd eaten, he turned his cell phone back on. There were two more messages from his mother. She had told Reed everything; Reed knew now; it was all out in the open and Eddie should *come home.*

His phone rang just as he finished listening to the messages from his mother. Only this time Reed was calling. Eddie hesitated before he answered. "Where are you, Ed?" Reed asked.

Ed. Even though Reed knew every shameful thing about him, he was still calling Eddie Ed. "I'm fine," Eddie said. "I told Mom that."

"Go home. I'll meet you there when I can."

Eddie said nothing. Strange to have everything out in the open. He didn't trust it.

"Listen, Ed." Reed's voice was quiet but firm. "I've talked to Mom. You're a juvenile. It's not like anyone is going to throw you in jail. You know that, right?" There was a long tense silence. "Ed, Jesus, are you listening? Tell me where you are and I'll come pick you up."

"Just tell Mom not to worry," Eddie said. "You know how she gets."

He hung up on his brother as well and turned off his phone again. He couldn't go home yet but he couldn't stay here. Reed was shrewd and might comb The Promenade. Eddie mounted his bicycle and started riding, and only realized after the fact that he was riding out of town, through undulating waves of heat, to the old deserted house he'd gone to with Tess, Danny and Soldier.

Back here, he thought as he stood in the heat, staring at the dilapidated, half-burned house. It looked pretty much the same as it had when he'd been out there only a couple months before, only now he was alone. He hid his bike behind a bush so it wouldn't be visible from the road, and stepped inside with a small lump in his throat. He moved cautiously through the empty, diminished rooms, half expecting a terrifying moment when he would come, at last, face to face with another man, a bum or a transient or the killer himself. But every room was a mild disappointment. Some ivy was growing up the wall in the living room that he didn't remember from before. The jar of peanut butter was no longer in the kitchen, but there was an empty bottle of whiskey and a half a bag of corn chips that had attracted some ants. He also found on the floor in one of the hallways a crumbled up, wallet-sized photograph of a woman who looked a little like what Tess might look like in twenty years. Eddie tucked the photo into his pocket.

Back in the living room, he paused and listened. The house was eerily still, emphasizing the sound of Eddie's own breathing. Beads of moisture glistened on the walls. The air around him smelled like fire. He lay down on the collapsing sofa and closed his eyes again. Waiting, waiting... He felt bottled-up and a little mysterious, even to himself. His mind drifted off yet again, and was dragged back to reality when he heard a thump inside the house. Startled, he sat up and watched a creature stumble into the room. The animal looked half-shaven, unlike any he'd seen before, like something hallucinated. The animal saw Eddie and bolted back out the door. He waited for his heart to slow down in his chest. What the hell was that? It had looked somewhat like a porcupine without its quills.

When he turned on his phone again, he saw another message from his mother. He ignored it and sat for a minute with the phone in his hand until his heart had slowed back to its normal rate. Then he dialed Danny's number.

"McGregor," Danny drawled into the phone. "So how was your night?"

Eddie felt nothing at the sound of Danny's voice. "The cops were out here a couple hours ago," Danny continued. "Your brother and some other fuck dragged my uncle into this. They seem to know stuff, or think they know stuff. They seem to have some *suspicions*."

"I suppose we should talk," Eddie said.

Danny sighed. "Yeah, sure, I *suppose* that's okay. We got some shit to straighten out."

Danny told Eddie to come to his place tonight after dinner, when everyone would be gone except, maybe, "the old lady." Eddie agreed to this. He understood he couldn't avoid Danny any longer. It was time for at least that reckoning.

*

Eddie remained at the deserted house until evening and then started riding his bicycle to the other side of town and back out into the country where Danny and Soldier lived. The ride was long, made more so because he wove his way across town in indirect ways, suspicious that Reed or his mother might have sent the cops out to search for him. But finally he was on the other side of town, riding past warehouses and open loading docks and the grim lot near where they'd gotten the flat on the night of the attack, before he curved onto the road that led to Danny's.

It was still quite hot but less so. A few cars passed but he didn't recognize any of them. Twilight closed in, the western sky a fierce red. Thick dark clouds were pushing in from the south. Eddie rode on instinct, not thinking much. He felt wrapped inside a deceptive calm, a very different calm than he'd felt when he'd first left his room after his days of self-exile. He pictured his mother sitting on her bedroom floor, legs folded in a lotus squat. He thought of Buddhists, rows of pacifist brown men in urgent white robes, and their imperial chanting.

A car passed him, slowed down to for a moment, and then pulled to the side of the road. Eddie stopped riding and looked toward the car. He had the sense of someone inside watching him: Buddhist or murderer or one of his friends, who could tell these days?

To his surprise, the car door opened and a man hurried toward him. Eddie was startled, so caught off guard that he just stood on his bike, mouth agape, as the man rushed over, his face so contorted in anger and pain that Eddie didn't recognize him at first. He stopped in front of Eddie and glowered. "Remember me?" the young man asked, his body leaning vehemently forward.

And Eddie's mind fumbled even as he shook his head, because of course he did know, did remember, the fading bruises on the young man's face enough of a reminder. The face that kept taunting Eddie in dreams. "*Do you remember me?*" Kip asked again, forcing the words, his face red and throttled.

"Yes," Eddie said, his heart pounding between his ribs.

Kip shoved Eddie hard enough so that the bicycle collapsed out from under him and Eddie fell to the ground, his legs twisted up with the bike. He just lay there on the ground, looking up at a pitiless Kip, the avenging angel. Eddie thought he'd never seen anyone so beautiful. "Miserable fuck," Kip muttered.

The passenger door of Kip's car opened and a young woman with purple hair stuck her head out. "Kip!" she cried out, aghast, and her voice was enough to pull Kip back from the edge. He stared down at Eddie for a moment longer, their eyes locked together and bordering on sorrow. Then Kip swore under his breath, hurried back to the car, and drove off before Eddie had managed to stand back up and right his bicycle.

Eddie wheeled his bike beside him for a minute before he mounted it and began riding again. His knees and elbows stung from his fall but he hardly noticed them. Kip's sudden appearance had broken through Eddie's detached calm and lit a small fire inside of him. His cell phone rang. "Eddie, where *are* you?" Iris asked. "It's almost night. Come home now. Please. No one's mad at you. I don't have a good feeling, you being gone for so long—"

"One more hour." Eddie was embarrassed he'd been trying on her clothes for half the summer and she didn't know, almost like he'd been taking advantage of her in some way, maybe even stealing from her. A summer of masquerade and betrayal, violence and murder, and the summer wasn't over yet. He listened while she continued to protest, to reason, to placate. Down the long stretch of road, Kip's car turned a corner and was gone. Eddie felt, once more, that peculiar loss for something he'd never had.

Eddie heard a man's voice saying something to his mother, probably Arnie's voice. "Okay, one more hour," Iris said. "If you're not home then, I'm sending someone out after you."

"Won't be necessary," he said and hung up before she could ask where he was.

When Eddie reached Danny's house, he saw only one dirty light on in the living room. The sun had set and the night was blanketed in a rapidly encroaching darkness. There was a murmur of God in the weeds around him, until he realized the murmur was just crickets. Eddie thought of communion, of ritual, of beautiful avenging angels, of dead fathers and flies zipped open in the night. The Sternes's dog was nowhere around that Eddie could see.

For some time he simply stood and stared at Danny's house. There was still time to turn around and head back home and forget. But by now he was curious to know why he'd come. The confrontation with Kip had just increased his resolve. He walked up to the house, his head bowed and hands in his pockets. The door was ajar so that Eddie could see through the screen door to a corner of the sofa, where Danny sat in front of the TV in the same way he normally sat.

As Eddie watched, Danny, unknowing, lifted up his T-shirt and wiped his face. Eddie caught a flash of Danny's flat bare stomach. A click like the release of the trigger of a gun went off inside Eddie's head. A crazy electricity shot through his blood, animating him.

He burst through the door. He felt as if his hands were burning, his entire self, burning. Surprised, Danny jumped up from the couch. "Fuck's sake, McGregor," he said, but before he could grasp what Eddie was doing, Eddie had charged ahead and punched Danny in the chin. "McGregor!" Danny said, half stunned and half laughing, as Eddie grabbed hold of Danny's T-shirt—that fucking sawed-off-at-the-arms T-shirt—and pulled him down onto the floor.

The burning within: it wasn't just fire Eddie felt now but something snarling, alive, on the attack. Eddie jumped on Danny to wrestle him, but Danny was too disoriented to fully fight back. First, Eddie caught Danny in a headlock, then turned it into a chokehold, his arm slung tight around Danny's throat, crushing his windpipe so that Danny could no longer laugh or say Eddie's name. Danny struggled against him, which only made Eddie squeeze tighter, his hold steadfast. *Let go,* Eddie told himself, and yet he couldn't let go, had no desire to let go, gripped by some fever, some death spell. He wanted Danny back in that area of breathlessness, in that suffocated place they'd shared in the abandoned house. Or whatever was rising out of Eddie wanted that—part serpent, part raging ape, part avenging warrior, part *Kip,* it was all a mess inside of him, struggling to become. Eddie threw his head back and squeezed until he thought, maybe, he wanted to snap Danny's neck altogether.

Because maybe he wanted Danny dead. Not Christian all this time, but Danny, whom he loved and hated in equal measure. Certainly his life would be easier that way.

Danny's struggles weakened. His tongue began to protrude from his gritted teeth. Upstairs, Eddie heard movement, a woman's cough, the flushing of a toilet. It was that sound alone—the lavatorial flush—that seemed to move through Eddie's blood and quiet him.

He released his hold on Danny. Danny rolled away from him and wiped spit from the corner of his mouth. He rubbed at his throat, his breath labored, as if he were trying to resuscitate the room. Finally, when he turned to Eddie—both of them still lying on their backs on the floor, both still winded from the exertion of the fight—Eddie couldn't make out the look on Danny's face. "Jesus, McGregor," he said. "You don't get it. You didn't let me talk first."

Eddie sat up. Talk: words pushed from his throat before he had a chance to consider them. "Mess with us again, I'll kill you," Eddie said, sounding like himself in the future.

Danny turned his head away, his chest heaving up and down. Eddie stood up, brushed off his pants, and walked out into the night. Thunder rumbled in the distance, a reassuring enough sound. "Not what you think," he heard Danny rasp, but Eddie had lost interest in anything he had to say, and wanted to leave the whole angry night behind him.

*

Eddie was riding his bike home, his mind lost in sobering thought, when a car approached from behind and idled next to him.

At first Eddie didn't glance over. Maybe, he thought, Kip hadn't finished with him yet. But after a solid tap of the car horn, Eddie turned and saw Reed behind the wheel, his car window open so that Eddie had full view of his brother's face—openly relieved, lit with a quiet authority but no accusation, no judgment. A few drops of rain spattered down from the sky, a light salty rain, not at all cleansing.

Eddie braked to a stop at the same moment that Reed pulled over to the side of the road. Reed motioned to Eddie and popped the trunk open. Eddie wrestled his bike into the back and then circled to the passenger side. He was reaching for the door's handle when he noticed that Christian was also in the car, sitting in the passenger seat next to Reed. Instinctively, Eddie climbed into the back seat. A raw tenuous silence hung between the three of them. Eddie's throat ached with the obligation to say something—he owed them that much—but the words wouldn't come. The brothers sat for several seconds in this way. Christian glanced at him through the rearview mirror and crossed his eyes at Eddie, the way they'd done when they were boys, before they'd learned to hate each other. Eddie crossed his eyes back at Christian. It was the most either of them could manage.

Only minutes ago Eddie had tried to snap Danny's neck. Only minutes ago he'd nearly crossed over, again. Now he was sitting here with his brothers, his arms still humming with violent tension, with a killing fever his brothers would never understand.

At last Reed broke the silence. "Onward, soldiers," he said, shifted the car into drive, and they started toward home, back to face what Eddie could no longer avoid.

(23)

The rest of August passed by quickly, although not quickly enough for Reed. He wanted the whole brutal summer over with. Eddie's role in Kip's beating and the subsequent attack on Iris's house were only the latest stark reminders that violence could erupt at any time, from any source. The Sternes boys and their friends, with one of those impenetrable "brotherhood" walls of solidarity, insisted that they had not been responsible for the "bombing" of the McGregors. Ticker and Alberta Sternes swore that Danny and Soldier had been at home that night, although they balked when Reed asked if they were willing to take a lie detector test attesting to that fact. "No bullshit machine can tell us where we was or wasn't" was all Ticker would say on the matter. And since no one had really seen the attackers, the police didn't have much to go on other than suspicion.

As for the attack on Kip, Soldier and Danny Sternes and their friends were backed into a corner on that one. With Eddie's confession, given to Reed and Arnie succinctly and precisely and with no self-pity, and buttressed by what Iris had been told by Alberta Sternes, Soldier's posse grudgingly admitted to their own culpability on that front. But only Danny and Eddie had really committed a crime, and they were both underage, and Kip, when told his assailants had been identified, repeated that he had no interest in pressing charges. So all those involved in the attack were let off with a stern warning and a little token community service, and that, apparently, was the end of it.

But Reed couldn't let it go. He'd known something was troubling Eddie during the weekend they'd spent together at the cabin, and yet, despite all his police training, he hadn't come close to guessing what that something was. And while there was no sound reason for why he should have suspected Eddie in Kip's attack, he still felt he'd failed them both.

In those last two weeks of August, Reed spent much of his free time alone and reflective. Alex was back in town to begin a new teaching semester, but so far neither one of them had phoned the other. Reed's working relationship with Casey continued down its strained and inarticulate path, made even more awkward by their most recent fight. Casey never apologized to Reed for the things he'd said the night he found Reed and Maggie sleeping together on the sofa, and once again neither man acknowledged the incident, preferring to bury the inconvenient memory where they didn't have to look at it.

A few days after the fight, when Reed first heard through the grapevine that Maggie had quit her job at the daycare center, moved out of the house, and flown to Oregon to stay with her friend Jasmine for an indefinite period of time, he felt guilty and shaken. He remembered the pleading way Maggie had looked that night when she was standing beside his car—what had she wanted from him, other than the impossible?—and it bothered him that she had left town so abruptly and without saying goodbye. But when Reed swallowed his pride enough to let Casey know he'd heard about Maggie, offering Casey an opening to talk if he wanted, Casey only nodded and said "I know" while staring somewhat fiercely through the windshield. And then, as a measured afterthought: "It's nobody's fault. We want what we want."

Despite what felt like an increased estrangement from the world, Reed wasn't as lonely as he imagined he could be under the circumstances. He discovered the pleasures of a solitary life. The week before Labor Day was Reed's vacation time but he didn't go anywhere special, just stayed in Barrow's Point and let time pass in its lazy and uneventful way. He had a couple of nightly drinks, listened to music, drove out to the lake, and considered how he was 29 now and still living in his hometown. It seemed a subtle warning of some kind.

Every now and then Reed drove around town at night to see what he might uncover. By some divine coincidence or fate, maybe he would catch someone in the act of a beating, of bombing or murder. But of course when he was driving through the streets, nothing much stood out. The ignoble heat spell had broken, and now there was rain or a thunderstorm almost nightly. The storms flushed the streets clean, and suddenly there felt like less of a threat in the air, as if the whole of Barrow's Point had exhaled. One night as Reed was driving around, he stopped at a downtown stoplight, and saw posted on a street lamp an old flier for the vigil, now crumbled and peeling away. Two months later and the vigil was already history. The red-shirted *VIGILANT* group seemed less visible these days as well, although maybe this was only his imagination.

Often after those futile but still oddly relaxing drives around the city, Reed would stop at Quench for a nightcap. He sat at the bar and kept his eyes open. Quench was often quiet and scant of patrons these days, almost as if men were having second thoughts about showing their faces inside Barrow Point's only gay bar. One night Reed drove through Barrow's Point and kept driving, all the way to a gay bar in Minneapolis. He ended up going back to the apartment of a recent University of Minnesota law school graduate. Theirs was a frank sexual encounter with little talking between them. At sunrise Reed left the man's apartment and drove back to Barrow's Point with a headache and an unclear sense of the man's name. Doug? Why couldn't he remember? He was as bad as the town he lived in, too quickly forgetting what most needed remembering.

*

And then, without warning, how easily and violently things could change, if only for an instant.

One early mid-September morning at the start of their shift, Reed and Casey were called to a farmhouse several miles outside town. A "domestic disturbance" of some sort was all they knew. The day was overcast with a hint of autumn chill in the air. As Casey drove past woods and ditches and farmhouses so familiar to them both, Reed stared out the window and tried to shake a vague sense that he and Casey had already responded to this call before. He couldn't quite put his finger on it.

"Maggie phoned last night," Casey said from out of nowhere, still staring ahead at the road.

This was the first time Casey had volunteered anything personal in a long while, or at least what felt like a long while. "That's good," Reed said. He wanted to say more but it was too early in the morning for him to come up with anything.

"I guess so. She's clearing her head. I'm just afraid I'm part of what's going to get cleared."

They drove the last mile in silence. A somewhat elderly woman in an old-fashioned gingham dress met them out by the road as they pulled up to the farmhouse. "I can't live this way!" the woman said as Reed and Casey stepped from the police cruiser. "I *won't* live this way. I will not be driven from my house by that ticking time bomb."

"Who's the time bomb?" Casey asked.

"*He*. He is. Jonny, my sister's boy. He's moved back in and taken over the house. Susan and I were doing all right before he came back and turned the place to garbage."

Casey asked her to slow down so he could take her name. "Cirie Grodin," she sighed, as if she couldn't believe they were sticking to formality when her life was sliding into such disorder. She was a short, rabbity-looking woman with thin white hair and an unfortunate balding spot at the top of her scalp. She had nervous, sharp little teeth. "Susan's your sister?" Casey asked.

"Yes! Please, this isn't why I called you here!"

"Where is she now?"

"Inside with the prodigal son." Cirie's eyes were bright and a little caustic. "Aren't you going to do something? Arrest him, maybe? I can't live like this, with such fear. Not an hour ago he ran me out of the house. Said he'd set me on fire if I came back inside. *On fire*."

"He lets your sister stay inside but not you?"

Cirie turned to Reed and looked at him for longer than was necessary. "She's his mother," Cirie said. "He needs someone around to scramble his eggs for breakfast and whatever else he wants to eat, and to pay the bills while he—" She pressed her lips together and didn't finish the thought. "Some nights he has other people over. I cry myself to sleep, listening to the things they say."

"Your sister wants him out of the house, too, then?" Casey asked.

Cirie frowned. "She thinks she can save him. That's part of the problem. She's delusional. He slaps her and she thinks she just needs to be more patient."

Casey met Reed's eyes, the both of them a bit at a loss about how to proceed. Cirie motioned for them to follow her, and she led them, not to the house, but to a small shed on an opposite corner of the yard. Reed noticed several dead patches of grass nearby. Inside the shed, a few small stuffed birds were mounted on the walls, as well as a couple of chipmunks, a squirrel, and a rabbit. The table standing in the center of the shed was heavy with tools of the trade: scalpel, handsaw, wire cutters, pliers, fleshing knife, needles and thread, a spray canister of Liqua-Tan. A small stuffed squirrel was standing up on its hind legs on the table, posed as if it were eating a nut while dressed up in a jaunty vest and a French beret. Large metal traps hung from hooks on an opposite wall, a couple of the traps open in such a way that they appeared to savagely smile with their serrated teeth. "The inside of Jonny's head," Cirie muttered, picking up what looked like a tuft of animal fur and tucking it into a pocket of her dress. "I remember a time when it was just teddy bears. He calls this *creative* taxidermy, but what I want to know is, is all this legal?"

Taxidermy: it was another of the world's appalling practices that enough lazy and wrong-headed thinking had turned into fashion. Looking around the shed, Reed didn't see creativity and art: he saw ego, control and ownership, fetishism with mutilation and death. In particular, the rabbit on the wall gripped him with its sorcerer stare. The rabbit looked ready to bolt if only it possessed the means to charge ahead.

"As long as he's not killing out of season, it's legal," Casey said and straightened the squirrel's beret with his thumb.

"I think it's supposed to stay cocked," Cirie said. And, as an afterthought, "Seasons! What does he care about seasons? He kills when and where he pleases."

He kills when and where he pleases: the words nudged at Reed but he was reluctant to make too much of them. For a moment Reed thought the teeth of the saw on the table were stained with blood, but when he stepped closer, the blood turned to rust. It was in the air still, the memory of death, the calculated taking of life. All summer they'd been receiving calls like this one, people wanting to report the suspicious behavior of neighbors, friends, coworkers, children, parents, spouses. The shadow selves had taken over and no one could be trusted. Of course, a death fetish shed like this was enough to short circuit anyone. "I was hoping," Cirie added, nearly in a whisper, "that maybe this would be enough."

"You really think he's a threat to you?" Reed asked.

Cirie considered this. "I don't know. Maybe. He's a threat to somebody, I have no doubt—"

They heard the screen door of the house bang open and shut, followed by a woman calling Cirie's name in a vigorous, accusing voice. Cirie turned pale and gripped her skirt. "Please help her see reason," Cirie whispered to them.

She left the shed and walked with reluctance over to the woman, who Reed assumed was her sister. Reed and Casey followed behind, still apprehensive about interfering in a family squabble. "Do you think it takes more craft to stuff a small animal?" Casey asked, although he didn't sound all that curious for an answer. "You know, like you need a more steady hand or something?"

"They probably require the same thing," Reed said. "You prefer the animal dead."

As soon as Cirie was within reach, Susan balled up her fist and struck Cirie's arm, not hard since Susan looked older and frailer than her sister. Still, Cirie shrank back. "She gets punchy when he's around," Cirie said grimly.

"You called the *police?*" Susan stared, appalled, at Cirie. "After all I've done for you?"

"What you've done for me, Susie," Cirie said, rubbing her arm, "is let the monster back into the house."

Susan turned to Reed and Casey and eyed them with nervous reproach. She was dressed hastily in oversized men's clothes. Reed had the sense that she'd tossed on whatever clothes were nearby before stepping outside, and those clothes happened to belong to her son. Thin lank strands of hair hung over her face, but this was not enough to conceal the yellow bruise that circled Susan's right eye. "Please go," she said, biting her bottom lip. "I'm sorry my sister has wasted your time."

Casey shrugged, almost in agreement, but a suspicion born out of instinct was growing stronger inside Reed. He glanced around the ill-kept yard, at the large black garbage bags heaped against a fence, and at the dusty car with its hood open parked under a tree with fungus growing on its trunk. The car; there was something about the car. He turned back to Susan. "What happened to your eye?" he asked her.

"My eye is my eye," she said. "You have no rights to this place! This is my property."

"Our property," Cirie corrected her. "Daddy left it to the both of us, certainly not to the demon seed—"

"You've never been a mother!" Susan cried, glaring back at Cirie. "You're jealous of my *child!*"

As the sisters argued back and forth, with Casey serving as half-hearted referee, Reed backed away and gazed again at the house. It was a nondescript house, for the most part, other than for all the windows with curtains drawn. Yet the house beckoned to Reed in its voiceless way. Or not quite voiceless, because the house was making a low but distinct humming sound, rattling and mechanical. Several trees towered over the house, casting it in perpetual shade. Rotting apples lined the ground under a dying apple tree, but no birds pecked at the dead fruit.

Without considering what he was doing, Reed started toward the house. He was at the back door before Casey called out, "Reed, where are you going?"

"Keep them outside," Reed said. "I'll just be a minute."

See what's inside, he thought. *Look in, not out.*

"We don't have a warrant!" Casey said, and Susan was shouting about violations and rights, and then she cried out in a strong clear voice, not an old woman's voice at all: "Jonny! The police!"

But Reed was already tapping on the screen door. "Coming in!" he said before he stepped inside. The first thing he noticed was the smell, the heavy smell of ammonia and rotten eggs. He paused a moment to get his bearings. The hall entryway was stacked high with yellowing, crumbling newspaper, with scattered unwashed laundry, with the clutter from crippled chairs, dead car batteries, and the clogged, disassembled pipes from kitchen sinks. Dust motes clung to the air, a thin veil that Reed had to pass through on his way to the kitchen, where the dust thickened and the air smelled even more corrosive.

Yet despite the strong chemical odor, Reed also smelled death, literally *smelled* it in the air, a repellent, almost sacrificial odor of animal flesh, of *cooked* animal flesh…was that the carcass of a dead rabbit, half-skinned and tossed aside in the kitchen sink? Reed turned away from the sight of it, and from unwashed dishes, and from broken plates scattered on the chipped and grimy floor. He ignored the cobwebs spun up in the ceiling corners, and the flies and moths caught in the web, while the unwebbed flies buzzed and hovered over the mess in the pans on the stove. A little patchy daylight managed to slant through the tears in the curtains, but once inside the house, the light was sullied. The kitchen table, cluttered with empty plastic containers and several empty boxes of *Lucky Charms,* looked as if it had been dragged inside from a dump. Reed felt tension knotting his body, now that he'd entered this rubbishy house without a plan. In the back of his mind a voice whispered that he shouldn't do this, not without a plan, and yet he moved forward anyway, pulled ahead by an almost supernatural will, driven by curiosity and the desire to know, to see, to dig deeper into the misery of this house.

As Reed passed into the small hallway leading to the living room, he said "Jonny?" in what he hoped was a nonthreatening way. No one answered, or precisely answered, yet Reed heard, or thought he heard, a detached, tinny voice mutter something. He paused and listened but heard nothing more. Reed stepped into the living room, also dimly lit, with heavy dusky shades pulled over the windows. This room, too, was in disarray, with cracked walls and mismatched furniture standing not quite where you'd expect, as if shifted out of alignment by an earthquake. A large aquarium filled with green murky water stood on a corner table, but there was no sign of life inside, just a couple of fish floating dead at the top. The air in this room also smelled pungent with the same corrosive stink, despite the several oscillating fans that were attempting to circulate the air. The TV was turned on to *The Price is Right*, but the sound was off and the image kept breaking apart, the spinning wheel flickering in and out of focus.

There was a ragged sofa in the center of the room, but no one was sitting on it. "Hello," Reed said and jumped when he heard someone say "hello" back in that same tinny voice. The voice was coming from this room, the very room he was standing in now, and yet the room was empty except for Reed. Then he saw the baby monitor on the coffee table next to the sofa. "Hello," he said, louder, and listened to the monitor echo his voice back, louder, to him.

A baby monitor? Reed walked over, picked it up, and turned it over in his hands. The baby monitor was smudged, a grubby-looking, manhandled instrument. Neither Cirie nor Susan had mentioned a baby. No, he was pretty sure there was no baby in the house. Then why the monitor? To alert someone to intruders? Reed set the monitor back down and looked around again. The room was so still, the kind of quiet that felt deliberate. The back of his neck prickled, and yet he still didn't leave. There was something he was missing, something he almost understood but that still eluded him.

The living room led into another, still darker room. Reed stuck his head into this room but couldn't see much. Boards and black plastic sheets were nailed to these windows, he saw that much, blocking out daylight altogether. This room smelled worse than all the other rooms, no longer a smell so much as a presence. A large motorized exhaust fan rumbled in a far corner. He fumbled at the light switch but there was no light. He clicked the switch on a second time to make sure. Then, maybe too calmly, he took a few steps forward. A string attached to an uncovered light bulb in the ceiling dangled in front of his face, so he tugged on the string. A dim and cautious light filled the room. A large table was pushed against the right wall, the table littered with empty containers of antifreeze, of drain cleaner and paint thinner and empty two-liter plastic jugs of soda with puncture holes near the top. A pair of rubber gloves lay on the end of the table, next to what looked like a respiratory mask of some kind.

Meth lab, he thought, or at least the beginning of one. He breathed shallowly, reluctant to inhale the room's poisoned air. He started to reach for the walkie-talkie attached to his hip when his eyes were drawn to the wall on his left. Newspaper covered it like discount wallpaper. Reed stepped closer, squinting, a catch in his throat. It hit him in a single swooping rush—not just random newspaper, but newspaper headlines and articles about the murders: *Local Man Bludgeoned; Second Man Murdered in Barrow's Point; Third Victim of Gay Murders*—on and on the headlines went. To complete the puzzle, the demonic maze he'd stumbled into, was the picture of Reed himself, holding the candle at the vigil. Something had been written over his face in a careless scrawl but he couldn't make it out.

All the breath felt punched from Reed's lungs, this compilation of the murder and mystery he'd been chasing for months. It was so troubling a sight, so disorienting that Reed was momentarily caught off-guard, and only felt the danger to himself a moment before he heard the whistling of air at his back. Still, trained for self-defense, he reacted on instinct, twisting just enough to one side so that the baseball bat didn't land across his skull but instead struck lower, near the back of his neck. An explosion went off inside his head, a bursting aura of hellish light. He crashed down against a small desk filled with books, a stack of paperbacks thundering down around him.

Blindly, his hand shot to his hip where his gun holster was, and he fumbled for the gun even as he saw the blurred shape of a man standing over him, his face frozen in a rictus of fierce concentration and bland indifference as he swung the bat at Reed's hand. Reed yelped in pain as the bat struck his fingers and he heard, *heard* the snapping of bones—his hand, dull and throbbing with pain, useless to him now. Reed kicked his foot out, trying to trip up the man with the bat, but he didn't have the right angle so his foot only stomped against the man's shin. The man raised the bat a third time and swung it toward Reed's face, but Reed deflected enough so that the bat connected with his shoulder. He yelled again, his body nearly in convulsion, a darkness passing over him as his body went numb...

Then Reed heard voices, and the man was yanked away. The bat clattered to the floor. Dimly, Reed was aware of Casey in the room, struggling with the other man, their bodies pushed against the wall and the table, knocking over chairs and things from shelves. The man's hands locked around Casey's throat, and Reed tried to stand up, meaning to help in some way, but that same darkness clutched at him. He couldn't feel his arms or his legs.

A gun fired. The explosion ripped through the air and reverberated inside Reed's head. Briefly, the room went dark and then surged to light again. Only someone had changed the scene. Now Reed's head was leaned against Casey's chest. One of Casey's arms was wrapped around Reed from behind, and with the hand of his other arm he held his gun at someone just out of sight. "Come on, Reed," Casey said. "Stay awake, my friend."

"It's him." Reed was almost panting. His lungs were forgetting how to breathe. "Don't let—him..." He meant to say don't let him go, but the words were stuffed down deep, a coil he couldn't unsnarl.

Without lowering the gun, Casey moved his arm enough from Reed so that he had his walkie-talkie in hand, calling for backup. Reed saw then, although barely, that Casey was pointing his gun at the man who had attacked him, now handcuffed to a leg of the table, his back bowed, no longer resisting, no longer fighting. Susan was crouched beside the man, her voice keening, "Jonny, what have you done? My baby!" She touched his leg, which was bleeding heavily from the calf. But Jonny said nothing to his mother, didn't even look at her, while the other woman, the sister Cirie, stood in the doorway with her hand at her throat, unable to stop looking, first at mother and son huddled on the floor, then at Reed and Casey huddled in their own way. She signed a cross in the air. Reed felt the warm drift of blood down the back of his head, turning him dizzy, staining Casey's shirt. The blood knew more than it seemed.

Reed heard Casey saying "*Merc, Merc,*" a call back to their boyhood. A sharp pain like a knife to his head made Reed wince, and yet he couldn't feel the rest of his body, only blood surging toward his heart with the force of a hot, panicked river. His vision turned cloudy. Cells danced in the air in front of him. Were those cells, corpuscles, strands of living things pushing against one another, melding and forming? It seemed, maybe, he was reliving a moment he'd never experienced before. Casey continued to encourage him to stay awake, to not drift under, and Reed nodded, straining to focus on Casey's fading voice, as if it were the last of what could save him...

(24)

The hospital. Darkness and light. Rising and falling. Pain and no pain. His body, so torn and beaten and broken, was on fire. Then he was more spirit than body, with no pain at all.

Doctors and nurses called to him. They hooked him up to machines. His brain was scanned; he was injected with sedatives; he sunk back into sleep.

Voices churned in and out. Hands young, careful, ancient ministered to him. At one point he knew Casey was in the room with him, too, unless they were both sealed in a car. A blizzard darkened their windshield: he remembered that much. Snow, ice, the howl of the bitter winds. He and Casey had held each other and waited for death. It was long ago or it was now, the moment he was trying to wake back into.

And Maggie. She was no stranger to snow. They'd packed it in their hands and thrown it at one another and were almost happy. But Maggie had gone away. He'd left her, now she'd left him.

Back and forth. Rise and fall. Someone else was in the room now, pleading for his life. His life? Men had died but Reed had forgotten their names.

Maybe he'd never known them. Maybe he was one of them.

He felt a prick in his arm. It carried him back down, again, to the warmth of an unseen resting place.

*

More people were in the room with him now. This was later, or maybe later still. Iris, Christian, Eddie. He could feel their presence. His eyes wavered, trying to see, but all he could make out were shadows—anxious, pleading shadows. Yet somehow he heard them, only not their words but their thoughts, as if he'd tapped into the stream-of-consciousness ticker tape of their subconscious. Reed heard his mother's racing thoughts, *Come back to us, I can't do this without you, Carl keep him safe, God keep him safe, I looked away, I did not see, I should have known the danger for you, too...* and Christian's, *You're strong, you're a champion, a warrior, the lynchpin of us, come on, brother, open your eyes, you're the one who will outlive us all...* and Eddie's, *Please hang on, I don't want you to go, any of you, to go, when you're better I'll make it up to you, erase every secret, every doubt...*

He heard Maggie, too, although a part of him remembered she wasn't in the room, she was far away, and yet her voice was clear, not distant, part of that same subconscious river he'd tapped into, *I love you, Reed, even if I can't say it, speak it, even if you can't return it, there's nothing to be done about what is, but I'm with you, I'm always with you even when I can no longer be there...*

And Casey, even in a symphony of voices there was still and always Casey's, *The one friend who never let me down, who I've let down over and over again, I'm your friend and always have been in my way, we are stronger than this gutter of hate, we can survive even this, Merc, we have always survived together, it's our blood...*

"Reed!" his father called, and Reed felt a chill down his spine, but he couldn't answer him, the words wouldn't come. His father didn't call again.

But other voices called, some that he recognized and some that he didn't, adding to the river. Then, shouldering aside all others, he felt the presence of the dead men, Solomon and Anthony and Ronald, like trembling light around him, his brothers who had not lived. He wanted to tell them that the killer had been found and justice delivered, and in that small way, there was payback. Only they seemed to understand everything already. They were silent, sober, and when at last they spoke, *Payback? There is no payback, for us.*

But I found him, Reed told them. *Casey and I, together we found him.* And the dead men said, *Are you sure?* When Reed hesitated, not understanding, they added, *Not just one. They are legion.*

"Legion." It took all of Reed's effort, his breath, to mouth the word.

"Reed?" Iris leaned down toward his bed.

*

A few hours later, when Reed briefly woke up, his head was clearer and he could feel his arms and legs again. A nurse smiled at him and stepped out of the room, and soon a doctor stepped in and said, "Namaste." The doctor was somewhat young and inexperienced, and his bedside manner sounded as if he were just trying it out. Reed's injuries were serious, the doctor said, but not as severe as they might have been. A concussion, a small fracture of the shoulder, and a broken hand were the extent of it. "Shock was the main issue," he said. "You're lucky."

Reed nodded his bandaged head as best he could. Although he was still a little divorced from the world, he also felt himself inching back toward it. "Lucky we found him," Reed muttered. "Took us long enough."

The young doctor half-smiled and scribbled on Reed's chart.

*

Reed slept again, a more sustained and restful sleep. When he woke, it was evening. Reed lay in bed for several minutes, his arm in a sling and his hand in a cast, staring at the window, his mind adrift. When Casey stepped into the room, he was no longer in uniform, having changed into a clean T-shirt and jeans. There was a large visible bruise on his right arm and a couple of gouge marks on his neck. "Ouch," Reed said. His eyes hurt to look at Casey.

"Are you kidding? Have you seen yourself lately?" Casey rested his hand on Reed's uninjured shoulder. "What an idiot I was, letting you walk into that portal of hell by yourself."

"It was my idiot idea to go in the first place." Reed couldn't even remember now what had compelled him to step inside the house alone. He'd simply done so without question. "It was worth it, though, to finally catch him."

Casey pulled a chair over from the corner of the room and sat down near the bed. He surveyed his hands and then dragged his eyes back up to Reed. "I'm not getting a good feeling," Reed said.

"He's not our man, Merc."

Reed nodded although his brain was still sluggish and he didn't fully understand. "Who?" he said.

"Jonny or whatever his name is. He's not the one."

Reed stared at Casey and waited for the meaning to change. "He checks out," Casey continued. "He has alibis for two of the three murders. He wasn't even living here then."

"His mother doesn't count as an alibi."

"Not his mother, Merc."

"He tried to bash in my skull." The back of Reed's head throbbed in dull pain.

"He was doped-up and paranoid and there you were, inside the house. He's an asshole, yes, a botched meth dealer, probably crazy too, and a creepy fuck in a shitload of trouble, but he's not the killer." Casey stared again at the bruise on his arm. "At least not the one we're looking for."

"He had all the newspaper clippings taped to the wall," Reed protested.

"One of those true crime buffs. Did you see all those books he had? When he wasn't running his junior meth lab or cutting up animals or terrorizing the old women, he was reading about any grisly murder he could get his hands on. Reading, apparently, not doing."

A silence yawned between them. Finally, reality sank in. Once again, in haste, he'd misread circumstantial evidence as fact. Reed breathed deeply, trying to rid himself of disappointment, but all it did was gave him a woozy sense of dislocation. He felt as if he'd lied to the dead.

Casey leaned back in his chair. "Christ, what a day," he said, rubbing his face. "Iris and the boys were here earlier. Do you remember?"

"A little." So they hadn't been a hallucination after all.

"The doctor sent them home once visiting hours were over."

"So why are you still here?"

The first hint of a smile crossed Casey's face. "They can't send me home," Casey said. "I'm the police, remember? Besides, I promised Iris I'd stay."

"You don't have to stay."

But Casey said that was exactly what he was going to do, stay. A fierce light gleamed in his eyes that looked almost devotional. "We've been through this before," he reminded Reed. And when Reed said he didn't have a clue what that meant, Casey said, "You're supposed to be getting rest, remember?" And then, quietly, "Dream, Merc."

(25)

It was night now, the kind of night that didn't come often, a night of shadow, trickery, drugs, and revelation.

When Reed opened his eyes after drifting off, the first thing he saw was that Casey had moved his chair back to the corner of the room so he could stretch out his legs. Casey's head was tilted to one side as he slept, and his knee was jittering a little. His was not, Reed would guess, a peaceful sleep. Reed watched Casey with fondness, with love, actually, although that love lacked the secret erotic charge he'd felt for Casey since their heady teen years. At last his romantic ideal of Casey was burning itself out, Reed's heart purged clean of it. In its place was born this new friendship, waiting for direction.

A blow to my head: it didn't seem real. Reed stood up with difficulty, slipped his feet into a pair of the foot slippers lying beside the bed, and walked out into the hall. He didn't know why, other than for the welcome feel of motion in his limbs. Despite the painkillers he'd been given, there was still a slight pain in his skull he couldn't shake, as well as in his shoulder and hand. Yet his heart beat strong and constant, in defiance of the day's terror and frustration.

The third floor hall was empty. Reed passed by a few rooms with closed doors. Inside one he thought he heard whispering, the whisper of prayer or self-reckoning, possibly the whisper of dream. He reached the small waiting area, but the nurse's desk was also empty. Reed saw the time on a clock behind the desk, but it wasn't the right time: 10:05.

He walked over to the long window near the desk and gazed out, but all he saw through the black-seeming glass was his own reflection and the reflection of a man stepping into the waiting room behind him. Reed turned back around and saw a hospital security guard standing a few feet away. The man was somewhat tall and appeared strong enough although not unreasonably so. Tuffs of premature gray in the man's hair made it impossible to get a clear read on his age. There was a small baton attached to his hip, but he was otherwise unarmed. "Do you need something?" he asked a bit tersely.

"No," Reed said. "I'm a patient down the hall," he added as if the bandage around his head, the sling around his shoulder, and the cast on his hand didn't make that already evident.

The security guard nodded but nonetheless eyed Reed with a thoroughness that was exhausting. "What happened to you?" he asked.

Reed shrugged. What was left to say?

A different look crossed the guard's face then, a leap toward recognition. "Wait, are you that gay cop?" he asked.

Reed didn't answer but it appeared he didn't need to. The guard stepped forward to shake Reed's unwounded left hand. "I've seen you around, I think," the man said with an affable grin.

Seen him where? At the vigil? In the newspaper? In a squad car? The guard's grip was on the verge of overzealous. "I was part of the Blue myself once," the guard said. "In Milwaukee, though, not here." He released Reed's hand, then removed a narrow pack of gum from his pants pocket, unwrapped a black stick, and popped it into his mouth. Black Jack—did they still make that brand? Reed expected the guard to offer him some, but the man tucked the gum back into his pocket. "I lasted almost five years before they asked me to leave the force," the man continued. "Nerves."

"Really?" The longer Reed talked to the guard, the more the man had the look of someone he'd nearly met once. "You look steady enough."

The man nodded his appreciation. "You should see me on the inside," he said. "Take an X-ray, I'm like a hurricane on radar." He smiled again, but it was no longer the same smile. "Working at a hospital is easier," he said. "Not the same pressure. These halls are pretty dead at night most of the time."

As if to confirm this, they both glanced up and down the desolate hall. For all Reed knew, he and the security guard were the only people awake on the floor. "Of course, there was that attempted burglary last year," the guard continued. "Some junkie broke into the pharmacy. Methadone, Xanax, Oxycodone, he was just cramming the shit into a bag and into his pockets before I caught him in the act. Lucky for me he was so wasted he had a fake gun instead of a real one. Otherwise I might be dead all over again. I didn't mean to break his arm like I done, but, you know, how was I supposed to know he was packing a toy gun?" The guard shook his head and looked at Reed's arm in a sling. "You remember all that? The cops had to come and take over."

Reed couldn't remember hearing anything about a theft at the hospital pharmacy, but for some reason he nodded as if he remembered what he didn't.

He couldn't help but notice how casually the guard mentioned breaking a man's arm.

"I tell you, being the police is tough work," the guard said. "I know what the pressure's like, day in and day out, and then having to try and solve those murders too. It was a good fight while it lasted."

Down the hall someone cried out. Then, someone stopped. "The fight's not over yet," Reed said. His head felt dreamy and light, as if he were on the verge of missing everything.

"Of course it's over." The guard sounded surprisingly emphatic. "It's been over for a long time. The killer went on some sort of rampage. Some hate or sickness got the best of him, but that ended and the murders just sort of stopped. Haven't you noticed?"

"It's not uncommon in cases like this for a murderer to stop for a while and go into hiding," Reed said. "Doesn't mean they won't kill again, or that they won't be found."

The guard nodded politely. "Maybe," he said. His tongue had gone black from the gum. "Or sometimes someone kills and then stops and disappears and you never hear from him again. You end up with one of those cold cases."

Reed felt as if air was leaking from the inside of his lungs. "If you haven't found him by now, you're probably not going to," the man concluded. Now his voice sounded almost gentle. "Yet another mystery we'll never understand."

Another mystery we'll never understand: the words thundered in Reed's head, as if born out of the fear dogging him for months—that a man could kill with such deliberate calculation and still not be caught. The bodies accumulated underground, restless and protesting, and yet there was no resolution, no ending. The guard's voice was like a clarion wake-up call that every fiber of Reed's soul meant to resist. "I don't believe it," Reed said. "A man can't just disappear into thin air."

"Unfortunately, he can." The guard kept looking at the clock behind the nurse's station, the one frozen at the wrong time. In a few hours, for a brief minute, it would be precisely the right time again. "Or worse, he doesn't disappear at all. He just blends in so we don't notice him when he passes us in the street. Too many trying to blend in and not be seen."

And those words, too, echoed with a familiar truth. The killing shadow Reed had imagined eluding and taunting him for the entire summer could well have vanished altogether or taken on another form he didn't recognize. He shook his head; it was as if he were bashing his head against the unknowable. A nurse appeared at the end of the hall and started walking toward them. The darkness outside the window on the opposite side of the hall had just begun to lighten. For the first time, Reed noticed how scuffed and raw the guard's hands seemed.

"What's your name, by the way?" Reed asked.

The guard's eyes lingered on Reed. Then he smiled that strangely placed smile, started to open his mouth, thought better of it, closed his mouth again, shook his head, and glanced back at the hamstrung clock. 10:05, 10:05, 10:05, there was no escaping it. At the same moment Reed realized the guard wasn't going to offer up his name, that, in fact, even one's smallest private choices are laced with impregnable mystery, the floor nurse walked over and stepped behind the desk. She peered over at the two men who stared at one another, both unmoving, connected as if by some unseen and nameless cord. "I hope there isn't a problem," she said.

About the author

Photo by Joan Jastrebski

Robert Schirmer is the author of the collection of short stories titled *Living With Strangers* (NYU Press) and the winner of the Bobst Award for Emerging Writers. His stories have appeared in a wide range of literary journals such as *Byliner, Glimmer Train, The Sewanee Review, Epoch, New England Review, Fiction, Confrontation* and *The Best of Witness*. In addition, he has won an O. Henry Award, a Pushcart Prize, a Walter E. Dakin fellowship to the Sewanee Writers Conference, and a fellowship from the Chesterfield Film Company Writer's Film project. His screenplays have been optioned by Amblin Entertainment and Warner Brothers. He has also been a Visiting Writer at the Southwest Writers Series and at Stetson University as part of the Tim Sullivan Endowment for Writing series.

Note:

Portions of this novel originally appeared in *Glimmer Train* under the title "Fag Killer."

Books from Gival Press—Fiction & Nonfiction

The Best of Gival Press Short Stories edited by Robert L. Giron
Boys, Lost & Found by Charles Casillo
The Cannibal of Guadalajara by David Winner
A Change of Heart by David Garrett Izzo
The Day Rider and Other Stories by J. E. Robinson
Dead Time / Tiempo muerto by Carlos Rubio
Dreams and Other Ailments / Sueños y otros achaques by Teresa Bevin
The Gay Herman Melville Reader edited by Ken Schellenberg
Ghost Horse by Thomas H. McNeely
Gone by Sundown by Peter Leach
An Interdisciplinary Introduction to Women's Studies edited by Brianne Friel
    and Robert L. Giron
Julia & Rodrigo by Mark Brazaitis
The Last Day of Paradise by Kiki Denis
Literatures of the African Diaspora by Yemi D. Ogunyemi
Lockjaw: Collected Appalachian Stories by Holly Farris
Mayhem: Three Lives of a Woman by Elizabeth Harris
Maximus in Catland by David Garrett Izzo
Middlebrow Annoyances: American Drama in the 21st Century by Myles
    Weber
The Pleasuring of Men by Clifford H. Browder
Riverton Noir by Perry Glasser
Second Acts by Tim W. Brown
Secret Memories / Recuerdos secretos by Carlos Rubio
Sexy Liberal! Of Me I Sing by Stephanie Miller
Show Up, Look Good by Mark Wisniewski

The Smoke Week: Sept. 11-21. 2001 by Ellis Avery
The Spanish Teacher by Barbara de la Cuesta
That Demon Life by Lowell Mick White
Tina Springs into Summer / Tina se lanza al verano by Teresa Bevin
The Tomb on the Periphery by John Domini
Twelve Rivers of the Body by Elizabeth Oness

For a complete list of Gival Press titles,
visit: *www.givalpress.com*.
Books are available from Ingram, Follett, Brodart, your favorite bookstore, the Internet,

or from Gival Press.

Gival Press, LLC
PO Box 3812
Arlington, VA 22203
givalpress@yahoo.com
703.351.0079

Made in the USA
Middletown, DE
11 October 2016